$\mathcal{B}$ARONESS

BARONESS

DAUGHTERS of FORTUNE

Susan May
WARREN

summerside
PRESS™

Summerside Press™
Minneapolis 55337
www.summersidepress.com
Baroness
© 2012 by Susan May Warren

ISBN 978-1-60936-631-5

Scripture references are from the following source: The Holy
Bible, King James Version (KJV).

All characters are fictional. Any resemblances to actual people
are purely coincidental.

Cover design by Peter Gloege/Lookout Design, Inc.
www.Lookoutdesign.com

Interior design by Müllerhaus Publishing Group
www.mullerhaus.net

*Summerside Press™ is an inspirational publisher offering fresh,
irresistible books to uplift the heart and engage the mind.*

Printed in USA.

For your glory, Lord

Acknowledgments

I am deeply grateful for the help of so many on this story! Thank you to my writing partner Rachel Hauck, who helped me sort out every chapter with her wisdom and patience. And Susan Downs, my fabulous editor, who cheers me on and partners with me in writing these stories. Thank you to Ellen Tarver, for her amazing attention to story flow and detail, and for knowing just how to advise me without making me want to jump from a tall building. And Rachel Meisel and the rest of the Summerside/Guideposts editing team who go above and beyond to read every word, over and over, until we get it as right as we can. Finally, thank you to my family for their support and willingness to put up with cereal for supper (and every other meal), especially my daughter, Sarah, who challenged me to write a 1920s book—"Not just about flappers, Mom." May you always know who you are, and where you belong.

S'ENVOLE

PARIS, FRANCE. 1923

Chapter 1

She no longer recognized herself in the mirror. Gone was the girl whose long black braids twisted in the prairie wind as she galloped her father's black Arabian across the Montana prairie.

Lilly Joy Hoyt Stewart stared at herself. She'd become a flapper—no, worse, a *charity* girl. Oxblood-red lips, kohl-black eyes, and rouged cheeks...she looked like she might be inviting danger.

She'd never be Parisian, no matter how her cousin Rosie dressed her up. And, if she bobbed her hair, she just might lose herself completely.

Maybe she simply didn't know who she was anymore, but she knew she hated the woman she had become since leaving Montana. The woman she couldn't seem to escape.

How could she hope to find her place in a world where she knew she didn't belong?

"No, Rosie. I'm not cutting my hair." Lilly stepped away from Rosie's hands, her dark hair falling free from where her cousin held it, just below her ears, as if seeing herself hairless might cajole Lilly into lopping off her braid, and taking the last step toward turning herself into one of the wild Parisian girls Rosie couldn't stop idolizing.

Apparently Lilly had become Rosie's pet project since arriving in Paris a month ago.

"Paris will be too sweltering in the summer to leave your hair long, Lils. Besides, short is all the rage."

Lilly took a cloth and began to wipe the dark lipstick from her mouth.

Rosie shook her head, sinking onto a gold velvet chaise, her own dark, bobbed hair shiny under the morning sunlight streaming in from the grand paladin windows of Lilly's boudoir. Dressed in a loose silk robe, knotted at her slender waist, all Rosie needed was an ebony cigarette holder to complete the portrait of a woman of leisure. If anyone could play the role, it was Rosie Worth, daughter of the infamous Jinx Worth, the widow of slain shipping baron Foster Worth. She had a certain *je ne sais quoi* about her that lured the attention of men and women alike. No one did tragic, misunderstood, and coquette quite like Rosie.

Except, few knew that Rosie was tragic and misunderstood. Since her brother disappeared in the war four years ago after her father was murdered and her mother publicly shamed, Rosie seemed to be the recipient of every morsel of scandalous reporting that appeared on Page Six of the *Chronicle*. No one truly understood that under that glamorous smile, Rosie was mere bits and pieces, one broken heart away from disintegrating. Except, of course, Lilly.

Although recently, even she didn't recognize Rosie, the way she threw herself into the bright, too-chaotic world of Paris. As if she were trying to forget the grief she'd left back in Manhattan. Maybe even recasting herself into a society girl who'd broken free of her family's scandal.

"I don't understand you," Rosie said, a pout in her tone. "We are in grand Paris! The home of Cartier and Boucheron and Maison Worth. Yesterday, during the showing of his new designs, you had your nose buried in a book. They served you canapés and champagne while the vendeuse tried to entice you, and there you sat, positively glum."

"I wanted to finish my novel. It's the newest Zane Grey—*To the Last Man*. I purchased it just for the journey."

"You've already finished it twice, *ma chérie*. It's time to take in the

City of Light, to enjoy the freedom of *jolie Paris*." Rosie intoned the last words with her crisp French accent, her brown eyes alight with mischief.

Lilly refused to rise to her charms. Rosie and her coy enthusiasm had the power to coax Lilly into nearly anything—hence, her painted face, and even the shapeless new dresses that hung in her wardrobe. What she really longed for, however, was a pair of britches and her boots, her father's old hat pulled low over her eyes as she rode Charity across their land. Sometimes she struggled to conjure up the aroma of the bitterroot flowers, the jack pines, the prairie grasses scenting the breeze. "I miss Montana."

Rosie's smile vanished. "I'm so tired of hearing about Montana and your precious ranch. You haven't been back for six years, Lilly. Your life is in New York. And Paris."

"I hate Paris." Lilly applied cold crème to her towel, began work on her eyes. The chiffon curtains blew in the traffic clatter and the dusty, smoky haze of the busy Champs-Élysées, tempered only by the faintest hint of the new horse chestnut blossoms along the boulevard. The luster of *la Belle Époque de Paris* had vanished the moment Lilly stepped out onto the balcony of the Worth family's Paris estate shortly after her arrival and discovered an encampment of hungry-eyed war orphans leering at her, yearning for crumbs of bread.

The gendarmes chased them away, and Lilly had the sense of prairie dogs scattering at the sound of a .22. She could have sent down her tray of *café au lait* and brioche. She longed for American fare anyway— perhaps a boiled egg, or even a piece of bacon.

The congestion of traffic outside her window—horses pulling carriages, buses belching out black exhaust, trolley cars and Citroens weaving in and out of foot traffic—reminded her too well of their view in New York City. It made her want to close her window, hide inside the safety of the brocade-papered walls, the crackle of the fire in the hearth.

"It might help if you and Aunt Jinx didn't insist on drilling French into my head. I cannot abide one more *bonjour* or *au revoir*. My tongue refuses the accent, and my ears curdle the moment I hear the word *mademoiselle*. Paris has made me mute, as well as illiterate."

Her eyes burned as she scrubbed. "I'd give my entire monthly allowance for an English bookstore, not to mention an English copy of the *Chronicle*. Must everything in this house be in French? Do you truly read the *Petite Republique*, and *Figaro*?"

"Of course. How else do you expect me to stay informed about the theater showings?"

"Please, Rosie. They're no better than the gossip pages of the *Chronicle*."

There went that annoying smile again. "I will translate for you, but you really should learn at least a modicum of French, *mon petit chou*. Otherwise, how will you understand the culture?"

"If you mean to turn me into a French flapper, I don't want to understand."

"Oh, Lilly. You are hardly in danger of dancing the night away with some lonely American doughboy. I'm just trying to help you fit in."

Fit in. Hardly. Lilly hadn't fit in anywhere since the day her mother stole her from her legacy in Montana, fitted her in a Gibson girl shirt-waist and skirt, threw away her muddy boots, and made her sit up straight at the table. Six years in New York, and still Lilly stared out her window overlooking Central Park and saw the big sky of the West.

It didn't help that her mother had settled without a look over her shoulder into New York life, running the newspaper with her new husband, Oliver. And in six years, not once had her mother mentioned returning home.

Lilly tried—really she did—not to feel betrayed.

But it also didn't help that her mother had packed her bags and sent her to Paris for the spring and summer with Aunt Jinx and Rosie. As if she didn't want her around anymore.

Just because Aunt Jinx pulled her aside and asked her to chaperone Rosie didn't lessen the sting.

Lilly finished wiping the kohl from her eyes and doused her face with the water in the basin on her dressing table. "I *do* want to understand Paris, Rosie, but here we are in the middle of history—with l'Arc de Triomphe right outside our window, and you'd rather spend the day on the Rue de la Paix looking at ostrich feathers. That is hardly French culture."

"It is *exactly* French culture. I can see Napoleon's masterpiece and the Eiffel tower from my window—what else is there? I suppose I can arrange for us to go yachting down the Seine, but as long as Mother and Bennett continue to pursue their fruitless, six-year search for Jack, I intend to throw myself into society, to take café at the bistros, to attend the theater and opera and to—"

"Drink Pernod and come home with the stink of cigarettes on your skin? If Aunt Jinx knew—"

"She won't know, and if she did, she could not stop me."

Lilly turned on her settee. "She could cut off your allowance."

"She wouldn't dare. Not after the scandal she put our family through. We would have never recovered if it weren't for Bennett's handling of Father's fortune."

Lilly drew in a breath, hearing the rancor in Rosie's voice. Clearly, her cousin still had to forgive her mother the sins that cost her a father, a brother.

"When is your mother due home?" Lilly turned, parted her hair into two sections, and began to braid. Behind her, Rosie uncoiled herself from the chair, got up, and paraded to the window, staring out on the street.

"I don't know. They didn't expect to be gone more than a day or two. But they cabled from Belgium, where many of the war records are kept, and said they might be a week, or even more. I fear that yet again, mother's hopes are for naught." Rosie drew in a long breath, one that shuddered out at the end.

Lilly knew that kind of breath—the kind that rattled grief through your soul.

"Jack always wanted to go to Paris. I wonder if he managed it," Rosie said quietly.

Lilly got up, slipped behind her, and circled her arms around her cousin's waist, resting her chin on Rosie's shoulder. Outside, a crowd gathered along the street, in anticipation of the day's procession.

Rosie cupped her hands over Lilly's. "I am forgetting my brother's smile, the sound of his voice when he teased me. He used to sneak into my room at night, after returning home from his outings, tell me about his adventures. He loved to read—like you do, Lilly—and he dreamed of being a hero. I shouldn't have been surprised that Jack left. He only needed a reason. And Mother *certainly* gave him one."

"I'm sure he's still alive, Rosie. Out there somewhere."

Rosie leaned her head back against Lilly's. "I think he may have fabricated a name so Mother wouldn't find him, otherwise, with the war over, he would have returned home. Unless…"

Rosie's fear hung in the crisp breezes of the morning. Her voice fell to nearly a whisper. "I'd do just about anything to find my brother and bring him home. I've written to the Department of War in America, and even London, nearly as often as Mother, and…I admit I look for his face as we walk the streets of Paris."

Lilly held her for a moment, wishing to shoulder her longings. No wonder Rosie insisted on going out on an excursion every day. "How about instead of attending the procession today, let's go for a stroll in Tuileries Park? Or to the Louvre? The last thing you need is a funeral."

For a moment, Rosie curled her hands upon Lilly's. Held them there. Then she detached Lilly's hands from her waist and turned. "This isn't a funeral." She swept her hand toward the crowds. "It's Sarah Bernhardt's bon voyage. We can't miss it."

"I don't know why you're so taken with this actress." Lilly stepped away from her, picked up a playbill of *Figaro* with Sarah's picture on the cover.

Rosie stood at the window, and Lilly considered that her cousin might just be brazen enough to step out onto the balcony in her robe. "She spoke once, in Brooklyn. I went to hear her—it was just after you arrived in New York. Sarah was mesmerizing, even then. The crowd hung on her every word. Even now that she's gone, look how they adore her."

On the street below, along the funeral parade route, Parisians held wreaths, some of them pressing handkerchiefs to their mouths, their eyes.

"Imagine, being able to capture the hearts of so many?" Rosie's voice fell to a whisper. "To be adored so completely."

"She was just an actress—"

Rosie rounded on her. "Just an actress? Sarah Bernhardt embraced life and everything in it. Did you know she lost her leg? She broke it during a performance and they had to amputate. But she never stopped acting." Rosie walked over to the balcony, gripping the curtains. "Never stopped living until the very end."

"Sarah's *life* was an act, a performance, Rosie. It wasn't real."

Rosie threw open the curtains. "That looks real to me."

A noise rose from the street below. Lilly watched as Rosie stepped out, garbed, yes, only in her chemise, although she tucked it tight around her. Lilly followed her, shaking her head at the things her cousin made her do. But the attention of the crowd settled, not on the two women in the third-story balcony, but on a decorated funeral cortege. A driver in full eighteenth-century livery drove a team of black horses pulling a floral-covered float, upon which lay Sarah's coffin, draped in yet more flowers. Walking beside it, a row of young girls held palm leaves, shading the float as it proceeded down the boulevard. As they passed, the mass of mourners closed in behind them, following them through the streets of Paris.

The drone could only be the mourning of Bernhardt's thousands of admirers.

"Quickly, Lilly, let's dress and join them." Rosie nearly pushed her back into the room. "I'm tired of grieving Jack. I want to live life big and bold. White hot and bright. Hurry, we don't want to be left behind."

"Rosie—"

"Don't you want an adventure, Lils? To break out of this life?"

Yes, actually, but—

"C'mon, let's join the crowd. It's time to become Parisian."

* * * * *

Rosie longed for the energy, the *joie de vivre* of Paris to sweep her up, to carry her down the Champs-Élysées, and into a different life. She might be attending a funeral, the mood more somber as she entered the surge of the crowd, but Paris never did anything without flourish. A band played as the spectacle of Sarah Bernhardt's grand, final procession urged onto the street all manner of observers. Sailors, dressed for leave, and displaced soldiers still lingering after the war, as if searching for something they'd lost. Frenchmen in bow ties and straw hats, matrons in pearls and furs, despite the spring air, and everywhere Rosie looked, young women in low-waisted dresses and felt cloche hats, and men in baggy suits all hustled behind the carriage.

"Lilly! Stay with me." Rosie turned, reached her hand back for Lilly's as she flowed into the crowd.

Rosie had rouged her cheeks, painted on lipstick, but haste demanded she forgo her black eyeliner and the pin curls. She'd return home before shopping this afternoon or venturing out this evening for dinner at the Ritz and dancing with Blanche and hopefully Dash. She heated all the way through with the memory of his hands on her waist.

Dashielle Parks embodied the zeal of the expatriates who had escaped New York for the onset of the spring fashion season, perhaps even the sultry Paris summer, in hopes of abandoning the rules of prohibition sweeping the country. They'd also abandoned the mores tethering them to high society, thirsty for something bold and shocking to sever them from its stiff-collared etiquette.

Her mother would keel over in a swoon if she knew Rosie had escaped their flat to join a throng of mourners.

Or perhaps not. Her mother, after all, had marched on Washington with the suffragettes. However, Jinx still cinched on her corset every morning, still wore her gloves and her furs, her diamonds sparkling against her broad décolletage. Still planned dinner parties and watched for suitors with a keen, matchmaking eye.

Rosie had no doubt that one of these days her mother might tote home some unfortunate chap she expected Rosie to marry.

Maybe Rosie would never get married. Look how marriage had turned out for Mother.

She wouldn't look too far ahead. Not right now. Not today. Not when she, too, thirsted.

She gripped Lilly's hand, pulling her cousin along behind her.

"Rosie, you're hurting me."

"Mother will simply murder me if you are lost. You know she won't allow us in the city without each other. Please, Lilly, keep up!" She glanced behind her. Lilly glared at her, her face unpainted, those annoying freckles thick on her crinkled nose. Lilly had barely had time to braid her long hair—why her renegade cousin insisted on looking like a savage from some Zane Grey novel...it was all Rosie could do to keep the gossips from inquiring about Lilly's heritage. So Lilly was part Crow Indian. It didn't mean she had to embrace it and ignore the privileges of being young and wealthy in Paris.

Like shopping, yes. But Paris offered more than simply a change of fashion scenery. They'd escaped into a new world. A freer world. A laissez-faire, come-what-may aura hued the conversations, the laughter. Women, even more than in New York City, wore their clothes loose, almost boyish. Only last week, Rosie was lunching at the Ritz, eating with Dash and Bradley "Tripp" Martin, Blanche Stokes, and Pembrook Stockbridge, a chap Dash knew at Harvard, when across the restaurant strolled a woman in trousers.

"She must be one of those art*eests*," Dash had said, his grin following his mangling of the French accent. And his gaze followed the woman without apology.

"Maybe you'd like to follow her all the way to the Left Bank, Dash," Tripp said, blowing out a curl of smoke from his cigarette. "We should slum over to the other side of the river, see what Boulevard Montparnasse has to offer. Go dancing at le Café Select."

Blanche reached for Tripp's cigarette. "Maybe we can talk Rosie into another glass of absinthe."

Rosie's face heated. "Blanche, that's not fair. I hadn't eaten—"

"What happened?" Dash said. He had a devastating smile, smoky dark, too-probing eyes, and a way of dancing with her that could make her stomach turn to warm milk.

Blanche laughed, blowing out smoke, handing the cigarette back to Tripp. "Two nights ago, she had a glass of Pernod—"

"They put water in it—it turned all green and milky. I thought it tasted like licorice," Rosie said quickly.

"Going down," Blanche said. Her gaze shot over to Pembrook, who seemed taken with the blond, his mouth slanted in a line of approval. "Not so much coming the other direction, I would guess."

For a delicious moment, Rosie lost herself inside Dash's amused smirk, not minding the chiding.

"Pernod is not for little girls," Tripp said, his mouth drawn down.

His words jarred her, and Rosie glared at him. "I'm no little girl."

"What are you, twenty?"

"Leave her alone, Tripp. Or I'll start telling her tales about your exploits at Harvard. Let's see, are you in your fifth or sixth year?" Dash said.

Tripp pursed his lips and turned away to watch a pair of flappers stride by, stockingless.

Little girl. Tripp's epitaph had clung to her all week, even cajoling her into letting Dash back her into a dark corner of the dance floor at the Napolitain. As the accordion player squeezed out a tune, Dash had pressed his lips against hers and whispered something dangerous into her ear.

She'd laughed, pushed her hands against his chest, but her heart stuck in her throat, watching him the rest of the night as he danced with Blanche and an Austrian tart named Lady Frances, whom he'd dubbed Frankie by the end of the night.

Not a little girl. Rosie had grown up the past six years, with the rest of the world trying to break free of the fear, the poverty of war. Grief did that to a soul—aged it.

She wanted to break free of the tentacles of grief, the specter of scandal. To feel every wild emotion layering Paris, to dance the Charleston and drink—yes, absinthe.

She wanted to live it all, in one big gulp. Even this funeral procession, this last hurrah to one of France's greatest performers, seemed alive and bold.

It was time for a new Rosie to emerge. She'd be like Sarah Bernhardt—

beautiful and adored. How hard was it to become an actress, to create a life on stage?

More crying—the sound rippled through the crowd.

"I don't like this. Let's go," Lilly said, tugging at her hand.

L'Arc de Triomphe loomed ahead. Rosie had no idea how long the procession might last—how deep into the Paris streets they might venture, but she held her cousin's grip. "Stay with me, Lilly."

How tired she'd grown of babysitting. Of Lilly's incessant whining, her refusal to behave when the seamstresses of Doucette attempted to measure her. Rosie had half a mind to let her buy her frocks off the rack in some peasant shop.

Worse, Lilly refused to visit the cafés with Rosie, or even take in the opera. Always the books, or writing letters to some ranch hand in Montana. Lilly was missing *everything*.

It was almost as if she'd forgotten she was the daughter of an heiress.

However, maybe Rosie should direct them through Luxembourg gardens, just to satiate her.

The crowd neared the Arc and surged forward, anticipating the narrowing of the parade through the gates. Some pushed, a woman screamed, and Rosie nearly fell. She released Lilly's hand. Immediately, Lilly sank behind. "Lilly! Stay with me!"

"No—I'm being suffocated!" Lilly turned, as if to escape the crush of the crowd.

"Fine! I'll meet you at the Café a la Paix!" They'd lunched there only yesterday—certainly Lilly could find her way.

She glanced for Lilly again, but the crowd closed around her.

"They called her Divine Sarah, did you know that?" A woman next to her held a handkerchief to her mouth. "I saw her in Shakespeare's *Antony and Cleopatra*. She made a heavenly Cleopatra."

Rosie found a sympathetic smile and only nodded. Clearly the woman considered Rosie to be French, and although her accent might be tolerable to the local garcón, she didn't want to try it out on the locals.

She followed the crowd to Père Lachaise Cemetery then stood on the edge, aware that she hadn't purchased the requisite triad of flowers.

The crowd had barely thinned by the time she snuck away, feeling— despite her attempts—a foreigner.

She inhaled the day as she returned to the Champs-Élysées. Regardless of the circumstances, the hour had a buoyant spirit about it— sparrows singing from the horse chestnut trees, the fragrance of lilac trees and pink dogwood blossoms, and the nutty smells of coffee twining out of the open cafés. Rosie lingered on her way back to the Boulevard, buying a new *Figaro* from a kiosk and a bouquet of pink tulips for her room. Lilly would be so angry with her, but for this brief hiccup of time, Rosie drank in the freedom away from her cousin.

Sure, Lilly pined for the frontier life she lost, but she'd been a wild-edged Calamity Jane when Aunt Esme decided to stay in New York and marry Uncle Oliver. Lilly should be happy to have a father after all these years. Rosie didn't understand the animosity Lilly bore toward Oliver— it wasn't like he had an affair with her mother, had disgraced the family name. Oliver was the co-publisher of the *Chronicle*. He had offices in Berlin, Amsterdam, and Paris. He'd made something of himself after growing up as a footman in the home of Esme and Jinx, their mothers. Lilly, the champion of the helpless and hunted, the bearer of all tales Wild West, should appreciate that.

Besides, Oliver adored Lilly. Or, at least it felt like that to Rosie. He shared Lilly's love of reading, showered her with books, and even gave her a camera and taught her to shoot photography. Not like Rosie's stepfather, Bennett, who looked at Rosie like he was seeing a ghost. She didn't resemble her father, Foster, that greatly, did she? Or maybe she was simply a reminder of the fact that her mother had chosen his brother over him.

Rosie tried not to hate Bennett. But he had an old-fashioned, even overprotective tendency, and the moment her mother married him, he'd enrolled Rosie in finishing school. Rosie felt like an antique as she walked across the room balancing a book on her head, or memorized French verbs, or learned how to waltz.

So that, what?—she might become more appealing in order that he could barter her off for a stake in some New York Knickerbocker family fortune?

Bennett didn't own her. And she didn't need his protection, or his affections. Let him direct them to her mother, finally happy after all these years, and her little half-brother Finley.

Finn, after all, could make anyone smile. Finn deserved to be loved.

"Rosie!"

The name turned her, and she looked around to see Blanche emerging from a hat shop, carrying a box. Rosie tried not to envy Blanche's platinum-blond bob, those green eyes that could hold a man captive. She had watched Dash dance with Blanche and finally took a breath when Pembrook cut in.

"Where's your tagalong?" Blanche swung the hatbox onto her arm. Her family had a fleet of servants, but Blanche had long ago emancipated herself from her mother's archaic expectations. Nichole Stokes had undoubtedly sent her daughter to Paris for the summer season in hopes of keeping her off the *Chronicle's* Page Six. But Paris had only ignited Blanche's joie la vivre. She smoked and drank like a man, and told jokes that made Rosie want to hide under the table. Her mother, Jinx, hated Blanche.

Rosie planned to spend every moment she could with her before Jinx returned to Paris.

"Lilly and I got separated in the funeral procession. I told her to meet me at the Café a la Paix."

"You went to the funeral?" Blanche stopped to purchase a handful of petite white daylilies from a youngster in a derby.

"Just the procession, but it seemed as if the entire city turned out. They loved her here."

"Paris loves a spectacle."

"No, there were real tears. Sarah Bernhardt was truly beloved."

Blanche lifted a shoulder. "And quickly forgotten, I'll wager. All of Paris is a stage and each of us players. We'll see who they mourn tomorrow. Come, let's track down Pembrook and Dash—I have a proposition for us all."

"I have to meet Lilly—"

"She's probably back in her room, her nose in a book. That girl has no sense of adventure." Blanche traded the flowers into her other hand and then wove her free arm into Rosie's. "What would you say to a trip to Auteuil, to the horse races? We can pack a basket with wine and sandwiches, be provincial and take the train?"

"Sounds splendid. When?"

"Tomorrow? Your parents haven't yet returned, but it seems our time is short."

"And Lilly? My mother would send me back to New York if she knew I'd abandoned Lilly for an outing to see the ponies. She nearly pledged on her life to Aunt Esme that we would keep Lilly safe and entertained."

Blanche smiled, tugged her close. "Perhaps she'll surprise us all and beg to join us. A day under the clouds, reading. She'll be no trouble at all."

"It's more likely she'll tuck up her skirts and leap right on a horse and gallop for the horizon."

"You don't like her much."

"I love her like a sister. She simply lacks the ambition to taste life. She hates Paris, or at least *my* Paris. If I allowed her to, she would wander the gardens of Luxembourg, lost in her memory of a life that is no longer hers."

"Montana."

"Her beloved ranch and her herd of buffalo."

"Buffalo?"

"Did you know that Lilly can shoot a pistol, ride a horse, and even swing a lasso? I know because she told me. Again, and again. She spends hours writing letters to a cowhand she left behind—"

"A beau?"

"More like an uncle. He runs their ranch in Montana, and before she moved to New York City, he took the place of the father she never had."

"Pity. What happened to her real father?"

"He died in a mining accident before she was born. Her stepfather, my Uncle Oliver, is the only father she's known, and she all but ignores him. No, Lilly has no interest in beaus, at least none in Paris. But I fear that someday Uncle Oliver will arrive home with the bookish son of his accountant and marry her into some austere flat on the outskirts of Manhattan. She will spend her entire gray life pining for a world she left behind and never truly live."

"I take it back. You *do* care for her."

"Of course. Who else does she have but me?"

Rosie stopped to look at a window display in front of Cartier's. She'd already perused their spring collection, but that long strand of pearls...

"Perhaps she will find a beau here, in Paris."

Rosie laughed. "No. Lilly isn't interested in love—it would have to get her attention and pull her nose out of her fairytale westerns and into the real world."

"But you might be. I saw the way Dash looked at you at the Napolitain. He kissed you, didn't he?"

He'd tasted of brandy, sweet and sharp, and for a moment, in his arms, Rosie had felt the bright lights of Paris shine through her. "Dash admires too many women for my taste." She added a shoulder shrug to her tone. "Not to mention himself."

"He does seem to relish his own reflection."

Rosie laughed. "I want a man who can't stop thinking about me, who will cross oceans and spend his last dime to woo me. A man who would surrender his life for me."

"You don't ask for much, do you, Rosie?"

"What's wrong with wanting everything?"

Blanche let her go, drew in the fragrance of her daylilies. "Because I fear you won't get it."

* * * * *

She couldn't possibly cross the Champs-Élysées without perishing. Lilly stood at the corner, the Café a la Paix crowded and loud and beckoning across the street, the name written in gold foil along a green canopy, and knew that if she stepped her foot out, some manner of bus or brougham or milk cart would mow her down.

But perhaps, if she navigated through the space of traffic, a moment at a time…how hard could it be? She used to herd buffalo on horseback. Certainly crossing traffic couldn't be that dangerous.

Besides, Rosie could be waiting for her right now. And while Lilly relished the moment she'd had wandering the gardens of the Palais Royal, feeling a bit like she'd finally escaped the congestion of Paris, Rosie might find herself in trouble if Lilly didn't meet up with her.

After all, who had been the one holding the chamber pot after Rosie's experiment with Pernod? Seen her dancing in the darkness with Dash? Watched the way Tripp's eyes raked over her?

It would help if Rosie didn't paint on her jersey sweaters along with her rouge. But Rosie's flirting was harmless. Dashielle's wasn't. She didn't for a moment trust Dashielle or Pembrook, and Rosie's friend Tripp could intimidate her, if Lilly were the cowering type.

But Aunt Jinx had nearly made her promise in blood that she'd stay with Rosie, keep her cousin from foolishness, and she intended to cross the street and keep her part of the promise.

She waited until a bus passed, saw a break in the flow, and darted out into the street like a chicken. A carriage nearly nipped her, the horse's hooves clomping like gunshots against the cobblestones, but she leaned away. Then—

"Are you trying to kill yourself?" A hand snaked around her arm, yanked her back. A Citroën nearly clipped her suede shoes.

Her rescuer pulled her back to the curb just as a trolley scooted into her spot.

For a slick, hot moment, her breath caught, her heart bulleted through her ribs.

She'd nearly died on the streets of Paris. A dramatic, tragic finale Rosie might have enjoyed, but...

Her arm began to burn where he gripped it.

"Let me go!"

"And watch you get run over?"

He moved her away from the edge of the boulevard where a fruit truck made a swipe too close to the curb.

Only then did she realize he'd addressed her in English.

Lilly shook out of his grasp, breathing hard, and looked at him.

He had dark brown eyes, the color of Parisian chocolate. They sank into her for a moment, sweeping away her words. Brown eyes, and light hair the color of parched prairie grass that curled from under a derby hat. He wore a tweed jacket, yet bore the tan of a field hand, the sunshine red upon his cheekbones and around his eyes. He looked in his late twenties, a little wear and tear around the eyes.

"I...I'm sorry," she said. "Are you okay?"

Her tone apparently flushed away the scolding in his expression.

"I'm alive," he said. "I suppose I shouldn't have handled you so roughly."

She refused to rub her arm in front of him. It would only accentuate her stupidity. Imagine what Abel would have said if he'd seen her throw herself in front of a stampede. Her face burned. "Thank you. I don't know what I was thinking."

"There are plenty of cafés on this side of Paris, I assure you." He had an accent, but not French. She couldn't place it.

"I am not hungry." Particularly. "I was simply trying to meet up with my cousin. We were separated, and she told me to meet her at the Café a la Paix."

"So darting across traffic like a jackrabbit seemed the best option."

A jackrabbit. She smiled at the comparison. And the way the rest of his frown eased from his face.

"I must find a way across the boulevard. My cousin will be waiting."

"I can't follow you around all day saving your life. I'm going to need some promises here."

The faintest excuse of a dimple appeared against what looked like a smattering of overnight whiskers, and as a smile emerged, her world slowed to a languid swirl.

"I...promise not to cross the road?"

He shook his head. "Nope. No good. I saw the look in your eye even before you stepped out on that curb. It scared the spit right outta me. I'm sorry, but you're going to have to accompany me to the nearest footbridge."

He held out his arm as if she would really take it.

"I don't even know you."

"Rennie Dupree, flyer and lifesaver at large."

She couldn't tell if he might be joking or not, his tone of voice solemn despite his white smile.

"Lilly Hoyt. Uh, daredevil." She wasn't sure why she said the words—both her former last name, and the moniker—in fact, for the last five minutes, it seemed she didn't recognize any of the words issuing from her mouth. But she hadn't seemed anything like herself since arriving in Paris—or New York for that matter. And she rather liked this title. It reminded her of who she'd once been, before her life had been stolen from her.

Most of all, she liked the way his smile settled into a smirk.

He seemed very much like one of Zane Grey's hero cowboys.

"Okay, Mister Dupree. You may walk with me."

"Rennie. Actually, it's Reynaud, but the chaps shortened it during the war."

He scattered blue-feathered pigeons before him as they walked down the street. A little boy ran up, dressed in suspenders, and offered up a handful of tiny budded flowers. She shook her head, but the fragrance followed her.

"Is this your first time in Paris, Miss Hoyt?"

"Lilly, please."

"For now, perhaps." He winked.

She could, she supposed, just return home. But, even as she walked in the company of this handsome stranger, she felt Rosie's tethers upon her loosen. Perhaps it was her too-brief stroll through the Palais Royal, perhaps the adventure that lurked inside her, fed by the pages of her Zane Grey novels.

She'd walk to the footbridge, be done with him, and harbor this tiny excursion in her heart.

"Your family is…," he asked, shoving his hands into the pockets of his baggy pants.

"Back home, in New York."

"I'm from just south of the province of Montreal," he said.

"You're from Canada."

"Originally from Winnipeg, although my family hails from the eastern side of the country. But I haven't been home since the war."

"Why not?"

He shrugged. "Too much life still to rescue, and nothing of obligation to call me home."

"What about your family?"

"I have no one. My brother was killed in the war, and my mother died shortly thereafter. My father died years ago from hard work and a bad heart."

"I'm sorry to hear that."

He lifted a shoulder. "He loved what he did. That's enough, I suppose, for any length of life. What brings you to Paris?"

"My mother sent me away with my cousin for the season—I think she hopes to knock the brooding from me."

"You're too pretty a girl to brood."

She glanced at him, his comment jarring her off her gait. Pretty? He had a nice smile, however, and seemed suddenly abashed by his own comment as he looked away.

Pretty.

She allowed his compliment to find soft soil in her heart. "It's just that, I don't much like New York. Or Paris. I don't belong here."

He made a face, shook his head. "Clearly, we'll have to remedy that."

Vendors hawking the *Chronicle* called for her attention. Apparently, they also beckoned her tour guide, because Rennie veered to the curb and picked up a copy. She read her mother's name on the masthead, along with Oliver's.

"I'd give anything for a novel in English," Lilly said, picking up a dime novel written in French. She was sounding out the headline when he sidled up beside her.

"*Wild Bill Cody and Calamity Jane.*" He translated the words. "The legends of the West. I wonder if they ever really existed."

"They're real. I used to live in Montana. You'd be surprised—"

He laughed. "Please. I grew up chasing prairie dogs and herding cattle. These stories are a bit more embellished." He eased the book from her hand, his eyes warm, knowing. "How would you like to find some real books?"

"In English?"

He smiled. "Of course." The little tuck in his cheek belied the mischief in his eyes. "If I promise to return you to the Café a la Paix, would you allow me to show you a bit of Paris? I believe you will find it not as wretched as you imagine."

His offer made her catch her breath. What if…what if she intentionally lost herself in Paris, just for a day? Tried to find the beauty, even her place in this world? Then she might happily return to Rosie's keeping.

No. Rosie might get into trouble without her.

Except, that seemed to be exactly what Rosie wanted—to be rid of Lilly. And Rennie Dupree might be just the joie de vivre that Rosie hoped for her.

At least for one delicious afternoon.

She considered him. He had a woundedness about him, something broken in his eyes, and they tugged at her.

Oh, how much trouble, truly, could Rosie find by herself for a day?

"It's becoming less wretched by the moment," Lilly said softly and slipped her hand through his arm.

Indeed, she might become Parisian after all.

Chapter 2

"Lilly isn't going to show up, Rosie. Let's go."

As she spoke, the smoke puffed from Blanche's mouth, dissipating into the clutter of conversation and commotion of the Café a la Paix. A bright wind had bullied away the clouds, and the sun burned down from a cheerful azure sky. Around them, patrons read newspapers or simply watched street traffic along the Champs-Elysees, most of them nursing a cup of café noir.

Rosie turned away from her, her own café au lait long finished, along with a plate of strawberry crepes, and scanned again the crowd that perched at the street-side tables. "Certainly we didn't miss her. We've been here for two hours."

"I told you that she'd probably gone straight home. I'll wager she's sitting in the alcove of her window, rereading one of those horrendous dime novels. I promise you that she won't mind an afternoon off."

"What if she's lost?"

Blanche switched her long, pearl-handled cigarette lighter into her other hand. "And what of it? She'll find her way home. Perhaps it might do her well to find a day to herself in Paris. Imagine if—"

"Imagine my mother packing us all up and sending us back to New York. That's exactly what will happen when she discovers I've abandoned Lilly. No, I need to go home, make sure she's arrived safely."

And then what? Rosie had no trouble seeing Lilly just as Blanche described her—tucked with her knees up under her skirt, reading in the sunlight. She'd be content for hours.

She wouldn't even miss Rosie, most likely.

"Dash and Pembrook have a tennis match this afternoon. Please don't tell me you'd rather retrieve your interminable cousin than see Dash be walloped by Pembrook."

"Dash will most undoubtedly triumph."

Blanche smiled, the sun touching her nose despite her hat. "Lilly is fine. It's Dash and Pem who need us. Who else do they have to show off for?"

Rosie found a grin.

Dash was up by two games by the time they threaded their way onto the bleachers at the Tennis Club de Paris. Pembrook looked smart and British in a pair of white flannel pants and a cardigan, his brown hair loose in the wind, his eyes darting to the stands long enough to lose the return from Dash.

"Rosie! Already my good luck charm!" Dash yelled into the stands, earning a glance from others in the gallery. He didn't seem winded in the least, his raven-dark hair slicked back, looking fit in a vest and dark flannel pants. He might stand shorter than Pem, but he had the shoulders of a football player. Rosie had heard rumors that he'd played the sport at Harvard last year.

The men's league filled up the courts today, although the official games had already occurred. It seemed Dash and Pem waged a gentleman's game as no linesman stood at the net for accountability.

"Trounce him, Pem," Blanche shouted, not caring what glances she drew. "Then he can owe us dinner."

Dash shook his head, pointing at Blanche with his racquet. "And if I win, you will owe me a dance."

She giggled, and Rosie refused to encourage her. But then Dash glanced back at her. "And the rest will be for you."

Oh, Dash.

However, "Only if you win," she shouted back.

He grinned, a row of perfect white teeth, and heat curled inside her. Rosie tucked her hands together as she watched Dash take the next point.

"I wish you knew how to play," Rosie said to Blanche as one of the men's courts opened up. The women's league started later in the day, and before her mother left for Belgium, Rosie had considered joining one for the summer. "We could have our own match."

"What about Lilly?" Blanche said.

"She tried, but the sport seemed too mundane for her." Rosie winked at Blanche. "No bucking broncos, no wild herd of buffalo. She does, however, long for the outdoors. Perhaps I could persuade her to take lessons."

With the wind rustling the chestnut trees towering over the clay courts and the sound of the racquets swatting the ball, the birds warbling around them, an afternoon game of tennis might aptly resemble a walk in the park.

Maybe Rosie could convince Dash to teach them both.

He backhanded his shot neatly into the far corner of Pem's court.

"Out!" Pem shouted.

Dash whirled around, another ball already in his grip. "Out? Pem, are you blind? That was in by a half-mile."

"Out," Pem repeated.

Dash glanced at the girls. "Rosie? You saw it, right?"

"Looked in to me." The voice came from behind her, and Rosie turned to see Lady Frances standing behind them. She carried her racquet, secured in a square, and wore a white linen dress that showed her ankles. A headband and a quaint blue-and-green checkered sailor's tie at her neck marked the colors of the club. She grinned over Rosie's head at Dash.

"See, Frankie says it was in," Dash yelled to Pembrook.

Rosie stood up. "I saw it. It was most definitely in. Dash's point."

"That's my girl," Dash said, but Rosie couldn't be sure to whom he might be referring.

Blanche glanced back at Frankie, shielding her eyes from the sun. "Are you in the women's league?"

Frankie nodded. "But Dash said he'd give me some pointers after his match, help me with my backhand."

She waved again to Dash as she walked away, toward the ladies' locker room. Rosie shot a look at her departing figure, slender and regal. "Where is she from, anyway?"

"Belgium. She was married to some count, but they divorced last year. I hear she's engaged to an Austrian of some nobility, but no one can track him down. She's got a fix on Dash, it seems."

"It seems."

The gallery of straw-hatted men in the far bleachers watched Frankie waggle by as she rounded the court and disappeared into a private entrance door.

"We'll glue his eyes back on you," Blanche said, leaning toward her. "Tomorrow at the pony races. You'll have him all to yourself. Pem and I will make sure of it." She followed her words with a wink, and Rosie wished she had Blanche's gall. Blanche had no problem showing her knees to Pembrook, or shooting back a glass of Pernod, or even learning the Charleston, the newest craze to hit Paris.

Rosie just wanted to keep up.

"Service," Dash yelled, and stretched as he threw his tennis ball in the air.

No, she wanted more than to keep up.

She wanted to win.

"What time does the train leave tomorrow?" she asked as Dash aced Pembrook for the game.

"Seven. I know it's early, darling." She leaned closer to her. "Perhaps we should simply stay up all night. Dance the night away at the Napolitain."

Dash and Pembrook met at the net and shook hands, although Pem wore a scowl.

"Oh dear. I will have to be on my best cheery behavior tonight if I hope to get a smile out of Pembrook." Blanche rose. "He is always so glum when he's bested in tennis."

Dash picked up a towel and his bag and came over to the fence. Sweat streaked down his face, and he blotted his forehead. "Wait for me? We'll dine at the Petite Rabbit tonight, near the Left Bank. It's supposed to be uninhabited by the American *étranger.*" He used his terrible accent, but added a wink. "We'll remedy that."

"I have to get home. I lost Lilly." But as soon as the words left Rosie's mouth, Frankie exited the locker room, swinging her racquet, heading back in their direction. Rosie didn't miss Dash's glance, then full attention upon the countess.

Frankie waved. "Dashielle!"

"Perhaps I'll wait," Rosie said. "Lilly is most likely at home, reading."

"I won't be long," Dash said, but Rosie caught Blanche's rolled eye expression.

"We'll be in the salon, for lemonade. Are you sure you don't want to join us?" Blanche slid her arm into the crook of Pembrook's.

"I'll wait for Dash," Rosie said, her voice tight.

The sun seemed extraordinarily hot for March, bleeding into her skin, turning it slick, despite the afternoon breezes as she watched Dash instruct Frankie, who knew perfectly well how to manage the backhand stroke, Rosie guessed.

It seemed that Frankie fit perfectly in his embrace. He had strong arms and even laughed once, the sound of it carrying across the lawn courts and simmering inside her.

Finally Frankie scooted off for her game and Dash found his way back to Rosie. "You're a good chap, waiting for me, Rosie." He nicked her on the chin with his finger. "I'm famished. How about a refreshment?" He winked. Undoubtedly he meant something more bracing than lemonade.

She got up and slipped her arm through his when he offered it. And glanced back at Frankie, lining up for her serve.

Lilly would be accompanying Rosie to the pony races if she had to drag her cousin by her long, annoying braids.

They found Pembrook and Blanche in the salon. Pem excused himself with Dash, and the pair retreated to the locker room to change.

"Try this, Rosie." Blanche handed her what looked like a lemonade. She took a sip and her lips puckered, the moisture sucked from her mouth.

"What is it?"

"A brandy smash. It's very chic."

Rosie wrinkled her nose but ordered the drink anyway. Thankfully, by the time it arrived, Dash saved her by appearing in a suit and bow tie and smelling of some exotic spice. He offered her his arm and didn't look back once at the courts as they left.

She'd hardly dressed for dining when she left the flat that morning, but by the time the shadows sunk around them, and they'd had to wait for their table at le Petite Rabbit—apparently the word leaked out about no foreigners—she'd forgotten that she hadn't colored her eyes or feathered her hair. Dash poured those smoky eyes into hers, however, and she barely tasted her roast chicken.

Or, thought once of Lilly.

They walked home along the Seine, Notre Dame Cathedral shining against the night, the stars above the bright lights of a grand performance.

Accordion and banjo music floated out from the cafés as they walked up the Rue du Cardinal Lemoine, the music mixing with the murmuring of voices of those dining on outdoor terraces. The moon came out to join them and hung low, peeking between the greening linden trees, the redolence of spring twining toward the blackened river.

A sailor tottered by, his arm about the shoulders of a girl wearing the war years in her young eyes. He carried a bottle of wine in his grip and raised it to toast them as they walked by, saying something to Blanche in a curdled British brogue.

"What did he want?" Dash said over his shoulder to Pem.

"He asked if we knew the way to Scotland."

They laughed, and Rosie felt Dash slip his hand into hers. Warm and strong, he wove his fingers through hers and tucked her close to him.

Pem and Blanche fell back, stopping at a wooden footbridge. It seemed as if Dash had no compunction to wait for them. He wandered down to a grassy patch and settled them on a bench. The Seine lapped against the shore, a whisper as the moon traced a finger down the middle.

"A guy could fall in love with you, Rosie, if you gave him a little encouragement." He ran his hand under her chin, drew her face to his.

"He could?" Oh, too much hope in her voice, but she didn't mind it when Dash smiled and leaned close.

"Could be halfway there, already."

Then, just as she hoped, he slid his hand to her face and kissed her. He tasted of wine and sweet dark chocolate, and she let herself into his arms, returning the kiss. He ran his arms around her and pulled her closer, deepening his ardor, and the adventure in it ignited something dangerous inside her. She curled her arms up around his shoulders and hung on.

He finally eased away, left her hungry for more, and smiled down at her. "You are a lovely thing, aren't you?"

"Am I?"

He tweaked her on the nose and winked, pressing another kiss to her lips as he caught her face in his hands. "Of course."

She leaned against him, settling into his arms, relishing them around her. "I went to Sarah Bernhardt's funeral today. All of Paris turned out for it."

He had his lips against her neck.

"Wouldn't that be grand? To see your name on a marquee? To have strangers throw you flowers and weep over you?"

He had his arm around her shoulders, drawing her back to him. She heard him chuckle, a low rumble in his chest. "Rosie. You have such fancy dreams."

She leaned away from him, turned. He met her eyes, humor in them.

"Don't you think I could be an actress? Maybe in the picture shows?"

His gaze dipped to her mouth, back up to her eyes. "I think you are a pretty girl on the loose in Paris who's had too much Pernod." He tried to touch his forehead to hers, but she jerked away.

"I haven't had a drop to drink tonight. Besides, you're one to talk, Dash. Fresh out of Harvard, your father's millions in your back pocket, idling away your life in Paris. You're the one who's had too much Pernod."

"C'mon, Red, don't be sore. Sure, you could be in the movies. It's just that I think you're destined for a different life. Your father has millions—"

"He's my stepfather—"

"And he'll want to marry you off to some wealthy duke who can give you a title and keep you in diamonds."

She wanted to slap him then, something brash and hot inside her. "What if I don't want that? What if I think marriage is outdated and *bourgeoisie*? What if I don't plan to ever get married?"

The last thing she expected was his slow, languid smile. "Doesn't mean you can't fall in love, right?"

When he kissed her again, she had already agreed. He confused her so, and her breath caught in her chest when he pulled away, kissed her forehead, her eyes.

"And what of you, Dash? Don't you dream big dreams?"

"I don't have dreams." He found her eyes, searching them for a long moment, smiled, something dangerous and intoxicating. "I have inspiration."

"There you are!" Blanche called down from the embankment as Dash broke away from her. "Come up here, you two. Pem is bleeding!"

Dash untangled himself from her, and she followed as he scrambled up to the street.

Pem sat on the sidewalk, his hands to his nose, blood on his linen jacket.

"What happened?"

Blanche knelt next to him, holding a handkerchief to his face. "A couple of sailors suggested something rude—"

"I'm a lover, not a fighter," Pem said mournfully. "But I gave it my best shot at defending her honor."

Blanche laughed, clearly unaffected by Pem's misery. "Good thing a gendarme happened by or he just might be defending me on the bottom of the Seine."

"Break my heart, will you, Blanche?" Pem turned to Dash. "I had it sorted."

"I'm sure you did. Want to point me in the direction of those sots?" Dash said as he hooked his hand under Pem's arm and hauled him to his feet as Blanche scrambled up beside him. Pem took the handkerchief, examined it.

Rosie put her hand on his arm. "Dash."

He glanced at her. "C'mon, Red. You're not going to let Pem bleed for nothing, are you?"

"I think I don't want you bleeding all over my new dress."

"I'll buy you another one." He grinned at her and tucked his arm around her waist, his voice low in her ear. "It's too early for the night to be tamed, don't you think, Red?"

Oh.

His voice could turn her to honey, and she kept hearing his words...

Inspiration.

She was his *inspiration*.

But it scared her a little too. She feared what his words might encourage if they continued their walk along the Seine.

"Take me home, Dash. There is plenty of taming yet to do this season. Besides, we have to get up early if we want to make the train."

His grin didn't quite meet his eyes, but he hailed a cab. They squeezed into the backseat, she sat on Dash's lap, and he let his hand linger on the small of her back, heating her through.

When they reached her house, he climbed out behind and walked her to the door. In the shadows he pressed a lingering kiss to her lips, suggestion in his touch. "The moon is still up, and Lilly is asleep."

"Dash—"

"You know I won't sleep a wink for thinking of you."

She pressed her hand to his chest, the doorframe in her spine. "Tomorrow—"

"Yes, tomorrow. We'll play the ponies for more than money." He winked. "I'll be by at six."

Her voice had vanished and she let herself inside, closing the door and leaning against it as she counted her heartbeats.

Then she smiled and pressed her fingers to her lips. Maybe she *was* just a pretty girl in Paris, maybe this was all she could dream.

But what if this was everything?

Lilly. She'd have to waken her and tell her their plans. Then pack a picnic lunch. Then lay out her clothing and bathe...

Perhaps Blanche had been correct—they should have simply stayed out all night.

Rosie shook away the smile and took the stairs lightly, then padded down the hall to Lilly's room. She wouldn't be surprised to find her cousin still reading, the light pooling over her pillows, or even before the hearth, a fire crackling to ward off the spring chill.

As she opened the door, an eerie silence breathed through her. No cracking fire, no slumber breathing from Lilly's bed. Lilly's *still-made* bed. Rosie turned on the light and stared, her heart loosening from its moors and dropping.

No Lilly. And from the looks of it, she hadn't returned all day.

Rosie didn't care that she awoke Amelia, or that the housekeeper was in her nightclothes. "Did Lilly come home today?"

Amelia shook her head. "No, ma'am. I thought she was with you."

Rosie pressed her hand against her breath, hot in her chest. "She's not here?"

Amelia shook her head then grabbed her robe to follow Rosie back to Lilly's boudoir. Rosie stood in the lit room, unable to purge the images too easily conjured. "Where could she be?"

She went to the alcove in the window, picked up the overturned copy of Zane Grey, and pressed her hand to the page.

Amelia stood at the door. "I'll brew some tea."

Rosie nodded then sat back, drew up her legs under her dress, and stared out into the graying night. *Lilly, where are you?*

* * * * *

Somewhere in the back of her mind, Lilly knew she should go home. That Rosie might be worried.

But the Cathedral of Notre Dame sparkled under the moonlight and the music floated down the dark, mysterious Seine, and for the first time in six years, she felt as if life might be more than what she left behind. She could taste it, the freshness of the breeze, smelling of freedom, of the sky. Maybe there was a place for her outside Montana, if she just looked for it.

"There are so many stars."

"If you think those are pretty, I should take you for a ride in the country. When the moon is full, waxing over a rolling French hillside, frosting the trees, turning the lakes to ribbons of molten silver. Glorious."

Rennie leaned over the edge of the bridge, the reflection of the moon in his eyes as he spoke, as if seeing something beyond the skyline of Paris.

"You sound like one of those writers I met today. But you're talking about flying, aren't you?" Lilly said.

"From the sky, everything looks so small. You can put your thumb over an entire river, a barn, or a house and make it disappear. Everything drops away except for the wind in your ears and the feeling that you are weightless, nothing to bind you to this earth."

She could sink into his voice—the way he described Paris, or his upbringing on the farm in Canada, not so far from her ranch in Montana. "Did you learn to fly in the war?"

"I went to England and signed up there with the RAF. They gave us a crash course and sent us over to France. I flew a Sopwith Camel with the 209th Squadron."

She wanted to ask, but instead, she stared into the black water of the river, watching a silhouette of a couple on the sidewalk walking arm in arm.

The charisma of the night seemed to wheedle from him a piece of himself, and he surprised her with his tone, intimate, and even a little sad.

"It was different, flying in the war. You went up knowing it could be your last time. The German Flying Circus had a chap named Richthoven who could knock anything out of the skies. They called him the Red Battle Flyer. He was finally taken out by my flight commander, Roy. Even then, he didn't crash, just set his plane down in a sugar beet field and died. Shot in the head."

The drama of the Great War had ended so soon after her arrival in New York, for Lilly the entire affair lacked the tragedy it should. Sure, she'd seen soldiers return home, some of them missing arms or legs, but mostly she'd seen the war through Aunt Jinx's grief over her runaway son, Jack. Lilly had only known Jack a day at most before the revelation of her aunt's affair drove him to war.

What if her cousin Jack was right here, in Paris, lunching at a café, or painting out of one of those suitcases along the river? Maybe she'd passed him in her tour of Paris, as Rennie charmed the day away.

She still couldn't believe she'd spent the day with a stranger.

Only now, perhaps not a stranger at all.

"It's a miracle you survived," she said as Rennie's words faded into the fold of night.

Rennie looked away from her. "I'm not sure I believe in miracles anymore. I saw too many friends burn in their planes to believe in miracles."

He straightened up from the railing, turned to her, and his eyes glistened. She looked away, the sharpness of his emotions cutting through her.

"Do you believe in miracles, Lilly Hoyt?"

She drew in a breath. "I didn't grow up with miracles. I grew up with hard work."

"Says the woman of nineteen formidable years."

She glanced at him, her gaze skimming quickly off his, his words stinging. "I don't suppose you saw a hint of God up there in the skies."

He stared at her, those brown eyes sifting through her words.

"Maybe it's not worth looking. Seems like heartbreak to put so much hope into something that might not even be there."

"You don't believe in God?"

"Oh, I believe in God. I just don't think He cares. In fact, I think He's abandoned us. Try flying over a battlefield and you'll see I'm right."

She had no words for this, churning them over inside. She hadn't given God much thought beyond the pews of her church on Sunday morning. If she looked around hard, however, she might agree with Rennie.

What use was God if He didn't show up for the important moments? Like saving her father? Or finding Jack? Maybe He had abandoned her. Maybe she had to figure out her life and where she fit into it on her own.

Rennie's hand slid into hers, warm and solid.

"Do you mind?" he said quietly.

"No."

He smiled then and tugged her over the bridge, back to the Quai de la Tournelle.

"I'm sorry I never got you back to Café a la Paix."

"I'll have to alert a gendarme, see if he will rescue me."

"I would put up a fight. They would have to arrest me and throw me in the Bastille."

She heated down to her bones. The guilt of not meeting Rosie had slowly sloughed off her, leaving only the niggle of shame, and with his words, that too vanished. Frankly, Rosie would probably applaud today's adventures.

"I would bring you crepes and books from Sylvia," Lilly said, laughing.

True to his word, Rennie had introduced her to a bookstore— Shakespeare and Company, located under the eyes of the cathedral in the Latin Quarter, on what Rennie called the Left Bank. Books crammed every cranny, tucked spine in or out, on their sides, or on end, massive walls with ladders climbing into the rafters to retrieve Homer and

Dante and Flaubert. There, he'd loaded her up with what he called "real books"—a novel by a new author named James Joyce, another by a T. S. Eliot. And poems by a woman named Gertrude Stein. "She lives right here in Paris and has readings at her salon."

He introduced Lilly to the proprietor, Sylvia Beach, and they drank tea, a spicy Indian mix that made her tongue sparkle in her mouth.

Then they strolled along the crisp gravel paths of the Luxembourg gardens, and Lilly lost herself inside this pocket of grace, abundant with cherry trees and leaf-strewn canals and thirsty willows. She drank in the flower gardens around the Palace and let Rennie buy her a cup of café au lait and a brioche as they sat at a wrought iron table, watching little straw-hatted boys dip their sailboats into the mirrored surface of the lake. Rennie then toured her through the Musee du Luxembourg to view the Cézannes and Monets and finally out the other side, to the Parthenon with its grand columns. They sat again at the original model of the Statue of Liberty.

"You can see the Eiffel Tower from here," he said, and she made out the frame of it against the setting sun.

They ate dinner at a café off the Boulevard Montparnasse—Rennie called it Mount Parnassus—and finished off a plate of oysters, although she turned down the frothy beer for a lemonade.

Then he had walked her back along the garden to the Seine.

Now he stood on the curb to hail a cab. "The truth is, I don't want to take you home."

She savored his words. "I really don't have a home anymore."

"I thought New York was your home."

"It's my mother's home. And my stepfather's home. My home is in Montana, on a ranch as big as this city. We have a herd of protected buffalo and a stake in a copper mine. But my mother owns the *Chronicle*, and she came back to New York to run it."

"Your mother is the publisher of the *Chronicle*?"

"Along with my stepfather. I think she hopes I'll take up the reins one day, but I have no interest in the paper. I intend to someday return to Montana and run our ranch. I'm only here because my mother decided I needed some culture, and my cousin Rosie needed a companion."

"Rosie is the one who left you during the procession?"

"She's probably out with her friends Dashielle and Blanche and Pembrook, glad to be rid of me."

He was staring at her, his eyes darkening.

"What?"

"I can't think of anyone who might be glad to be rid of you."

His words made her throat fill, conjured up emotions too long bottled inside. "I'm trapped in this life and I don't know how to get away. Today is the first day since we've arrived in Paris I've felt like I can be myself. Or maybe the me I'd *like* to be. Someone who Rosie doesn't have to doll up to keep from embarrassing her."

She ran her hand across her cheekbone, wiping away the wetness there. "I'm sorry. I'm just tired of feeling like I don't belong."

Rennie stared at her a long time, until she finally looked away.

"C'mon. I want to show you something."

He held out his hand and waved to a passing taxi. They climbed into the backseat.

"Aéroport de Paris—Le Bourget, s'il te plait," he said.

"Where are we going?"

"To show you where you do belong."

They drove north out of Paris until the carbon lights of an airstrip dotted the horizon. The round lights bordered the roofs of two long buildings and fanned out across a grassy, flat field of amber grass.

The driver let them off and Rennie handed him a roll of francs.

Then he took her hand and walked her across the grassy field toward the hangar.

"Rennie—"

"Trust me."

A row of planes sat parked outside the hangar, the moon shiny on their wings. He walked up to a biplane, ebony black, and ran his hand down her side. "This is Lola."

"After your girlfriend?"

"My dog." He grinned at her. "But don't tell anyone."

The plane had two cockpits, and he reached into the front and pulled out a leather helmet and a pair of goggles. "Your eyes will go dry if you don't wear these."

Her hands shook as she took them, but she tugged on the leather hat, the goggles, then took his hand to climb up onto the wing and into the front cockpit.

It sat her low, almost to her ears.

He climbed on the wing and leaned in over her, drawing a buckle across her lap.

As he leaned away, he again said, "Trust me."

Oh, how had she gone from a flapper to a fool in just a day? But the peril stirred a dormant spirit inside her, and she nodded to him.

He donned his own goggles then headed to the front of the plane. Giving a jerk on the prop, he let it go, and it spluttered then roared to life. The power of it filled Lilly's ears, the wind blowing into her face.

The plane had begun to move without Rennie in it. "Rennie!"

He jogged around the wing, letting the plane catch up, then flung himself inside the second cockpit, settling down into the seat. "Going somewhere without me?"

She laughed, but it came out too high, too much fear in it. She hung onto the sides of the cockpit as he maneuvered the plane out from the hangar and toward the grassy runway.

Already, the exhilaration of sound and wind filled her belly. She gulped it all in, tasting something fresh and whole.

They gained speed and she held in a scream as they lifted off, leaving the ground for the heavens.

Her stomach stayed earthbound, however, and she covered her mouth with her hand to stave off her surprise.

The light fell away from them as they ascended into the darkness, toward the stars. The farmland below darkened, buildings flattening, roads bleeding into the vast plane of shadow. In the distance, she made out the twinkling lights of Paris.

She couldn't speak over the roar of the plane, so she simply took in the wash of starlight above and below. Rennie turned the plane, and she held on, fighting another scream—this one more from delight, as they headed toward Paris.

Now this was how a girl should see the Eiffel Tower. It lit up, a beacon all the way to the top, arching over the city, spilling light onto the river, blue-black under the glow of the big bridges.

Beyond that, the city fanned out in sprinklings of light, the boulevards like rivers of fire through the city.

She put out her thumb and blotted out the tip of Notre Dame, then the Eiffel Tower. With her hand, she laid waste to entire districts. The Latin Quarter, then the Champs-Élysées, the Hotel de Ville.

She heard him laughing behind her, and when she turned, her braids wrapped around her. For the first time, she pondered cutting them off.

Then her leather flying cap would fit better.

Rennie arched the plane around the Eiffel Tower and then back toward the airfield, but she turned in her seat. "Please! Let's go around again!"

He must have heard her, because he grinned and nodded.

She settled back for another turn.

I'll show you where you belong. Rennie's voice hung in her ears, beyond the drone of the propeller, the sting of the breeze on her face.

Here she'd been thinking she belonged in Montana. Could it actually be in the heavens?

Chapter 3

He wore a black tux, a creamy white shirt, and a gray ascot at his neck, and seemed so real as he extended his hand for her, Rosie wasn't sure if she was dreaming or not. She wore gloves, and possibly an opera dress, for she heard the sounds of *Figaro* deep inside her mind.

Dash smiled at her, his eyes caressing her as he drew her up the stairs then lowered his mouth to ear. "A guy could fall in love with a girl like you if he only had some encouragement."

She lifted her face to his and—

"Rosie!" A horn blared from the street outside, jerking her from the swaddle of slumber and into the misty gray dawn. She'd fallen asleep on Lilly's velvet chaise lounge. Someone had pulled a blanket over her.

She looked up, expecting Lilly's form in the bed, but it lay smooth and unrumpled.

"Red!"

The voice, deep and husky, drew her to the window. She threw open the sash, letting the cool, misty air of the morning leak in, and looked down. "Dash! Shh! You'll awaken all of Paris."

"It's a grand day to be awakened," he said, looking cheery in a derby hat, green cardigan, and tweed trousers.

She ran her fingers through her hair, thankful that she'd long ago cut it to a manageable length, then threw another glance at Lilly's empty bed.

For the first time, fear wound a hand around her throat and squeezed.

On the landing, she opened the door to Dash leaning with one arm against the frame, looking and smelling as if he'd had hours of unencumbered sleep. Where was his promise to lay awake all night thinking of her?

His expression fell when he saw her. "You're not ready? No matter, we'll wait."

She looked past them to Blanche, riding in the front seat beside Pembrook, who had taken out his family's Citroën for the jaunt to the station. Blanche wore a low-brimmed silk hat—possibly yesterday's purchase, and a low V-necked blue dress. She leaned over Pembrook. "Rosie, why aren't you ready?"

"It's my cousin. She hasn't returned from yesterday."

Blanche had the grace to look concerned. "She stayed out all night?"

"I don't know. I feel I must go out to look for her—"

"She probably met some nice chap and fell in love, is sailing away with him at this moment." Dash winked at her.

"That's not funny, Dash. She could be hurt, or lost. Or..."

"Shh, pet. She's fine. C'mon, we have a train to catch."

She stared up at him, nonplussed. "I can't go without her."

"Why not, you spent all day without her yesterday—"

"And she failed to come home!"

Dash's eyes darkened, his voice lowered. "And how many times have you come sailing in nearly at dawn?"

Her jaw tightened. "But I was with you. And Lilly was there too."

He sighed then turned to the car. "Pem, I think you'll have to go on without us. Don't lose too much of my money."

He turned back to her, held out his hands. "I'm at your service. Let's find your cousin."

Oh, Dash. The fact that he had suddenly sacrificed his day...

that Lilly had ruined everything again. "Dash, you should go with them. Don't let my cousin wreck your day. I can manage. I'll send our house-boy out to look for her, and maybe I'll go back to the Café a la Paix." She closed her eyes. "If she doesn't return soon, we'll alert the gendarmes."

Dash's voice softened. "I'm sure she's fine. We'll find her."

"Oh, even if she is, Mother will send us back to New York if she finds out about this."

"I hope not." He lifted her chin, and she opened her eyes to find his soft. "We were just starting to have fun." He smiled down at her, and clearly she needed more sleep, because her legs turned soggy.

She had a good mind to go with him, to forget Lilly. But what if she was truly hurt, or worse? Reckless, selfish... She drew in a deep breath. "You should go with them," she said again. "Don't let Lilly ruin your day." She signaled to Pembrook, now arguing with Blanche, most likely about the outcome of the day's activities. "Take Dash with you!"

He stared down at her. "No, Red, I'll stay."

She pressed her hands on his chest, pushed him back. "Go, Dash. Win me something." Then she stepped up and pecked him on the cheek.

"Are you sure?"

No. But what choice did she have? She didn't want Dash to see her as a weight around his neck. "Pem, try and keep him out of trouble!" she said as Dash slipped into the back seat. He waved as they drove away.

She closed the door, ran her hand against the panel.

Lilly.

She wanted to be angry, but fear tempered her emotion into worry.

She found Amelia in the kitchen, meeting with the cook, a French woman named Annette, who had worked for Bennett for two decades. They looked at her with concern.

"Perhaps I need to alert the police that my cousin is missing."

Amelia nodded. "I'll get Pierre and have him take care of it."

"And then send Leo out to Luxembourg Gardens—she's always wanted to go there. It's possible she wandered across the river onto the Left Bank and then couldn't get home. I'll go to the café, in hopes that she found her way there."

She turned to Annette. "Perhaps some coffee? *American* coffee."

"Right away, ma'am," Annette said in her accented English.

Rosie was on the second-floor landing, about to enter her room, when she heard the door open, the light footsteps up the stairs.

Lilly appeared, looking flushed and rumpled, wearing a smile.

It dimmed when she saw Rosie.

"I can explain," she said without greeting.

Rosie bit back a sour word she'd heard Blanche use. Kept her voice steady. "Amelia! She's back!"

Lilly removed her hat, then her jacket. Her hair had unraveled from her braid as if someone had combed it backwards, and her cheeks appeared sunburned.

"Where have you been?"

"Rosie, listen. It's not what you think. I…met someone, and we toured Paris—"

"You toured Paris? All *night*?"

"He took me flying, and that took up the rest of the evening…."

"You went *flying*?" Fatigue, and not a little disbelief, had loosened all grip on her volume. "As in an *aeroplane*?"

"I really am quite exhausted, Rosie. I'll tell you everything when I get a few winks."

"Are you kidding me? I've been worried sick about you, not to mention that I was supposed to go to Auteuil today with Dash and Pembrook."

"Oh." She at least had the decency to look sorry. "You can go. I'll stay here. Really. I am quite fatigued, and Reynaud said he couldn't pick me up until evening—he's teaching all day."

"Reynaud?"

"He's a pilot. And, he was in the war…. Oh Rosie, I had such a delightful day!"

Rosie stared at her, at the way Lilly began to loosen her braids, working her fingers through them, at the windburn—she realized it now—on her cheeks, at the sparkle in her eyes—carefree and without a hint of trouble in her expression.

In that moment, with her cousin so bright, so without a care—Rosie couldn't stop herself. She slapped her.

Lilly jerked back, her hand to her cheek, her mouth open. "What—"

"You ruined my day, my entire trip to Paris! I can't believe your mother made us bring you, or that my mother insisted on me escorting you around town—I'm so sick of you tagging after us like some sorry, hungry mongrel. You don't belong in Paris."

Lilly's eyes flared. "You're right. I hated it here—all your shopping and dancing and drinking Pernod and acting like some floozy charity girl and making me do the same. I'm not that girl."

"Clearly!"

"I'm not about to pretend I'm something I'm not."

"Is that what you think I'm doing—pretending?"

"I dearly hope so! Because I'm not sure I like the Rosie you're becoming. And I'm not sure you know her either."

"Well, fear not, Lilly, because you haven't changed one morsel. I thought that Paris might turn you into someone charming and witty. You're simply…bohemian!"

"I'd rather be bohemian than a tramp."

Rosie wanted to hit her again.

"And by the way, I was sent to Paris to escort *you*."

Rosie had no words for that, or for the handprint exposed when Lilly removed her hand from her cheek.

The wound took a measure of steam from her. "Go to bed, Lilly. You're relieved of your duties."

Rosie turned toward her room.

"What are you doing?"

"I'm going to catch up with my friends."

"Your mother said—"

Rosie slammed her door on Lilly's words.

She stood in front of the mirror and saw that tears had streaked her face. She scrubbed her skin with the water in the sink, but glanced at the clock and realized she hadn't time to bathe.

She would slap Lilly all over again.

Rosie dropped her dress on the floor and picked out a white, wide-collar blouse and a checkered skirt. She added a long-sleeve cardigan, cinched it at the waist with a belt, and grabbed a sailor's hat with a wide bow at the brim, pulling it down to her eyebrows.

She added lipstick—no time for proper makeup—slipped into a pair of low heels, and dashed down the hall.

Lilly's door was closed, and she refused the urge to stop, to mend their row. Perhaps tomorrow.

Or next week.

Rosie debated asking Pierre to warm up the Peugeot, as she ran down the stairs, and decided that a cab might be faster.

She closed the door behind her and a cab almost instantly appeared as if it might be fated.

She directed him to the train station in her worst French ever then leaned into the seat, wanting to direct him through traffic as they pulled out onto the boulevard.

Wouldn't Dash be surprised? Rosie let the memory of his smile soothe away her row with Lilly. With luck, she would catch them just as they were leaving, and they'd make a glorious day of it. They'd purchase the racing forms and study them side by side, make their picks on the journey out, and then visit the paddocks to cheer on their mounts. She imagined the noise of it all, the raucous cheering of the crowd, the fleshy, earthy smell of the horses in the dirt, the noble colors of the jockeys' silks. They'd stand at the rail and root on their ponies together, and when their horse won—or not—they'd celebrate with a picnic under the blue skies of the French countryside. Perhaps Dash would lie down beside her and let her nest her head in the crook of his arm.

And then, she'd help him dream. Because that's what inspiration did.

"Faster."

Her cabbie ignored her. Around her, the city had come to life, the flower vendors lining the sidewalks with all manner of carnation and roses and lilies, the fruit vendors pulling out their carts, the newspaper kiosks opening their doors, new copies of the *Chronicle* thick on their shelves. Men and women already gathered for breakfast, eating crepes or a brioche, drinking a cup of café au lait at the sidewalk cafes.

Today, she would give Dash a bit more encouragement. Because even she didn't quite believe her own words yesterday. *What if I don't want to get married?*

Maybe she didn't belong on stage. Maybe she belonged on Dash's arm.

Finally they pulled up at the station. She paid the cab driver and jumped out, nearly running past the columns, under the awning into the tiled central hall. A sign listed the trains and their platforms and she located the one to Auteuil.

No time for a racing form, or even breakfast. She lined up at the ticket booth and tried not to bark. "One for Auteuil, please."

Taking her ticket, she walked as fast as decorum would allow toward the far platform. The train had already pulled in, green, with gold-fringed shades at the windows. Relief leaked out of her, but she hustled her pace.

As she drew closer, she saw passengers lined up to board, many of them still clumping in conversation. Race-goers carried picnic baskets, wore sporting suits with leather or flannel jackets, women in wide-brimmed hats and gloves. Men in straw hats and derbies smoked cigarettes.

She glanced through the crowd for a glimpse of Dash or Pembrook.

There—she spied Pembrook at the far car, Blanche beside him, holding their picnic basket. Dash appeared, stepping from behind Pembrook to let them pass as they handed the conductor their tickets.

Pembrook helped Blanche up the steps then followed.

Rosie hustled her pace, wanting to wave. She bumped into a woman holding the hand of a little boy. "Excuse me."

They glared at her.

She turned back to see Dash—

He was helping someone onto the train. Rosie slowed, watching the woman turn, seeing her regal, slim figure in a pair of trousers and a white blouse. She smiled down at Dash and put her hand on his shoulder.

Frankie.

Rosie slowed, her heart caught in her throat.

He pulled himself up on the steps behind her. Then, they disappeared into the car, Dash's low-throated laugher trickling out like a stain upon the day.

Rosie stopped, her heart thumping, the ticket in her hand deformed as she closed it around the paper.

But…

"Ma'am, are you boarding?"

She shook her head and moved aside for an elderly gentleman in a suit and fedora to pass. She glanced up toward the train.

Blanche stared out her window at her. She met Blanche's gaze, then shook her head.

She saw Blanche turn away, and couldn't stay for the humiliation. Turning on her heel, Rosie headed for the exit with more dignity than she felt. Behind her, the train coughed, lurched, then began to pull out.

By the time she reached the street, her eyes were blurry, burning. She strode out of the station, crossed the street, and found a bench.

She sat until she stopped shaking, watching travelers arrive, luggage in tow, watching carriages and footmen unloading crates, pigeons fighting the squirrels for sunflower seeds.

Lilly did this. Lilly and her whining. Lilly and her foolishness. She'd shown up in New York City and invaded Rosie's life.

Rosie had taught her how to dress, to act, to talk, and introduced her to her friends. And Lilly repaid her by going flying. Flying.

She could have been killed, and who would have borne the blame?

Rosie got up, walked over to a flower vendor, and purchased a bouquet of lilacs, breathing them in.

Lilly was a chain around Rosie's neck, suffocating, pulling her under. It was time to cut the chain and let her drown.

* * * * *

"Rosie hasn't spoken to you for five days?"

Lilly tried to place the name of the redhead who'd posed the question—she'd met so many people in the past week, she struggled to keep them all straight.

Darby she remembered, because of his soldier's uniform. Irish and tall, he had flown with Rennie and now worked at the embassy. She liked his brogue and well-bred manners, unlike Rennie's pal Hem, who'd shown up last night with his pregnant wife. Hem knew Darby, and all three soldiers shared a darkness they refused to discuss. Brooding and dark, Hem drank too much and had danced most of the night with a coquette girl who sported some fancy title. Baroness Raymonde, or something. Rennie called her Ray and teased her enough that Lilly had to work to laugh at her jokes.

There were others—Scott and his drunken, pretty wife, who cursed like men in a shipping yard and had nearly embroiled her husband in a fight over her honor, and two women who dressed in trousers, suspenders, and white oxford blouses and danced together, their derbies cock-eyed upon their bobs.

As for the redhead…Paige, maybe? She couldn't remember her name, but clearly she had an interest in Lilly and her moaning about Rosie and the fact that since she'd left her handprint on Lilly's check, Rosie had behaved as if she didn't exist. Shopping, lunching, even dining out and clubbing with Blanche and Pembrook without even a fare-thee-well to Lilly.

Although, for her part, Lilly hadn't exactly followed her cousin down the hall to make amends. Not after her first attempt ended with the door in her face.

How was she supposed to chaperone a cousin who loathed her?

"She's angry with me."

"Why?" the redhead asked. Yes, it must be Paige. Or Patty?

"Because she doesn't need her anymore, Presley." Rennie slid onto the chair next to Lilly, set his arm around her shoulders. "Because Lilly has discovered Paris on her own." He picked up her glass and winked at Lilly.

Oh, she wanted Rennie to kiss her. Every day, he seemed to nudge his way deeper inside her soul, until it felt as if he belonged there. She had lingered last night as he'd let her off by her door, caught in his smile, hoping he might sense her acquiescence. But Rennie was a gentleman, all the way through to his core, and although he'd taken her out every night and taught her to dance, he hadn't once pushed for more.

Maybe tonight. She'd silently begun to thank Rosie for her efforts to attire her in the latest fashions as she'd picked out a sleeveless sequined tunic dress with large orange and red poppies, and a matching headband that, admittedly, Lilly never dreamed she'd wear. She had also forgone the braids and twisted her hair into a knot at the back of her head, amazed at how thin it made her neck appear.

But this week had been one of new discoveries, each moment igniting inside her something new. New laughter, new passions, new daring pursuits. Something about being away from New York, eyes upon her, the daughter of mighty Esme and Oliver Stewart, the publishers of the *Chronicle*, meant that she never went anywhere without the specter of fame.

But here—here she tasted the freedom she'd forgotten, was slowly becoming the daredevil she'd named herself. She never dreamed she'd learn the Charleston, thanks to Presley—yes, now she remembered her name. Or find herself in a smoky dance club, listening to a dark-skinned American croon out a song from stage, something sultry, as if she were listening to chocolate. It made her wish that Rennie might pull her back onto the dance floor, wrap his arms around her.

She never thought she'd be the kind of girl who let a man fill her thoughts, invade her dreams.

Perhaps she never really had dreams, before Rennie. Just sorrows. And, she *hadn't* discovered Paris on her own.

Rennie had given it to her.

"I think you should just forget about your cousin," Presley said, smoke trailing from her cigarette holder. "She sounds like a bore."

"Rosie? Oh, hardly. She's a lot of fun, and very kind, really." Lilly put her hand to her cheek, the bruise still upon her heart. "I think she'll forgive me, in time."

Her gaze went to Rennie, talking to a brunette seated on a stool at the black zinc bar. She wore a dark lace dress that stopped just above her knees, and a pair of matching sheer stockings rolled just below the hem. She played with a long string of pearls as she smiled at Rennie, running her other gloved hand down his arm.

He held Lilly's lemonade in one hand, his absinthe in the other, but made no move to turn away. He was so handsome, it could steal Lilly's breath, the way his straw-blond hair fell over his eyes, adding a hint of dangerous mystery. She longed to twirl her finger through the curls at the nape of his neck. Tonight he wore a pair of tweed trousers and a shiny vest over his collared white shirt. She wanted to smile at the way he laughed at the brunette's words, his expression so full of life, the brokenness draining away from him on nights like this.

"I see Ginny is still trying to get her fingers back into Rennie." Presley sipped her glass of champagne then shook her head. "You'd think she'd had enough."

"What are you talking about?"

Presley gestured at the pair. "Lady Virginia Fontenbreau. The former Ginny Dupree. She and Rennie were married a couple of years ago. They have a son—Duffy."

Lilly stilled, the words sliding hot through her. "Rennie was… married?"

Presley glanced at her, frowned. "How well do you know him?"

"We met this week—he took me flying."

Presley smirked, rolled her eyes. "Of course he did."

Lilly's chest began a slow squeeze. "What do you mean?"

Presley shook her head. "You're such a nice girl, Lilly. Too nice. I can't figure out what you're doing with Rennie." She threw back the rest of her champagne. "I'm going to find someone to dance with me before this night is a waste."

She slipped onto the dance floor, and it didn't take but a few moments for a chap to swing her into his arms.

Lilly watched Rennie peck his former wife on the cheek and turn back toward the table.

She couldn't look at him. Around her, the music turned raucous, and the dance floor filled. She slid off her chair and disappeared into the crowd, heading for the door.

She just needed some air, a fresh breeze to clear her head, sort through Presley's words.

"Lilly!" His voice spurted out behind her, but it bled into the jazz and she ignored the tug to return. She didn't have the voucher to retrieve her coat so she pushed out onto the street and gulped in the night air.

The lights from the marquee of La Rotonde bathed the night in white and red, and outside the club, couples spilled out of taxis, dressed in sequins and pearls, feathered headbands, the men in suits and shiny silk vests.

She strode down the Boulevard Montparnasse, the music spilling from La Select and the Dome, and from them more partygoers, most of them wildly tight, their tongues soaked with absinthe and preening loudly about life.

She clasped her hands to her bare arms, brushing away the goose-flesh. What was she doing here, in this world? She should go home, back to Rosie, apologize, figure out how she'd let Rennie—

"Lilly!"

She didn't turn, but heard his feet scuffing down the sidewalk. He grabbed her arm, stopping her, breathing hard. He must have run all the way from La Rotonde. "What are you doing? Where are you going?"

She ran her hand along her cheek, keeping her face away from him, hating her tears. She didn't need Rennie or his—

"Lilly-Peach, what's egging you?" He'd stopped her fully now, putting himself in front of her, grabbing both arms. "You're freezing out here."

He shook out of his suit coat and settled it on her shoulders, searching for her eyes. She looked away, but he touched her chin, brought her head up.

"What did that snipe Presley say?"

Lilly's jaw hardened. "Was she your wife?"

"Who, Presley?"

"Don't mock me."

"Fine. Yes. For three blissful weeks and eight agonizing months. We're better as friends."

"And parents?"

He shook his head. "Duffy? He's not mine. Ginny was already carrying him when I met her. I thought I could change her, but she's her own person. In the end, she didn't want me."

"It looks like she wants you."

"She wants what she can't have."

Lilly could hardly bear how those words weakened her. How she wanted to throw herself into his arms, to press her lips to his cheek, to sob out her apologies. Instead she drew his suit coat tighter around her. "So, you're not…you're not going to throw me over for Lady Virginia?"

"She's a dish all right, but she's not my Calamity Jane." He tucked his hand along her cheek. "Forgive me for not telling you? It didn't even occur to me. That's how little she means to me."

She found the courage to meet his eyes then, and drank in the apology in them.

"Presley said…she said I was too nice to be with you. I don't understand."

"There's nothing to understand." He ran his thumb down her jaw. "You make me better, Lilly. Make me the person I should be."

She didn't understand him, not at all. But it didn't matter then, because he leaned close and hesitated only a moment, question in his eyes, before he kissed her.

She closed her eyes because she'd seen it done that way and let his lips whisper against hers, lightly. He tasted of licorice, and at his touch, a tingle shot through her entire body. She stilled, but when he slid his hand behind her neck, when his lips moved against hers, she relaxed. After a moment, she even found the courage to respond, to explore his kiss with her own.

She didn't realize he'd put his arms around her, tucking her close to him, until he leaned away, leaving her body buzzing, her mind still caught in his smell, his touch.

He smiled. "I've been wanting to do that all week."

She had no voice. It had simply abandoned her, and she could do nothing but stare up at him, drink in his affection.

"Have you ever been kissed before, Lilly?"

She shook her head.

He made a face. "I hope...I hope I didn't frighten you."

"No," she squeaked, and was mortified.

He grinned. "Oh, you are a peach, aren't you?" He swung his arm around her, walking her back toward the Rotonde. "What would you say if I asked you to run away with me?"

"Flying?"

"No, Peach, somewhere grander. Hem and some others are talking about taking a jaunt down to the bullfights in Spain. They just started in Pamplona. It's too early for the running of the bulls, but we thought we'd all take a look at the sport. Hem wants to write about it for some American journal." He stopped, looked down at her. "You could write an article for the *Chronicle*."

"No. I never want to write for the *Chronicle*."

He held up his hand. "Forget I suggested it. Come—it'll be a grand diversion away from Rosie and her pouting."

"I'm afraid Rosie won't allow me to. It's one thing to squirrel away the night with you and Presley and the other chaps. It's another to go to Spain."

But the idea lit inside her like a flame. Bullfights. It sounded rough and raw, and the sense of it conjured up memories of Montana and helping Abel with the cattle drives.

"Then don't tell Rosie. We'll sneak away, and by the time you return, she'll have found other pursuits to distract her. She has to realize sometime that you don't need her."

She didn't need Rosie? Perhaps not. Perhaps she didn't need anyone. Except, of course, Rennie.

Lilly looked up at him, smiled. "When?"

"Hem is making the arrangements. Perhaps in a week?"

She found herself nodding before her mouth could make the reply. "Yes. Of course. Yes."

Rennie's smile could feed her for a week. He stopped her right there, under the streetlights, and kissed her again, this time something hungry and urgent in his touch. She curled her hands up around his shoulders and pressed into him, freeing herself to kiss him in a way that stole her breath. Oh.

"I have finally discovered what I love best about Paris," he said into her ear as he let her go.

She warmed down to her toes, not even needing her coat when he fetched it. He hailed a cab and she snuggled into the cradle of his arms as the taxi drove her home, past the lights of Luxembourg Park, then over the bridge by Notre Dame, past the Hotel de Ville, and finally to her house on the Champs-Élysées.

A light burned from deep inside, a faint glow through the window bars onto the street, prisms of light against the darkness.

"I have lessons all day tomorrow, but I will fetch you in the evening, for dinner." He pressed a kiss to her forehead. "Spain," he said softly.

"Spain," she replied, grinning. She let herself out of the taxi and waved as it pulled away.

Spain. The word settled inside her like a live coal.

She would tell Rosie, of course, but not ask, not invite. Frankly, Rosie might not even care. She hadn't seemed to even notice when Lilly left every night, bidden by the honking of Rennie's horn.

She opened the door and noticed that Rosie had left the light to the parlor burning. It squeezed out under the door.

Lilly opened it to extinguish the light and froze.

Aunt Jinx sat on the divan, Uncle Bennett behind her, his hand on her shoulder. Rosie looked away from them on her perch in a straight chair, her face drawn.

"Welcome home, Lillian Joy," Aunt Jinx said. "You're just in time."

Chapter 4

Rosie had declared herself a fool the moment she stepped foot into the Pre-Catelan, the infamous outdoor restaurant and cabaret in the creamy white Bois de Bologne. She stood in the entryway, took in the gold wallpaper, the dark zinc hostess stand, the round gold fabric divan, and then saw him standing across the room, at the foot of the long, red-carpeted marble stairway.

Dash seemed startled, and on his face formed a hurt smile. He could be so very dangerous in a black tailored suit, a gray tie, his dark hair slicked back, especially when the smile vanished and his brown eyes watched her as if they'd never met, as if she amused him.

She refused to betray her traitorous, thundering heart.

A pianist at a white baby grand peeled out some jazzy, fresh tune from the cabaret behind him, and from the open doors to the terrace, the smells of the night twined through potted ferns.

Rosie slipped her arm through Tripp's elbow and stoutly ignored him. But every cell in her body alerted her to his presence as they passed by him, her skin tingling as he said softly, "Hello, Red."

She brilliantly refused to look at him, her gloved hand pinching Tripp's arm.

"Red?" Ah, that's what she wanted to hear, the hue of confusion.

She glanced over her shoulder. "Hello, Dash. You're sporting a bit of sunshine. I take it the races agreed with you?"

"I lost every single one."

"Shame. Next time you'll have to bring along a bit more luck."

Pembrook rose from a round table in the corner and they threaded through the room, eyes upon them. Dash reached around Tripp to pull out the fabric-covered chair for her. She ignored him and settled into the seat Tripp offered.

Dash sat on the other side, ruffled.

And right then, she prayed that Pierre might not see the telegram Rosie had left for him to send to her mother, suggesting Jinx might return home and rein in her wayward niece. Because, as Dash fiddled with his fork and ordered a shot of vermouth, she knew she could win him back. Only this time, she'd keep enough of her heart not to be wounded by his other temptations.

Two days of fury and not a little self-examination had told her she'd brought this on herself. She'd let Frankie best her.

Blanche had filled her in on the particulars. How Frankie met them at the station—surprise!—and wheedled her way into Dash's attention. How she bet against him, teasing him, and then won. How it bruised Dash's ego.

How he'd fawned over her, as if begging for redemption all day.

It occurred to Rosie then that perhaps instead of fearing Frankie, she might learn from her.

The minute Dash had returned to Paris, he'd motored back to her doorstep, pressing the bell until she thought she'd have to call the gendarmes. Finally, Pierre managed to send him away, but Dash had sent flowers both days, and tonight, a vellum card inviting her to dinner.

She'd acquiesced, but she intended to make him reach for it. Too much encouragement clearly spoiled a man.

She'd attired herself in something daring and chic—a short white dress of lace with a peek-a-boo neckline with just enough revelation to encourage a second look, her stockings rolled just below the knee, black T-strap shoes, and a feather boa around her shoulders—hoping to remind him of everything he might have forgotten while gazing into Frankie's regal smile.

She'd taken her time, lined her eyes, rouged her cheeks, powdered her entire body with a new fragrance, and painted a shocking, tantalizing shade of red upon her lips.

Inspiration, indeed.

Now that she had her bearings, the last thing she needed was her mother returning home to destroy everything. *Please, Pierre, ignore the missive.*

She wanted Dash firmly in her pocket and begging for her hand in marriage by the time her mother returned. After all, how could her mother deny her daughter true love after all she herself had suffered?

And, even if Dash might not be Rosie's true love, he seemed enough for now.

As the garcon attended them, she let the games begin. Dash suggested the Fois de Gras, and she chose the roast duck. He ordered her a brandy smash, she drank Tripp's gin and tonic. Dash asked her to dance, twice, and only on the third request did she extend her hand.

"You're making me crazy," he said into her ear, and she played with the hair at the nape of his neck.

Tripp drove her home, pecked her on the cheek. She dove into the house and to the hallway side table where she'd left her instructions for Pierre.

They were gone.

She spent the next day at home, bracing herself for a call. By the time Dash appeared on her doorstep—shortly after Lilly had snuck out with her new beau—she'd decided that her mother was too busy hunting down her vanished brother to supervise her wayward niece.

Never mind check in with her formerly distraught daughter.

Perhaps the Paris girls would escape with their indiscretions unhindered.

"Forgive me, Red? I've missed you so much," Dash said two days later, as they strolled through Tuileries Garden. He had his jacket around her shoulders, the smell of beer on his breath.

"I know," she said softly and let him atone for his sins under the statue of Renommée and the glorious wings of Pegasus while the lights of Paris sparkled behind them. They stopped at the basin, the water reflecting the night.

"Won't you throw in a coin?"

"Why?" he said quietly, pulling her against him, his lips at her neck. "I already have all the luck I need."

Perhaps she was ready for her mother's arrival, after all.

Rosie didn't, however, expect to see Jinx seated on the red velvet divan in the family room, little Finley asleep in her arms, Bennett reading a book in the Queen Anne chair. Rosie closed the door, nearly breathless with the taste of Dash's touch on her lips.

Jinx always knew how to command a room, from the moment she married Foster Worth and became the doyenne of society, even at seventeen, to now, a lady of society in her midforties married to his brother, shipping baron of Paris and New York, Belgium and London. Jinx knew what to wear, what to say, how to throw a party, and how to silence her daughter with a look.

Even now, after midnight, in their stiff Parisian parlor, Jinx looked regal in a dark skirt, white shirtwaist, and a string of pearls at her neck. Her coat lay draped on the back of the divan, as if she and Bennett had only just arrived. Rosie paused when she saw her mother's dark bobbed hair, tiny pin curls delicate around her face.

"Welcome home, Rose," Jinx said quietly. She smiled but it didn't meet her eyes.

"Hello, Mother," Rosie managed, and walked over to kiss her cheek. Jinx reached up, caught her daughter's cheek against hers. Held it.

As she pulled away, Rosie saw the results of their investigation in her mother's eyes. "You didn't find Jack."

Amelia came into the room, sleep still on her countenance, tying her apron on as she entered. She curtsied to Jinx then took her coat from the room.

Finley roused on her lap and Jinx looked at Bennett, who put down his book and crept over to them.

"Hello, Rosie," he whispered and scooped up Finley in his arms. He kissed Jinx on the cheek. "I'll be down presently."

"Wait," Rosie said, and turned to Finley, pushing away his hair and kissing him on his pudgy, six-year-old cheek. She inhaled the reckless, innocent smell of him and then let him go.

"Sit, please."

"Mother, I can explain."

Jinx began to tug off her gloves. "Imagine my surprise when I arrived home moments ago to see you outside on the front street—in the view of all of Paris—in the grope of some man. You've been busy." Jinx shook her head. "Your rash judgment, Rosie...it's going to get the best of you someday."

"Mother, please. I was in the company of Dashielle Parks. I do believe he's smitten with me."

"Smitten, or in love? Does he hope to marry you?"

Rosie sank down onto the Queen Anne chair. "Perhaps."

"He's been courting you? He should have asked your father."

"Times have changed, Mother. Men don't ask to court women anymore, they don't line up to fill your dance card, don't drop vellum calling cards on the trays for you to choose from. This is Paris, and we are a different generation—"

"A generation that will find themselves in dire trouble—"

"Besides, Bennett is—Not. My. Father!" She wasn't sure how the argument had escalated so quickly, but her voice reverberated through the room and drew Jinx upright.

Her mother removed the other glove. Folded them together in her hands. Drew in a breath. "No, he's not. But he's a better father than Foster ever was."

Rosie shook her head, refusing to trudge back into the darkness of the years with her abusive father. "Mother, Dashielle is in love with me, and…and if he must approach Bennett, then I will tell him so."

"Don't hold your breath, Rosie."

"You don't believe he will?"

"I know the type. I even married the type. I fear Dash will push you as far as he can and then find someone more willing. Unless, of course, you've already let him—"

"Mother!"

Jinx drew in a breath, her eyes sad. "Dash is only out for Dash, my darling. Do you know why Dashielle is in Paris and not at his father's bank, learning the business?"

"Because he just finished college and he needs a holiday?"

"Not hardly. Dashielle's father is settling a rather…seedy affair that Dashielle left in his wake at Harvard. Apparently Dash may be the father of a child recently birthed by a local hussy who worked at a nearby pub."

"That's a lie."

"Perhaps, but it is costing his family's estate dearly, and according to the whispers, he just may be cut off."

"Dash might be charming, but he's no rogue."

"He's exactly that, and completely unsuitable for a member of the Worth family."

"Mother! We are not of the high society set anymore. I hardly think the Worth name has the merit you'd like to claim. Thanks to you."

Jinx cut her voice to low. "You cannot be so ignorant as to understand why I didn't love your father. You heard his words, saw the bruises he left. However, trust me when I say that I never intended to disgrace our family name, and I can only hope someday you come to understand that."

Rosie matched her tone. "I understand that you always loved Bennett, even when you were married to Father."

"And I was always in love with her," Bennett said, standing at the door.

He could startle her sometimes, the way he looked like her father, his voice so similar, a calm tenor. Tall and regal, like her father, but Bennett had lighter hair, and eyes that could smile when he wanted to. Still handsome at fifty, he could turn the eye of even her friends. He came in now and settled his hand on her mother's shoulder. "And you can believe her words, Rosie. Your mother is an honorable woman." He kissed the top of Jinx's head. "And she worries about you."

"And Lillian." She held up Rosie's telegram. "It's time this nonsense came to an end." Jinx pressed her hand on Bennett's. "There will be no more meetings with Dashielle Parks. And as for Lillian, clearly, summer in Paris is an abysmal idea for the both of you. I knew I should have hired a chaperone. I simply didn't expect to be gone so long. Nor, of course, to have my daughter behaving like a flapper in Paris!"

"Mother!"

"Rosie, I promise, I only have your best in mind. Besides—" Jinx looked up at Bennett, a smile on her face. She returned her gaze to Rosie, and the gentleness in her expression left Rosie without words. "I believe I've found a suitable man to court you, in Belgium. A duke. Perhaps even a husband. He'll be here in a few days to meet you."

Rosie's hand tightened around the arms of her chair as she heard voices outside. Laughter. Then the sound of a car driving away. Rosie stared at her mother, the blood draining from her face as the parlor doors opened and Lilly appeared, her cheeks flushed.

Lilly froze, her gaze landing on Jinx, Bennett, and finally Rosie. Rosie couldn't look in her eyes.

"Welcome home, Lillian Joy," her mother said. "You're just in time."

* * * * *

Lilly stood in the parlor, staring at her three keepers, and for a long moment, simply debated turning around and running.

Rennie couldn't be that far away, could he?

But her legs wouldn't work. She simply stared at her aunt, something cold sliding through her.

"Hello, Aunt Jinx." She glanced at her uncle Bennett, and he simply gave her a tight, grim nod.

Her aunt rose, walked over to her. Lilly was as tall as Jinx now, but it didn't stop her from feeling like an incorrigible child. And to think, just moments ago, she'd considered herself a woman.

She refrained from pressing her fingers against her lips and met her aunt's kiss, first on one cheek, then the other.

"I'm so glad you're safe."

Lilly shot a look at Rosie, who still didn't meet her eyes. "Of course I am. Why wouldn't I be?"

"Lilly." Jinx patted her hand on Lilly's cheek, shook her head. "You're so much like your mother. Sweet and without guile. I hear you've met a fella."

Clearly, Jinx didn't know her at all, for Lilly sank onto the opposite divan and plotted, even now, how she might escape, track down Rennie, and run.

Her aunt would never let her go to Spain. And Rosie—clearly, she could never trust Rosie again. Lilly drew herself up. "Reynaud. He's a flyer from Canada. He gives flying lessons."

"Mmm," Jinx said as she lowered herself onto the divan. "I'm glad you've had your fun and are no worse for wear. But I'm afraid you'll have to leave a card for your young man, tell him that you are unable to see him further."

She expected it, but it still felt as if Aunt Jinx had smiled at her then skewered her with a penknife. "But you don't even know him."

"I don't have to. I have only myself to blame. I should have never left you in Rosie's care. Nor, I see, she in yours."

Lilly flinched, and for the first time, Rosie's head came up. See, she hadn't been lying about her assignment to chaperone, and she tried to communicate that in her glance to Rosie.

Aunt Jinx had cut her hair. In fact, the style made her appear not much older than Lilly. Perhaps this beguiled Lilly to lean forward, to press her case. "There is no harm done here, Aunt Jinx. Just allow him to introduce himself—"

Jinx held up her hand. "Your mother trusted me with your honor this summer, and I know she would be distraught to know of your behavior."

"I've not betrayed—"

"Thankfully your father is already on his way to Paris to fetch you."

Lilly froze. Oliver?

She couldn't breathe. She swallowed, managed, "When?"

"I suppose he'll be here by the end of the week." Jinx looked away as she spoke. "I was forced to cable your mother, and she agrees that you should leave with him."

"No."

Jinx looked up at her. "What?"

"No." Lilly found her feet. "No, I will not leave Paris. I—I am in love with Reynaud Dupree, and he is with me. I will not leave him!"

Rosie was staring at her. "You've only known him for five days."

"And you, Rosie? How long did you know Dash before you allowed him to corner you on the dance floor, to steal kisses—"

"He did not kiss me on the dance floor!"

But Jinx already looked stricken. "What has been going on here in my absence?"

"Enough to know that we are all leaving Paris as soon as I can tie up my business here," Bennett said quietly. He turned to Lilly then to Rosie. "There will be no more dancing, no more shopping. We'll be ready to go by the time Oliver arrives."

Lilly stared at them, at Rosie, then she turned and drew in a long, calming breath. "I understand. Of course, I've been foolish. I will pack my things. I trust your trip went well, Aunt Jinx?"

She didn't wait for a reply as she turned and shut the door behind her then climbed the stairs.

She'd simply have to get word to Rennie to move up their trip to Spain.

And then she'd have to figure out how to escape.

Lilly held herself together until she reached her room then shut the door and pressed her hands to her face. *We'll be ready to go by the time Oliver arrives.*

She'd leave them all, run off to Spain with Rennie.

Rennie loved her. Her words reverberated back to her. *I am in love with Reynaud Dupree, and he is with me.*

She had to get word to him. They couldn't imprison her in her room, could they? She went to the window, looked down, measured the distance.

A knock came at the door. She drew in a breath, steadied it. "Enter."

Lilly had no more words when Rosie stepped into the room, closing the door behind her, her face still ashen. "I...I'm sorry."

Lilly tightened her jaw against the tears that burned her throat. "It's no matter. Of course you had to cable your mother—"

"I was angry. And worried. And...well, Lilly, you nearly wrecked everything when you didn't come home." Rosie rubbed her hands on her arms, settled on the chaise lounge. She wore a lacy white dress, something fancy, and a boa around her shoulders.

Lilly sank down on the settee opposite her. "You mean I nearly wrecked everything between you and Dash."

Rosie whisked her hand across her wet cheek. Nodded. "But I fixed it, and I ran home that night and hoped that Pierre hadn't sent the cable."

"But it was too late."

"And now they have forbidden me to see Dash, and my mother has picked out a husband for me. A duke or someone she met in Belgium! He's coming here to meet me!" She met Lilly's eyes. "I always feared my mother would arrange my marriage. I'm trapped."

Lilly stared at her, the tears welling in her eyes, and the ache of their estrangement broke inside her. "No, you're not. Come with me—to Spain."

Rosie stared at her, as if not comprehending.

"Rennie and I and Hem and a few others are going to the bullfights in Pamplona. They just started, and—"

"Are you crazy? Spain? With Rennie? You don't even know him."

Lilly drew herself up. "Clearly I shouldn't have said anything." She got up, but Rosie caught her arm. "Lils, are you sure about him?"

Lilly stared at Rosie's hand on her arm, heard the texture of concern in her voice, and it conjured up those early days in New York when Rosie had been her only friend.

Rosie still might be her only friend. Outside Rennie.

Lilly sat back on the settee. "Oh, Rosie, if you only knew how he makes me feel. For the first time in my life I don't feel like...well, like I'm a buffalo in the middle of New York. He understands me, and he wants to be with me. He makes me feel alive. I—I meant what I said."

"About him being in love with you?"

"About me loving him." She took Rosie's hand. "I am going to Spain with him, Rosie. Come with me."

Rosie looked at their clasped hands. "Do you forgive me, Lils?"

"For telling your mother?"

"For trying to make you be someone you weren't. I was just..."

"I know. Trying to help me fit in. I forgive you."

Rosie swung her legs from the chaise, touched her hand to Lilly's cheek, and shook her head. "I'm not going with you to Spain."

Lilly closed her eyes.

"But if it's what you really want, I will help you run away."

* * * * *

It couldn't have worked out more perfectly if Rosie had planned it herself. Like fate had drawn it, the idea simply materialized, right there before her, like a gift.

Rosie didn't believe Lilly's acquiescence to Jinx's plans for a moment in the parlor, and knew her cousin had a lie brewing. So, Rosie had listened to her mother gush about the duke she'd dug up, then excused herself to discover Lilly's secret.

Spain. Rosie slipped out of her lacy dress, tied on a robe, then sat down at her dressing table. She dipped her facial cloth into the cold crème and began to wipe away her makeup.

Of all places to run away...and to see bullfighting? A crass, bloody sport that made a game of killing animals—not to mention the men who were gored. She'd heard Dash and Pem talking about it and declared the entire subject repulsive.

Whoever Rennie might be, he clearly hadn't the dignified tastes required of a man suitable for Lilly's breeding. She was the daughter of Esme Price, due to inherit millions.

And this Rennie chap probably knew it.

Rosie finished with her eyes, cleaned them with another towel, then began to wipe the blood-red lipstick from her mouth.

As soon as Lilly suggested Spain, however, Rosie's own rescue appeared, fully formed, in her head. She'd help Lilly escape…and then betray her to Oliver.

For Lilly's own good, of course, because even Rosie could see destruction and heartbreak ahead. He'd get Lilly pregnant, and then demand the Price family millions.

She'd be saving Lilly from a disastrous life.

Rosie finished with her lipstick then smoothed the crème over her face and neck, her hands.

She had three days to divert attention off herself and onto Lilly. Three days to convince Lilly of her sincerity and to push her on her journey.

Three days to supplant Lilly's plans with her own.

Most of all, she had three days to convince Dash that they should elope.

Picking up her brush, she ran it through her hair, thankful that she didn't have to wrestle with her long tresses anymore. Even her mother had joined chic society. No doubt she'd eventually see that Dash was exactly the man for Rosie.

She dropped her robe over her velvet chair, climbed into her bed, and turned off the light.

The starlight of Paris twinkled against the floor of her room. She lay back into her pillows and pondered how to cajole Dash into marriage.

He just needed some more encouragement, perhaps.

Or…and she drew in a breath at this…Lilly wasn't the only one with a healthy allowance at stake. She heard her mother's voice again, the one suggesting that Dash might lose his inheritance.

Forgive me, Red. She closed her eyes, feeling his hands on her back, his mouth against hers. He made her feel beautiful, as if only she could satisfy his hungers. Someday he would love her—maybe he already did.

Dash is only out for Dash, my darling.

No. He cared for her. She'd do whatever it took to keep him.

Her mother might want to cut her off, but she wouldn't, not after losing Jack. Aside from Finley, Rosie was all she had.

It would work, she knew it.

Mrs. Dashielle Parks.

She was just falling into slumber when she heard a knock, then her door opening.

"Rosie? Are you awake?"

The last person she expected to walk into her room, dressed in her robe and night dress, was her mother. Jinx, too, had wiped off her makeup, and smelled of cold crème as she sat on Rosie's bed. She reached out in the darkness and ran her hand over Rosie's short hair.

"Mother?"

She heard Jinx's breath, and then stilled, not sure what to say when her mother lay down beside her. She tucked her arm over Rosie.

"I missed you," she said quietly.

"I—I missed you too," Rosie said, surprised at the truth in it.

Jinx said nothing for a long while. Then, "I was seventeen when I married your father. He was so handsome, and I thought we would be happy. But I wasn't enough for him. He had a thirst inside him that I couldn't quench. Nothing could quench it—not his yachts, or his homes, or his power, or the women…even you, I'm afraid. Although I know he loved you."

Rosie's eyes burned.

"I'll never forget the day you were born. He came into the room and picked you up. It was the first time I'd seen him be gentle with anyone in years, even Jack. He stared at you for a long time and then kissed your forehead. Then, without looking at me, he handed you to Amelia and said, 'This one's mine.' I didn't realize then that he knew—maybe he didn't. Maybe he just meant that you belonged to him and he expected me to take care of you."

A cold tear pooled in Rosie's ear.

"I'm still trying to do that, daughter. Because you're mine too." Her voice softened. "I'm sorry about Dash. I know you care for him. But please, trust me."

Rosie tightened her jaw.

"I love you, Rosie. And I'll do anything to make things right. To fix what I've broken."

She said nothing more, and the silence fell around them, Jinx's arm growing heavy across Rosie's waist.

Just as Rosie began to drift off, she heard the soft shudder of an intake of breath. She threaded her hand into her mother's as she realized... her mother was weeping.

Chapter 5

Lilly felt like a criminal, and drank in the illicit taste of escape as Rennie loaded her valise into the train compartment. Two leather bunks bordered each side of the private room, a table between them. Two more bunks folded up above them to allow seating.

Lilly stood in the doorway, peering out the window at the platform, expecting any moment for Uncle Bennett or even Oliver to show up with the gendarmes to carry her away. Her heart thundered in her chest as she scanned the crowd.

"Are you well, Lilly? You are perfectly ashen." Presley eased past her into the compartment, wearing a pair of trousers and a tweed vest. She handed Rennie her bag. He stashed it with Lilly's then turned and smiled.

It calmed the racing in her chest, the churning in her belly.

"She's just ready for her big adventure." He stepped up to her, ran his hands down her arms. "I'm so glad you came."

Lilly wished she'd worn something more daring than her shirt-waist and skirt. She had, however, left behind her Zane Grey book on her writing table.

Presley had pulled out her cigarette case. "Rennie said it was some clandestine escape." She tapped the end of the cigarette on the case then inserted it into her holder. "The entire escapade sounds very Sir Conan Doyle to me."

"Indeed, I am amazed we pulled it off," Rennie said, and took Lilly's hand, pulling her down onto the seat next to him. Then he reached over to light Presley's cigarette.

Presley grinned, a hunger in her expression, and leaned back into her seat. "Do tell."

Lilly didn't know whether to be relieved or annoyed that Presley would be joining them. Of course, she'd needed her for her plans, and Lilly didn't exactly hope to be alone with Rennie, but Presley had the eyes of a minx, always on him, and it raked into her memory Presley's words that night at La Rotonde.

You're too nice, Lilly.

Not anymore. She'd run away with her...well, lover wasn't the term. But perhaps simply run away. She didn't have to answer to anyone, not anymore.

"It was Rosie's plan, really," Lilly said. "Although Rennie caught on fast."

"Especially when I drove up to fetch her two days ago and she was waiting for me at the door."

"I knew if he rang, Uncle Bennett would find him and send him away for good. So I waited for him and snuck out. I told him to go, but gave him a note that explained exactly how we'd get away."

"And?"

"The scheme went off without a hitch. Right now, I'm supposed to be at Jardin des Tuileries with Rosie and my nephew Finn, floating one of his toy boats in the pond." She curled her hand around Rennie's arm. "We've been taking him there for the past three days, with Aunt Jinx or Amelia. Only today, we took him alone. Rennie met me at the edge of the park."

"I hope everything I picked out for you fits."

"Thank you, Presley. I will secure my own wardrobe when I get to Spain."

"I have no use for the dresses anymore. You may keep them." Presley gave her a wink. "It gives me an excuse to order more."

"All the same, I have my allowance. I'll manage."

"Suit yourself," Presley said.

"So we're all here, then," said a voice in the doorway.

Presley looked past her, toward the opened door. "Hello, Hem. Are you all settled?"

"Mike is here, and Bob is ever the pompous mule." Hem was a handsome man, Lilly supposed, a rumpled, no-nonsense way about him, in his patched tweed jacket, his canvas pants and tennis shoes. He wore his hair long and irreverently mussed, and every time he looked at her, it seemed he might be probing for something deeper. She felt childish and naked around him, and couldn't shake the feeling of his disdain.

"Hem is just upset that Bob's footing the cost of the trip for him," Rennie said. "Or should I say, Bob's wife, Annie, has paid them both to jaunt off and leave her to her own devices in Paris. Oh, the ails of being married to an heiress."

Lilly shot him a look.

Presley, however, picked up the explanation. "Annie's father is in shipping in England and possibly could purchase this entire train. Which Hem hates, don't you?"

"Bob needs her cash to run *Contact Editions*, his new press," Hem said without emotion. "And if I write for him, then I write for her."

"And Hem just can't bear being bought by the establishment," Rennie said.

Hem made a noise, and Lilly shifted in her seat, hoping he hadn't heard her comment about her allowance. "I didn't know you were a writer," she said.

"If you call holing up in a hotel garret every day scribbling out poetry—"

"That's enough, Rennie. You're only here because we need another hand at bridge. I didn't realize you were bringing your kid sister with you, however."

Lilly couldn't quite figure out if Hem was kidding or not, but his words slicked through her like acid.

Rennie slipped his hand into hers. "He's just being surly because Hadley's at home, too sick with his child to tag along. Leave her alone, Hem." He glared at the man, and Lilly tucked close to Rennie, a surge of warmth at his defense.

Still, she lifted her chin, met Hem's gaze, inviting his dark eyes to challenge her.

He considered her for a moment, then suddenly smiled. "Don't mind me. I am surly. The bulls will cheer us all up. There's nothing better than drama, tragedy, and some danger to brighten a man's spirit." Then he winked at her, and she didn't know what to make of it as he moved away.

The train lurched, and she caught her breath. Rennie tightened her hand in his.

"Men are such children," Presley said. "A woman has to know how to handle them. It can be so fatiguing. Hadley is lucky to be rid of him for a few days." The sun hung low on the horizon, a golden wash of light upon the city. Long shadows draped across the platform like fingers, groping for the train. But it moved forward, away from them, and soon left the sunlight behind. All that remained was the orange glow of twilight on the leather seats and the fire of adventure before her.

"I'm so proud of you, Lilly," Rennie said, putting his arm around her, pulling her back against himself. "You surprised me, yet again."

"Why? Didn't you think I'd come?"

He pressed a kiss to her head. "It's just that bullfighting can be a rather…brutal sport. But perhaps you are as brave as you profess."

"But she's not here for the bullfighting, not really, are you, pet? You've come for the adventure of running away, haven't you?" Presley inhaled on her cigarette, glanced at Lilly, then turned her gaze on Rennie. "Spain, after all, can be quite the life-changing experience."

Behind her, she felt Rennie tense.

She frowned at Presley as the woman held her gaze, blowing out a stream of smoke. "In fact, Spain can turn a girl into a woman, if she has the courage." She winked, then turned away and stared out the window as they left Paris behind.

* * * * *

Rosie tried not to think of the unpardonable sin she'd committed and focused on Finn and his triumphant smile as he chased the mallards around the pond at Jardin des Tuileries. She kept glancing at the statue of Rommende, the outstretched wings of Pegasus, warmth curling through her, remembering Dash's whispers of apology.

Yes, it was worth it. And Lilly wouldn't get far, anyway. She'd enjoy a day or two of freedom, and then Oliver would track her down and rescue her from Rennie.

How difficult could it possibly be to find her at the bullfights in Pamplona? And if it took two days or more, all the better.

Rosie and Dash would be long gone by then.

"Can I put my boat in?" Finn ran up to her, fetching the wooden sailboat he'd brought to float in the pond. The wind picked up his hat, nearly blew it off his head, and he grabbed it, stowing it in her lap.

"Hang onto the string, Finn. You don't want it floating away."

She glanced again at the statue. Dash had promised, through Blanche, to meet her here, finally, and it took no small amount of conniving to assure her mother that she and Lilly would keep Finn safe, no escort necessary. Jinx hovered over her youngest son like he might be made of glass.

"Rothie, look at my boat!" Finn pointed to the schooner as it drifted from shore. He grinned, pushing his tongue through the gap between his front teeth. With the sun in his blond hair and with his blue eyes, he appeared a miniature version of Jack, so much joy in his smile she could lose herself in it. Finn was the balm that soothed their cracked hearts, and with him Rosie felt the world drop away. To Finn, she didn't have to be anyone—not a flapper, or an heiress—just Rothie, Finn's sister.

However, she still couldn't wipe the sound of her mother's sobs from her mind. She'd rolled over, held her mother as her grief turned Rosie brittle. She couldn't bear to feel this grief, not anymore.

Dash could make her forget it all.

Another gust of wind lifted Finn's straw hat from her hands and tumbled it across the grass. "Oh!" She got up, glanced at Finn, then took off after the hat, chasing it as it rolled away from her.

"I'll get it!" Finn said, and started toward her, dropping the string that tethered him to his boat.

"Stay there, Finn!" she said, and turned back to find the hat.

She plowed into its rescuer. "Oh!"

The man caught her before she took them both down, one arm wrapped around her waist as he stepped back to absorb her weight.

"I'm so sorry!" She disentangled herself from him and looked up.

His blue eyes could stop her heart. They looked down at her, a smile in them, as if amused. She swallowed, tried to find her voice.

He beat her to it. "Is this yours?"

"It's my little brother's." She glanced back to where Finn had now hunkered down on the shore and begun unlacing his shoes. "Finn, what are you doing?"

"My boat. The string got away from me!"

"Oh dear." She took the hat from the man. "I need to rescue his boat."

"I don't think so," the man said, and strode toward Finn. "Stay here, sailor." He slipped out of his shoes.

"Oh no, sir, please—"

But he shucked off his socks then rolled up his pant legs before stepping into the pond.

Rosie made a face. "Is it cold?"

"Like ice," he said, and glanced at her over his shoulder.

Oh, he was handsome—she couldn't help but notice that as he waded into the water after the loose string. Wide shoulders, a chiseled chin, aristocratic lines, dark-as-night hair that fell over his eyes. And an accent that sounded British. He reached out and snagged the end of the string then held it between two fingers as he reeled in the boat. Finally, he picked it up by its sail and trudged back to shore.

She watched the water slough off his ankles and pool around his bare feet as he knelt in front of Finn and tied the end of the string around his wrist. "A sailor never loses control of his craft," he said, then winked at Finn. "Let's relaunch her."

He handed the boat to Finn, who set it back into the water. The sailboat drifted from shore.

Rosie walked over and fitted Finn's hat back on his head, running the strap under his chin. Then she turned to the man, now seated on the bench, drying off his feet with his socks before slipping them back on.

"You didn't have to do that."

"What, and let your little brother lose his vessel? I think not." He slipped on his shoes and stood up.

Again, those eyes, and they had the power to render her silent. "Thank you for your gallant service," she finally managed, and felt the fool. "I don't know how to repay you."

"Fear not. I believe you might find a way." Then he winked at her.

She stood there, a strange warmth simmering through her. He extended his hand. "Rolfe Van Horne," he said.

"Rosie Worth," she said.

He smiled. "I know."

She stared at him, nonplussed. "What—"

"Red!"

She turned and spotted Dash coming toward her from the direction of the statue. How could she have missed him? "Dash," she said, more surprise than enthusiasm in her voice. She cleared her throat, brightened. "I didn't see you there!"

"Clearly," he said, and his gaze shot to the man next to her.

"Nice to meet you," Rolfe said, then nodded toward Dash.

"Nice to meet—you—too...." But he had already turned his back to her and was walking away.

Dash caught up to her. "Who was that?"

"Some man who helped Finn get his boat back." She turned to Finn. "You stay here on shore while I talk to Dash, okay, Finn?"

He held up his arm, the one with the string attached. "I'm a sailor!"

"Indeed you are, little man." She turned to Dash, who still had his gaze on Van Horne. "Forget about him. I'm so glad to see you!" She slipped her arms around his waist, not caring that she might be making a spectacle.

He closed his around her shoulders, but she felt stiffness in his response. "What's this all about, Red? I show up at your house, and you won't see me, and then Blanche sends me this cryptic note about meeting you in the garden." He pushed her out to arm's length. "I thought we were having fun."

She frowned. "It's not what you think, Dash. My mother and stepfather came home the other night. They—they don't want us to see each other."

He made a face. "Sounds about right. I wondered when the news from Page Six would find them."

Oh. "So it's true?"

He lifted a shoulder. "She says so. I don't know."

Rosie stared at him, coldness sliding through her. "You...you slept with her?"

"Rosie, come on, don't be like that. I'm here with you, today." He took her hand and tugged her down onto the bench. "Now, tell me how we're going to sneak out and have some fun." He traced a finger down her cheek.

She swallowed back her hurt, forcing a smile. "You're right. It doesn't matter. It's nothing." She leaned into him and raised her chin. "How much did you miss me, Dash?"

He pecked her nose. "Terribly. I've had no fun at all the last few nights. Tell me that you'll find a way to come 'round with us tonight."

She fiddled with a button on his jacket. "What if you could have me all the time? Would you like that?"

A dangerous smile tweaked his face. "What do you mean, Red?"

She drew in a breath, tried not to rush. "Do you love me, Dash?"

"Sure, darling. I love you lots." But something sparked in his eyes.

"Me too." She couldn't look at him. She pressed her hand against his chest. "Let's elope."

He stilled under her touch. "Now, Red—"

"I have an allowance, Dash, and we'll be fine. Mother wouldn't dare cut me off, and we can leave tonight if we have to. I have a plan."

He caught her hand on his chest, pulled it away. "Rosie—"

"I know you need money. I can give that to you...."

Dash sat up, scooted away. "Rosie, I'm my father's only son. I promise you, I don't need your money." His tone had changed, added a chill.

"Fine. Of course you don't need my money. But..." She feared what she'd see in his eyes. "My mother wants to marry me off to some duke from Belgium. I want to be with you." She looked at him then, and her heart died at his expression.

"Rosie, I don't want to marry you." He drew in a breath.

She held herself fast, willing her voice calm. "But you said—you said I was your inspiration."

"Oh, Red. Of course you are. Look at you. You're a dish, doll, and you look good on my arm. But we're just having fun. You're my good-time girl. But I don't want to get married. I'm sorry, I guess, if that hurts you." He reached to touch her face. "Don't blame me. You said you didn't want to get married, if I recall."

She had said that. Because that's what he'd wanted to hear.

She pushed his hand away. "Finn!"

"Red, don't be like this. You know I like being with you. We have the whole summer—we'll figure something out."

She marched over to Finn, began to drag his boat in.

"Rothie! I want to stay."

"No, we're going home, Finn. Our walk in the park is over."

Dash touched her on the arm, and she jerked away, losing her balance. She fell and hit the water, her hand sinking in to her elbow, the cold bracing upon her skin.

"Let me help—"

"Get away from me," she hissed. "Just...get away."

He held his hands up in surrender. "If that's the way you want it. Good luck with your duke, Red."

"You swine."

Finn reached up and tried to help her out. He wore fear in his eyes as he glanced at Dash, who was backing away, shaking his head.

Rosie climbed out, turned her back to him. Her eyes burned, and she sank down beside Finn. She began to tremble, her hand over her mouth. Her breaths began to shudder through her.

No. No. She wouldn't break down, not here, not—

Finn put his arms around her neck, burying his face in her shoulder. "I love you, Rothie. Don't cry."

She pulled him tight against herself, holding onto his tiny, strong body, so full of grace, and wept into his shoulder.

It wasn't until she had found herself again, mustered her composure, until she'd pulled the boat to shore, that she saw Rolfe Van Horne watching her from across the pond.

She ignored him, gathered up Finn and his boat, took his hand, and trekked toward home, the sunset bleeding into the horizon.

She should have known Dash would turn on her. Should have known he was just using her, that he didn't truly love her.

In fact, she'd never met a man who truly loved her. Her father hadn't—not with the way he treated her, as if she were a reminder of his unfaithful wife. And Jack—well, if Jack truly cared for her, he would have never run away and left her. And Bennett—how could he possibly care for her after what her father did to the woman he loved? Besides, she wasn't his daughter.

She had Finn, of course, but he was too young to betray her.

No, she shouldn't expect anything from a man, except to use her for what she could give him.

"Rothie, you're hurting my hand."

She loosened her grip. "I'm sorry, Finley." She stopped at the edge of the park, crouched down to face him. "Listen, let's keep my... conversation with my friend a secret, okay?"

"And your crying?"

"That too." She reached over, scrubbed dirt from his face with her thumb. "I'll be fine. I was just sad."

"I'm sad when you're sad," he said, and looked like he might cry.

"Thanks, Finn."

She stood up and took his hand. They crossed the street and headed down the boulevard. She bought a bouquet of peonies and drank in the smell.

No, she'd never trust a man again. At least unless she had something to barter, something to keep his love.

As she entered the house, she bent down to unbutton Finn's jacket, take his hat. "Run and tell Mother we're home."

"We're in here."

Jinx sat in the parlor, her needlepoint on her lap. She looked up at Rosie then frowned. "Where's Lilly?"

Where was Lilly? She knew the question would come, but still, it stripped her. "Lilly?" she said, as if she'd never heard of her cousin before.

Jinx set down her needlepoint. Stared at Rosie. Then, her voice dropped, realization in it. "Oh no, what have you done, Rosie?"

"Uncle Oliver!"

Rosie heard Finn's greeting down the hallway.

"Finley! You've grown a mile since I saw you last."

Rosie closed her eyes. Drew in a breath. She hadn't expected him until tomorrow, or later.

He always scared her a little, his history as a stringer for the paper, living on the streets in his eyes. He knew how to make his own way and bore it in his demeanor. "Hello, Rosie,"he said as he walked down the hall, holding Finn's hand. "Amelia said you were in the park. Is Lilly up in her room?"

Rosie saw Jinx's mouth tighten around the edges. She got up just as Finn looked at Uncle Oliver and said, "No, Lilly left with that man. At the park." He looked at Rosie. "'Member?"

Oh, yes, she remembered. And as long as she lived, she knew she'd never forget the darkness that washed over Oliver's face, nor the way he turned to Rosie and said, "Tell me where she is, Rosie. Right. Now."

* * * * *

Lilly had never seen such courage—or foolishness—as the fatal ballet between the midnight-black bull and the young matador. The matador moved with grace through the sand of the amphitheater, as if the entire event might be choreographed, his crimson robe a partner as he danced around the bull.

"He's going to get killed."

"I know. After three or four of the bulls are down, you can smell the blood," Rennie said.

She'd been near blood during the cattle drives of her youth, during the castrating of the cattle, the birthing of calves.

But this taunting of danger wheedled inside her, churned up something ugly, even repulsive, as the bulls became angrier, the matadors more daring.

They'd started the *corrida* with six bulls and three toreros—older men who paraded into the ring all in bright pink or white. And then came the young one—possibly still a teen, dressed in a shiny gold vest and dark pants, a bright yellow shirt that would surely emphasize his blood. He stared into the audience with the rest of the toreros and, for a second, met her eyes, almost with a dare. Then he moved on to the other side of the stadium, whipping the crowd's adoration to life.

Behind them came the *cuadrilla*, the team of bullfighters mounted on horseback, and the flagmen, to keep them safe.

When the bulls trotted out, their white horns sharpened into a fine point and pawed the ground, Lilly gripped her seat, leaning forward and holding her breath.

"Look away," Rennie said as the picadors stabbed each bull, letting the first blood run.

Lilly had the strangest urge to cry.

"It makes them lower their head, a more daring charge for the matadors."

"It's cruel."

Presley, beside him, laughed.

"Just wait," Rennie said, and echoed Presley's laughter. He had beer on his breath from the hours before in the café, and in the hot sun it probably only soaked into him.

The young matador flicked his cape as the bull swung around him then let it charge so close she thought the horns had grazed him. But he held his ground, and the *banderillas* closed in with more barbs.

"I can't bear it. They look like buffalo." She held her hand to her mouth, turning her head away as the matador waved his cape on the long dowel, moving it from one side to the next as the animal charged him.

The crowd roared as the bull chased him, but he turned at the last moment then let it pass.

"He's magnificent," Hem said.

Presley clapped.

"You'd better turn away again, they're about to stab the bull through the shoulder blades and pierce his heart."

She stared at Rennie. He didn't seem to be kidding. She got up. "I—I don't feel well." She moved to leave, and fast.

Rennie got up to follow her, but Presley put a hand on his arm. "I'll go with her." She rose. "Trust me, after a few days of gore, you'll get used to it. That, or enough beer to not care anymore." She winked.

"No—I'm fine." Lilly managed a smile. "I'll find my way back to the hotel."

She stepped past Rennie before he could stop her and climbed down out of the stands. Already, her head felt less hot, her stomach settling, away from the blood and violence.

She wanted to cry at her stupidity, at the fear and revulsion that had risen inside her. What would Rennie think? But the entire event conjured up the brutality of the buffalo massacres she'd read about in the West. She hated it.

Lilly walked through the grounds toward the gate and noticed the traveling cages that had transported the bulls from their ranches outside the city. Some of them were empty, but others hosted bulls still waiting to be let out into their corral. Did they know that they would be released only to their deaths?

One of the bulls nudged up against the bars. She saw the hairy, black head, and one dark eye, wild with fright.

She'd known better than to get near the buffalo on her ranch back home, but sympathy welled up inside her, and for a second she reached up—

"*Alto!*"

She jerked as a wrinkled man wearing a basque beret strode up and slapped her hand away.

She curled into herself and hurried out the gate, onto the street.

Her hotel was located on the plateau behind the city, and she ordered a carriage from the man at the gate and gave the name. The carriage drove her through the city, a plume of white dust rising to obscure her view of the bullrings. Everywhere she looked, bougainvillea twined up whitewashed buildings, chickens ran through the streets chased by little girls in bandannas. Clouds hung in the distance over the far green mountains, and the farther she went from the bloodletting, the stronger she became.

She thought of the young matador, the way he played with the bull, his face tight, his eyes growing. The bull had charged, and he'd barely moved, unshaken. If she didn't let the blood and gore turn her away, she might see the courage.

She longed for that kind of courage. Thought she'd had her hands around it once again over the skies of Paris, and in the last week.

Clearly, she wasn't the daredevil she hoped to be.

Yet.

The carriage bumped along the dirt road, up the hill toward the hotel. She'd paid for her own room—insisted upon it, after hearing about Hem's lack of fortune. She feared Rennie might be in similar dire straits, although they'd all had a rich lunch of poached fish and hard bread and cold cucumber soup. She'd stuck to lemonade again, while Presley led the men in consuming frothy cold beer that teared down the sides of the glass. Presley offered Lilly a sip, and her mouth puckered at the bitterness.

Maybe she'd never be Presley, brash and smart, looking beautiful in men's clothes and a jaunty beret. But perhaps she didn't have to. She had Rennie, after all, and he'd made this clear when he'd taken her hand in his while they walked through the streets.

Back at the hotel, she found her room freshly cleaned, the linen curtains blowing in the smell of rain from the darkening clouds. Hopefully Rennie would return before it began to deluge the bullfights. She looked forward to sitting with him under the stars, maybe talking about where they'd go next. Perhaps Madrid.

She ordered gazpacho and ate it on the Juliet balcony outside her window and wished for writing paper to recount the day's events for Rosie.

If only Rosie had come with her. Lilly feared for her, at home with Jinx and the news of Lilly's escape, but Rosie had assured her that she could manage without betraying her.

Rosie had been so distraught over slapping her that Lilly believed her. And, perhaps, after this week, Aunt Jinx would realize that Lilly was her own person, that she didn't need the supervision of her elders. Perhaps they would allow her to stay behind in Paris after the summer season.

Maybe she would marry Rennie. Yes, *of course* she would marry Rennie.

A knock came at her door just as the sun dripped into the black mountains. Rennie stood at the door, a sunburn on his nose, a smile curling up one side of his mouth. One whiff of him suggested he'd stopped at a cantina on the way back to the hotel to finish off a carafe or two of beer. "Hello, peach."

"Rennie. Are you okay?"

He came into the room, took off his derby, and flung it onto the bed. "Never better." Then he sat down on the edge. "Have you put yourself back together?"

"Yes. I'm sorry. Perhaps tomorrow I will be a better sport. It's just so…maudlin."

"It is," he said softly. "C'mere."

She slid into the comfort of his embrace, expecting words of sympathy, even understanding. He said nothing, however, and pulled her down to him. He tasted of beer and garlic, and she didn't relish it. But this was Rennie, and she could forgive him of his vices. Especially in Pamplona.

Besides, hadn't he come up to inquire after her?

He curled one hand around her back, the other behind her neck, and in a moment had pulled her down beside him on the creamy eyelet bedspread.

"Ren—"

"You're so beautiful," he said, lifting his head, his eyes dragging over her. "Young and beautiful."

She didn't know what to think when he leaned over her, kissed her again. This kiss she didn't recognize. It lacked the gentle ardor of before, it was reckless, and sloppy, his breath hot and dark against her mouth, then her neck. But perhaps this was what happened to a man when he drank.

Then his hand traveled down, and she stiffened. "Rennie, please. Stop." She caught his grope, but he pulled out of her grip.

His eyes had a storm in them as they raked down her, back to her face, and she froze, a spark of warning now touching her core. "I thought you wanted an adventure." Before she could respond, he leaned down, close to her ear, pleading. "Please, Lilly. I'm in love with you."

She swallowed, her throat burning. When he leaned over and kissed her again, his touch had gentled, but panic had already reached up to suffocate her.

"No...I... Please, Rennie—I can't." She pushed on his chest, but he again covered her mouth, as if desperate.

She twisted beneath him, fear spearing through her limbs. She didn't even think as she reached back and, with everything inside her, slammed the palm of her hand against his face.

He reeled back and stared at her, his hand to his cheek. She pulled together her mussed clothes and scooted back from him, breathing hard.

He moved away from her and she expected an apology—something—but he just shook his head and got up, off the bed.

"Rennie, please, understand. I...I'm not ready. Shouldn't we be married first?"

He held up his hand, as if to silence her, then he opened the door. He stood in the frame, the hallway dark beyond her room, his back to her, his shoulders rising and falling.

"I should have listened to Presley. She told me you weren't ready for Spain. This was all a terrible mistake," he said finally, and shut the door.

The sound of it shook her through.

Rennie. She drew up her legs on the bed, feeling sick, and touched her fingers to her stinging lips.

This was all a terrible mistake.

His words turned to acid inside her. *You weren't ready for Spain.* What had Presley told him?

She had the sick feeling that Presley had once been in Rennie's arms, maybe even here. In fact, maybe that's where Presley—not Lilly—still belonged.

Maybe Rennie knew it. Maybe he was still in love with Presley. Then why had he invited her? Why had he made her feel as if she belonged here, with him?

Maybe she did. He'd made her feel bold and alive, and with him she became someone who traveled to Spain, who watched the bull-fights, and who went flying.

Lilly stood up, stared at herself in the mirror. She'd braided her hair today, but it was mussed and tangled, and she looked like a schoolgirl in her plain shirtwaist and skirt. She worked her braids free then retrieved a brush and ran it over her hair, turning it shiny and full.

She already felt older. More daring. *Men are children. A woman has to know how to handle them.*

She opened the valise of Presley's clothes and found a black-fringed dress, sleeveless and low. She slid into it, and although it bagged on her, it showed more of her than she ever had before.

Spain can turn a girl into a woman, if she has the courage.

She went without stockings, slid into a pair of heels, and stared at herself in the mirror. Rosie would most likely approve of this outfit, would probably suggest adding a string of pearls to her neck. Oliver had presented her with pearls on her eighteenth birthday. They still sat in the velvet box in her trunks back in Paris.

She put her hand to her bare neck. If she had them, she'd wear them now, swing them in her hand for courage as she sauntered downstairs to where the men played bridge at one of the white wicker tables on the stone terrace.

The sun had set, and electric lights and torches trickled dark shadows upon Hem and Rennie's faces as they held up their cards.

Presley sat on one of the chairs also, hunkered in tight between Hem and Rennie, reading both their hands. She glanced at Lilly as she got closer, a frown darting across her face—quickly replaced by an expression of sadness. She nudged Rennie. "Look who showed up."

Rennie set down his cards. She expected a smile, something of apology, even appreciation, but she couldn't read his expression as he scanned her, head to toe, then back to her eyes. "Looky here. Who is this?"

"Rennie..." Lilly said softly.

His mouth tightened into a knot, his eyes hard.

She advanced another step. "I'm sorry, Rennie."

He laid his cards down, glanced at Presley, who raised a thin eyebrow. Then back to Lilly.

She smiled, but the edges of her lips quivered.

Then, his eyes softened, a smile barely edging—

"Lilly!"

The sound of her name behind her shook her through. No.

Her breath came fast and sharp. She turned, and a whimper escaped. Oliver.

He looked wrung out, his dark brown eyes red-rimmed, his black hair mussed, wearing a suit he must have slept in, but the disarray only made him appear ferocious. He stared at her, the entirety of what she'd become, and she had the urge to cover herself.

Then he advanced toward them, setting down a case on the terrace. "I've been to every hotel in Pamplona."

She swallowed.

Behind her, she heard a chair rake against the stonework. Rennie. Oh, sweet Rennie. He'd stand up to her stepfather, would tell him that no, she wasn't returning with him, that Rennie loved her. That she belonged with him now.

"Who are you?" Rennie asked.

Oliver cut him a look.

She almost wept with relief at the way Rennie came to stand beside her. She wanted to take his hand, but she couldn't move.

"I'm her father," Oliver said, and could melt a lesser man with the heat in his eyes. "Who are *you*?"

She glanced at Rennie and offered a little smile, even a nod for encouragement.

Rennie stared at him, and she wanted to answer for him. Heard the words in the beating of her heart, felt it in the heat of her held breath.

"I'm no one."

His words fell upon her like a blade.

Then, as if to remind her just how foolish she'd become, Rennie turned to her, his eyes hard and cold. "Go home, Lilly. Your adventure is over." He returned to the table, sat, and picked up his cards.

She stood there, and the tremble started deep inside, found its way out. She wanted to slap him, to—

"Lilly." The voice was too gentle for her against all the rage boiling inside.

She turned to Oliver, and words churned a long moment before she could latch onto the right ones. But they were exactly right, and came from a place she hadn't had the courage to speak from. Until now. "I hate you. You stole my life from me. Again."

She brushed past him and fled back to her room to weep.

Chapter 6

"Will you never forgive me?" Rosie tried to keep the anger from her voice.

Lilly stood at the rail of the steamer, staring into the ocean breeze, the shadows of the night pocketed into the wells of her face, sallow from tears. Her long braids twisted in the wind as she knotted the front of her steamer blanket hanging over her shoulders with a fist. She didn't acknowledge Rosie's question.

Behind them, in the grand ballroom, the orchestra played as first-class passengers danced and lounged. Bennett and Uncle Oliver had retired for an after-dinner cigar while her mother went to oversee Finley's bedtime. Ten days on the ship had lost its allure to her, especially since most of the first-class passengers were businessmen traveling home from Europe. None of her set would come home until the end of August, when the season in Paris ended.

Rosie pulled her own steamer blanket up over her shoulders, shivering as the ocean winds scuttled across her arms. She'd forgotten the chill of the open sea—that, and the briny feel of the salt layered upon her skin, woven into her hair. She felt grimy and old, weary and torn through with the chop of the sea, the brisk wind, and the unrelenting cold front from her cousin.

"Oliver gave me no choice," Rosie said, grasping the rail.

Lilly's face hardened.

"You should have seen him, Lils. He looked undone and tired, as if he'd swum across the Atlantic to get to you. I tried to hold out, I even went to my room and locked the door, but he stood outside it and knocked and knocked—he kept pleading with me. He told me how much he loved you. It was horrible. I know I said I wouldn't tell him, but...I didn't realize how much he cared for you."

A muscle pulled in Lilly's jaw, her dark eyes tracing something in the mysterious darkness beyond the bow where they stood. Early stars hung over the darkness, and a half moon had risen to cast an eerie glow upon the silver waves.

"I finally opened the door. He'd pulled up a chair and sat there, holding his head in his hands. I thought he was crying, but then he just looked up at me, and I think, had I not been a woman, he might have taken me by the throat and throttled the information right out of me. But he just stared, something so desperate in his expression...I had to tell him, Lils."

Okay, so yes, she'd planned on betraying Lilly, but once she'd returned home, her own heart in pieces, it felt so wicked, for a moment, she debated holding onto her secret.

Rosie wished she had someone who might break a door down for her.

Lilly swallowed. Drew in a breath. "Rennie loved me, Rosie." Her voice emerged sharp and brittle. "And if Oliver hadn't shown up, I'd be with him in Madrid, right now. Oliver destroyed everything."

"You don't know that. Rennie might have tired of you—"

Lilly rounded on her. "He wasn't Dash! Rennie wasn't playing games with me!"

"Of *course* he was playing games. That's what men do! They play games. They only want a woman who will fit into their world, who will give them what they ask for, become the thing they want. Our job is to beat them at their own game and get what we need in return. None of it is real, Lilly, and the sooner you figure that out, the sooner you'll realize that Oliver did you a favor."

"No. He didn't. I don't know why, but Oliver is set on destroying my life."

"Oliver loves you."

"If he did, he would have left me alone to be happy instead of dragging me back to a city I hate, a life I loathe." Lilly turned back again to the dark pane of night. "I'll never forgive him."

Rosie looked down, at the way the steamer lights skimmed the ocean, leaking out like puddles upon the oily surface. The dull thud of the waves against the hull sounded like a heartbeat. "And me?"

Lilly drew in a breath. From the ballroom inside, the orchestra played Mozart and the music drifted out to season the night. "Being out here helps me forget. The stars dripping on the ocean, like fire. Look— there's a falling star."

Lilly pointed to the sky, but Rosie couldn't find it, lost among the glitter of the Milky Way.

"It's not really a star, you know," Lilly said. "It's a meteoroid. A big rock that passes through the earth's atmosphere. We're seeing the earth burn it up."

"Did Rennie tell you that?"

Lilly shook her head. "I read it in the *Chronicle*. Some German astronomer wrote a paper on it. He also wrote an article on black holes. He said that when a star dies, it leaves a black hole so large the magnetic force pulls everything around it into the darkness."

Rosie searched again for the meteor, but her attention fell to the lights of New York, twinkling in the distance. Tomorrow they'd dock, disembark to New York City. Then, Rosie planned on forgetting everything about Paris and Dash any way she could. Perhaps Mother would pack them up and they would spend the summer in Newport, at Rosehaven.

"The sky is so big, it reminds me of Montana."

"Everything reminds you of Montana, Lilly."

"I'm going back there, you know."

"Of course you are."

"I will convince Mother to send me back. To let me work the ranch. She's not the only one who can move out West, create a life. I am just as capable as my mother. I don't need her help—or Oliver's. I can do this on my own."

Rosie drew in her words, the robust fragrance drifting off the sea. "Look, you can see the Statue of Liberty from here." She pointed to the glow emanating from the harbor.

"I saw the real one in Paris, at Luxembourg Gardens," Lilly said, her voice bitter again.

"This is the real one, Lilly. That's just the model. This is the one that means freedom and liberty."

Her own words fell through her, settled like a fist over her heart.

As long as her mother dictated who she married, where she lived, and controlled her allowance, she'd never have liberty.

She'd end up marrying some Russian count, or Belgian duke.

She needed to be more like Lilly, standing at the rail, fierce and strong and headed to freedom.

The lights along the harbor pulsed into the sky, like a marquis. Beyond that was Broadway, the theaters.

She almost flinched when Lilly's hand slipped into hers and folded between her fingers. She expected it to be cold, but Lilly's grip warmed hers. They stood at the rail in silence as the ship anchored just outside the city, waiting for tomorrow's arrival.

"Someday I'll earn your forgiveness?"

Lilly glanced at Rosie and now offered the barest of smiles. "Yes."

* * * * *

The plan had churned inside Lilly all week, once they'd left port in France. Until then, a sort of numbness spread throughout her body as Oliver forced her into a taxi and then to the train back to Paris.

She hadn't seen Rennie—not once after she'd fled from him. She'd sat in her room at the hotel all night, the paint around her eyes turning into a mess, waiting for him to knock.

Instead, Oliver had banged on her door—it felt like he might be pounding on her soul—demanding to see her.

She locked the door, refusing him. What might he do but offer reproof at her actions?

As the sunlight finally tipped over the sash in her bedroom, she cleaned herself up and found a resolute expression. Oliver sent a porter to fetch her bags, but she had nothing. She left Presley's clothing folded in the satchel and took only her reticule. She didn't even have her Zane Grey book to occupy her mind as she stared out the train window.

Oliver sat across from her in a private car, his gaze turning her flesh to cinders.

Oh, how she hated him. Hated how he made her feel a nuisance. And now, as if she might be tawdry.

"He didn't hurt you, did he?" he'd asked once, devastating the padding of silence.

She'd shot him a look. "Never. Rennie cared for me."

Oliver gave her a look she couldn't comprehend and she glanced away, her eyes burning.

Funny how her mind played games with her, one moment impressing on her the moments—flying, and walking along the Seine, the next, impaling her with Rennie's cold, brutal words. *Go home.*

He didn't mean it, and if Oliver hadn't arrived…

Lilly watched him now, on the dock below, paying a porter to fetch their trunks. By the time she'd arrived back in Paris, Aunt Jinx had all her belongings packed and en route to port.

She couldn't believe it when Aunt Jinx, Finn, and Rosie left right behind her and Oliver. She bit down a sluice of satisfaction.

So Rosie had lost Dash. He was trouble for her anyway, slick, with his gray reptilian eyes, his smooth smile.

The bustle of New York seemed less refined than Paris, the workmen along the docks thick with muscle, the stench of their work on their skin. They tied up the steamer like brutes manhandling a whale, their words raw and ugly. For as far as she could see, piers stretched out into the wharf like fingers, great twisted ropes falling from masted yachts, barges, and tugboats, fastening them to shore. The reek of oil and fresh fish curdled the breeze. Beyond that, upon the long stretch of harbor, motorcars and carriages huddled like beetles, ready to whisk their charges away.

Immigrants queued up to be ferried to Ellis Island and processed, their belongings in crates and burlap and trunks. Most wore their journey on their faces, children draped over the laps of their older siblings.

Beyond the docks, the city rose with alarming alacrity, blotting out the sky, dust hovering between buildings.

Her mother would no doubt be at work at the Chronicle Building in midtown Manhattan, and surely Oliver would take her there before delivering her home. Back to their chateau along Fifth Avenue, where from her window she could stare out at Central Park and make believe it might be a prairie.

On the docks below, Oliver finished his business and glanced up at the ship. Lilly looked away from him, searching for Aunt Jinx and Uncle Bennett. She'd seen Amelia disembark with Finn and knew they couldn't be long behind. Rosie she hadn't seen since last night on the bow.

Since she'd tried to smooth out the disaster of Paris. *Someday I'll earn your forgiveness?*

Perhaps. Yes. Today, however, the sting of Rosie's betrayal bit into her, reminded her why she couldn't be with Rennie.

However, if Lilly's plan came to fruition, she might find it easier to slough away the memory of Paris.

To forget Rennie.

But she'd never forget the taste of freedom, the sense that she could be more than what she was in New York.

"Lilly!"

She glanced down where Oliver had been standing, and found him gone.

"Lilly!"

She found him striding up behind her, looking every inch the powerful owner of the local press in his black suit, a derby hat. He and Mother made a fetching pair, if she didn't let herself remember the pictures of her real father back on the ranch. And, she could admit that Oliver made her mother happy. As if, when Esme met him, she'd breathed for the first time in years.

"Oliver."

"The porter will transport our belongings. Are you ready to go?"

Lilly manufactured a smile but didn't take his arm, choosing the rope instead to steady herself down the long gangplank to the dock.

She simply had to time her performance well. Throw herself into her mother's arms, plead her loneliness in Paris, and beg to return to Montana before Oliver scandalized her with his version of her escapades in Spain. Perhaps, even if he did, Esme would be so grateful to have her back, safely, that she would relent. She might even convince herself that Lilly was safer, far from the city, in Montana.

Her mother could stay in New York.

And, she'd be just fine on a train to the West—after all, hadn't she gone to Pamplona, the bullfights, on her own?

Of course she'd miss her mother, but Esme had seemed willing to send her to Paris, without her.

Oliver loaded her into a taxi then climbed in the other side.

Sure, her mother longed for her to join her in the newspaper business, but Lilly wasn't a businesswoman or a writer. She wanted adventure. To live life, not write about it.

Esme, a woman who'd left New York and headed to Montana at the very same age Lilly was now, should understand that.

They drove into the arteries of the city, past women shopping, their jackets raked by a spring wind, motorcars and buses, the elevated train, and not a few delivery carriages. They passed the Flatiron building, its shadow darkening the pavement, then turned down Fifth.

"Aren't we going to the *Chronicle*? I don't want to go home yet."

Oliver didn't look at her, drawing in a breath. "There's a reason I came to get you, Lilly, one that had nothing to do with…your excursion to Spain."

They passed a newsie on a street corner waving a copy of the *Chronicle*, or perhaps the *World*.

"I don't understand."

"I know." He looked at her then, and for a moment, the expression on his face struck her silent. His dark brown eyes seemed pained, his mouth tight and lined at the corners. It stirred in her the uncanny feeling of wanting to take his hand, to squeeze it.

It scared her.

"Your mother isn't in the city, Lilly. We sent you away in the faint hope that by the time you returned, she would be better, and that she could come home again."

Lilly's chest began to knot, slow and tight.

"We both felt it was time to come and get you. However…her condition is progressing and we are unable to stop it."

"Where is she?"

"She's convalescing at a private sanitarium in the Adirondack Mountains, on Saranac Lake. It's really quite peaceful, and…" He swallowed; his voice hitched. "They've had good results from the fresh air and climate in the mountains and offered a great hope. She's been there since you left. We're going right to the train station."

The words slipped out a little louder than a breath. "What's wrong with her?"

He tucked his hand into hers and she didn't even flinch, just let him hold it as he said, "Lilly, your mother has tuberculosis. She's dying."

* * * * *

It seemed more a vacation spot than a hospital where people came to die. Lush, green grounds, fragrant pines, and wide-trunked oak trees, the whisper of hope on the wind. The lake rippled along the shore, such a rich blue Lilly thought it might be painted. A flag fluttered in the scant wind from the white pole in the center of the grounds, and the sun in the cloudless sky winked down at them as she climbed the wide stairs to the brown-bricked administration building.

Oliver had directed their belongings to a boardinghouse in town, pointing it out to her as the taxi took them directly to the Adirondack Cottages.

Inside the reception hall, Lilly found a room filled with straight-backed chairs and the cheerful pictures of patients smiling into the camera, as if, indeed, they might be on an extended holiday. A nurse in a smart white dress and green cardigan greeted them and handed them passes. "She's curing at her cottage," she said.

Oliver nodded, as if he understood exactly what she meant, and led Lilly out to the grounds.

"What is that—curing?"

"The consumptives spend a great deal of the day wrapped in blankets, resting on the open porches. It's part of the regimen."

He pointed to a row of children, bundled and lounging on what appeared to be canvas chairs. "These are called cure cottages."

They walked down the path bordered by marigolds, the air seasoned with the fragrance of optimism. They passed a cluster of small red houses with white trim and tiny porches. Farther back on the lawn, larger houses with expansive porches suggested group lodgings.

"Are they taking good care of her?"

"They feed her well. Milk and eggs and pork chops for breakfast, dinner at noon is roast beef, baked potatoes, corn or peas—sometimes I've even seen them serve rice pudding for dessert. She eats four or five times a day. Even so, brace yourself. She has lost a great deal of weight."

"Is that part of the disease?"

"It comes from the fatigue of so much coughing, the night sweats, the fever."

"I knew she had a cough, but…how did I not know?"

"They only diagnosed it a couple of weeks before you left. She'd lost so much weight, and we thought she simply had the flu, or fatigue from the paper…."

He cut up the path toward a large house with a stone foundation and rolling roof. Pink peonies poked from the garden on each side of the steps, just starting to push open blooms. A lilac tree in bud waved as if in greeting. "I shouldn't have allowed her to work so hard."

Her throat felt tight, scratchy.

They climbed the stairs, and even as they drew near, she heard the coughing, then voices. Oliver stopped, one hand on the screen door. Then he met her eyes. "I'm sorry."

"Don't say that."

He nodded and opened the door.

She always liked her mother best from the photos taken on her honeymoon with her first husband, Lilly's father, Daughtry Hoyt. In them, Esme was tall and regal, her thin neck boasting a choker of pearls, her hair piled into a proper knot at the nape of her neck. She stared into the camera without a smile, as if it dared capture her.

Lilly had surely inherited her independence from her mother.

She'd heard the story about how her mother fled to Montana after her sister Jinx had married Esme's fiancé, Foster, how Esme had built a newspaper in a town called Silver City, just west of Butte, Montana. How she'd stood up to the Copper Kings—the mine owners who wanted to bankrupt the workers—and that she'd learned to run a mining operation. She'd inherited a ranch and a herd of Buffalo from Lilly's father, then built her paper to three more towns. Most of all, she'd kept alive her deceased husband's legacy for her fatherless daughter.

Then she'd moved to New York City, helped prove her sister Jinx innocent of the murder of her husband, taken the reins of the largest paper in New York. She'd married Oliver, the publisher, and helped him expand the *Chronicle* to Europe.

Esme Price Hoyt Stewart was beautiful, brilliant, always buoyant, and possessed the ability to light up a ballroom or stop the presses.

The person before Lilly was not her mother.

This person lay on a bed, her eyes reddened, her skin nearly bled of color, her straw-blond hair dry and wispy, her body mere bones, the flesh wrinkled upon it like tissue. This person waged a losing war with the disease ravaging her body.

This person lay upon death's door.

A nurse moved away from the bed, a tray of bloody spittle in her hand. "She's been holding on for you," she said softly as she turned to the sink in the room.

Her mother looked up at Lilly and smiled. "You made it."

Lilly had no words, nothing but a moan escaped from her as she shuffled toward the bed. She looked for help from Oliver, but he'd walked to the other side of the bed and drawn up a chair. Esme turned her head. "You are so handsome."

He kissed her forehead before sitting down. He took her hand. "And you can still take my breath away." But his eyes glistened.

Lilly bent down to kiss her cheek, but Esme closed her eyes, turned away. "Wear a mask, Lilly. Please."

"I'm not going to get ill—"

"Please, Lilly. If you don't already have this, then I pray you don't get it from me. If I give you anything, it's a future with Oliver and the *Chronicle,* not this."

A future with—Lilly shook her head even as she sank onto a chair. The nurse handed her a mask, and she fitted it over her nose. Oliver took one also, his mouth a pinched line before it disappeared beneath the cloth.

"Mother, you're going to be fine." She ran her thumb over Esme's hand, the bones brittle beneath her touch.

"No, Lilly. It's gone too far. I feel it in myself. I'm fading." She glanced at Oliver. "I'm so sorry."

Oliver pressed her hand to his lips. Shook his head.

She turned back to Lilly. "How beautiful you look, tan and strong. Paris agrees with you."

Oh, Mother. She glanced at Oliver, but he was lost in a place she couldn't yet go. Apparently, he hadn't told Esme anything of Lilly's misbehavior. She might forgive him just a little because of that.

Never mind that Aunt Jinx had lied to her. She surely hadn't cabled her mother with the news of Lilly's behavior—not with her mother in this condition.

"I should have never gone to Paris. I should have been here, with you."

Esme smiled. "No, my darling. I wanted you to see Paris. Isn't the Eiffel Tower glorious? And Notre Dame. Please tell me you saw it at night."

I saw it from the air. But she couldn't say that, not with her mother crumpled in this tiny bed, the cotton sheets barely outlining her fragile body.

"It's beautiful. I walked the Luxembourg Gardens, and Rosie and I took Finn to Jardin des Tuileries so he could sail his boat in the pond."

"And the Champs-Élysées? You ate at the cafés?"

"Café au lait, every day. So many crepes my mouth would water just at the sight of them."

Esme smiled. "Your father took me there on our honeymoon."

"Oliver is not my father." The words were out, quick and sharp, before she could stop them.

Her mother closed her eyes. Took too long to open them again. "I know. But he's the only father I can give you, darling. And he's going to take care of you now." She looked at Oliver, nodded.

Lilly refused to look at him.

"You two will run the paper together." Esme had a softness in her expression when she turned back to her. "The newspaper business is in your blood, Lilly. You will be a newspaper baroness and change the world with the pursuit of truth. The *Chronicle* is my legacy, Lilly. And now I give it to you."

Lilly's breath stilled in her chest, but what could she say? Her eyes burned as she nodded. "Yes, of course, Mother."

A sigh trickled out of Esme.

"But just until you are well."

A smile edged up Esme's face. "That's my girl. Always the feisty one."

The cough began deep inside, but it rumbled out of her like a train, bending her over, racking her body so that Lilly thought she might fracture every one of her delicate bones. Oliver wound his arm around

Esme's back and pushed her upright, and she bent over double as the nurse ran and shoved the spittle bowl under her chin. Lilly turned away when blood dribbled from her mother's mouth.

Esme held a rag to herself as she collapsed back into the pillows.

Her eyes had sunken into her head, sweat dotted her forehead. "This isn't how I'd planned to leave you both." She looked first at Lilly, then at Oliver. "But long ago I committed my plans to God. I trust Him, you know. And He blessed me with you."

Oliver pressed his hand to her cheek.

"And you, daughter."

Lilly's jaw tightened and she looked away, out the window, at the green lawn, the clear, shiny sky, the glint of sunlight on the lake.

Why trust a God who didn't show up when you needed Him?

Rennie's words drifted back to her, latched on.

Her mother's voice whispered through her, into her thoughts. "Whatever happens, honey, don't forget who you are. Don't forget the blessings God has bestowed upon you. Don't forget your name and where you belong."

Lilly tore off the mask, then, meeting her mother's blue eyes, bent and kissed her on the forehead. "I love you, Mother."

Then she turned and escaped to the porch lest she suffocate.

Her own breath felt traitorous as she sat on the porch steps, listening to her mother cough away her strength, her blood, her lungs, as the sun sank into a crimson and gold puddle beyond Saranac Lake. Fireflies came out, twinkling like stars against the velvety darkness. The trees whispered secrets, and across the grounds, young people called to one another, playing games.

The screen door finally whined and Oliver stepped out onto the porch. He was wiping his hands on a towel as he sat down beside her. She drew up her legs and thought about how just two nights ago she'd stared at the stars with Rosie. How one unlatched from the heavens, plummeting to earth, and how a black hole might suck everything that mattered into it.

"She's asleep, but she's so fatigued, they don't expect her to wake again. She won't last through the night."

Lilly sank her chin into her hands, covered her mouth.

"I'm sorry, Lilly." Oliver's voice shook. "I'm so sorry."

"I know." She longed to go back inside, to climb in bed with her mother, to drape her arm over her body. But she might lose what remained of herself if she gave over to the grief tearing through her. She steeled her voice instead. "I want to bury her at the ranch. It's where she belongs."

Oliver drew in a breath. "Her life is in New York. We already have a plot in the family cemetery. She'll be buried next to her father."

"And what of my father? She loved him too, you know."

Oliver said nothing, and she traced the pattern of the fireflies as they burned against the darkness. It seemed the golden hour had passed, and they'd begun to fade.

"Of course she did. But she left that life behind when she married me."

"I didn't. I don't want to be here. I don't want to run the *Chronicle* with you, to be a newspaper baroness—"

"You told your mother—"

"She's sick. She doesn't realize…" She turned to Oliver and refused to be shaken by the wretched expression on his face. "I don't belong in New York City. I belong in Montana, and I'm going back there. I *have* to go back there."

Oliver's mouth fell to a tight, pained line, and for a second he appeared as he had when he'd found her in Spain. Hurt? Furious?

Then, "I'm sorry, Lilly, but your mother instructed me to sell the ranch. She already signed the paperwork giving me power of attorney, and I've handed it over to our solicitor. It's only a matter of time before we find a buyer."

Lilly stared at him, her breath shuddering, her body shaking, words tumbling over in her head. She couldn't get a fix on even one. She shook her head.

"It's for the best, I promise. It'll be good, you'll see—"

"No!" She bounced up, away from him, down the steps, onto the cool grass. "I'm not going to let you sell the ranch. I'll buy it—"

"With what?"

His cool words landed like a slap. She stepped back, reeling, the reality of her life settling like poison into her bones. Her voice dropped, and she let the venom drip from it. "I—I hate you. You did this. If she hadn't come to New York, hadn't found you, we would have been back home, and she wouldn't be sick."

"Lilly, that's not true." He kept his voice soft, like she might be a skittish mare, and she hated him for it. "She's been sick for years—she's probably had this since Montana—it's probably those miners who gave it to her—"

"That's a lie!"

He stood up, advanced toward her.

"Stay away from me."

He stopped, held up his hands. "Lilly, I know I'm not your father but—"

"You'll never be my father! My father was noble and kind and he loved my mother!"

"I loved her long before he did! I've loved her since I was six years old. I was her footman, remember? I came first!"

"Then why didn't you come after her? Why did you let her run away to Montana?"

A muscle pulsed in his jaw. "Because I was a coward." His eyes had darkened, his hands shaking. "Because I didn't think she wanted me."

"She didn't."

"She thought I was dead, Lilly—"

"I wish you were." She let the words land and relished his flinch.

Maybe now he'd stop following her, leave her to live her life. "I'm not going back to New York City."

"Don't be foolish. You're still a child, you need someone to take care of you."

"I'm not a child—"

"You're only nineteen years old."

"I'm the same age my mother was when she ran away from New York. From you."

Again, the hurt flickered in his eyes. But he held up a hand. "I understand, you're tired. We're both tired." He covered his eyes with his hands, his voice scraped to nothing but a whisper. "Please, Lilly. I can't bear to lose you too."

And right then, as she watched him shudder and reach for the porch railing, she felt it—a splinter of compassion, something soft that resembled pity.

Or, affection?

No. Never. She stepped away from him, farther down the path. "I'm going back to the boardinghouse."

He looked up at her. "Your mother—"

"Call me immediately if she revives."

He nodded, and she turned, half walking, half running down the path.

The fireflies had vanished, and in their place appeared a smattering of smooth stars. She followed them past the registration hall and out to the town, the "City of the Sick." The shops had closed; she had only the streetlamps to light her way as she walked in and out of the puddles of light.

Her breath constricted in her chest, her eyes burning.

If only Rennie were here with one of his airplanes.

By the time she reached the boardinghouse, she had her hand pressed to her mouth. She barely found her voice as the landlord directed her to her room. Inside she found her trunks and cases, but she ignored them and lay on the double bed, pushing her face into the eyelet pillowcase, letting the night—cicadas, the rush of the wind—scream into her room.

The Chronicle *is my legacy, Lilly. And now I give it to you. You will be a newspaper baroness.*

She let those words thunder inside her as she pressed the pillow to her mouth.

No. She didn't want this life.

Especially without her mother.

I'm not going back to New York City.

She let those words fortify her as she drew up her legs and curled into a ball.

The change of sounds, from night to the chirrup of birds, awakened her. She'd slept hard, her eyes swollen and heavy. Early sun, tinged with orange and gold, filtered into her room, along the wooden floor, across the coverlet on her bed. She lay there for a moment, getting her bearings.

The boardinghouse. In Lake Saracan.

Her mother. Lilly sat up, put her bare feet on the cool wooden floor. Her second-story room overlooked the backyard garden, an oasis meant possibly for the heartsick relatives of the infirm. A pathway edged in stones meandered around the yard, lavender and crimson pansies, pale orange begonias, pink impatiens, all caressed by the wind in raised beds. The wide embrace of a maple hovered over a bench in the center of the garden.

On it, his back to her, sat a man, his wide shoulders hunched into himself, his hands pressed to his face, his black hair unkempt. He wore his white shirt untucked, his sleeves rolled up at the elbows.

She watched his grief as recognition rolled over her.

Oliver.

Pressing her hand to the windowsill, she let the sight of him move her, the fact that he'd returned to the boardinghouse seep realization into her.

Mother.

She let out a breath, and it became more of a moan. Without thinking, she fled downstairs, through the kitchen, and out to the back.

The door slammed behind her, and Oliver jerked. She stopped right there in the wash of golden sunlight, her eyes watering with the glare. "Tell me."

He looked wrecked, his eyes red, dark whiskers brutal upon his face. "She's gone," he said, his voice hitching. "It's just you and me now."

A whimper escaped and she folded her arms over her chest, holding herself tight. Another whimper—

"Lilly, it's going to be okay. I'll take care of you." He stood and came toward her, his arms open, but she backed away from him, her breaths fast, hard.

Then, she turned and scrambled back to the house, her world breaking apart before her. She swept through the parlor, opening the drawers in the desk until she retrieved what she'd been searching for.

Gone.

Just you and me.

I'll take care of you.

She was shaking as she reached her room. Shutting the door behind her, she pressed the palm of her hand on it, steadying herself. She drew in a breath. Let it out. Another.

Then she locked the door.

She knew exactly what she wanted, but since Jinx had packed her cases, it took a moment to find it.

The pearls still lay in the black velvet case, untouched since her birthday last year. *Pearls make a girl into a lady,* Jinx had said as Lilly opened them. Oliver had stood behind Esme, beaming.

That was also the first time her mother had called Oliver her father. As if her affections could be purchased.

She hadn't wanted to pack them for Paris, but Esme insisted.

She hadn't changed from her trip, still wearing her traveling clothes, her white suede traveling shoes. But she didn't bother with it now. Grabbing a satchel, she shoved inside an extra shirtwaist, her necessaries, a skirt, and her nightgown. Then she retrieved her wallet and counted the last of her allowance. Enough to buy her a ticket west, maybe not all the way back to Montana, but far enough. She'd figure out the rest. Just like her mother had.

She picked up the velvet case and considered the pearls. Her mother had brought her choker strand of pearls to Montana to purchase her new life. Certainly she wouldn't begrudge her daughter the same freedom? She shoved the case into the top of the satchel and closed it, then stared, finally, into the mirror. *Go home. Your adventure is over.*

No. It had just begun. And if she wanted an adventure, she'd have to be someone...different. Someone bold and daring. Someone she didn't recognize. Taking a breath, she picked up the scissors she'd retrieved from the parlor.

She gripped her first braid, set the scissors right below her ear. "I'm not going back to New York City," she said out loud as she snipped them hard and fast against the hair. The braid slumped in her grip.

She put the scissors to the other ear. "My mother was my age when she ran away to Montana." The braid fell into her hand.

She laid both braids on the bureau then tugged on her hat, the one with the wide brim and rosette in front.

Glancing at the window, she saw Oliver, again seated on the bench in the garden, staring into the day as if he had no idea what to do with it. She heard his stricken voice. *It's just you and me now.*

"No," she said as she picked up her satchel. "It's just me."

Then she closed the bedroom door behind her, crept down the stairs, and let herself out the front door to freedom.

THE SUICIDE LOOP

SOUTH DAKOTA, 1923

Chapter 7

Lilly had hoped to make it farther than Mobridge, South Dakota. Worse, it seemed as if she might not be escaping this dustbowl cow town anytime soon. But she refused to turn around and go home.

Not that New York had ever been home. But even less now. Especially since she hadn't shown up for her mother's funeral. Somewhere near Chicago, the regrets had awakened her, and she'd disembarked at Union Station just to check the schedules back to New York. But she'd traveled too far to return—the Chicago *Chronicle* captured the funeral on their front page. Apparently her mother had made the arrangements long ago.

No, she couldn't turn around. Not with the taste of shame in her mouth. But, obviously, she couldn't go forward, either.

"It can't possibly be two more weeks?"

"Sorry, Miss Hoyt." This from the Milwaukee Road Railroad representative, an immigrant from Germany with large hands and kind blue eyes. "They're waiting on supplies from Minneapolis."

Lilly managed a smile, digging it out from behind her frustration, and wandered back down the wide, dirty main street with the greening cottonwoods, the dented Ford trucks along with lazy horses parked outside the hardware store, the café, the feed and seed, the soda fountain. Dust sank into her pores like crème, layering her skin with grime, turning her hair to glue. She'd traveled back in time when her train chugged to a halt here, the last stop before the rails trekked over the Missouri River bridge and out to the great frontier.

A bridge inconveniently washed out by the spring flooding.

It seemed that Mobridge, South Dakota, had one foot in the frontier, the other edging toward civilization, with everything from a saloon-turned-tavern to a Sears Roebuck outlet. Surrounded by ranches and the Standing Rock Indian reservation, it hosted a railroad hub that ferried in goods and workers, but precious little in the way of escape. Mrs. Garrett's tiny boardinghouse had electricity, a small luxury she gave thanks for when she discovered that the privy was outside the back door and down three steps. A navigation that, in the middle of the night, had turned her ankle and caused her to lounge for a week on the front porch, reading every book she had within reach while she mended.

Now, after three weeks, Lilly was running out of money, patience, and time. However, she had come to know the fair citizens of Mobridge.

"Howdy, Miss Hoyt." Curtiss Latham tipped his hat to her as she entered the soda fountain, the bell over the door jangling. He wore a layer of prairie around his mouth, embedded in his blond whiskers, and he'd been there at Lang's every afternoon for the past two weeks, his booted feet hung over the lower rungs of a counter stool, ready to inquire about her day.

"Curtiss," she said. He looked about twenty, his cheeks reddened with too much sun, his forearms tanned and strong. He bore the look of the land on him, something honest and rough, and for that, she liked him enough.

Even if she refused his suggestions that she might find other pastimes than reading a book on the porch of her boardinghouse.

Maybe she should have turned around three weeks ago when they shut the line down, but returning to Minneapolis to be rerouted only seemed opposite her goal of heading *west*. And, despite her moaning, they hadn't sent a train to fetch her. Her money had only bought a one-way ticket, and even if she scraped together enough funds to hire a car, carriage, or pony to take her west, no one seemed to be headed that direction.

"A vanilla phosphate," she said, and pulled out a nickel from her reticule.

"It's Tuesday. I thought you liked cherry on Tuesdays," said Harvey, sweating in a white shirt, dark bands about his upper arms as he mixed her drink.

"I'm full of surprises," she said.

He handed it to her, and she nodded to Curtiss before taking her drink to an alcove by the door.

Thankfully, Mrs. Garrett's boardinghouse hosted a fine collection of Zane Grey. It was the only thing that kept grief from swallowing her whole.

Sometimes, the brutality of her rash actions could curl her into a ball in her single bed, make her shove her sheets into her mouth to stave off her sobs.

Was this how her mother felt when she left New York City so many years ago, believing the man she loved dead?

Don't forget the blessings God has bestowed upon you.

What blessings?

Lilly read page twenty-four three times before she turned it, and right there at the beginning of chapter six, she heard it—a low, choppy buzz.

Almost like—

"There's an airplane driving down Main Street!" Curtiss jumped up from his stool.

Lilly put her book facedown. Sure enough, a fine-looking biplane with red wings and a sleek white body made a low pass along Main Street. And in the front seat, a woman sat, waving.

Lilly got up and pushed past Curtiss onto the boardwalk as a car sped down the street bellowing out, "The Flying Stars Air Show! Only one dollar per car to watch! Tonight at the fairgrounds!"

The plane made another pass, this time waggling its wings, and just for a moment, she was airborne with Rennie over the brilliant skies of Paris, touching the heavens.

"A buck a car." Curtiss shucked off his hat, shook his head. "Too rich for my blood."

"You got a car, Curtiss?" she asked.

"I got my boss's truck," he said.

"That'll do," she said. "But you have to take a bath."

Two hours later, with the sun still high, the evening cooling after a thorough baking, Lilly sat on the back of Curtiss's pickup on a blanket. She cupped her hand over her eyes, watching with a crowd of Sunday-best-dressed ranchers as the Flying Stars air show flyers lined up their biplanes.

An announcer introduced himself from a makeshift podium as Marvel James and welcomed the crowd. A fleet of planes took off behind him, sweeping into the air. The sound of it rumbled through Lilly's bones, the dust from their wheels exploding in a fog that rolled into the crowd like a stampede.

Airborne, they became magnificent red and white birds, with a constellation of the Flying Stars etched on their tails. She counted a total of four, all winging through the sky with dips and turns and rolls, eliciting the awe of the audience before landing back on the ground and bouncing over the untended field like chickens.

Only then did she realize she'd been holding her breath.

"And now, ladies and gentlemen..." Marvel had the voice of a ballyhoo and wielded it well as he spun the dangers of the next act. "Truman Hawk, the Baron of the Air, famed World War I pilot, will perform his death-defying engine stall, operating a dead stick—"

"What's that?" Curtiss said.

"I think he turns the plane off while flying...."

"Jeepers, that don't sound like he's got a full basket."

She agreed as they watched the pilot climb then cut the engine and fall to the earth. The crowd began to scream long before he neared the ground. As Lilly closed one eye, he touched the plane down in a graceful landing.

Her hand was sweating as she let go of the blanket.

A mechanic popped the prop, then Truman Hawk, the showman, buzzed the crowd, waving.

Three more planes took off, waging a mock World War I battle in the sky. Then, two parachutists jumped from the front wings, falling like rocks and pulling their chutes nearly too late in a breathtaking display of idiocy. A trail of white followed them like smoke.

As they floated down, Lilly could nearly feel the wind in her teeth, tangling her hair, the delicious sense of letting go, of flying.

They dropped a pair of guinea hens and let the children chase them across the field, then staged a motorcycle show—jumping it through a circle of fire.

"And for our final act, the Flying Angel will perform a death-defying wing walk!"

"You mean some dame is actually going to get out on that wing and walk around?" Curtiss said, his voice close to Lilly's ear.

Lilly had no words as she watched a woman in a white jumpsuit climb into the front cockpit. She shut her ears against Rennie's voice. *I'll show you where you belong.*

Still, she easily imagined herself in that seat, goggles over her eyes, anticipation like a live coal in her belly.

The plane took off, did a loop and a roll, then leveled as the Flying Angel climbed out onto the lower wing, a white speck against the blades.

"That's gotta be the stupidest thing I ever seen a woman do," Curtiss said, but he didn't take his eyes from the spectacle.

The woman walked out on the wing and waved to the crowd, then crossed to the other wing. Then, as the flyer circled back around, she climbed to the upper wing and sat down.

Lilly nearly wept with horror when the plane dove and the woman raised her hands over her head, as if to plunge face-first into the earth. The pilot pulled up then did a barrel roll, with the woman's hands still over her head. Lilly pressed her hand to her stomach.

Then, he turned upward, into an inside loop, and Lilly finally had to look away.

"She's a real tart, that one, to put up with his shenanigans," Curtiss said, enough awe in his voice for her to know that he would be lining up after the show to catch an up-close glimpse of the Flying Angel.

The woman finally climbed back to the cockpit, and the pilot brought the plane to a bumpy, grandiose landing, motoring it around to face the audience. The Flying Angel jumped out, ran around to face the audience, and as the prop fizzled out, bowed in a flourish.

The audience erupted, honking, cheering, until finally the pilot joined her. Truman Hawk took her hand as they bowed together then joined the rest of the troupe to wave.

"Well, ain't that the darndest thing? I never seen an aeroplane, let alone the tricks it can do." Curtiss climbed off the back of the truck, held out his hand. "Now how 'bout I show you some of my tricks." He winked at her.

She gave him her best society smile. "Oh, Curtiss. I believe our time together is over. I will walk back to town."

"It's nearly a half mile. And you got them fancy white shoes on."

She folded up his blanket, handed it back to him. "See you at Langs?"

He managed something of an acquiescing smile, and she didn't look back as she headed toward the airfield.

Twilight skimmed the shiny wings and their sleek red bodies as she finally broke free of the departing spectators and lost herself among the airplanes, parked in a neat row before a long white tent. Inside the tent, lamplight flickered, voices of the pilots tumbling out onto the grassy field. Parked alongside was the red roadster she'd seen barrel through town, and a truck with THE FLYING STARS painted on the side, a trailer attached to the back. A man in a gray jumpsuit stained with grease sat on the running board smoking a cigarette, the ash a red eye in the encroaching darkness. A mongrel with a mangled ear lay at his feet.

She wandered between two planes, feathering her hand over the painted canvas of the wing. Bracing herself on a wheel strut, she pulled herself up to look into the cockpit.

"Please! Let's go around again!"

She heard her voice, high and bright, laughing into the wind.

Perhaps she did belong in the heavens—

"Moseby, listen to me. It's not any more dangerous than an inside loop—"

"Except it's my head you'll decapitate."

Lilly slunk down behind the plane, her heart in her throat.

"Bertie Jones did it just a week ago, in Kearney!"

She could see them now, charging across the field toward the planes, the woman in the jumpsuit and a man in a leather flight jacket, his dark hair tangled from the wind. Tall and lean, he had wide shoulders and reminded her of someone, although she couldn't place who.

The woman rounded on him, stabbing him hard with her finger. "Then get Bertie to do it. Or…pay me more."

"You're already getting ten dollars a show—"

"And every week you come up with another cockamamie trick that's liable to get me killed." She leaned close to him, and Lilly held her breath to hear. "Maybe I will go fly with Eddie. At least he's nice enough to take me out for dinner once in a while."

"Is that what you want—a steak dinner? Flowers? For the love of Pete,

Mose, it's not like you have to actually *fly* the plane. Do you have any idea how hard it is to keep the plane level with you climbing all over the wings? All you have to do is hang on—how much talent does that take?"

Oh, he deserved a slap, and Lilly braced herself for the sting of it in the air. But just a breath sucked in, something sharp and then—

"You know what, Truman? If you think it's so easy, why don't you find someone else to walk across your precious Travel Air?"

Footsteps crunched through the grass, and Lilly began to back away from the plane.

"And who would I get to take your place?"

"How about her?"

Lilly froze, the voice too close to be ignored. She glanced over her shoulder.

The Flying Angel had her hands on her hips, staring at her, a dangerous smirk on her face. In the dusky night, she looked even more ethereal, a lean, shapely body, dark hair curling out of her leather cap. "Yes, you. What are you doing here?"

"I—I wanted to see the airplanes." Oh, she sounded like a child.

"Did you now?" This from the pilot, who came up behind Moseby the Flying Angel, and ran his hand along the tail of the airplane. She put his face with the name—Truman, the Baron of the Air. The showman. The daredevil. And he looked it, with that rakish, smug smile. "Ever been up in one of these?" He raised an eyebrow, almost like a dare.

She'd had enough of arrogant flyboys. "Thanks, but I'm not getting tangled in your quarrel—"

She turned, but Moseby's voice reached her. "See, Truman. You scared her off. It shows you that you can't get just anyone to wing walk. They have to have courage."

Lilly stopped, and for a second called herself a fool, but Moseby's word itched her, and she rounded on her, her voice cool. "Yes, actually.

I have been up in an airplane. Over Paris, in fact." She stared hard at Moseby. "Certainly wing walking can't be as difficult as riding a horse at full gallop, bareback. Like he said, all you have to do is hold on."

"You don't look like a cowgirl." Moseby walked up to her.

"I grew up in Montana—"

"With those shoes, you look like you grew up in Minneapolis," Truman said. "Nice and proper."

She met his eyes. Grayish-blue, like the sky at storm, except they held a trace of humor, proof that he was laughing at her. A long curl of dark hair hung over his eyes, and for a moment she thanked her fancy-now-dust-slathered heeled suede shoes, because she might have otherwise been intimidated by his height. He had the raccoon eyes of a flyer, a dark shadow of whiskers upon his chin, and a husky smell of leather and sky that blew off him.

Lilly folded her arms across her chest. "I grew up in Montana. And New York. And I could run a race across that wing." The last part she said for Moseby because she reminded her of Presley, just a little. Then she smiled. "But, like I said, I'm not getting into your quarrel."

She turned and set out across the grass.

"Wait—"

This from Truman, and she didn't slow as he jogged up behind her. He stepped in front of her and blocked her path.

She nearly plowed into him. "What?"

"You really think you can wing walk?"

It was the way he said it, half challenge, half admiration, that nudged her. As if, in his eyes, she might not be a child, someone to care for, but…

"I'd rather learn to fly."

He stared at her a long moment, one she felt to her bones, then suddenly he gave a laugh. "Fly. Really?"

"Why not?"

"Women can't fly."

"I'd slap him for that," Moseby said from behind her. "But it wouldn't matter. He's so arrogant he wouldn't feel it."

She hadn't released his gaze, however. "I could fly, if someone taught me."

"I could teach you to fly." He breathed in, cut his voice low, and something about it sent a trickle of heat through her. "If you really wanted." He raised an eyebrow, cocked his head. For a moment, his gaze roamed her face, settled on her mouth, then finally found her eyes again, a new spark in his.

Her mouth dried.

"Truman, leave her alone." Moseby nudged up next to him. "Don't mind him, he's just trying to scare you."

Truman's gaze broke away, and he glanced at Moseby. The grin he gave her looked distant, even angry. "She's too young anyway. I have a feeling we'd have the law on us as soon as we left town."

"I'm nineteen."

"See, a child," he said, his smile gone. "Go home. This adventure isn't for you."

Moseby looped her arm through Truman's. Smiled at her. "But if you change your mind, we're headed west in the morning." She winked then drew Truman away.

"What did you say that for?" Truman said into the night.

"Because you're a fool," Moseby replied.

They headed back toward the tent while Lilly stood there and felt his words.

Go home.

Her feet screamed in agony by the time she managed her way back to Mrs. Garrett's boardinghouse. She removed her shoes at the bottom of the stairs then sighed relief.

"There's a plate with roasted chicken and cabbage for you in the oven," the woman said as Lilly climbed to her room.

"Thanks," she called over her shoulder, but she just wanted to put a pillow over her head, bury herself in it.

Flicking on the bedside lamp, she walked over to the bureau, pulled out the top drawer, found the velvet box.

She hadn't tried them on since that day, when she turned eighteen. Now she took out the pearls, looped them around her neck, then again, and finally a third time, pulling them tight like a choker, letting the rest dangle.

Stared at herself in the mirror. *Don't forget your name and where you belong.*

She sat on the bed, taking off the pearls, letting the strand run through her fingers. *Mother, I miss you.* Tucking the pearls under her pillow, she lay back on the bed and closed her eyes, wishing away the burn.

Maybe she *should* return to New York City. Perhaps she could hitch a ride with the next supply train that came in, apologize to Oliver...

Then what? Become a reporter, a newspaper baroness like her mother hoped? Or, more likely, Oliver would arrange for her to marry a banker, and she'd be trapped in a life she loathed.

The door creaked open.

"Thanks, Mrs. Garrett, but I'm not hungry."

"That's no problem, you can eat on the train."

Her eyes opened, and she sat up. "Mr. Stewart, what are you doing here?"

Oliver's father bore his same dark looks, although her mother's former butler wore his hair close cropped, an almost regal bearing to him. "My son sent me to find you. I'm sorry it took me so long." His eyes betrayed a benevolence that made her want to trust him. "Oliver is very worried."

She stood up. "He needn't be—I'm fine."

"I see that." He came in and closed the door. "But I suspect you are running low on your allowance and, according to the railroad, there will be no train for two more weeks."

"I'll manage."

"And then what, miss? A trip to Montana, if you make it, to run a ranch you haven't seen in years? A ranch that doesn't belong to you?"

"It should belong to me—Oliver stole it from me."

Mr. Stewart gave no sign of flinching. "You may want to hear his side of the—"

"No. He stole the ranch, just like he stole Rennie from my life. I have no intention of going home with you, and you can tell him—"

"Miss Lillian, I will not tell him anything. You will return home. You are out of money, and your father will not give you one more penny if you should continue this behavior."

"I don't want his money and he's not my father."

"Very well then." Mr. Stewart moved over to where she'd stashed her valise and picked it up. He opened her wardrobe.

"What are you doing?"

"Taking what belongs to Oliver." He pulled her skirt off a hanger, shoved it unceremoniously into the satchel. Then he reached for her only other shirtwaist.

"Those don't belong to him...."

The butler turned to her. "Indeed, they do. He's given you everything you have. And unless you intend to travel to Montana in just your skin, you may want to rethink your position."

"Oliver would be furious if he knew how you were treating me."

Mr. Stewart raised an eyebrow. "You'll be free to tell him in a few days."

"Get out!"

"I'll be back in the morning to help you finish packing." Then he tucked the valise under his arm and stood at the door. "I'll keep this with me in case you contemplate sneaking out into the night." He stood at the door, then, and sighed. "It's time to stop running and come home where you belong, miss."

She put her hand on the first thing she could find—the Bible Mrs. Garrett had set beside her bed—and flung it with everything she had at the door. It hit the frame and fell with a thud, the binding cracking.

Mr. Stewart shook his head and shut the door.

She sat there, listening to his steps in the hallway, her heart thudding.

"I'm not going!" she yelled at the closed door. Oh, how she hated Oliver. His belief that he belonged in her life, that she couldn't live without him. When would he understand? He *wasn't* her father.

The lamp cast a dingy glow on the throw rug, upon her bare feet, her grimy, now nearly black, white travel shoes. She looked up, stared at herself in the mirror. Her hair had grown a little after the shearing of her braids, and she looked bedraggled and misbehaved.

Like a child.

A petulant child who had thrown a tantrum after her mother died. She'd fled on a train, taking Oliver's money, hoping it might prove that she'd grown up, could live her own life, make her own way.

Moseby's words pinged inside her. *If you change your mind, we're headed west in the morning.*

She snaked her hand under her pillow, closed her fist around the pearls.

Don't mind him, he's just trying to scare you.

She wasn't that easily scared. Not anymore.

He's given you everything you have.

Pulling out the pearls, she found the velvet case in the top drawer of the bureau and tucked them inside. She set it in plain sight. She'd just have to find another way to pay for the ranch.

Certainly he'd let her keep her shirtwaist, her skirt, her shoes, a jacket. She wrapped up her necessaries in her pillowcase—she'd just have to owe Mrs. Garrett—and scooped up her shoes, carrying them as she tiptoed down the stairs. For a second, she stopped on the landing, listening.

Her mistakes echoed inside, tugged at her. But this wasn't a mistake. She just wanted to return to the world where she belonged.

Don't forget your name, her mother had said. Indeed. She was a Hoyt, a girl of the West of adventure and courage, and she didn't need Oliver Stewart—or any man—interfering with that.

She stepped out into the darkness and hiked barefoot out of town.

The new moon cradled the old one, a crescent thumbnail as she walked out to the airfield. It shone upon the white tent, a beacon amidst a sea of night. The planes lined up like sentries with stout arms. Her feet crunched in the grass as she moved toward the planes, rehearsing her words, settling on the most plain. *Please, take me with you—*

"Well, if it isn't Miss New York. What are you doing here?"

She stopped, searching for the voice, needing no identifier. "I'm... I came to take you up on your offer, Mr. Hawk."

He nearly startled her out of her skin as he rolled out from under a wing, found his feet. He wore a dark canvas shirt, rolled up at the arms and open, flapping in the wind, his hair askew, as if he'd already been asleep. "What offer?" he said, too much darkness in his voice.

She hitched the pillow onto her other hip. "You're not going to make this easy, are you?"

He smiled, and she felt it behind her breastbone. "Nope."

"Fine. Take me with you. Please."

He leaned back against the plane, crossing his ankles. His shirt blew open in the wind, and she looked away. "Why should I?"

"Because—because you need me. You need another wing walker—I can learn."

She glanced at him. He raised an eyebrow.

"And I—I need you. I need to leave, head west, to Montana."

"Running from the law, are we?"

She drew in a breath. "No." But her voice emerged shaky enough to elicit a drawn breath.

"Really. You're not on the lam, are ya?" he said, softer now.

"No. Nothing like that."

He narrowed his eyes. She looked away, hating suddenly how he had her whole world in his fist.

"Fine. And we'll see about the wing walking. For now, you run concessions. I'll talk to Marvel in the morning." He came over, reached for her pillowcase.

"What are you doing?"

"Tucking you in. We sleep under the planes when it's nice out. Don't we, Mose?"

"C'mere, doll." A voice chirruped behind her. "You can sleep next to me. That way Truman won't forget and leave without you."

Lilly crouched down and found Moseby on a blanket under the belly of the next plane. She made out the forms of other pilots, performers in the shadows beyond. Moseby pulled a blanket from a rucksack at her feet. "Good thing it's warm out." She tossed her the blanket, and Lilly spread it out beneath the wing. Then she hunkered down, shoving her "pillow" under her head.

"We leave at dawn," Truman said, settling back into the darkness.

Overhead, the stars sprinkled light upon the prairie. Lilly drew up her legs, folded them into her dress.

"What's in Montana?" Moseby asked quietly.

Lilly watched a star break free, cast to earth. The wind tickled her hair at her neck, and in the distance, a coyote bawled. "Everything," she said quietly.

* * * * *

New York City, 1923

Rosie just wanted to hide in the cool, velvety padding of the Mark Strand Movie Palace and disappear inside Colleen Moore's newest movie, *Flaming Youth*. It seemed that the actress might have reached right down inside Rosie's heart and plucked out the storyline of betrayal, lost love, and heartache in the role of Pat Fentriss and the story of a girl who longed for the flapper life, only to find herself in over her head.

"Pat should have known that Leo only wanted one thing from her. He was a fella, after all." Lexie Wilson bumped her way down the row past the plush red seats as the lights from the grand swinging chandelier flickered on, washing away the surreal and plunging Rosie back to reality.

The one where her mother wanted her help packing for a salvaged summer season in Newport, a useless and grand hope that they'd shake free of the grief that still held the family hostage.

First Esme, then Lilly. Gone. And Uncle Oliver—Rosie could admit a growing well of pity for him. He seemed barely human when he shuffled to their house for dinner night after night, shuttering himself into Bennett's office afterward. Jinx finally moved him into their apartment in the Warren and Wetmore building after discovering that he'd taken to sleeping on his sofa at the *Chronicle* office.

Oliver couldn't go home to an empty house—Rosie heard him confess it to Bennett while standing on the steps of Grace Church the day of the funeral—and over a month later, the words seemed a prophecy.

Rosie understood Uncle Oliver's sentiments exactly, and if she'd had a place to hide away every day, she would have fled to it to escape the grief that held their household in a cadre grip.

She doubted that three months on the seashore would temper it.

God had been unfair, taking Jack and her father, then Esme, and finally Lilly. She still couldn't believe Lilly hadn't returned for her mother's funeral. It piled even more tragedy upon the event and stirred wretched imaginations of Lilly's fate.

Rosie couldn't bear to entertain the thought that perhaps she deserved the loneliness, the despair after her wanton behavior in Paris. And, because of her flaming youth, as Colleen Moore had put it, Rosie had nothing with which to bargain the Almighty for Lilly's safe return.

Hence, she only had the dark, sultry escape of the movies.

"I want to stay," Rosie said as she followed Lexie into the aisle.

Lexie hooked her arm, the smell of her tonic drifting over Rosie and conjuring up images of Blanche, or even Frankie. "No, you don't. I promised Sherwood we'd meet him tonight at the Cotton Club. Besides, the next show is *A Woman of Paris,* and we both agreed you were going to erase that episode from your mind." She tugged Rosie along. "Paris has you all balled up. We need to take your mind off that scoundrel Dashielle Parks."

"Dashielle who?" Rosie said, forcing a grin.

Lexie laughed and Rosie let herself fall into it. Yes, perhaps a night out at some jazz club, listening to a sultry-toned singer, watching the dancers, letting some handsome banker parley her with something hot and smooth, might help her forget.

Hide.

Especially tonight. Because Colleen Moore's story of a girl wooed by independence, who ran away from home, burned inside her.

Lexie led them out of the theater hall and into the lobby. "I'd never fall for a sailor like Pat did." She made a face at Rosie. "I want a man who can take me to the club and dress me in tinsel."

"Darling, you have enough tinsel to sink a ship."

Lexie Wilson could counsel a fleet of flappers on how to wheedle furs, jewelry, and adoration out of men. With her ebony black cap of hair, her dark crimson lips, her lean body, she had been the first among Rosie's set to roll down her silk stockings and powder her knees, to teach Rosie how to make pin curls out of her short cap of hair, how to smoke, and even do the Charleston. And while Rosie had escaped to Paris, Lexie made headlines by moving out of her parents' Fifth Avenue chateau to take a room at the Algonquin Hotel.

Rosie had never been so happy to see her finishing-school friend as the day Lexie pulled up, two weeks after the funeral, driving her own roadster, a smart riding cap perched on her head. She'd practically thrown a rope to Rosie's window to effect her escape back into society.

"New York City is alive, and it's time to stop moping," Lexie had said as she dragged her from the apartment. Rosie had bit back any sort of argument and let Lexie's plans balm the wounds inside.

Now if Rosie could just convince her mother to allow her to summer in New York. She had a sick feeling her pleadings would fall on deaf ears.

They exited the theater with the crowd and Lexie hailed a cab. Yes, Rosie needed a night out to forget, and maybe this time it would take. Because regardless of how many nights she spent letting the jazz into her bones, she always returned home to the quiet of her room and listened to Dashielle lie to her.

A guy could fall in love with you...

They settled inside the cab, and Lexie pulled out a compact mirror, added another layer of lipstick.

"But what about true love? Isn't that really what Pat was looking for?" Rosie wasn't sure why she had to press the issue—especially since she sounded pitiful and heartbroken and wanted to bite back her words the moment she spoke them.

Lexie closed her lipstick, smacking her lips. She sighed and dropped the tube into her reticule. "There's no such thing, doll. It's all a game." She leaned over to Rosie, a smile tweaking her face. "And the gal with the most tinsel wins." She winked. "Besides, we're not the marrying type. What, I'm going to settle down, pop out an heir and a spare, start decorating and hosting dinner parties? I don't think so. I'm not the marrying type. I'm a good-time gal, just like you."

A good-time gal. Dashielle had certainly thought so.

Outside, New York had turned to dusk, shadows draping over the buildings to clutter the street. Fruit and vegetable carts had already packed up, shops drawing the drapes of their storefronts. The Broadway marquees from the Hippodrome, the Heilig, and the Orpheum glittered into the twilight, turning the night to jewels.

Lexie pulled out a cigarette, offered it to Rosie, who shook her head.

"Suit yourself." Lexie inserted it into the long ebony holder and lit it.

Rosie read the billings on the theater doors as they crawled by. "The Follies will open soon." Her mother had never permitted her to attend Ziegfeld's show, but someday…

"Oh, doll, I completely forgot. I have someone you absolutely must meet. I told him to meet me at the club, hoping I could persuade you to tag along." She glanced at Rosie's shirtwaist and skirt, her head adorned with a basic brown cloche hat, then leaned forward to the driver. "Pull over up here." She pointed to the Algonquin. She looked at Rosie. "We're stopping by my room before we head over to Harlem."

"Why?"

Lexie leaned back in her seat. "Trust me."

The cab pulled up to the red brick and limestone hotel across the street from the Hippodrome. Down the street, roadsters and sedans edged up in front of Delmonico's, white-gloved attendants helping patrons from the vehicles.

Once upon a time, Rosie's family made Sunday afternoon lunch a tradition at Delmonico's. Now, her mother and stepfather lunched at home on Sunday, after attending church. She hadn't attended church with her family since Aunt Esme's funeral.

Rosie followed Lexie through the dark oak-paneled lobby, past the gold velvet chairs, past the Pergola room, and to the gilded lift. An operator closed the cage behind them and pulled the third-floor knob.

"I can't believe your mother let you take a room."

Lexie pulled off a glove then the other. "I didn't ask her permission. It's my life—"

"It's her money."

"I simply reminded her of a few secrets that I've been keeping for her over the years." Lexie glanced at Rosie then pursed her lips, her gaze darting to the white-gloved attendant. He gave no hint that he might be keen on the backdoor behavior of the city—politicians, bankers, Wall Street investors who frequented the Algonquin for lunchtime trysts.

Lexie's word latched onto her. Secrets. Like the kind her own mother had harbored about her affair with Bennett? Yes, that might make a mother surrender to the whims of her daughter.

The doors opened, and Rosie followed Lexie down the hall to her room, the numbers in gold on the dark-paneled door.

The twilight burned against the filmy white curtains, the long, green velvet drapes cast open.

They'd walked into the sitting room—a sofa, coffee table, chairs with the discarded remains of a room-ordered breakfast on the credenza along the wall.

"What happened to the maid? Is she asphyxiated in here somewhere?" Rosie followed Lex into her boudoir, pushed aside a crimson silk robe, and lowered herself onto the velvet settee.

"I only have service once a week. My request. They bang on my door at all hours of the morning—"

"Disturbing you and whoever you might be entertaining." Rosie raised an eyebrow.

Lexie's smile tweaked up one side. "Oh don't be such a Mrs. Grundy." She dropped her gloves onto her cluttered bureau. "For all your talk, you're still so naïve."

Rosie walked to the window, stared at her reflection. She'd lost weight since Paris, and dark wells hung under her eyes. "Not as much as I was. But I never thought I'd be the girl whose heart is broken."

Lexie came up behind her. Tucked her chin on Rosie's shoulder. "Tonight, you get to be someone different."

"Who might that be?"

"Anyone you want to be." Hands on Rosie's shoulders, Lexie turned her. "And I have just the dress to be anyone in."

Rosie had only heard of the Cotton Club, never actually found the courage to leave Manhattan and venture north to Harlem, and as they pulled up, a thrill buzzed through her. She got out and tried not to adjust the low-cut sleeveless dress Lexie gave her, the lime-green silk shiny under the marquee lights. Somehow, although she'd worn nearly the same style dress in Paris, it lacked the scandal of this outfit. The silver headband and peacock feather hit the door of the cab as she climbed out. She hung onto Lexie's pearls swaying from her neck and tried to look older.

A man in a tuxedo escorted two women to the door, where a dark-skinned doorman let them in.

"Are you sure we can get in?" Rosie said, cutting her voice low.

Lexie wore an organza white dress and long gloves, a striking contrast to her dark hair and red lips, the beaded white headband. "Trust me," she said again and led the way to the door. When she reached the doorman, she leaned up and whispered into his ear.

He glanced at Rosie, back to Lexie, then opened the door.

Rosie felt the doorman's gaze on her, burning as she walked past him, and didn't want to know what Lexie told him.

Inside the club, round tables covered with white cloths and flickering candles surrounded a large show floor, and upon it, a woman with dark-as-night skin swayed to music, her smoky voice rising to fill the room, adding a sizzle of anticipation to the evening. Behind her, a full band played under the direction of a tuxedo-attired conductor.

Lexie led Rosie across the room, where she saw two men rise from their chairs. Both appeared ten years her senior, the first lean and tall, his brown hair brilliantined back, shiny against the dim lights. He wore a pair of black tails and a bow tie with a white vest—a real dapper that made him exactly the sort Lexie might prefer. He took Lexie's hand. "You look delicious." He kissed her cheek.

"Sherwood." Lexie patted his cheek. "Sorry we're late. We had to freshen up."

"It's a lady's prerogative to be late, isn't it?" This from the other man. He looked Italian, with black curly hair close-cropped to his head, groomed sideburns, dark eyes that seemed to match the music and settle upon Rosie like heat. He wore power in his expression, and more than a little appreciation as his gaze roved over her. She took a breath at his appraisal but didn't hate it.

Dash was a child compared to this man. He held out his hand to Lexie, his gaze finally flicking to her. "Hello, Alexis."

"Cesar." Lexie took his grip, glancing at Sherwood, her smile speaking approval. She gestured to Rosie. "I want you to meet my friend—"

"Red," Rosie said. She wasn't sure where the impulse originated, but suddenly she *did* want to be someone different. Someone bold and daring. Someone without heartbreak on her countenance.

A woman who deserved Cesar's appreciative look.

For a second, she heard Dash's voice when Cesar took her hand and said, "Red. Nice to meet you."

Then Dash vanished and only Cesar remained to pull out her chair and settle in beside her.

He smelled good—something expensive, and wore a ring on his pinky finger, just enough tinsel for a man.

"Sherwood said that Lexie would be bringing a friend. *Bella*, you are worth the wait." Cesar slid his hand behind her chair.

She smiled, no, giggled, and remembered the lessons she'd learned from Frankie. A woman too interested in a man just might lose him.

Interested might not be the correct word, but Rosie had had enough with losing. She leaned her elbow on the table and reached out for his drink, smelled it. "A martini?"

He had his eyes on her as he raised his fingers and snapped. She let him order for her while she sipped his drink.

The gin burned and she wanted to cough, but held it in behind her smile. "I thought alcohol was forbidden."

"Just the sale of it. But if you have your own supply..." He raised a shoulder and retrieved his drink, watching her over the edge of the glass as he sipped. She heard his accent now, less refined than those on Fifth Avenue, with a huskiness inside it that buzzed just under her skin.

"You own a supply of gin?"

He leaned back. "You might be surprised what I own."

"Indeed."

Sherwood had his arm around Lexie, tracing his finger along her jawbone, whispering into her ear. Rosie reached over and retrieved Lexie's purse, pulling out her cigarette holder. Lexie only glanced once, then forfeited a smile as Rosie pulled out a smoke.

Cesar provided a lighter, and she drew in the haze, another moment in Paris fleeting through her, then out again. "What do you own?"

The waiter came and pushed a martini in front of her.

"Ever heard of Valerie's?" Cesar said.

"It's a jazz club in Manhattan. Lexie told me about it."

"Did she mention that it has the hottest acts in the city? Our stage is twice the size of the Cotton Club, twice the spectacle. A real classy joint."

Rosie refused to betray the way her heartbeat ratcheted, glad she had a cigarette to keep her hands from shaking. "Then what are you doing here?"

He leaned in, met her eyes. So dark, so focused, she had the sense of something reaching out, pinning her fast, stealing her breath. "I came to meet you."

Oh.

"Lexie told me a lot about you." He glanced at Lexie then back to her, his eyes darkening.

This time she couldn't hide the tremble as she brought the cigarette to her lips.

The singer finished her set, and a troupe of sequined women danced out to a fast jazz tune from the orchestra. Rosie recognized the famed Charleston, and watched the footwork of the dancers for a moment.

"I have always wanted to dance like that," she said, almost under her breath.

"You're a dancer?"

"Not formally. But someday I'm going to be in show business. I can sing. And act."

"Really."

She lifted a shoulder. Looked away. But his low voice filled her ear. "Come work for me, Red. I'll make you a star."

She turned to Cesar, studying his face. His dark eyes twinkled now, a smile edging up his face. And, as he leaned back, he held up his hands in surrender. "No strings, I promise."

"You want me to sing for you?"

"And dance. You'll be my main attraction."

She glanced at Lexie, who was grinning at her. Lexie reached out and took Rosie's cigarette from her, took a drag, and handed it back.

"Of course she will, Cee. Won't ya, Red darling?"

Yes. For a moment, her future hung right there, on the edge of Lexie's smile, the way Cesar touched her arm, sending a tingle to her bones. She could be Red, an actress, a star, her name in bright lights, making her forget about—

"Rosie, what are you doing here?"

Rosie stilled, the voice slapping her out of the role she played as she looked up.

Jinx stood over her, her eyes on Cesar, then Lexie. She shook her head. "I should have guessed."

Lexie rolled her eyes.

"What are *you* doing here?" Rosie said, but her voice emerged weak, and she couldn't bear it. Her mother, dressed in a black scooped-necked dress and dark cap, gave her a look that could sear her through.

"Bennett is here on business. I saw you walk in. Funny, I thought you had to be twenty-one to get into a club." She directed her words to Cesar, then Lexie.

Lexie lifted a shoulder. Rosie couldn't look at Cesar.

Jinx pursed her primrose lips. "A word with you, please?"

Her mother had powers she couldn't escape, and Rosie followed her into the hallway, where the noise dimmed. "And you wonder why I worry about you," Jinx said, flashing her socialite smile for a couple entering the club.

"Mother, you worry about everyone but me. Please."

"Really? Is that why I managed to salvage your affront to the Duke of Lexington and get you a meeting with him?"

The duke? Oh, she'd thought she'd escaped the European snare when she left France. "He's here?"

"Arrived last week, and he still wants to meet you."

"Mother, no. I don't want to marry a duke."

"Would you rather be a cigarette girl, flaunting yourself in front of men who want nothing more than to ogle you?"

"No." But her mother made her aspirations sound so tawdry. "I want to be an actress," she said thinly.

"Same thing," Jinx said.

"You embarrassed me just when I was being offered a job."

"A job?" Jinx took the cigarette from Rosie's fingers and threw it on the ground as she gestured for their driver.

"I'm not leaving."

The door opened, and suddenly Bennett appeared, dark and furious. "Jinx, what's going on out here?" He shot a look at Rosie. "Do you have any idea who you were sitting with back there?" Bennett looked positively ferocious in the wan light, his blue eyes sparking. "That was Cesar Napoli—the son of Vito Napoli, the Italian mob boss. He's nothing but trouble."

Jinx shook her head, folded her arms across her ample bosom.

"He said he ran a club," Rosie said, but her voice sounded thin.

"If that's what you want to call it. More like a burlesque show. He's dangerous, and we forbid you to go near him."

She stared at Bennett, trying to get a handle on his words. "We?" She shook her head. "I'm done listening to either one of you. You destroyed my life with your...tawdry affair. No wonder my brother ran away. Jack didn't—"

Jinx pressed her hand to her mouth.

Rosie ignored it, losing herself to the fury. "And you—" She pointed at Bennett. "Who do you think you are? You're not my father—"

"I should have been," he said softly. His jaw tightened. "I wanted to be."

She had nothing for him, her body frozen.

Their chauffeur pulled up to the curb in their Rolls Royce.

Bennett opened the car door.

She stared at it. Then, suddenly, she turned and stalked toward the door to the club. "You can tell the duke I'm not available," she snapped. "Don't wait up for me. I'm going home with Lexie." She entered the club and didn't turn to see if they'd followed her, just weaved her way back around the tables to where Cesar and her friend sat. She sat down, reached for another cigarette, her hands shaking.

Cesar slid his hand along the edge of her chair. "You okay, doll?"

"Your job offer still good?" She blew out an arrow of smoke, watched it curl toward the ceiling, hating the way her eyes smarted. Then she found a smile and gave it to him, sweetening her question.

He pulled a card from his jacket, slid it over to her. "Show up tomorrow and I'll make you a star."

Chapter 8

"Seriously, Truman, does this look west to you? Because according to my map, Minnesota is *east* of South Dakota." Lilly turned and glared at him, the prop now sputtering out.

"Flaunting that finishing school education again, are you, Lilly?" Truman climbed out of the cockpit, sliding down to the ground. No, he didn't offer to help her out, but she didn't really expect it after the past two weeks. He acted like she might be a stray he picked up from one of the dusty North Dakota towns he kept hopping them through.

At this rate, she'd be back to New York long before she ever set foot in Montana.

"Truman, I'm talking to you!" Lilly threw one leg over the edge—*thank you, Moseby, for the pants*—and held on as she slid down over the side of the plane. She scrambled behind him, pulling her goggles from her eyes. He'd already gained twenty feet on her across the grassy airfield.

"I thought I made it clear that I needed to head *west*." She pointed, just in case he couldn't figure it out. "The direction of the *setting* sun."

"I never said I was a taxi service." He stopped, looked down at her, only not quite, because his gaze skittered off her, away, as if he couldn't meet her eyes. "In fact, the only thing I ever said to you was 'go home.'"

"I'm trying. But you keep flying us to every backwater hole-in-the-wall in North Dakota."

He held up a finger. "We're in Minnesota now."

"I don't care if we are in South Carolina. We're not heading *west*."

"We go where the crowds are," he said, striding toward where Rango and Suicide Dan had parked the van.

"What crowds? The last two towns were washouts. We barely made enough to cover our gas, repairs, and a night in a hotel."

He rounded on her. "You have any great ideas on how to bring in the crowds, I'm all ears, New York. The more money we make, the sooner I get you to Montana."

She didn't flinch at the mocking. "How about letting Moseby teach me how to wing walk? Two wing walkers will be a bigger draw. I remember a conversation about that too."

"No recollection of that." He started to stalk away.

She grabbed his arm. "What I don't understand is what you're so afraid of. You told Moseby that anyone could do it."

"Not you." He looked down at her hand on his jacket. She didn't remove it, so he shrugged out of her grip. "You run concessions."

"I run everything that isn't in the sky. I clean spark plugs, fill gas tanks, repair wing covers, take tickets, round up spectators, and run around with programs and soda pop and sandwiches. I keep people calm and convince them that you're a safe pilot and help them into the cockpit. But I can do more, Truman. I could wing walk. I could even learn to fly. What about that—a female pilot in your show?"

"I don't call the shots on this one." He still wouldn't look at her, instead watching Eddie fly in, Moseby in the front seat.

"But isn't this your circus? Because you're the one that seems to be in charge of the repairs—repairing wings, changing oil, grinding valves—whatever needs to be done to keep the planes in the air. Not to mention the daily hovering. Did you really order Eddie and Beck to mind their mouths around me?"

"They can run a blue streak that will part your hair once they start drinking. I also told Rango to keep you away from any overzealous spectators, yes."

"And that was you last night, the creak I heard outside my hotel room door, wasn't it? Jeepers, you're the big brother I've never had."

Something hot sparked in his eyes. He hadn't really looked at her since that morning in Mobridge when he'd returned from town on the truck, shoved a gas can into her hand, and told her to learn how to gas up his plane. She'd obeyed, and only after that did he hand her a helmet and pair of goggles and point to the front cockpit.

Now, the heat in his eyes shook her, along with his quiet words. "I don't own the circus. I don't even own my plane. I just fly for Marvel. He can cut me loose anytime, for any reason." He moved away from her. "Make sure you get your gear out of my plane before I start doing hops. They're already lining up. Guess you won't have to wing walk to stir up a crowd." He winked, but there wasn't any warmth in it.

Sure enough, a trail of sedans headed down the road, churning up a tail of dust as they motored toward the assembly of planes. Between Lucky Eddie, Beck, and Truman, they could ferry over three hundred passengers in an afternoon. At five bucks a pop, that kept them in supper, if not steaks and flowers. It was Lilly's job to keep the courage of the patrons aloft as they neared their turn. She usually regaled them with stories of Paris, of the bright lights, omitting Rennie, and focusing on the feeling of soaring.

Unfortunately, it seemed her stories were as close as she would get to wing walking or flying, or doing anything that might help this circus earn enough money to get her back to the ranch. She could still hear Truman's voice in her head, two days out of Mobridge. *"She's not wing walking—absolutely not. Over my dead body."*

She'd been standing outside the tent as Truman's voice rattled the poles, no consideration given to the fact she might hear him.

"She wants to, Truman—she keeps saying she's willing to do anything to help us draw in the crowds."

Rango. She wanted to hug him. A year older than her, Rango could fix an engine with his eyes closed. He helped run concessions with her at the events, walking through the hot sun with a food box as the flyboys chased each other through the skies. Propeller, the mongrel, belonged to him, although she'd discovered the animal would turn over and expose its belly for anyone on the slightest provocation.

Rango, like her, had no one else. And, he too wanted to fly— or parachute—or anything to help their struggling band of air circus performers. If only Truman might give him the chance. It shouldn't surprise her, probably, that Rango had taken up for her.

"Why not? You *could* use two wing walkers."

"I don't need anyone else getting killed," Truman growled. "Stay away from it."

That had stumped her for two days until she cornered Rango after a show, in the kitchen of the boardinghouse, sneaking a glass of milk.

He drank it from the bottle as the night drifted through the kitchen. "Bette Leary. She was a wing walker with the Heavenly Aces. Was doing a ladder act and got tangled. She couldn't get back up. Dragged to death in front of a thousand people."

"So, I won't do the ladder act."

Rango took another sip of his milk, then wiped his mouth with his sleeve and capped the bottle. "It's not just that. There's extra weight on the wings when a walker gets on them and it offsets the plane, not to mention that your foot could go through the fabric, and you could get tangled on the wing wires. If that happened, the pilot couldn't land— you'd crash for sure. And, don't forget, one slipped hold and you're flying off into air, no parachute."

"Maybe I'd wear one."

"They're too big for you. Besides, that's a surefire way to get tangled. Wing walkers go without the pack. But they don't have a long life expectancy." He offered her the milk.

She shook her head, but his words sloughed through her now, lingering as she headed toward the truck.

"Hey, Lilly, there's a small tear on my wing—can you take a look?" Lucky Eddie intercepted her, tucking his helmet under his arm.

Apparently, she'd become a doctor as well. But repairs consisted of fabric, glue, and patience. She retrieved her belongings—a satchel that Moseby lent her, along with a pair of boots—*thanks, Rango*, and pants that Marvel's wife once owned. She didn't ask what happened to the wife. Then she headed over to Eddie's plane. A piece of fabric slapped in the wind on the top leading edge of the lower right wing, a tear that could compromise the entire wing under stress. She retrieved the glue from the supply truck and pasted it down. By the morning's show, it would hold steady, no more rips.

She found Moseby in the tent, stirring a pot of beans over a portable stove. On days when the takings were thin, Moseby and Beck would pull out their beans, spices, and some version of meat and make a stew that usually kept their spines away from their bellies.

Lilly squatted down opposite her.

"Marvel's in town, checking on the advance promotion. He came out here a month ago, set up signs. Says we're in for a record crowd tomorrow."

"No more beans?"

Moseby smiled. "I was thinking of trying that outside loop Truman and I were talking about." She offered Lilly the spoon. "Just to give them a thrill."

"How close to the ground does he get?" Lilly slurped off a taste. "Needs salt."

"About twenty feet. I figure there's room enough for my head." Moseby adjusted the seasonings. She had elegant hands, the kind that reminded Lilly of her mother's. Piano fingers. Or maybe just strong hands.

"How do you plan to stay on?"

"I've rigged up another rope. I'll loop it around the front of me as I sit down. I'll hold tight to the other going up the backside."

"Isn't what you're doing enough?"

"Not to compete with the Flying Aces. They have two wing walkers who actually change planes."

"How?"

"They use a rope ladder."

Lilly shook her head. "I heard about Bette. Does that happen a lot?"

Moseby capped the pot, turned down the flame. "Enough. Mostly with parachutists, though. Dropping from the sky like that? Not safe."

Lilly's gaze shot of its own accord toward Suicide Dan. Sometimes, in an evening show, he would drop in the dark, shining a light on his descent and pulling his rip cord at the last moment. Lilly never watched to the end.

Moseby pulled out a burlap bag and from inside retrieved two loaves of bread. "Got these in our last town from a church lady who said I should probably stop my foolishness and get married." She handed them over to Lilly to cut.

"Why don't you?" Lilly moved to the folding table, began to saw off pieces of the creamy bread.

"I haven't found anyone I could fall in love with, let alone stop flying for."

Lilly glanced over her shoulder. "I thought you and Truman were—"

"Nope." Moseby got up, dusted off her hands. "Truman is a distant cousin, so that puts me off right there. But more than that, he lives to fly. He lives for the adoration of the audience, the thrill of near death, the every-moment-could-be-his-last adrenaline. He doesn't have room in his life for anything else."

"But he stays here, eats beans with everyone else."

Moseby began piling the bread on a plate. "That's because Truman is also a realist. He knows he needs us to protect his reputation. Especially after the accident."

"He wrecked a plane?"

"Killed his kid brother. He'd made a name for himself barnstorming across the Midwest, and returned home like some sort of celebrity. Took his brother out for a ride, and his plane caught fire. Flames and belching sparks from the exhaust ports are normal, but when you see it coming from the engine—well, he thinks one of the mechanics left an oily rag in the oil breather. The plane ripped apart before Tru could land. His brother died, Truman broke both arms and was in a coma for three days. But he lived. He's never forgiven himself, and it didn't help that the paper claimed pilot error. He got a job in Wichita, working on Jennys, and Marvel caught wind of him. He's the best flyer I've ever seen, but I'm afraid, if Tru could, he'd just set out for the heavens, doing loops and rolls until he ran out of fuel and deadsticked into the ground."

"That's terrible. No wonder he's such a loner."

"Oh, don't get me wrong, darlin'. Truman Hawk has no problem making nice with the ladies." She winked. "Just be careful he doesn't make nice with you."

Lilly pulled bowls out of a crate. "Don't worry. I fell in love with a flyer once, and—"

"He broke your heart?"

"Almost."

"Those flyers are all alike. They promise you the stars." She glanced up, and Lilly followed her gaze to Eddie, standing outside the tent talking to Rango. A soft smile touched her lips.

Eddie, with his curly blond hair, his aw-shucks smile, didn't have to work hard to win a girl's heart.

Moseby turned away, her face red.

Lilly lowered her voice. "Are you sure you haven't found anyone to love?"

Moseby shook her head. "Eddie told me that he wanted me to wing walk for him. That we'd make a great team." She glanced at him again. "He brought me flowers last week after the show."

"He's sweet on you."

Moseby shrugged.

"Do it." Lilly put her hand on hers. "It'll be good for Truman. Show him that he doesn't own you."

Moseby gave her a wicked smile. "And that he might expand his horizons." She held up the spoon.

Lilly blew on it and tasted the beans. "You're a good cook."

"I think you're not too bad yourself."

Lilly slept in her bedroll under the wing, waking to dew on the grass and the sound of buzzing in the air.

She climbed out from under the plane, cupped her hands over her eyes, and found Eddie's red and white biplane circling the field.

"Are you kidding me?" The noise must have awakened Truman because he scrambled out, standing beside her, his shirt flapping, his hat shadowing his eyes as he watched Eddie do a barrel roll. And then—

"I'm going to kill him."

He stood with his hands on his hips, shaking his head as Moseby climbed out of the front seat and toward the wings. He added a bit of color to his opinions, but Lilly said nothing, just watched as Moseby edged out onto the right wing, wearing the new red suit Marvel had ordered.

"She looks like a bird, a cardinal."

"Birds can fly, Moseby can't," Truman snapped. "Was this your idea?"

"You give me way too much credit, Truman. I just hand out tickets."

"Sure you do," he said, his jaw tight.

The plane circled the field then did a barrel roll, coming up late out of the turn.

"He's not ready for her weight on his wing."

Perhaps Eddie had figured this out, because Moseby started to make her way back to the cockpit. He leveled out across the field.

"I'm getting some breakfast," Truman said, his tone surly.

She ignored him.

Then, "Truman—stop." She may have even put a hand on his arm as she watched Moseby's foot shatter through the right wing. She couldn't hear it, but she imagined a terrible, wrenching rip as the fabric separated.

For a moment, only Moseby's legs dangled through, a macabre dance as she tried to hold herself up. Then the fabric gave way and she dropped to the earth.

Lilly screamed. She ran toward the plane as Moseby hit the ground, crumpling.

Truman passed her, his long legs doubling her pace. He skidded to his knees beside Moseby. She lay at a cruel angle, one leg splayed, the other bent beneath her. A bone protruded from her thigh. Her eyes were closed and blood bubbled up from her mouth.

"She's still breathing. Get help!" Truman turned to her, his eyes wild. "Run, Lilly!"

But she didn't have to alert anyone. Marvel was already in the truck, barreling over the grasses. Eddie had managed to put the plane down, had started calling her name as he leaped out of the cockpit. She wanted to weep for him as he landed beside Truman, rocking back and forth, almost in a wail.

"She's still alive," Truman said as Marvel pulled up. "Let's get her into town."

Rango produced a blanket, and Beck and he slid Moseby's broken body onto it as Dan tossed out their remaining supplies. Oil cans and hoses, fabric, glue, signs, tires—everything that kept their fleet alive.

They loaded her into the cargo area, and then Lilly was standing alone, in the field with Truman as the realization slid through her like poison.

This was her fault.

* * * * *

Cesar Napoli made Rosie glitter inside. A hot sparkle that lit in her every time he met her outside the dressing room, bidding good night to the other chorus line girls. Often he held a single red rose between his sausage fingers, that too-cocky smile on his lips, as if he knew exactly the way her heart gave a little start when she saw him.

She might not be a headline yet, but on his arm, she felt like a star, shiny and bright. Sort of how she should have felt with Dash, if she hadn't always felt she had to keep up, impress him. With Cesar, all she had to do was smile.

"There's my gal," he said as she emerged from the dressing room, pushing up from the wall and handing her the flower. He wore a three-piece suit with thin gray stripes and matching gray vest, his dark hair slicked back. "You were a smash tonight."

"I was in the back row," she said, adding a pout to her words. He responded best when she gave him a little drama. She sniffed the rose. "When is this show going to end, Cesar? When am I going to be your star attraction?"

He took her hands, met her eyes, his dark and with a magnetic power that could steal her thoughts. "Soon, doll. Soon." Then he held out his elbow for her to slip her gloved hand through.

She hid her disappointment, sharp in her throat, as they walked through the club.

"A chorus girl is not a star," she'd said after she discovered the role he'd landed for her. She'd watched the girls perform and her heart sank. How was she going to prove anything to her mother if she didn't earn top billing? Worse, on a chorus girl's salary, she'd never make enough to keep a room at the Algonquin, where she'd escaped after the Cotton Club, with Lexie.

"Don't you worry, kitty. I'll keep you in your digs." Cesar had peeled out a wad of bills. Of course, she still had her last monthly allowance, tucked away in her bank, but she took the green anyway. He owed her for the broken promises. And, he still made her feel as if she might be made of tinsel, something to decorate his arm. Wherever they went, doors opened, gloved attendants handed her champagne, and men eyed Cesar with envy.

Perhaps being *treated* like a starlet would suffice, for now.

In the daylight, Valerie's looked worn, even drab: black tablecloths, an unlit bar, an empty stage, saggy velvet curtain tied back with fraying golden ropes. But at night, with the chandeliers lit, Mickey at the bar, the cigarette girls hawking goodies, and men drinking old-fashioneds, the crimson shine from the glasses like firelight, the place sizzled. She loved the hum of conversation, a thrill curling inside her stomach as she painted on her face in the dressing room before her performance. She was born for the stage, and if she had to room with Lexie and make her tidy up now and then....

At least she was on her own, her mother's matchmaking behind her. Hopefully the Duke of Lexington had already returned home. She could find her own beau—and besides, Lexie's words became truer every night. Rosie wasn't made for marriage.

She was made for Cesar's arm.

Outside, rain had washed away the day, leaving a murky smell on the street where his Rolls waited. He held open the door, and she climbed inside. He settled next to her on the velvet seat.

Cesar gave the address to his driver as she settled back in the pocket of his arm. It wasn't long before he began to smell her neck, press his lips to her skin. Different from Dash—who made her feel bold and independent—Cesar's touch drew her into a world of sultry danger, a feeling that could frighten her if she allowed it. She turned in his arms and let him kiss her, drawing some security in the fact that they were in the car and that he wouldn't dare soil her makeup before they arrived at whatever party he'd scheduled.

Still, when his hand moved to her décolletage, she caught his wrist.

"Cesar." She pushed his hand away, adding a giggle. "No."

He didn't smile, just touched her face. "Pet. You're so beautiful, it makes me lose my mind."

She put her hand to his clean-shaven chin, something he must have done after her show. Met his eyes. "Later, perhaps."

Indeed, a dangerous game she played, because later she'd have to find another ploy, something else to divert his attention.

In the back of her mind, she'd known there'd be a trade-off, something in barter for her role, despite his "no strings attached" declaration. But if she became his lead attraction, singer-dancer-actress, then she had something of a commodity from the deal. Maybe someday she could even land a role at one of the bigger theaters—the Hippodrome, or the Select.

Even Hollywood.

Cesar's eyes grew dark, and for a moment their texture changed from desire to something that put a fist in her gut. Then, abruptly, he formed a smile. "Later," he said and leaned away from her.

She puckered her lips, hoping he hadn't mussed her lipstick.

The Rolls splashed through the shiny streets, past the other clubs, toward Fifth Avenue, across from Central Park. Esme had once lived here, in a grand chateau. Imagine what Lilly might think of her now, an actress on a stage, just like Sarah Bernhardt.

They pulled up to a well-lit mansion, with men in livery attending. She allowed one of them to help her out. "Where are we?"

"This is my father's house," Cesar said. He offered his arm but didn't look at her. "He's having a little party."

Indeed. The place swam with men holding martinis and whiskey— apparently, someone had raided the local prohibition office's confiscations. Most in suits, a few had shed their jackets, rolling up their sleeves. There seemed to be a wrestling match of some sort happening in the parlor, the furniture cleared back. She watched a blond-headed man best a dark-haired brawler.

Cesar pulled her into another room, a sitting room of sorts, with men smoking cigars, bedazzled women, with low-cut fringed dresses like her own, on their arms, or laps. In various stages of clothing, some wore dresses, others just slips, and even a couple, silk robes. Her stomach tightened as they went in search of a drink. Cesar walked up to a robust man entertaining two ladies, one on each leg. He smoked a cigar, his eyes glinting with satisfaction. "Cesar."

"Happy birthday, Papa."

"This your girl?"

Cesar pushed her forward, his hand pressed at the small of her back. "Red, meet Vito Napoli."

She smiled at him. The man inhaled a long time, his gaze running over her. Then, finally, "Nice-lookin' gams." He winked at Cesar, and heat climbed up Rosie's cheeks.

Cesar grinned and moved his hand down to rest on her backside. She looked at him, but he didn't remove it. In fact, he turned to her, bent close to her ear. "Why don't ya find me a brandy, pet?" She frowned at him, his words a fist in her chest. But nothing burned as much as the tiny spank he gave her.

She jumped then moved away from him, her eyes on the ground.

More commotion erupted in the parlor. She watched for a moment as the blond man squared off with yet another opponent. They circled for a moment then leaped at each other. No punching, just rolling and grabbing and one man's arm snaked around the throat of another. The blond brawler finally twisted the other man's arm behind his back.

She realized she'd been holding her breath when the victor finally freed the beaten man.

Brandy.

She wandered into the dining room and found a group of men playing poker, their "dates" standing behind their chairs. In a large anteroom, a few couples danced to the small band set up in the corner. The doors to the terrace were open, and lights glowed on the verandah.

She meandered into the kitchen, usually located in the basement, but in this house, on the ground floor, and stood for a moment amidst the bustle of waiters. The smell of roasting pork could turn her inside out, and she couldn't remember the last time she ate.

"What are you doing in my kitchen?"

She found the voice, bruised by his tone, his crisp French accent.

"I was looking for a glass of brandy?"

He rolled his eyes. "Ramone!" The rest of it was in French, something so fast she couldn't unravel it. But moments later, a glass of brandy appeared on the tray of a waiter.

"Thank you," she said. She exited the kitchen the way she came, back through the anteroom. But the redolence of summer tugged her out onto the verandah, just for a moment. She stood there, staring at the tiny city garden, the crimson climbing roses, the marmalade marigolds, the hosta lush with color, an oasis.

"Plotting your escape?"

She turned at the voice, found it attached to the blond from the parlor. He stepped out on the verandah beside her, his skin glistening, his hair—more auburn than blond in this light—tousled, his shirt wrinkled from the hand-holds upon it. Up close he had a rough energy about him, something raw and simmering right under his skin. The sense of it drew her in, held her there.

"No," she breathed then found her voice. "I just got here."

"Hmm," he said, and began unbuttoning his shirt.

"What are you doing?"

"I'm sorry, miss, I just need to cool off."

"Not right here!"

He looked around, behind her, then finally met her eyes. "I don't think anyone is going to care."

"I care."

He smiled, stopped unbuttoning, and leaned against the rail. "Do you now?"

He had a funny accent, flat, nothing of New York in it.

"It's just—I don't think it's right to undress in front of a lady."

His gaze traveled down her, back up. "My apologies."

It was his tone, mocking, that stirred her. "What does that mean?"

"Just what I said." He buttoned his shirt back up, but not before she glimpsed the chest of a man familiar with hard work. "I'm sorry. I have to admit that I mistook you for one of the Napoli bimbos. Apparently, you're from different stock."

She drew herself up, considered her current job title and chose, "I'm Rosie Worth, daughter of Foster Worth. And you are?"

"Guthrie Storme." He held out his hand, and she clasped it.

"Guthrie," she said, aware of the strength of his hand. "Do you work for Cesar?"

She expected something simple, something perhaps within the Napoli world. Deliveryman, or perhaps security enforcement. She wasn't ignorant of Cesar's empire, or its activities. She just preferred to focus on the club.

"Hardly. I play baseball. For the Robins. Vito's a big fan and invited us out for his bash."

She considered him. Taller than her by a few inches, and shoulders that looked more suited for a dockworker, he didn't look anything like the type of man who would play baseball in the hot sun all day. "What position do you play?"

"Pitcher. I throw a mean knuckleball." He put his right hand in his fist and then pretended to throw an imaginary ball into the darkness.

"Really? Then what was that back there?"

"Aw, that? That's just for fun." He lowered his voice. "And a few extra smackerels." He pulled a wad of cash from his shirt pocket and winked. "That's what having three brothers gets you."

She liked him. He had an aura that suggested he didn't take life too seriously. Someone that, indeed, she could escape with. If she wanted to escape.

"I have to find Cesar and bring him his brandy."

His eyebrows rose. "You're Cesar's girl?"

She smiled, feeling glittery again. Nodded.

"Of course you are."

Her smile dimmed. "What does that mean?"

He turned his back to her. "Just, either you're slumming, or you're not quite the lady I pegged you as."

She stared at his broad shoulders, not sure how to respond. Finally, "Good night, Mr. Storme." She turned and walked away, his words sour in her stomach.

Cesar had vanished when she finally found her way back to the smoking room. She stood there, holding his brandy like she might be a servant, and searched the room for him, eyes upon her. His father disentangled himself from two girls and a conversation and said, "He left."

He left?

"Try the poker game."

But he wasn't there, or with the crowd of men, now betting on two different grapplers. She looked for Guthrie and didn't see him.

She stopped a waiter in the foyer. "Have you seen Cesar?"

He glanced past her, up the stairs, then shook his head.

Perfect. She climbed the stairs, feeling like a fool to chase him around the house, carrying his brandy. She had a good mind to take a sip of it.

The first door to the left hung ajar and she moved toward it, her hand on the knob when she heard a giggle. She froze, listening.

"In my next show, doll. The main attraction. Your name in lights."

Then silence, and Rosie had a good guess at what had followed. She stood there, gripping the glass, her hand shaking, when suddenly the door creaked. She must have pushed it, for it swung open.

And then she had a perfect view of Cesar and one of his girls tangled together on the leather sofa. He looked up, and she expected surprise, even remorse. But Cesar didn't even bother to put himself back together. Just a vicious, "Get out!"

She recoiled, stung.

"You hear me, Red? Get out!"

She started to back away, to reach for the handle, when suddenly, she stopped. Then, with everything she had in her, she threw the brandy glass at his head.

It went wide and smashed on the bookcases behind him. The girl screamed. Cesar pushed himself off the sofa, menace in his face. He advanced toward her, and she backed away, but not fast enough. His hand snaked around her neck. Just tight enough that it stifled her breathing, turned her weak. He pushed her out of the room, against the far wall, and put a finger in her face. "I told you to get out."

She put her hand to his wrist, tried to push it away, but he held it, moved close to her ear. "Remember, you're just a chorus girl. You can be replaced." He let her go, and just when she thought he might slap her, he pressed his hand to her face. "Wait for me downstairs."

Then he turned, closing the door to the library behind him.

She couldn't move, everything inside her turning to liquid.

"You okay?"

Down the hall, a few feet away, Guthrie stood, his fists tight at his sides, his face solemn.

She put her hand to her neck and rubbed. "I think so."

"You want to get out of here?"

Her gaze went to the closed door. *Wait for me downstairs.*

"Please," she said softly.

Guthrie took her hand and pulled her down the stairs to where a few guests had assembled to watch the spectacle. He left her in the foyer, dashed into the parlor, and grabbed his jacket, his hat. Then he returned and offered her a smile.

It was so kind, she wanted to weep. He held the door open for her as she shot one more look upstairs then stepped outside. The rain had resumed, the night sky weeping.

"That was a fabulous throw, by the way." He shook out his jacket and held it over her. They stepped out onto the sidewalk. "Ever think of trying out for the majors?"

She laughed, more of a bubble of relief than humor.

"C'mon," he said, "let's get you something to eat."

This time of night, the city appeared deserted, streetlights glistening against the wet sidewalks. They crossed the street, then to the corner where he told her to wait. "I'll get us a cab."

She stood, holding his coat over her head, shivering, and then saw him splash back, his shirt soaked through, water dripping into his eyes. But a car pulled up behind him, and Guthrie opened the door, ushering her in.

"Marshall's café on Eighty-Second." He took his coat from her, shook it, then folded it beside him on the seat. "They serve amazing eggs all hours of the night."

They pulled up and she could hardly believe the crowd, the after-clubbing assembly of socialites, men in tuxedos, and workmen pulled up to the tables or seated at stools at the long bar.

Guthrie found them a table in the back, and they slid in the booths.

"Eat here much?" she asked.

He lifted a shoulder. "Enough." He raised a finger to a waitress. "Goldie, a couple of coffees?"

She nodded and disappeared through the swinging doors into the kitchen.

Rosie ran her hands up her arms, still shivering.

"I'm sorry my jacket's wet, but you can have it if you'd like."

"No, I'm fine. I'm just..." She shook her head, looking away, and drew in a breath that seemed to touch her bones. "My father used to push my mother around sometimes. I never really knew how helpless that made her feel until tonight."

He folded his hands on the table, and they turned white. "That's not the first time I've see Cesar get rough with a dame." He met her eyes. "He's done worse, I promise."

She swallowed, caught in his green eyes. Then, wishing to push the night away, she found a smile for her rescuer. "So, Guthrie, where are you from?"

"Kansas City. Actually, I grew up on a farm and started by playing stickball. I played some in high school, then got lucky in the minors, got traded to the Yanks, and they moved me up to the show last year. Still can't believe I'm sitting on the mound throwing to Babe Ruth."

"What's your position again?—that's what they call it, right?"

"Pitcher."

She made a face. "I'm sorry, I don't know much about baseball."

"Aw, you're killing me here, Red."

He called her by her stage name, but on his lips, it felt almost natural. As if it belonged there. He took the salt shaker, the pepper, the napkin holder, and the sugar bowl and put them out in a diamond on the table. "This here's the infield. You got home plate"—he picked up the napkin holder—"then first, second, and third. Your job is to hit the ball and get your man on base before the other team throws you out. My job is to make sure you don't get the hit."

She had heard of baseball. Once upon a time, Jack had asked her to go to a game. But it seemed a bore to sit in the hot sun watching men stand in a field. "I'm sorry. I've heard of the Robins. I just don't know much about them."

He shook his head again, a smile playing on his face. "Now you're breakin' my heart. Next to the Yanks, we're not too bad. We won the pennant a couple years ago."

"The pennant?" She raised an eyebrow.

"The league championship? Played in the World Series?"

"I'm sorry. Is that something important?"

He shook his head, his expression pained, but a smile edged up his face.

Goldie returned with their coffee. "Order?"

"A couple fried eggs for the lady, and a stack for me."

He added sugar to his coffee, offered her some. She shook her head. The brew went down and settled in her stomach, heating her through.

She hadn't realized how cold she was. Her stomach growled with the addition, and she was mortified.

He smiled but said nothing. Then, as his smile fell, he ran his thumb along the handle of his cup. "How long you been dancing for Cesar?"

She had spilled her coffee and now reached for a napkin. "Just a couple of weeks."

He nodded, seemed to consider that. Then, "Why?"

"Why do I dance? Because...because I want to be a star. And he promised..." She looked away, feeling the fool.

He leaned forward. "And why do you want to be a star, Miss Worth, when you already shine so bright?"

Oh. Her throat filled. She didn't feel bright. Not tonight. Cesar had turned off the shimmer, made her dull inside.

He leaned back. "You get any days off?"

"I have every day off—I work in the evenings."

"Perfect. I got a game tomorrow afternoon. I'll give you a free ticket if you come."

"To a baseball game?"

"Don't say it like that, I'm liable to think you're offended by my offer." But he chased his words with a smile.

"It's just...I've never been to a baseball game. I wouldn't have the slightest idea what to do."

"Just show up. Eat some popcorn. Watch me throw a no-hitter. Maybe even hit a homer."

"A homer?"

"I'll show you what that is if you'll be my lucky charm."

His lucky charm. "You don't know anything about me. How could I possibly be your lucky charm?"

"I just got a feelin'," he said.

Goldie served up their breakfasts and Rosie nearly devoured her food, not stopping until she looked up, saw Guthrie considering her over his cup of coffee. "What?"

"I've just never seen a lady eat so fast."

"Maybe I'm not a lady."

He sipped his coffee. "You're definitely a lady."

She frowned at him then finished her eggs. "My mother is a lady. And she wants nothing more than to marry me off to some Duke of Lichtenstein or something."

"What do you want?"

She took a sip of coffee. "Not to marry a duke, that's for sure."

He smiled, dug into his pancakes. "You're an interesting bird, Red. Most girls would do anything to marry into money and title."

"I'm not most girls."

He forked a mound of pancakes into his mouth. "I think I'm starting to figure that out."

She finished her coffee as she watched him eat. He propped his arm on the table, the plate in his embrace as he sopped up syrup with each forkful. Away from the theatrics of the Napolis, Guthrie seemed less on edge, easy, like someone she might have known all her life, except her sort didn't mix with farm boys from Kansas.

He had large baseball player hands to go with his strong arms, and she could admit that he had a sort of rough beauty about him, with that blond, tousled hair, the square cut of his jaw, the blush of a burn on his nose and arms.

She might be eating dinner with one of her mother's footmen. Still, he made her feel safe. The chill of the rain on her skin had vanished.

He finally finished his meal, wiping his mouth and settling back in the seat. "Have I talked you into a baseball game?"

She played out the silence for a bit, then, "Yes. I'll go. But only if you meet me afterward so you can explain everything to me."

"It's a date."

A date. "Perhaps we should call it something different."

He signaled Goldie, who slipped him the tab, then reached into his wallet, pulled out cash, and left it on the table. When he stood up, he extended his hand to her. "Nope. It's a date."

She took his hand and let him lead her out onto the street, not willing to correct him. So, let it be a date. Cesar didn't own her.

"Where do you live?"

"I share a room with my friend at the Algonquin."

He hailed them another cab. Light began to dent the cap of darkness over the city, and as she sagged into the seat, his arm curled around her. She wanted to lean into the cradle of his arm, to rest, but she wasn't sure, and...

"We're here, Red. Wake up."

His hand on her arm jolted her. She blinked, sat up. "Oh!"

"I'm sorry to wake you. I made the driver go around twice, but I'm running out of money." She turned in his arms and he met her eyes, a softness in them.

Would it be so terrible to kiss him? She had the sudden, inexplicable urge to lean forward and touch her lips to his. For a moment, she willed him to move his hand behind her neck, to lean in, but he just pushed back a hair that had fallen in front of her eyes and climbed out.

She followed him onto the street, startled when he extended his hand. She slipped hers into his grip and he leaned low, his voice in her ear. "Game starts at one."

Then he was gone, leaving her in the street, the night turning to silver around her.

She turned to enter the lobby of the Algonquin when her gaze fell on the Rolls parked under a leafy oak.

Her mouth dried.

Oh, let him not have seen Guthrie. She resisted the urge to glance after his taxi and refused to flinch as she heard a car door slam, footsteps down the pavement. "Red! Where'd you go? I was so worried."

If ever there might be a time to act. "You got a lot of nerve, Cesar Napoli, coming down here after dumping me for that floozy. What did you expect me to do...stick around?"

Her heart thundered inside her as she narrowed her eyes at Cesar.

Cesar just came at her, his hand slipping behind her neck, kissing her fiercely, his touch hard and possessive, the piquant taste of brandy on his lips. He met her eyes, his dark and with a glint of danger. "Whatcha doing with that bozo?"

Her breath squeaked out a little, and she braced her hand against his tuxedoed chest. But she lifted her chin, shrugged as if Guthrie might already be an afterthought.

"I was hungry. He took me out for breakfast. It's nothing."

Cesar's mouth tightened, and he glanced behind her, at the retreating taxi. "I see." He moved his hand down to hers, caught it. Held it until it hurt. "Just remember. You're Cesar's girl now. You belong to me."

Then he let her go and abandoned her to the wet street.

Chapter 9

All Lilly had to do was hang on and ignore the echo of her arrogant words in her head. *"I'm going to save your sorry hide."*

She clung to the cockpit edges of the biplane, the wind whistling in her ears, and rewound twelve hours, to the moment she'd found Truman in the bar.

A hole in the wall with a saggy wooden floor, the reek of whiskey embedded in the walls, and Truman saddled up to the counter, looking wrung out and testy as he considered another shot of whatever amber liquid he had in that glass.

"I think I understand now," she'd said without greeting.

"You don't understand anything," Truman said, picking up his glass, studying the shiny liquid under the lights of the bar. A cigarette burned in the ashtray before him, a long char of untapped ash. He put down the glass without drinking and ran his thumb and forefinger through his eyes. "What could you possibly understand?"

"Why you don't want me to wing walk." She slid onto the bar stool and waved away the barkeep as if it might be completely natural for her to saunter into the seedy digs, as if she hadn't spent nearly thirty minutes outside O'Paddy's, willing herself the courage.

But, what did Marvel say as he drove out of town to Duluth? *The show must go on.*

Especially since they needed the money to pay for Moseby's hospital bills. Lilly touched Truman's arm. "She's going to live."

"She may never walk again." He looked at her hand on his arm. "I should've checked Eddie's plane before she went up. It's my responsibility to oversee all repairs."

Repairs. Like the ones she'd done on the wing. "I'm so sorry, Truman."

He closed his eyes. Drew in a breath. "I checked your work on Eddie's plane after we returned from the hospital. It wasn't your fault. The glue on your repair held. Moseby went through a different tear. The fabric was just weak, should have been replaced long ago. That's on me."

"Truman—you can't protect everyone. Accidents happen, especially in flying."

"Spoken by a person who doesn't fly."

"Then teach me."

He gave a laugh, edged like a knife. "I don't think so."

"I'm not afraid."

"Of course you aren't."

"You need me. We already had to cancel the Detroit Lakes show. If you want Duluth to be a hit—if you want to pull out of the financial abyss we're in, you need a wing walker. Me."

A muscle pulled in his jaw. He took a drink then looked at her, his red eyes glassy. "Why do you want to throw away your life so much?"

She met his eyes then eased the glass from his hand. Set it on the counter.

"I don't want to throw away my life, Truman. But you seem to want to." Then she moved over to him, tucked her arm around his waist. "I'm taking you back to your plane. And in the morning, you're going to take me flying so I can save our little show."

"You're going to wreck everything," he said.

"I'm going to save your sorry hide."

Her voice churned inside her now as she heard Truman's voice, shouting over the roar of the engine, accompanied by a violent tap on her shoulder. "It's time. Do it just like I told you. And be careful, or I'll kill you."

They'd practiced on the ground—or rather, what he called practicing and she called berating—as she'd climbed out of the cockpit and touched her foot to the wing.

"Stay on the ribs. If you step foot on the fabric…"

"I know," she said, the wires digging into her fingers.

"Figure out where you'll put your foot. It might be easy now, but not at a thousand feet, and look out for the propellers. There will be a wash from them, and I won't be able to hear you. I'll have to teach you the hand signals."

He'd bathed after his run-in with the dark side of whiskey, his ebony hair shiny in the sun, and he smelled of soap. He wore a clean white T-shirt that stretched over the muscles in his arms as he showed her the signals. In his jeans and bare feet, his skin golden in the sun, he looked like a farmhand, and only the raccoon suntan from his goggles betrayed him. "Don't forget to look at me."

Please, there were days when she couldn't take her eyes off him. But now, with the worry on his face, he seemed suddenly human.

"Climb back into the cockpit and let me measure you for rope."

He fixed a knot around her waist, then the other end to the cockpit.

"This is supposed to save me?"

"This is supposed to keep you from hitting the ground. If you fall, you'll have to climb back into the plane yourself."

He raised an eyebrow, as if waiting for her to back down.

She had borrowed a pair of Moseby's canvas gym shoes and tucked her shirt tight into her pants before donning the leather helmet and goggles. "All set."

Not quite, because with the wind whipping through her shirt, the earth dropping away, the propeller blades cutting the air, her stomach doing flops, she realized that no, indeed, she had no idea what kind of courage it took to climb out onto the wing.

She had only her pride to propel her.

She glanced back at Truman. He didn't smile, and if she shook her head, she had no doubt he'd circle around and land, no questions asked.

She gripped the cockpit walls and stood up. She hadn't appreciated the well that protected her—the wind nearly blasted her over, filling her mouth, blinding her eyes. The propeller wash burned her face with wind shear. She went deaf, and she had to lean into the wind to keep from splatting onto Truman's windshield.

She could do this. Throwing her leg over the side, she held onto the wire and stepped onto the wing spar. The wind growled around her and tore at her goggles, ripping them sideways. She freed a hand to adjust them, but the wind whipped her backwards and she nearly peeled off her perch.

Shouting, or perhaps just the roar of the props, filled her ears now. She could only see out one goggle eye. She grabbed the next wire, pulled herself onto the wing, and set her legs.

Just stand. She could just stand. Not look back at Truman for hand signals, not creep out to the leading edge of the plane and sit down like Moseby. Just stand there and call herself a fool.

She was going to die.

They circled the field, and he seemed to pull back on the speed, because her balance returned to her. Perhaps she could edge out onto the wing. She moved her foot to the next rib, sliding her hand down the wire toward the strut.

The rope around her waist snaked into the wind, slapping her, nearly dislodging her as she worked her way to the edge. Her eyes teared, her breath stolen.

She reached the strut and held on with both hands, frozen.

How did Moseby manage to climb to the upper wing and hang on while Truman did his stunts? Oh, she was a fool. Arrogant and headstrong and—

She couldn't do this. She couldn't ride the wings, waving at spectators, or perch on the upper wing like a bird while Truman twisted in the air.

So much for the feeling of freedom, the ethereal sense of breaking free. So much for learning how to fly.

Lilly turned back toward the cockpit, hand reaching for the wire. But when she tried to move, the rope tugged at her waist. She yanked at it, but it wouldn't give. With her clear eye, she followed it back to where it had snagged in the wires, wrapping like a snake. She pulled again, but it wouldn't budge, and she didn't dare reach for it without tumbling off the wing.

She turned to look at Truman for the first time. She couldn't read his eyes, but his mouth pressed tight, his face white.

I can't land the plane until you're off the wing. She remembered that part of the instructions.

Her words burned through her: *"I'm going to save your sorry hide."*

No, she was going to get them both killed. With one hand, she began to work the knot at her waist. He'd tied it tight, and thick, but she edged one loop out, then the other, her hand shaking, grabbing at the wire when she felt her body start to pitch off the wing.

She finally pried it free and the rope fell away, flapping behind her. Her eye on the cockpit, she ground her jaw to keep from screaming and stepped on the ribs, working her way back to safety.

At the spar, she stood for a moment, paralyzed. It was one thing to walk hand over hand across the wing. Getting back into the cockpit required her to throw her leg over the edge then let go with both hands and fling herself back inside.

Moseby had a good six inches of leg on her. No wonder she could dart in and out of the cockpit like a monkey. Lilly held tight and reached out her leg, clipping the edge.

It slipped, and she nearly plunged off the wing.

Oh, God, please.

She took a breath, threw her leg up again. Something caught her ankle.

Truman had reached up, grabbed her leg, was holding it fast. He maneuvered it into the cockpit enough for her to get a hook around the edge. Then, with a cry that the prop ate, she lunged for the opening, grabbing at the rope still attached to the cockpit. She tumbled in, not caring that she scrubbed her face on the seat, that it might not look graceful.

She righted herself then drew up her knees and curled into a miserable ball as Truman brought the plane down to a smooth landing.

The prop sputtered out, and for the first time she heard her sobs. Gulping and hot, they coursed through her, shaking her out.

She tore off her goggles, pressed her hands to her wet, windburned face.

"I'm sorry."

She heard his voice above her and couldn't look up. Oh, he must be laughing, and she couldn't bear the mocking on his face, those stormy eyes that told her she was a fool.

"I guess the rope was a bad idea. Maybe we'll use a parachute next time."

What—?

She peeled her hands away, looked up at him. He stood against the sun, staring down at her with an expression she couldn't unravel. A frown, but nothing of anger, more curiosity.

"I—"

"Don't beat yourself up, New York. The first time Moseby wing walked she threw up in the cockpit." He leaned over her. "You're less messy, that's for sure."

She sat up as he climbed out. Then he reached over and lifted her out of the cockpit. He didn't put her down. "I don't want you to collapse on me."

She stared up at him, the kindness rattling her more than the wing walk. He held her as if she weighed nothing, and his smell washed over her as he walked her toward the tent, the scent of the air, wild and clean and free. As if he might be a piece of the sky.

He reached the tent and looked down at her, still something enigmatic, even intimate, in those blue eyes. "Ready to stand on your own?"

No. But she nodded.

He put her down. She clung to his arm.

Oh...uh... "Truman...I don't know if I can do that again. It's..."

"Terrifying?"

She drew in a breath. "I thought I was going to die."

He put his hands on her shoulders. "I did too, the first time I tried it. In my case, we nearly did. The pilot couldn't compensate for my weight, we nearly did a loop into the ground."

"I just...I thought I was...stronger."

He took his hands from her shoulders. Propeller ran up to them, his tail slapping against her legs. Truman bent and rubbed the dog around the ears. He didn't look at her. "You were the one who wanted to do this. It's your call, New York." He rose and met her eyes. "I personally don't want to see you as a grease spot on the grass." He said it like it might be humorous, but something of pain sparked in his eyes. "Let's get some grub."

Beck and Rango were cooking oatmeal when she entered the cool tent. They looked up at her, and she caught the quick shake of Truman's head that clearly silenced any comment about her morning adventure. She took her breakfast outside, sat on the ground alone, and tried not to cry.

They packed the tent and the trailer, and Truman gassed the planes as Rango went to retrieve Eddie from his vigil at the hospital. Rango returned empty-handed, shaking his head. Suicide Dan slid into Eddie's cockpit.

"I didn't know he knew how to fly," Lilly said as she gathered Moseby's belongings. She stood beside the plane, her pile of gear tied into a bag, and wasn't sure what to do.

"We'll come back after the Duluth show and check on her," Truman said, and took the bundle from her, securing it in Dan's cockpit.

It took everything she had to climb into Truman's plane, the sense of nearly losing herself so fresh she could taste it. But she buckled in and hunkered down, wanting to cry again at the loss of everything she'd discovered in Paris.

Rennie was wrong. She didn't belong in the sky after all.

* * * * *

Lilly must have fallen asleep because it happened so fast. One moment they were flying blue skies, the next the sky began to weep, a slow drizzle that turned the air to a murky soup. Water bled across the windshield, and a trickle of wispy clouds turned into fingers of white, wrapping around the plane.

Fog. She'd heard Truman and Beck talk about it before as zero-zero. Zero visibility, zero ceiling. And often fatal, as airplanes misjudged their landings and slammed into the ground or buildings, or even simply ran out of fuel, looking to break free of the mist.

She glanced back at Truman. He shook his head at her, his lips tight, and she felt them descending. The fog thickened as they fell toward earth. He pulled up higher, but the rain only turned to icicles, shearing her face.

He dove again, lower and lower, the rain turning to mist off the wings as he tried to get under the clouds, to find the ground, but the fog only turned less milky.

"We have to land!" She barely made out his words and turned so she could see his mouth. "I can't see anything!"

She leaned over the side of the plane, wishing she could shoo away the clinging fog. If they were over a town, electrical wires and church spires would be fatal. Maybe if she...

A few extra feet of visibility might give them enough to find a landing. Moseby had told her a story of how, in exactly these same conditions, she'd guided Beck to safety.

If she didn't do it, they could die. Lilly glanced back at him. "I'm going out on the wing!"

If he heard her, she didn't know, because his expression didn't change.

She slipped a leg over the edge of the cockpit.

The plane dipped, as if he might not be expecting her weight, and she grabbed for the wires. Without her gloves they cut her hands, but she ignored the burn.

The rope that Moseby held for her stunts on the upper wing flapped in the wind. Attached to the trailing edge of the one wing, it looped forward and down around the front strut, across to the other, then back again to the trailing edge of the opposite wing. She'd seen Moseby climb up above the cockpit and use the rope to pull herself up. Now, Lilly mimicked her moves, hooking her leg around the upper strut, grabbing hold of the rope. Icy and slick, it slammed her fingers into the fabric of the plane, but she hung on and scrabbled to the top of the plane. Wrapping her legs around each rope, she lay spread eagle across the top of the wing, holding to the rope across the leading edge.

It gave her a few extra precious feet. But she'd have to sit if she wanted Truman to see her directions. She kept her feet clamped around the ropes and slid herself forward, to her knees, and then settled back into a sitting position, her hands white on the rope.

The rain spit on her, and the props buzzed right below her dangling feet. But this felt more secure than standing on the wing, her hands embracing a front strut. Here, she could tuck herself into the plane, be a part of it.

Grow wings.

And, it gave her even more of a vantage point. She gestured that he should descend, and Truman must have throttled back, because the plane sank down into the fog. She caught a glimpse of darkness and waved him to the right. A wire along their left, then a tree—which told her they might only be fifty feet from the ground.

Low enough to plow into hill, a building, a cliff.

He continued to descend, and she made out an expanse of gray blue. A lake. Looking back at him, she saw him glance at her, then over the side, then back. She directed him left, back toward toward the trees—maybe she could guide him through the forest until they found a field.

He obeyed her, and she took them through a winding, bumpy ride, even ascending up into the fog as she saw walls rise up before her.

Then, as quickly as it had thickened, the woolly fog dispersed. All at once they were through it, and below lay a thick tangle of pine and birch. And in the distance, carved out of the forest, a swath of pasture with a muddy landing strip and a wooden shack, the words DULUTH AIRFIELD painted on the roof.

She was going to turn around, to climb back into the cockpit, but Truman held up his hand.

Stay? She thought she recognized that.

She hung onto the rope, her heart clogging her breath as he brought them down to a smooth, albeit grimy, landing.

He taxied them into the grass. The prop fizzled out. She just clung to the rope and breathed.

Truman stood up in the cockpit just as she turned. He stripped off his goggles, and the look in his eyes turned her dumb.

"You saved our lives, New York."

She managed a smile.

"That was the stupidest thing I've ever seen."

Oh.

He climbed out of the cockpit and came around the front of the plane. Stared up at her. Then, suddenly, he turned away, his hands on his knees.

She thought, for a moment, he might lose his oatmeal.

"Truman."

"Just…give me a minute here."

He finally turned and held out his arms. She wasn't sure what—

"I'll catch you."

He did, but didn't hold her, just lowered her to the ground. Then, he took his thumb and wiped her cheek. She looked at his hand. Mud.

He shook his head, and again that look—curiosity? Amusement? Yes, but something more too.

"What?" She wiped her hand across her other cheek. Oh, she'd need an entire bath.

"I guess the only question left is…what are we going to call your act?"

* * * * *

"No, you are absolutely not going." Lexie grabbed the white slacks from Rosie's hand and threw them on the bed. "Have you lost your mind? One close call isn't enough?"

"It's just a baseball game—"

"To see Guthrie Storme play!" Lexie went to the window, looked out as if Cesar might be parked downstairs in his Rolls. "Maybe I need to remind you exactly who Cesar Napoli is."

Rosie put her hand to her throat. Although the tenderness had subsided, she might never forget the pressure of his grip. "No. Actually you don't." She sighed and stared at her closet, some dresses purchased with Cesar's money and some, her own, ferried to the Algonquin by porter from her mother's house. "But Guthrie's team is just back from a road trip to Boston—"

Lexie flopped down on the bed. "Why do you want to wreck a good thing? Cesar likes you."

"Cesar likes himself. And if I make him look good, then he'll keep me." Rosie shut the closet door then settled beside Lexie. "I can't believe that a week ago, Cesar actually made me believe…" She sighed. "Well, that I was special."

"You are, baby," Lexie said. "The world just hasn't figured it out yet." She propped herself up on one elbow. "But they never will if you start missing rehearsals and attending baseball games."

Rosie sighed. "But I actually enjoyed myself." Indeed, that glorious day in the summer sunshine and stands of Ebbets Field, sitting with the girlfriends and wives of the players, seemed almost magical. She'd cheered Guthrie on, her cheeks heating when he waved at her, and she'd even managed to figure out the basics of the game by the end. But the magic didn't come from the game, or the crowd, the popcorn, or even the fact the Robins had defeated the Giants, their rival team from Manhattan. It was Guthrie, and the fact he'd made her feel, not glittery, but perhaps simply…enough. As if she didn't have to be anyone but herself for him.

He'd met her outside the stadium with cotton candy, and she'd eaten it while he walked her through the streets of Brooklyn, talking about the game with his hands, acting out his favorite moments, making her laugh with antics from his fellow ballplayers in the dugout.

When it came time for her to return to the club, he hailed her a cab, gave the address and a wad of bills to the driver. Then he leaned in through the window. "That homerun? That was for you, Red. You are my lucky charm." He didn't try to kiss her, just touched the tip of her sunburned nose with his finger and patted the cab on its way.

The sweetness of his words, his actions, only churned the desire to see him again. And, after over a week on the road, the Robins had a home game tomorrow.

"What's with this guy anyway? What do you see in him that Cesar doesn't have?"

You are my lucky charm. "Guthrie makes me feel safe. As if I don't have to try. He likes me. Just me."

"Are you sure? You are a Worth, after all." Lexie's question was serious.

"He doesn't care about money. Besides, he has no idea who Foster Worth is. He just wants to play baseball. Would you believe he hasn't even tried to kiss me?"

"And a good thing for you, if Cesar saw! But still, what a shame. He does have delicious shoulders."

Rosie threw a pillow at her. But Cesar's warning had hung in her ear every day for nearly two weeks. *You're Cesar's girl now. You belong to me.*

She got up and went to the bureau, stared at herself in the mirror, tugging at her hair.

"I like the peroxide look," Lexie said. "It makes you stand out."

"Cesar's suggestion," she said, trying to decide if she liked herself as a blond. "Guthrie hasn't seen it yet."

"And probably it's best if he never does." Lexie sat up, crossing her legs on the bed. "So, whatcha gonna wear to Cesar's party?"

Just like his father, Cesar was hosting a birthday party. "I don't know.

Cesar bought me a dress to apologize for sleeping with that bimbo, but I already wore it. He won't notice if I wear it again, though. He's consumed with the party. He's ordered live peacocks to stroll the grounds of the club."

"Oh, he'll notice you. Especially if you wear something swank. Why don't we go shopping? We'll charge it to Cesar's account."

Well, she *was* Cesar's girl, or so he said.

The matron at Barney's showed them into the private rooms, gilded with mirrors and red velvet chairs, where attendants offered them juice (if they were in Paris, they'd be drinking champagne) and sandwiches while store models displayed the latest fashions. Lexie wore a pair of black slacks and a white blouse, her dark hair perfectly marshaled in gentle waves. She smoked a Lucky Strike in a long black cigarette holder, peering at the models as if they might be lying to her.

Rosie finally chose a long pale pink dress with a drop waist and an embroidered bodice, separated from the skirt by a satin sash. When she tried it on for Lexie, her friend gave her a saucy, approving wink.

She would prefer to wear it for Guthrie, but since Cesar's money purchased it, she'd wait until his party. She added a gray felt cloche hat, pale shimmering silk stockings, and a pair of black suede shoes.

The store clerk packaged it all up and sent them home with a porter, in the store's car.

Rosie nearly dropped her bundles when she spied Guthrie sitting in the lobby of the Algonquin. He looked tanned, his hair burnished by the sun.

"Guthrie!" she said, her voice a little too bright.

"Hey, Red...or should I say Goldie? Wow." A smile touched his face. Indeed, how could he be anything but devastatingly handsome, with that dimple in the center of his chin and the way he could grin, real slowly, and make her feel beautiful? He got up and pulled his derby off his head. "You look real pretty."

She didn't care that he had to be lying, because she had barely kohled her eyes or powdered her face. At least she'd remembered to apply lipstick before leaving the store. "I thought I wouldn't see you until tomorrow, after the game."

"I wanted to see you."

She let those words seep inside, leaned into them.

"I was hoping we could…maybe go for a stroll?"

She turned to look at Lexie, who was shaking her head. "Take my packages."

"You've got a show tonight," Lexie said as she reluctantly held out her hands. "Don't miss it."

Rosie frowned at her. Turned back to Guthrie. "Where are we going?"

"Ever been to Coney Island?"

She'd been to Paris and Newport and the Berkshires, but never across the bay to Jersey and the shores of Coney Island.

They walked along Surf Avenue under the glittering lights of the shows, then onto the newly laid boards of the Reigelman Boardwalk, the sea air and cotton candy sweetness adding a tang to the summer night. Picnickers and bathers still kicked up the waves, and at the fair end, the Parachute Tower loomed above them, a giant steel tower with a pancake across the sky.

Screams from the steeplechase drifted in the air, mingling with the music from the band shell.

"This is the perfect hot dog," Guthrie said, handing over her doctored Nathan's dog. The wind found her skin and sent a whisper of chill over it as she maneuvered the hot dog into her mouth. Ketchup and mustard squeezed from the sides.

Guthrie reached out and wiped the edge of her mouth. "A little extra there."

She licked her lips. "Delicious."

"I still can't believe you'd never had a hot dog. Or attended a base-ball game."

"My brother tried to talk me into going once. Back right before the war. But...it didn't work out."

"Maybe next year, I can get him tickets."

She made a face. Oh, how did she do that, bring up Jack, when all she wanted to do was run from the topic of her lost brother? "No. Jack... Jack never came back from the war."

It was easier said that way than to explain that Jack ran away from home after hearing about his mother's adultery and the fact that Jack's uncle was suddenly his father. Or that he hadn't been heard from since.

This explanation made Jack sound like a war hero.

"I'm so sorry, Rosie." Guthrie drew in a breath. "I lost my oldest brother in the war. I didn't know him real well, but his passing surely made a loss in our family. My mother would sit for long hours in her rocking chair, holding our family Bible, just staring out the window, as if he might appear from between the cornrows. I couldn't bear it and started playing as much ball as I could, just to stay away. Pretty soon, it became my entire life, was all I had. Playing kept me numb, made me feel untouchable."

Rosie looked at the long shadows over the boardwalk. "My mother crawled in bed with me a couple of months ago and sobbed herself to sleep." She hadn't shared that with anyone, hadn't really been able to acknowledge it herself. "We've been grieving for a long time."

The rush of the waves, the caw of gulls, and children's voices filled the silence. "My parents fought a lot when I was young. My father was..." She drew in a breath. "He could be so cruel. Sometimes I could hear them in the parlor, hear things break, hear my mother screaming, and I'd climb into the wardrobe in my room and shut the door."

"Oh, Red."

"My brother, he knew where my hiding space was and sometimes, when he was home, he'd sneak down the hallway and hide in the wardrobe with me. We'd play rock, paper, scissors, and have thumb wars, and he'd tell me stories about the boys at his academy. He told me it would be all right." She glanced at Guthrie. "It wasn't. And then he left. It hasn't been okay since."

Her appetite had vanished, so she threw away the hot dog, wiped her mouth. "I just can't take any more grief in my life. I don't want to feel this way anymore. I want to live." She looked at him. "Is that a terrible thing?"

"I think that's a normal thing. The question is—how will you live?" He was looking at her with those green eyes, and they seemed to hold a power she couldn't bear. She looked away.

"I think I have to get back to the city. I'm on stage at ten o'clock."

He blew out a breath. "Red, I need to ask you something." He put a hand on her arm.

She stopped, and watching the tension on his face, her chest tightened.

Then, suddenly, he dropped to one knee, right there in the middle of the boardwalk. "Guthrie—"

He took her hand. "Just listen to me, Red. I know we haven't known each other long. Certainly not long enough for me ask this, but the truth is, I'm in love with you. I think I was the minute I saw you on that verandah. And maybe we don't yet love each other the way an engaged couple should, but I know that I can't stop thinking about you, and the thought of being traded and moving to Chicago—"

"Traded? Moving? What are you talking about?"

"Red! I'm in the middle of something here!"

She closed her mouth.

"So, it looks like I might be getting traded, maybe even to the Sox. Like I said, I can't bear the thought of leaving you behind, so I was wondering…"

She held her breath as he reached into his coat pocket. He produced a little velvet box. "Red, will you do me the honor of marrying me?"

Oh. My. He opened the box. A simple silver band with a chip of a diamond lay in the center of it. She stared at it.

"I know it's not very big, but who knows. Maybe I bat in a few more homers next year, land myself an end-of-the-year bonus—"

"Shh, Guthrie." She put her hand over his. "It's beautiful." She took the box, ran her finger over the ring. Oh, how she'd like to try it on. Keep it on. She looked down at him, those kind green eyes searching hers, and she saw in them a future filled with a home and children, and—

"I told you, I'm not the marrying kind, Guthrie. I'm a chorus girl, and I'm headed for show business, and—"

But he was shaking his head. He got up, took her face in his hands. "Red, you're an amazing, beautiful woman, and I would love to spend the rest of my life with you. You're exactly the marrying kind."

What girl did he see? Because she saw a good man giving out his heart to a woman who didn't know what to do with it. Who perhaps didn't have the capacity to love him. Hadn't she just been shopping for Cesar's birthday party? And three months ago, she'd been ready to give her heart away to Dashielle Parks.

"I'm a good-time girl," she said, shaking her head. "I think it would just end in heartbreak, Guthrie."

"What are you talking about?"

"Did you hear nothing of my story? My life is a tragedy. My father was murdered, my brother is lost, my aunt recently died, my cousin—who knows where she is? Everyone I love leaves me. And I finally figured out why. Because I'm not worth enough to keep them around. Jack and Lilly could have stayed for me, and my father—if he truly cared for me, would he have destroyed so many lives? Not to mention Dash—he just wanted a girl who liked to have fun."

"Dash?" A darkness edged Guthrie's eyes.

"Dashielle Parks. He's no one, now. But see, people only want me if I can give them something. Like Cesar. But you—you don't need anything from me. And that's a recipe for disaster."

"Oh, Red," he said softly, and tipped up her chin. "I do need you. Didn't I tell you that you're my lucky charm? You're beautiful and intriguing, and I'm thirsty for your smile. You're not just enough, you're everything." Then he bent and kissed her. It was so sweet she wanted to weep with the gentleness in his touch. He wove his hand along her face, tilted it up, and ran his thumb down her cheek. She couldn't help it—the way he touched her made her curl her arms up around his shoulders and mold herself to him.

Right now, right here, she was thirsty for him too.

He tasted tangy, like ketchup, and sweet like soda pop, and when he made a little sound of contentment, it made tears edge her eyes.

Yes, she could love this man.

Until, of course, he left her for someone or something that could give him more. She buried her head in his chest, blinking away tears. Then she untangled herself from his arms, turned her back on him, and walked away, to the edge of the boardwalk, staring at the waves, one by one pounding the shore in a tremendous frothy roar.

He was silent behind her. Finally, "That's a no, isn't it?"

She drew in a breath. Nodded.

She heard him slip the box back into his jacket. Then he came to stand beside her. "I leave in a week, on the 6 a.m. train, if you change your mind."

She wiped her eyes. Bit her lip. Hated her life, her choices, the Rosie she'd become. But that's what she wanted, wasn't it? "I won't change my mind."

Chapter 10

Truman had changed. It wasn't just that he had stopped leaving camp in the evenings after a show to brood in some dark hole where he'd drown away his regrets. No, he seemed more…alive. As if her ability to hang off a wing and put her face into the wind had awakened something inside him.

And, he smiled.

He smiled when he plucked her out of the cockpit to bow before the cheering crowd. He smiled when he poked his head up out of an engine and found her there, holding a feeler gauge. He smiled when he landed after each hop, looking to her for their next customer.

And he smiled now as she came up to him, his shirt sleeves rolled up, sitting on a crate, blue paint dripping from a brush. "What do you think?"

"Lola," she read. "The Flying Angel."

"If you don't like it, we can change it. It's just that you told me the first time you went flying, it was in a plane called Lola. I thought…" He shrugged. "I thought you'd like it."

She had told him about Paris and the plane, and conveniently left out Rennie, whom she thought about so rarely, what with learning new tricks and handholds, ferrying the equipment from one town to the next, repairing planes, promoting shows—in fact, she couldn't remember the last time Rennie had edged into her mind. So, "Yes, I like it." She squatted down beside him, took the paintbrush. "But the *L* needs a bit of flair." She added a curl and extended the bottom line of the L across the sign, under the word Angel. "It's a pin curl." She handed the brush back to him, and again he smiled.

Her stomach could do a barrel roll off that smile.

"We're about ready to head out—I just wanted to fix the sign before the next show."

"What's Moseby going to think?" She'd been writing every week to the hospital in Detroit Lakes, where Eddie had rented a small house and started working as a mechanic. Moseby still recuperated, her leg and hip in traction, her ribs on the mend, her broken arm in a cast.

"I think Moseby will be relieved that we have a new angel. She isn't unaware of the costs of this show."

"The show must go on, right?"

"There's my star performers!" Marvel strode up to them, his suit coat off, his sleeves rolled up. "I'm leaving for Eau Claire. I'll see you there." He handed Lilly a flyer. "Thought you'd like to see the new lineup."

She read the bulletin. "An Air *Pageant*?"

Truman stood up next to her. "Air races, daredevil stunts, parachute drops, mock battles, and…an aviation ball?"

"The Eau Claire city leaders are partnering with us on this event. They already have our bulletin, and their Lions Club is selling advance tickets. We'll have a sell-out crowd."

"I guess that means steak and flowers for you, darlin'," Truman said as he handed the flyer back to Marvel.

"Just teach me to fly."

He regarded her for a moment.

"You promised, Truman."

He made a face, but she saw acquiescence in it. "I guess you're ready. Get your gear."

She nearly sprinted to the pile where they'd stashed their gear while dismantling the tent. Grabbing her helmet and goggles, she stowed her bag into the cockpit then reached for her canvas jacket. Despite the early August heat, a cool wind shifted through the trees. And in the sky, the wind could be brutal, even if it was warm on the ground.

Truman came up behind her, his jacket open, his gloves tucked in his belt. He tugged on his helmet.

"Here's how flying works. As the air flows over the top of the wing, the wind separates. Top layer has to travel faster, creating lower pressure above the wing. Planes are literally sucked into the sky by the low pressure created by the vacuum of air as it travels over the wing. The pressure causes the lift and pulls the plane up. Your job is to maintain enough airspeed to keep low pressure above the plane. Get in."

She climbed into her cockpit while he boosted himself onto the wing, pointing out the controls inside. "This is your stick, but it only controls your flaps. It noses the plane up and down. You steer with the pedals at your feet. Give it a try."

She moved the stick back and forth then tried the pedals.

"This is a tail dragger, so as you go down the runway and pick up speed, the tail comes off the ground. That's when you pull the stick back and it'll take you up. The key is to go full throttle on takeoff."

He reached in and flicked up the magneto switch. "We have contact. I'll prop it. Remember, stick goes forward to nose down, back to ascend. To slow down, you pull back, to speed up, nose down."

"I'm flying *now*?"

"Why not?" He pulled down his goggles. "Just don't take off without me."

He snapped the propeller and the spark caught, jerked the engine to life. The plane began to bump across the ground with the power of the prop. Truman jumped inside, leaning over to talk in her ear.

"The crosswind could shimmy the plane, or even cause you to ground loop. As you're taking off, steer into the wind!"

"I'm taking off?"

"Let's go, New York!"

Wait a doggone minute— "I can't—"

"Yes you can! You were born to fly. Take us into the air. I'm right behind you."

She stared at the controls—the throttle, the stick, the pedals... not sure where to—

"Push the throttle forward, get us to the landing strip!"

She pushed the throttle away from her and steered with her feet toward the landing strip. "Now, center it up and push the throttle forward again, all the way. Remember not to pull back on the stick until the tail is up."

"How—?" She held her breath and eased the throttle forward. The plane began to shimmy and pick up speed. She held onto the throttle and the stick as it thundered down the runway.

And then she felt it, the tail rising in the back, and realized that yes, she recognized the feeling. Had experienced exactly this rhythm every time Truman took off. She eased back on the stick and...

They began to rise.

"Steer into the wind!"

The plane began to drift to the right so she veered it left with the pedals as she continued to work the stick. They rose above the strip, clearing the outbuildings, then the trees. Higher, until the runway turned to a ribbon below them.

"Now, head south!"

South? Which way was south? But flying with Truman had also taught her navigation—enough to know where the sun was, and how to point the plane in the right direction. She felt him take control of the stick as they banked south. She leveled it off.

And just like that, she was flying. The stick rumbled in her hands, her feet shimmering on the pedals. But she had control of this plane and...

She did belong in the heavens.

She breathed in the power of it, that ethereal sense of freedom. Above, the sky had turned such a rich blue she could drink it in, and the sun on her face nourished her.

She'd worry about landing later.

Out of the corner of her eye, she saw another red and white plane, THE FLYING STARS painted on the tail. Beck waved to her.

She lifted her hand to wave back. One-handed flying. Next she'd be doing loops.

She kept Beck on her right wing and followed him as they left Spooner and hopped from lake to lake on their map, south to Eau Claire.

Her hand grew numb with the buzzing of the stick, but as her confidence grew, she dove, then climbed, then dove. She tried to turn once, pushing the pedals, but the plane seemed to slip in the air, as if it might be on a skidded surface. Truman barreled over the back of her seat and grabbed the stick, moving it with the turn. They banked, and the force settled her back into her seat.

He patted her on the shoulder as he sat down, and she caught her heart before it slid out of her chest.

She practiced banking until she had that too, and finally the Eau Claire airport appeared below. The landing strip was a wide river, and Beck settled his boat easily upon the tarmac, pulling up beside the small wooden hangar.

She could hear her own breathing in her ears. Certainly Truman didn't expect—

She felt another tap then the controls leaped to life under her hands. She wanted to kiss him.

Or...something. The thought swept through her as she let go of the controls and Truman landed the plane. Kiss him. Or throw her arms around him, or…

No. She couldn't have feelings for Truman. She knew better than to fall for a flyboy. She'd heard the rumors—women called them sky gypsies because they stole hearts then flew away.

No, she wasn't giving away her heart to another pilot. After Rennie, she was smarter than that. They were too unpredictable, could too easily break her heart. Besides, Truman would always love flying more than he did any woman.

He taxied them over to the grass where Beck was already climbing out of his plane. Behind them, Marvel and Dan landed on the strip.

She climbed out before Truman could help her and stripped off her helmet.

He landed next to her on the grass. "You're a natural, New York. You belong up there. You're amazing—you can do anything you put your mind to. Wing walk, fly. What's next?" His grin was white against his tanned, handsome face.

She managed to smile back. "A suicide loop?"

"Forget it. But you did great on that coordinated turn. Just have to watch the bubble. Next time, maybe you'll land."

Next time. She nodded, too aware of how the breeze brought his scent to her, too aware that yes, she wanted to throw her arms around him, to thank him for keeping his promise.

Too aware that she would have to work hard—very hard—not to fall in love with Truman Hawk.

They set up camp beside the hangar and waited for the truck to arrive. Sometimes, it took a day or two for Rango to find the right roads to their destination. But he pulled in shortly after twilight with their gear and supper.

"The town's already buzzing about the show," Marvel said as he drove them in for dinner. A real dinner. And a real hotel. With a real bed.

Pre-ticket purchases must have been lucrative. "They can't wait to see Lola, the Flying Angel."

Lilly smiled, her gaze shifting to Truman. He wore that strange expression again, the one she longed to untangle.

They dined at the Chestnut Hill Supper Club on roast chicken and potatoes. Grand windows overlooked the Chippewa River, and a fire crackled in the magnificent river-stone hearth. For a moment, Lilly's life in New York returned to her in the white-gloved waiters, the gold chandeliers, the fancy flappers with their sequins and feathers striding in on the arms of dapper men in tuxedos. She saw herself in the dress Rosie had purchased in France, the one with the embroidered poppies, saw pin curls in her hair, perhaps captured by a feather headband.

From this vantage point, she could admit to liking the look.

She should write to Rosie. Tell her where she was, that she had learned to fly. But her cousin might betray her to Oliver, and the last thing she needed was Mr. Stewart showing up to drag her home like a child.

Only, she wasn't a child, not anymore. She sat at the table with her fellow performers, a part of the show. She'd helped pay for this meal, and not because of Oliver's help.

"A toast," Marvel said, and picked up his glass. "To the Flying Stars and their newest angel."

She picked up her glass, and Truman added, "To a safe show tomorrow." He met her eyes, a shine in his.

Marvel had secured them all rooms at the Fairmont Hotel downtown, and he himself escorted Lilly to her room. "We're all retiring early, darlin'," he said as she made a face. "You can dance tomorrow night." He winked, and she wasn't sure what to make of it.

The dance. She sank down on the edge of the eyelet coverlet of the bed and stared in the mirror. She looked scraggly, thanks to her helmet, and had raccoon eyes—pockets of white around them, the rest of her face a dark tan. She'd lost weight, it seemed, but in her trousers she couldn't tell. Her nails were dirty, grease dug into the pores of her hands.

She looked like a man.

Marvel answered on the second knock. He was already in his T-shirt. "I told you, we're staying in."

"I need my pay. At least for the last few weeks. I know you have it, Marvel, and I need it."

He pulled up his suspenders, leaned on the door. Once upon a time, he'd been a daredevil flyer like Truman, but promoting the show had added a paunch to his gut, a sag in his face. "Why?"

"I don't have to tell you why. It's my money."

"Sure it is, doll, but we need enough for gas and these fancy digs—"

"These fancy digs are your choice, not mine. But if you must know, I need a dress."

He raised an eyebrow.

"You don't want Lola the Flying Angel to show up in a flour sack tomorrow night, do you?"

He disappeared into his room while she waited at the door. He returned with a handful of dollars. "That's last week's take. I'm going to have to owe you the rest."

"Yes," she said. "You will."

She took a bath and scrubbed everything, picking the oil out of her fingernails.

What she needed was a hairdresser. Or Rosie. She knew how to make perfect pin curls. Sneaking out of her room right after breakfast the next morning, she left a note for Marvel, telling him she'd meet him at the field. The hotel clerk helped her place the call, allowing her access to the back office. She gave the number to the operator and heard it ringing on the other side of the country.

Amelia, her aunt's housekeeper, answered. "Worth residence."

"Amelia? It's—it's Lilly."

She heard an intake of breath. "Miss Lillian. We've all been so worried, your stepfather is here—"

"I'm calling to talk to Rosie. Is she in?"

Silence, then Amelia said, "Perhaps it is best if you discuss this with your aunt Jinx."

His tone tightened her chest. "Why? What's happened to Rosie?"

"Nothing, ma'am. She's well. Only…Miss Worth is currently unavailable, but I expect her back within the hour. Perhaps I could get a number?"

"Amelia, where is Rosie?"

Silence.

"I'll hang up and never call again."

"She's no longer in touch with us. I believe she's a showgirl in the city somewhere."

A showgirl?

"Thank you, Amelia."

"Where can we reach you, ma'am, if I may ask."

"Tell Aunt Jinx I'm well." She hung up before the desire to pour out her adventures to someone—even Amelia—might prove too tempting.

The barbershop had a line of men but posted a sign: HAIR BOB-BING, OUR SPECIALTY.

She waited, poring through a magazine, then pointed to the picture on the front cover when they called her name.

Fischer's dress shop had a number of styles, nothing Rosie might fawn over, but Lilly found something she could wear—a black dress with silver beading along the bodice and a drop waist, with a skirt made of long ribbons of flowing fabric.

If only she still had her pearls. Instead, she purchased a long silver scarf.

And gloves. Her mother had taught her that much.

Her fancy New York shoes would have to do. She had already scrubbed them in the sink, turning them a silvery gray.

She hid the trousseau in her hotel room, tucked her new hairdo into her helmet, and danced on the wings of Truman's airplane to thunderous applause.

She didn't remove her helmet all afternoon.

She couldn't bear to ride in Marvel's truck to the dance, so she hired a cab with the last of her allowance. The stars overhead glittered like diamonds cast before her, and the classical music of an orchestra drifted out onto the lawn as she exited the cab.

She'd forgotten the allure of looking like a woman, of wearing silk stockings, even if she had rolled them down below her knee, and smelling of a freshly picked bouquet. She would have to start demanding better digs, perhaps her own tent.

Although she could admit to loving the romance of sleeping under the wing of her airplane, counting the shooting stars.

A gloved footman opened the door for her. Inside the dining hall where she'd eaten last night, women and men dressed in their Sunday best danced, others sat at tables, hopefully discussing the day's show. She spotted Marvel seated with two men, probably the local Lions Club members.

She smoothed her dress, more nervous, suddenly, than when she'd climbed out onto the wing of Truman's plane, and stepped into the ballroom.

Right then, for a moment, she became Lillian Joy Hoyt Stewart again, daughter of an heiress. The music twined around her, and her finishing school lessons returned to her, useful for the first time. She recognized the waltz as an Irving Berlin tune. Her mother loved to play it on the piano. From the stage, a crooner pealed out the sad words. "The birds ceased their song, right turned to wrong, Sweetheart, when I lost you."

"Jeepers, Lilly, you sure do clean up." Rango, freshly bathed and in a clean white shirt and pair of wool pants, his dark hair brilliantined back to a shiny cap, came sauntering up to her from the open porch on the side. "I barely recognize you."

"Is that a compliment?"

He smiled, something like chagrin on his face. "Yep." He glanced at the dance floor, back to her. "I'm useless, except for the spiked punch. I can't dance a lick."

"That's okay, Rango. I don't need to dance."

"Yes, actually, you do."

She knew Truman's voice so well, it seemed impossible that it might have such an effect on her. A deep, calm voice, the kind that could reel her back to the cockpit or make her laugh with stories of flying. This voice could curl deep inside her and turn her body weak.

Lilly turned. "Hello, Truman." She smiled, something she dug out of her finishing school years also, because it felt unnatural and too bright.

He made it difficult to breathe. Truman had turned into a New York banker, bathed, his hair combed back except for that dangerous, annoying lock that tickled his blue eyes. And where did he get that suit, not to mention the tie, the silver vest, the fedora?

He looked...dapper.

And the look he gave her matched the mischief in his smile. He ran his eyes down her, back up, pursing his lips. "Wowsa, doll, you *are* from New York, aren't you?"

Oh. "I..."

He leaned close, his lips right next to her ear. "You take my breath away." Then he held out his arm. "I, unlike Rango, know how to dance. If your card isn't filled up...?"

"I can sneak you in," she said, and let him sweep her to the dance floor.

He indeed knew how to waltz. Then, the band changed tempo. "Do you know how to foxtrot?"

"Of course," she said, and thanked Oliver for the first time for tormenting her with dance lessons.

A soft breeze finally lured them out on the verandah and Truman fetched her a glass of punch. "Spiked?"

"You're safe," he said. They walked out, down to the river, and watched it sparkle under the moonlight.

"It was a good day, a good crowd," Lilly said.

"They loved you," he said.

She searched for a falling star.

"Do you suppose you ever might…" He sighed and looked away. "Ever might consider opening up your own show?"

She couldn't help the laugh. "With what? My own wings?"

He gave her a wry smile. "No, with—with me."

"You have a plane I don't know about?"

"Not yet." He seemed suddenly so…so *not* Truman, it rattled her. Question, even fear in his eyes.

No, he couldn't be serious. Start their own show? "I—I like flying, but I'm headed to Montana. I have to get back there."

He nodded, stared away from her. Finally, "Why? Why is it so important to get back to some ranch you haven't seen in seven years?"

She turned to look at the club, saw others drifting out into the night. Beck was on the verandah with a blond, leaning in, one hand perched on the railing behind her.

"Have you ever seen a buffalo, Truman?"

He glanced at her, frowning.

"They're really large cows that roamed the prairies, once upon a time. They're huge, about two thousand pounds, and they look like large, docile animals. They graze peacefully in their pasture for years. Every once in a while, however, they get a wild hair and have to roam, and when they get it in their blood, they can push down any fence, or traverse almost any obstacle. They're bullheaded. And yet, sometimes, when the pioneers crossed the country, they traveled for miles with them, tame as cats. "

"And you know this how?"

"I'm one-fourth Crow Indian."

"What?"

"Crow. My father was half-blood, and my grandmother, full Crow. My mother was a socialite from New York who ran away from a forced marriage. She fell in love with my father and married him. He died before I was born."

"I'm sorry, Lilly."

"It was a long time ago. But the point is, my grandmother knew the buffalo were being killed to the point of extinction, so she started a private herd. They live to be about thirty-five years old, so some of the calves who were born under her hand, and my father's hand, were the same ones I tended."

"You herded buffalo?"

"I love buffalo. They're majestic animals. But the important thing is that they were being hunted, and they needed a safe place. We gave them that, and if my stepfather sells the ranch, they'll have nowhere to go. That's another reason why I have to return. My grandmother intended to protect the herd, and that's what I'm going to do."

"You'd give up flying to protect a herd of buffalo?"

"I'd give up flying to be a part of my family's legacy."

He stared into the night. "I came from a family of farmers. I think they wanted the same for me. But I wanted something bigger for my life." A muscle pulled in his jaw when he turned to her. "You made me see, for the first time, what that might be."

He touched her face, running his thumb down the side of it. "You really are breathtaking, Lilly," he said softly. "I can't keep up with you.

You're brave and smart and…we're a good team, right? We put together a spectacular show, you and me."

"I—I don't know." She pressed her hand to her forehead, moved away from him, but he caught her, turned her.

"We could save our money—I already have a stash put away—and I could buy Eddie's plane from Marvel. I know he needs the cash. And then…then one day we fly away. We start our own gig. We'd make a name for ourselves."

"Hawk and Lola?" She tried to make light of it, to temper the earnestness in his expression.

"Truman and Lilly," he said softly. And then he kissed her. Nothing like Rennie's kisses, Truman's had a sweet desperation in his touch, a sort of hunger that she understood. He tasted tangy, sweet from the punch, and he cradled her face in his strong hands, his smell cascading over her, his touch perfect as he deepened his kiss.

And right then, she became a fool and kissed him back. She dropped her punch cup and wound her arms around his waist, holding on. He was so much taller than she was, she had to rise on her tiptoes, but he bent for her, wrapping his arms around her, pulling her tighter.

She'd never been kissed like this. Yes, Rennie had been…urgent. But Truman kissed her like he'd lost her. As if she'd gone tumbling off the side of his plane, only to be recovered.

He kissed her like they belonged together.

Maybe she could fly with him. Maybe this *was* her future.

As the music waltzed out into the night, and as his lips whispered against her neck, she molded herself to him, feeling a new kind of flying. "How about Lilly and Truman?"

Chapter 11

"You got married?"

Lilly sank down on the metal lawn chair beside Moseby's wheelchair, where Moseby sat basking in the sun, a bottle of lemonade sweating in her hand, her eyes closed, her dark hair pulled back in a rag headband. Overhead shone a glorious blue sky, one of the precious few before summer vanished into the sharp winds of autumn. Indeed on the August Minnesota wind, Lilly smelled the hubris of autumn, and a few of the early crimson maple leaves splotched the grass like droplets of blood.

"Eddie asked, and I said yes. I figured, he felt so guilty about the accident that this might be the only time, so I took my chance." She opened her eyes and glanced at Lilly. Held out her hand. "Go figure, he already had a ring." A plain silver band encircled her left ring finger.

"But what about your career, wing walking, the Flying Stars?"

She leaned back. "The fact is, Lilly, once I said 'I do,' it felt right to give it up. I want to stay here with Eddie and make a life, have babies. I never thought I'd end up in Minnesota, but these are good people, and this is where I am, so I'm going to hold on for the ride, with Eddie. Besides"—she looked over and winked at Lilly—"they have Lola, the Flying Angel. They don't need me." Nothing of rancor hued her words.

"Congratulations."

"Thanks."

Eddie and Moseby rented a tiny one-bedroom saggy blue house on the edge of town, but across the weedy road, the lake glistened, beckoning, waves combing the shore. Beck stood in the sand, his feet tunneled deep, the water sloshing at his ankles, looking as if he might be contemplating stripping off his pants and diving in. Rango, Dan, and Truman had gone to town to help Marvel put up bulletins in a desperate attempt to resurrect their show.

"So, how did you convince him to let you wing walk?"

She looked at Moseby. "Convince who? Marvel?"

"You know who." Moseby gave her a look. "I can't imagine that after my accident Truman was thrilled to let you climb out on that wing."

Lilly drew in a breath. "I'm not sure, actually. I found him wet to the gills down at some bar, dragged him home, and the next morning, he took me up. Gratitude, maybe."

"Or maybe he thought you'd get it out of your system."

"I nearly did. It's terrifying."

"And exhilarating." Moseby smiled.

Lilly smiled back. "That too."

Moseby shook her head. "I remember the first time I got on the wing. I thought I was crazy. I held the wires so tightly they ripped into my hands. But I told myself that I wanted this, and I kept hanging on, one flight at a time, until I became the Flying Angel. Still, I can't believe he let you take over the act. I thought for sure my accident would drag up demons."

"He hasn't had a drink since then either."

Moseby raised an eyebrow. "He's up to something."

We put together a spectacular show, you and me.

Truman's words niggled at her. He'd said nothing more about his offer since that night, almost a week ago, as if he'd forgotten. Instead, he found times to steal her away behind the tent to kiss her, moments when he swept her up into his strong arms and took her flying.

"Lilly?"

Oh. She shook away the memory of his kiss and smiled at Moseby. "What?"

Moseby considered her for a long moment, her green eyes running over her face, before she pursed her lips and looked away. "That scoundrel."

"What?"

"Oh, Lilly, this is a bad idea." Moseby reached out, took her hand. "Please tell me he hasn't gotten you into his...well, cockpit might be the right word."

Lilly yanked her hand away. "No...what? No. Moseby!" But her entire body burned. "He's not that kind of guy."

"He's exactly that kind of guy. I love my cousin, but Truman cares only about Truman. Everything he does is about him and advancing his future. About flying. It's more important to him than anything. Even..." She raised her eyebrows, nodded. "You know."

Lilly couldn't breathe, just stared at her until the words formed. "I used to think that, but it's not like that. He..."

"Cares about you? He *loves* you?"

Her tone bit at Lilly. "I don't know...maybe."

"More importantly, do you love him?"

Lilly watched Beck roll up his pant legs higher. Well, it was better than stripping off his britches.

"Lilly?"

"I don't know, okay? I'm not sure I know what that is. I thought I loved Rennie, that he wanted to be with me, but I was a fool. And now, maybe I can't recognize love when I see it."

"I'll tell you when it shows up—when you agree to do stupid things because he asks. Like wing walk across an old, broken plane. And say yes to tricks you know will kill you."

"I wouldn't do that. And Truman hasn't asked me to do anything—"

"Not dangle from a ladder? Because he came up with that cockamamie trick once, and I had to shoot him down."

"No."

"Not jump from Beck's plane to his, midair? Another of his brilliant ideas."

She glanced at Beck, now stripping off his shirt. "You can do that?"

"Apparently, but I told him no. How about the outside loop? He ask you to do that yet?"

"No, and he won't, Moseby. It's not like that. He hasn't asked me to do anything dangerous. I'm the one who's coming up with all the new stunts, not him. It's…we're…"

"Aw, shucks, you *do* love him."

"No! I just have more faith in him than you do."

"I have every bit of faith that Truman will do exactly as Truman wants. Flying is all he has, and he's not going to give it up for anything… or anyone. Just make sure you remember that before he gets you killed."

"I thought you trusted Truman. You wing walked for him."

"I wing walked for myself." She met Lilly's eyes. "Why are you doing it?"

Lilly stared at her. Listened to her heartbeat. Why, indeed. Because… because…

"Please tell me it's not to impress Truman."

Lilly couldn't answer for the way her chest tightened.

"To find the person I want to be," she finally whispered.

"You think you have to search for her," Moseby said. "But you can be that person now, Lilly. Be who you're looking for. Don't spend your life looking for what you want to be, or you'll never stop searching. You are who you commit to be, doing what you commit to doing, not what Truman or anyone else tells you to do." She reached out and touched

Lilly's hand. "And don't you dare let him talk you into something fool-ish." She waved to someone behind Lilly. "Eddie!"

Lilly turned to see Eddie striding toward them over the uncut grass. He carried a brown sack. "Hello, Angels. Saw Marvel and the guys in town. They're drumming up business for this weekend." He opened the sack and drew out a brown bottle, handed it to Moseby. She popped the lid with an opener she had in the stash of necessaries next to her chair and handed it to Lilly.

"Did you see Truman? He went in with Rango and Dan."

"I saw him go into the telephone station." Eddie sat down in the grass, pulled out another bottle, and opened it. He gestured to the tent setup down the shoreline, not unlike their own, the flaps pulled back like curtains. "They started yet?"

"I saw a few cars pull up. They won't get rolling until tonight." Moseby shaded her eyes to look at the spectacle.

"What is it?" Lilly said.

"A revival. There's a preacher here from Minneapolis. Revs up the crowd and starts pouring out the hellfire and brimstone after the sun goes down. Sometimes we can hear him from here." He took a drink. "They've been at it all week. The entire town empties out for it. I guess everybody needs a tune-up once in a while."

A tune-up. She hadn't thought about God, or religion, or church since...she took another drink. *"But long ago I committed my plans to God. I trust Him, you know. And He blessed me with you. And with you, Daughter."* Her mother's voice threaded through her.

"Whatever happens, honey, don't forget who you are. Don't forget the blessings God has bestowed upon you. Don't forget your name and where you belong."

"Maybe I'll go."

"You? Religious?" Eddie picked up a rock, threw it at Beck, who was wading now, waist deep in the water, edging toward a duck. The duck startled, flew away.

"I grew up attending church, it's just that I have a few questions." Like why God had taken her father before she could meet him. And why He'd yanked her mother away just as she started to need her. And while she had the ear of the Almighty, she might add a few questions about her cousin Jack.

Most of all, what had her family done to make God abandon them? Her mother might think He'd blessed them, but Lilly saw nothing of the sort.

In fact, she was probably better off without Him in her life, just like Rennie had said.

She got up and walked over to the water, standing at the edge as Beck finally dove in.

* * * * *

The revival began just around twilight, with hymn singing and clapping. The cars pulled up to clutter the field around the lake, much like the Saturday afternoon air show. Lilly watched for a while from her window, her courage a tight ball inside her.

When the hymns finally seemed to die into silence, she slipped into her skirt and shirtwaist and walked barefoot out to the tent.

Beck and Rango—and she supposed Truman, also—had headed into town for more entertaining—and perhaps sinful—pursuits. In fact, Truman hadn't even returned from town after his phone call, and she dearly hoped she wouldn't have to sneak back into O'Grady's tonight and pry him off the bar.

She understood the darkness inside him that made him want to forget. She just hoped that flying—flying with her—had given him a hint of light.

The grasses by the lake tickled her feet so she stayed nearer the water, padding through the dark creamy sand, surprised now and again by the lap of the waves, chilly upon her dry skin.

Truman cares only about Truman. Everything he does is about him and advancing his future.

Moseby's words hung in Lilly's mind. Along with her warning. *Truman will do exactly as Truman wants. Flying is all he has, and he's not going to give it up for anything...or anyone. Just make sure you remember that before he gets you killed.*

She didn't want to know how Moseby knew this. But this time, Moseby was wrong—Truman hadn't even mentioned her running away with him to start his own show. And, he'd been...mostly a gentleman.

Like last night. After the clouds blotted out the stars, he'd crawled over to where she lay wrapped in her blanket under the wing of Eddie's plane. He'd propped his head up on one elbow, traced his hand down her cheek. She'd stilled, seeing the look in his eyes. Not heat, but something tender. Then he'd kissed her, quick and fast.

He'd snuck away then, dissolving into the night, leaving her confused, at best.

No, if Moseby's warnings about Truman were true, then he would have behaved like Rennie had, right?

Moseby might have faith in his flying, but Lilly had faith in the man.

She wound her way around the cars, the lights from the tent glowing like it might be on fire under the canopy of darkness. Inside, maybe two hundred faithful—or lost—sat on long, roughhewn benches. Outside, a group of men hung onto the tent posts, their cigarette butts burning in the night. The skeptics, perhaps.

The words of the preacher, not quite hellfire yet, drew her in like a hook. She stood on the edge of the flap, watching, listening as a tall man, lean and bony, gestured from the stage. Sweat glistened off his melon head. He'd shucked off his suit jacket, rolled his sleeves up to his elbows, and held a worn Bible, which he alternately used to point with and then reprove with as he read it out loud.

"'For I am persuaded, that neither death, nor life, nor angels, nor principalities, nor powers, nor things present, nor things to come, nor height, nor depth, nor any other creature, shall be able to separate us from the love of God, which is in Christ Jesus our Lord.'"

Lilly slid in, sat on the end of the bench. Beside her, a farm wife held a sleeping baby on her lap, the little boy's blond curls sweaty against his skin, his lips askew.

"You know why, people? It's because when God adopts you into His family, you belong to Him. He stamps His name on you. A name that comes with His protection. And His birthright, which is eternity and the power to live with joy on this earth. It's all yours, just as if you'd always belonged. But the Good Word says that to have this, you must repent."

He looked down at his Bible. "'For to all who came to Him, He gave the right to be called a child of God.'" He pointed across the audience. "Are you a child of God tonight? Are you standing firm in that belief, in His embrace? Or has life pushed you out of His arms?"

Caught in the passion of his words, Lilly couldn't help but scan the room, right along with him. A figure standing just outside the open flaps along the far wall caught her eye. He stood with his face only half-illumined, but she recognized it like she might recognize her own.

Truman.

"The good news is that all you have to do to belong to God, to get the Almighty to stamp His name on you, to climb into that place of steadfast love and joy, is to repent. To see that you need Him, turn around and let Him forgive you. He wants to—"

Truman turned and walked away.

Lilly listened to the preacher outline just how one might confess and the various deeds they might confess, and then slipped out into the night.

Truman strode past the cars, along the beach toward town.

She darted after him, not raising her voice, waiting until she could catch up—

He ran the heel of his hand across his face.

He wasn't...crying? She couldn't stop herself. "Truman!"

He paused, glanced back, and she was glad the darkness hid his expression, because she didn't want to see his dismay. She had the overwhelming urge to pull his head down to her shoulder. To tell him that—

What? She loved him? No, maybe just that they were a team. That he could trust her.

"What are you doing here?"

She caught up with him, until she could trace the outlines of his face, his dark blue eyes in hers, terrible with some unshed emotion.

"I was at the revival. I—I saw you there."

He looked away. "They were making a racket. I wanted to see what it was about."

She slid her hand onto his arm. "Truman—"

"Bunch of liars." Truman shook his head. "That hokey about nothing being able to separate us from God's love—maybe for the preacher man. But what about the rest of us? The ones who make mistakes, and..." He held up his hand. "Forget it. Let's get out of here." He hooked his hand around her elbow and pulled her beside him, across the gritty shore.

She caught his hand, walked with him in silence, her heart thundering.

Finally, long after they'd passed Moseby's, as the moon rose behind them, he spoke.

"My folks were religious. Loved to go to prayer meetings, and took me and my brothers to church every Sunday. My father thought we should all be farmers, like him, and my older brother stayed on the farm to help. He expected me to also, but…I couldn't."

"You wanted to fly?"

"I wanted to live my own life. I wanted to explore the world. I left home when I was fourteen, worked on the railroad until one day we were set up in a small town doing repairs and a barnstormer flew in. I ran fuel for him all day and offered my free services if he would teach me to fly. I spent about two years with him, and then the army called. I wheedled my flying skills into a job and flew Sopwith Camels over Germany. When I came back, I thought I was a hero. I bought my own plane, and by then, I knew a few tricks and had made a bit of a name for myself."

He stopped, let go of her hand, turned to the lake. "Then I went home."

She stayed very still.

"I was so proud of myself. I flaunted my new plane in front of my family, then I took my brother up."

He went silent so long, she had to say it. "Moseby told me."

He closed his eyes.

She touched his arm.

"The thing is, my brother was scared to death, and I told him I'd take good care of him. That I wouldn't let anything happen to him." A muscle pulled in his jaw. "And then I killed him."

"Truman, flying is risky—"

He rounded on her. "Not for me. I knew what I was doing. It was a freak accident and—" His eyes glistened. "I destroyed my family. Sure, they forgave me, but my father died of a heart attack about six months later. Mom, she's never really recovered. I slunk out of town as soon as I was able, and I've never been back."

"I'm so sorry, Truman."

"This is what you gotta understand. I'm on my own now, Lilly. There's no forgiveness for me. What I do, what I make of my life is on me. I don't have God's love. And frankly, I look around this world, and I wonder if any of us do."

His words resounded inside her, sounded too much like Rennie. Maybe everyone who tasted loss wondered the same thing.

He shook his head. "Do I need God's love? I don't know. I don't even know if I want it." He turned to her. "What I do know is that we got something good going with us, Lilly. Something powerful and right. And I'm not just talking about flying." He stepped up to her, put his arms around her, leaned close, and whispered into her ear, husky, his tone vibrating through her, "Marry me, Lilly. Right now. We'll put our act together and set out on our own."

Marry him? She touched his face, his whiskers against her palm, his skin wet.

"We couldn't assemble our own show, could we?"

He touched his lips against her cheek. "Trust me, will you?"

She closed her eyes against the closeness of him, letting him pull her against himself, holding on as he lowered her onto the beach, the sand cold against her legs. "What about Montana?" she whispered.

"We'll get back there, I promise." He ran his hand down her face, his gaze stealing her power to think. "We belong together, Lilly. You and me. Please say yes. Marry me."

Then, he kissed her into the soft sand, weaving his fingers through hers, knitting them together under the stars.

Yes.

* * * * *

Cesar Napoli knew how to throw a birthday bash. He'd closed down Valerie's and turned the club into a wonderland of lights and music and pretty, glittering dames, chorus girls joining the ranks of their cigarette girl sisters, dressed in outfits designed to please the guests—men in Cesar's employ, and other businessmen in town. Thankfully, he'd canceled the peacocks and instead cleared the floor and put a boxing ring in the middle, dragging in prizefighters for exhibition rounds. The famed Jack Dempsey was supposed to take the ring tonight. The place reeked of sweat and cigar smoke and enough bootlegged whiskey to send Cesar to the clink for half a lifetime. Rosie wore the pale pink dress and looked like cotton candy on his arm all night, fetching him drinks, smiling at his lewd jokes, allowing him to occasionally draw her near and put his hand low, past the small of her back.

But she wore a smile, because what other choice did she have?

She refused to consider Guthrie's proposal. Move to Chicago? Become a baseball player's wife? Enter the world of domesticity? No, she was a good-time gal and tonight she sparkled. At least on the outside. Inside, she kept hearing Guthrie's voice, warm and settled into her bones. *I do need you. You're my lucky charm.*

He was leaving tomorrow morning, a 6 a.m. exit from her life. Now, she sat in the crook of Cesar's arm on one of the curved sofas, watching him finish his old-fashioned. Across from him, a businessman she didn't know had pulled a cigarette girl named Nicey into his lap, tucking his arm around her while he talked, gesticulating with his drink. Behind them, more prizefighters warmed up. Soon, another round would begin and she'd have to be on her guard as Cesar mock-punched his way through the match, his fists flying wider with each round.

Not to mention that he had bets on every fight and seemed to be raking in enough green to suggest he'd rigged the entire shebang.

She couldn't follow his current conversation—something about politics or business—until, "Did you hear I'm opening a new show?" Cesar's voice rose more with each drink. She pushed away and looked at him.

"That's right, doll," he said, his eyes obsidian, even fuzzy. He stood up, wobbled, but then found his feet. He pulled her up beside him. "C'mon."

His hand slipped down to hers, vised it, and sent a scurry through her stomach as he pulled her toward the center ring. Then he moved aside the ropes and climbed inside. She followed him.

"Ladies and gents!" The din in the room subsided. "As you know, Valerie's has a new show every season, filled with drama and singing and dancing. And I'm pleased to tell you that I've found our new lead actress. May I present to you, Miss Red Worth!"

Her breath caught as he turned to her and smiled. It seemed genuine, even sweet. He leaned close. "See, Red, I keep my promises."

She threw her arms around his neck. "Thank you, Cesar. I'll be amazing, I promise."

"Yes, you will," he said into her ear. Then he let her go and held up her hand in a victory gesture. "It seems the lady is rather thankful."

The crowd laughed, and her face heated. Still, their applause soaked into her, stirring to life a spark inside. She waved to her audience and heard Cesar chuckle beside her.

"Already a starlet."

Indeed. This was what she'd waited for, why she'd endured Cesar's threats and occasional gropes. Lead actress. Top billing. As his star, worthy of his adoration.

They climbed off the stage as the fighters took their positions. But even as the bell rang and the audience's attention diverted to the fight, she buzzed with the *fait de accompli*. The other chorus girls eyed her with suspicion, but she hadn't given enough of herself away for her to feel shame.

Instead of settling them back on the sofa, Cesar steered them toward his office, behind the bar. "I have something I want to give you," he said.

He closed the door behind him, the sounds of the fight muffling. His office always reminded her of her father's, back when they lived in the chateau. Dark mahogany panels, a matching desk, leather smoking chairs before a marble fireplace. Velvet drapes framed the window, where outside, rain spattered on the sidewalk. A gilded mirror hung over the mantel, reflecting the office back on itself.

Cesar let go of her hand, turned, and sat on the edge of his desk.

"You're very beautiful tonight, Red. I'm sorry I didn't tell you that sooner." He took her hand and pulled her to himself, his lips at her neck, trailing up to her face.

She let herself surrender to his kiss, drifting away to a different place, a windy boardwalk, the smells of the sea. When he was finished, he let her go, wiping his thumb along her lips. "I smudged you."

"I can repair it," she said, producing a smile. After all, she was an actress.

"You please me." He ran his hand down her arm. "You're so beautiful, so refined. Not like the other chorus girls—floozies, really. You've got real class, Red, just like Lexie said." He stood up, put his hand to her throat. "I'm really sorry I scared you a few weeks ago." He let his hand sit there, heating her, rousing the memory as he met her eyes. His were almost black, they held her fast, as if searching for her forgiveness.

She wasn't sure whether to believe his words, but she offered it anyway with a nod. "I should have listened to you."

"Yes." He moved his hand to her face, cupped her cheek for a moment, then turned and walked around the desk. "I think you need to replace the memory of my hand around your neck." He opened a drawer and pulled out a wide, long velvet box.

She stared at it. Held her breath. He came back around the desk and handed it to her. "To my leading dame."

She opened it, and everything stilled inside when she saw the pearls.

An immense rope of them, enough to loop around her neck two, maybe three times and still dangle down to her navel. She looked up at Cesar. "I don't know what to say."

His expression softened. "You're pleased, then."

She nodded, no acting necessary. What a kind thing he'd done. And he did look apologetic for his crimes. "Cesar, these are so beautiful."

He reached over, pulled them out. "Let me put them on you." She turned to the fireplace and saw herself in the mirror as he stepped behind her and put the pearls around her neck. Smooth hands, nothing like Guthrie's—she shooed that thought away. Cesar looped them again, and finally a third time, until they stacked on her neck then fell to a grand loop at her waist. He settled his hands on her shoulders and met her gaze in the mirror.

"There's my girl." They looked good together. Flashy, with her peroxide hair so blond it shimmered in the light, and his dark, regal Italian. Maybe she did belong to him.

She turned and wrapped her arms around his neck, smelling on him the cigar smoke, the starch in his suit. "I am your girl, Cesar."

His hands circled her waist and held her for a moment. Then he moved her away. "Perfect."

She nearly glowed as they exited his office, moving back through the crowd. The fight had finished the first round, heading into the second, and a few guests took the time to congratulate her—a few of the men directing their congratulations to Cesar, with appreciative glances flashed her direction. She tucked her hand into the crook of his arm and held on.

The night folded away into more drinks, more fights, more politics, and the occasional whisper of his lips across her cheek. Cesar kept a firm grasp on her, sending her away only to refill his drink, and even then he looked for her when she returned.

His leading dame.

She glanced at the clock, saw it edging past 2 a.m., and refused to count the hours until Guthrie's train left. Not that it mattered. She belonged here, with Cesar.

She was a starlet.

The crowd began to thin, and then, abruptly at three, Cesar rose and bid everyone good night, almost shooing out the crowd. Men peeled out of corners, cigarette girls attached to their arms. Others left with some of his chorus girls, and she saw Nicey on the arm of her suitor. Mickey at the bar began closing up, and the remaining wait staff collected the debris of the night. The band started to pack up.

Cesar sat on the sofa and watched it all, his eyes blank.

"Cesar, are you okay?" She drew up her knees beside him. "You look tired."

He glanced at her. "I'm thirty-two years old, and what do I have?"

"What are you talking about? You got this great place, a swell show, all these friends turning out to wish you happy birthday."

"These ain't my friends. These are leeches—they all want something from me." He picked up the end of her pearls. "Even you, doll. You don't really love ole Cesar." He watched her with milky, dark eyes, waiting.

Deep inside, a socialite knew the right answer. "Sure I do, Cesar. I'm here, aren't I?"

He touched her cheek. "Prove it, baby. Can't you prove it?"

She shrugged and leaned in, gave him a kiss on his cheek.

He leaned his head back, smiled. "You can do better than that, can't you?"

She grinned, despite the whirl in her chest, then kissed him on the lips. He cupped his hand behind her head, held her there, exploring her lips. He tasted of brandy and smoke, and his kiss was sloppy, but she felt in it a longing that allowed her a measure of pity. He was just drunk.

"C'mon, Cesar," she said when he let her go. "Let's get you into your office and onto the sofa. You need some sleep." She stood up and wrestled him to his feet. He hung his arm over her shoulder but managed to walk on his own to his office. She opened the door, turned on the light, and struggled to help him to the sofa. He kicked the door shut on the way.

He tumbled onto the sofa, his arm still tight around her, bringing her with him. She landed beside him, ingloriously stabbing her elbow into his chest. Her arm was pinned beneath her, the other still bracing herself on his shoulder. He laughed, so she did too, until suddenly, he rolled on top of her. Too fast for a drunk man—this was a move from someone seasoned.

She lay pinned under him, his body large over hers. She pushed her free arm against his chest. "Cesar, let me up."

He laughed again, and that's when she knew he'd tricked her. He caught her hand above her head, pinning it to the edge of the sofa. Then, he leaned close, put his nose to her neck, and drew in a breath. "I like that smell," he said softly. He lifted his head, looked into her eyes. "Do you belong to me, Red?"

She bit her lip, not sure if she should scream. "I—I don't know."

His eyes darkened, and suddenly, he slapped her, a backhanded blow across her cheek that rattled her teeth and bruised her cheek-bone, her eye socket. The pain flashed in her eyes, and she cried out. She began to squirm away, but he held her wrist fast, tightening his hold. The other hand he cupped to her neck. "Would you like to try again? Do you belong to me, Red?"

Her breath wobbled inside. "Yes. Yes, of course, Cesar."

"Say it."

"I belong to you."

He smiled, incisors showing. "Yes, you do."

And then he kissed her. Hard, without kindness, bruising her lips, crushing them to her teeth. She twisted to get away. "Please!"

He held her face in his grip, his mouth at her neck, his hand at her hem. She kicked and thrashed. "No, Cesar—stop!"

But he had his hand on her thigh, and she knew no one was coming to stop him.

Think, Rosie. She heard her heartbeat rushing in her ears as she twisted away from him, only to have his hand burn her wrist, his mouth return to hers for more punishment.

In the thrashing, her pinned arm broke free, and while his hand groped for her clothing, she clawed the floor for anything. Her hand hit the table. She searched it and found something hard.

An ashtray. She put her hand around it, and when Cesar came up for air, she brought her knee up hard. He snarled, and with everything she had, she clocked him across the face. He roared in pain, blood spurting from his nose, onto her dress, now ripped and mussed. He reared, both hands on his nose as he wailed, cursing at her. She scrambled back and landed a kick in his chest.

He went over the side of the sofa with a thud. She didn't even pause to look behind her, just leaped over the sofa and ran for the door.

"Red! You come back here!"

She escaped into the now dark bar, heading for the street.

Heading—please God—for Chicago.

* * * * *

She just had to get to Central Station. Rosie huddled in an alleyway, her arms wrapped around herself, shivering, soaked all the way through to her bones, waiting for the car to pass. She had no doubts that Cesar sent his men out looking for her. No doubts that when he found her, she might not ever be able to take the stage again after he worked her over.

She'd spent the last two hours remembering the stories she'd heard from the other girls. She'd been so naïve to think he wouldn't turn his dark side toward her.

Her mother's words that night outside the Cotton Club echoed inside. *He'll only hurt you.* Why hadn't she listened to her mother—Jinx knew the type, having been married for nearly two decades to a man who abused her. The car splashed water onto the sidewalk, dribbling mud onto her dress, her stockings. She probably looked like a street waif, bedraggled, dirty, starving. Her hair hung in strings around her face, and she hadn't stopped to retrieve her coat as she escaped Valerie's. She had, however, fled with the pearls, an oversight Cesar wouldn't forget either.

The car turned the corner, and she stepped out of the alleyway and quick-walked down the street. The sun had begun to turn the day dismal and gray, the sky overcast with the pallor of death. Rain spit on her skin, and a cruel wind licked through her soggy, ruined dress. The rain had stirred the dank smells of dirt and rot from the alleyways, and she could still taste the tinny rinse of blood in her mouth from where Cesar slapped her.

Another car passed her and she jumped and turned away, but it didn't slow.

Six more blocks to Central Station. Six more blocks to Guthrie and his proposal.

Six more blocks and she'd leave behind Red Worth, actress, and try on a new life as Mrs. Guthrie Storme.

If Guthrie would still have her. She wiped her face, her eyes blurring as she ducked her head into the icy rain. Why hadn't she said yes? Why hadn't she looked into his eyes and let herself surrender to the kindness there?

"I'm not the marrying kind, Guthrie. I'm a chorus girl, and I'm headed for show business."

Not anymore. Not if Cesar found her. And certainly not in New York.

But it could never work between them. Guthrie was kindness and chivalry and sacrifice. She simply didn't know what to do with that kind of affection. She needed the kind of affection that could be bartered, the kind she could control.

But now, she needed escape more. And she was willing to barter her heart for it.

A taxi shot by and she held up her hand too late, only realizing then that she had also left without her reticule.

Four blocks.

She passed an unlit storefront, mannequins in the windows, another with a display of jewelry.

What if she went home? The thought scurried inside her. She could return home, throw herself at her parents' feet, apologize, and beg for their protection. Bennett surely had the power to keep her safe.

Except...except Cesar's hand extended into every pocket in the city. She'd seen the men attending his party this evening. Aldermen and lawyers, businessmen and cops. They all drank his whiskey, toasted to his health. They all owed him favors.

And one day, regardless of how she hid in her home, Cesar would find a way to punish her. Maybe through her mother. Or even... She put her hand to her mouth, shaken by the thought. What if he hurt Finn?

Two more blocks. She tucked herself into an alcove of a building as another car passed, and behind it a delivery truck. She had to get off the street, and soon. She could see Central Station from here; the massive Corinthian columns, the grand clock rising above 42nd Street told her she hadn't yet missed the train.

She just might make it.

She waited until another sedan passed then crossed the street, put her head down, and tried to conjure up some explanation for Guthrie that wouldn't send him to the police, or worse, back to Cesar's club with his fists cocked.

What if she'd simply...changed her mind?

She had. Between Valerie's and the entrance to Central Station, she knew exactly what she wanted. No more show business. She would marry Guthrie and figure out how to help him with his world, his baseball career. Didn't he call her his lucky charm? She could give him that much, and more. She'd cheer him on, like the other wives, and learn how to build a home for him.

And someday, she'd also learn how to love him.

She nearly wept when she opened the massive doors to Grand Central Terminal.

Cesar wouldn't know. He wouldn't guess.

The expansive ticketing area, with the domed ceiling of the skies, the massive chandeliers dripping light upon the vast emptiness, hollowed her out. She didn't see him anywhere.

She walked into the main waiting area, the rows and rows of pews lined up like a church. A few sailors, a family of five, the children sprawled over their belongings as they slept, an elderly woman holding her valise as if someone might run by and yank it from her grip.

What if he'd already left? She pressed her hand against her roiling stomach.

Or... It was only five. Perhaps he simply hadn't arrived yet.

She found a place in the back, a place that allowed her to survey the entire room, and scooted in, folding her arms around her. The cavernous room devoured any heat, and she shivered as she looked for a vent.

"Is this seat taken?"

She looked up at the voice and found it attached to an elderly woman, only her doughy, wrinkled face showing from the folds of her habit. Rosie frowned, looked at the empty bench beside her, the rows and rows of unoccupied spaces, and could only shake her head.

"Very good, then," the nun said and sat on the bench, setting her valise beside her on the marbled floor. "I find it so lonely to wait for the train, and you looked like you might need a friend."

Rosie tried to fit herself back together, hoping the bruise Cesar left behind hadn't yet formed. She noticed the mud on her stockings, the way the gauzy rose-colored fabric of her dress had turned transparent in the rain so that perhaps even her undergarments bled through.

She put a hand to her hair, tried to smooth it.

"I see you were caught in the storm," the nun said.

"Something like that."

A gentleman walked into the waiting area. Not Guthrie. Her heart sank.

"My name is Sister Mary Susan."

"Re—Rosie Worth." She eked a smile from the despair inside.

Sister Mary Susan said nothing for a moment as a family entered the waiting area, the mother pushing a pram.

"Where are you headed, Miss Worth?"

Rosie rubbed her finger and thumb into her eyes and pulled away kohled fingers. She couldn't imagine what a horror she must appear. "I hope to Chicago."

"What's in Chicago?" Sister Mary Susan leaned over, her cross swinging forward as she opened her valise.

Rosie watched a couple enter, the man carrying two suitcases, the woman in a coat and hat, dressed for travel.

Oh, what would Guthrie think when he saw her, bedraggled, dressed for a party? Surely he'd know she was desperate, and then what? Would he believe she really wanted to be with him?

"I'm supposed to meet someone here. He's traveling to Chicago, and I'm hoping he'll allow me to accompany him."

Sister Mary Sue continued to rummage through her valise. Her silence indicted Rosie, and she added, "But he asked me to marry him already. We'd be *married*."

A smile tweaked the sister's lips as she sat up. She held a white wool cardigan sweater and draped it over Rosie's shoulders. "I can't bear to see you shivering so."

Rosie stared at her. Hazel eyes with flecks of gold, they bore a gentle humor.

"Please, just until you warm up."

Rosie nodded, pulling the sweater around her. Warmth seeped into her.

"So, is your young man late?" the nun asked.

Rosie refused to voice her fears. "He'll be here." She played with a button on the sweater. "At least he told me he would. I—I hope he hasn't left already."

"Certainly he wouldn't leave without his fiancée."

"We're not exactly engaged...yet. He asked me, but I haven't agreed."

"I see. But now you are ready to agree?"

Another man walked in, stood with his briefcase in the center of the room, then made his way back out to the ticketing area. She glanced at the clock. Five thirty.

"Yes," she said. "I—I realize that I..."

"That you love him?" Sister smiled. "That God put you together?"

Rosie didn't think God had anything to do with their match. In fact, she felt pretty sure He hadn't been watching any of her activities of late. Still, this was a holy woman. "Perhaps. Guthrie is a good man. Kind. And he cares for me."

"Those are the sort worth waiting for," the sister said.

Rosie nodded, stifling a yawn.

"You look exhausted."

"I was up all night." She hoped the nun didn't ask why, although it wouldn't take much to do the math.

Mary Susan regarded her for a moment. "If you'd like to lie down, I will watch for your young man. Tell me what he looks like."

"Oh, no, I couldn't..." But she was so tired. And maybe if she could just rest for a moment, she might be able to untangle her panic, breathe deep, figure out how she got here.

"He's tall and blond, with the kindest green eyes and magnificent shoulders—he plays baseball for the Brooklyn Robins."

"Does he now?" Sister Mary Sue smiled. "I'm a fan."

"Maybe I'll just sleep for a moment." She scooted away from the woman, lay down, cradling her head on her hands, drawing up her legs. "Just ten minutes. You'll wake me?"

"Of course, dear."

She drew in a long breath, finally feeling the warmth of the sweater touch her bones. "I don't know why you're being so nice to me."

The nun patted her. "Because God loves you, Daughter."

Rosie shook her head. "Trust me, I haven't done anything to earn His love."

"It's a good thing that it can't be earned then. The Holy Scriptures say that when we were yet sinners, Christ died for us. That settles peace in my bones at night."

Rosie's eyes flickered shut. "Please, Sister. You don't have anything to worry about."

She heard a huff of air, perhaps a chuckle. "We all have something to worry about, child. We all go to God hoping to bargain, only to discover we are fools. But it's in our foolishness that we discover grace."

"I'd love to know what that might look like," Rosie said, the darkness closing around her. She still felt the nun's hand on her shoulder.

"Shh. Rest now. I'll make sure you find your beloved."

Rosie was out long enough for the memories to assault her. Cesar, angry as he slapped her, then Lilly on the boat, pledging to forgive her. Dashielle in the garden, laughing at her proposal, Finn's cry as his boat drifted away.

No, not a cry. The sound of a train whistle. She opened her eyes, feeling the edges of her hands imprinted in her face. Pushing herself up, she found the clock.

"Six thirty! I've missed the train." She rounded on the sister. "You were supposed to wake me." She wiped her face, knowing she was only making it worse.

"I have kept my word," Mary Susan said, her face a picture of calm.

"But the train left! Are you saying he never showed up?" She got up, moved out of the pew, hating that she'd put so much into this wild hope of catching Guthrie, hating that she even needed rescue. She stood there dwarfed in the nun's sweater, soggy and looking like she'd slept in an alley, and despised her weakness for putting her heart in the hands of Jack, then Dashielle and Lilly, of Cesar and Guthrie. Of Sister Mary Sue.

Of God.

She put her hand over her mouth and tried not to whimper, not wanting to consider what she might do next, how she might return to the Algonquin, or perhaps straight to her mother's home, dragging Cesar and his thugs with her.

"Red?"

She stilled. Swallowed.

"Don't go. I brought you coffee."

She turned, and he was there. Wearing his ball coat and a pair of dark pants, a tie, his blond hair glistening, clean-shaven, those strong arms holding two cups of steaming coffee. He offered a slight smile, his eyes so sweet she could weep right there.

"Guthrie," she breathed. "I—I thought I'd missed you."

He glanced at Sister Mary Sue, who dusted off her habit, picked up her valise. "I believe my train is about ready to board," she said as she stood. She met Rosie's eyes, hers golden and bright. "So lovely to meet you and your fiancé," she said quietly. She glanced at Guthrie and leaned close. "I believe God would approve."

He would? Rosie offered the faintest smile. Then, "Your sweater—wait."

The sister turned, shook her head. "Let it keep you warm on your trip. I will make another."

Rosie couldn't help it. She threw her arms around the sister. "Thank you."

When she let her go, it seemed the nun's eyes glistened. "It's my pleasure to serve a child of God." She patted Rosie's cheek before she moved away.

"We have a train to catch too, Red."

Guthrie's voice stilled her, and she just stood there, dumb at her turn of fortune. "But I thought the train already left."

He handed her the cup of coffee then reached into his pocket. "Not the train to Kansas City. My mother called and hoped I could come home. I would love for her to meet you." He stepped closer and wiped the handkerchief down her cheek. "You're a little smudged there."

She winced at his touch, pain spearing through her. "Ow."

He peered closer, and she wanted to shy away. "Red, did someone hit you?"

She stared at her coffee.

"It was Cesar, wasn't it?" His tone bruised her, a hiss to his voice.

She nodded.

He looked away, his jaw tight. "Where is he?"

"Guthrie, no. Listen. I—I made a mistake. I should have said yes to you right off, but I—"

"So that's what this is about." He stared at her with such sadness she wanted to look away. He shook his head. "I came in and this nun started waving at me. I couldn't believe it when I saw you there, sleeping on the bench, as if you'd actually been waiting for me—"

"I was—"

"Then she told me to go get you some coffee, and...you don't even have a suitcase, Red. You didn't plan this. You came here because, what? You got in a fight with Cesar?"

She looked away from him, her teeth on her lip, because yes, his words sounded right, but—"No. Yes, he hit me. And more—"

"More?"

"I'm okay. And yes, he scared me. But that's not why I'm here, Guthrie. I..." She closed her eyes, willing herself to say it, finding it easier than she thought. "I want to marry you. I want to be your wife."

Silence. She waited for a reply, anything, but when he said nothing, she opened her eyes.

He had put down his cup on the bench. Had his hand tented over his eyes, as if he might be crying. Or so angry that—

"Yes." He looked up, and yes, his eyes were wet. "I don't want to know why you're here, why you'll marry me. Just that you will." He got up, took the coffee from her hand, set it beside his on the bench. "And in case you need another reminder..." He got down on one knee. "Red Worth, will you be my wife? I promise to love you for as long as I live."

She touched his cheek, unable to speak, and nodded.

He smiled. "Very good. Because I already bought your ticket to Kansas."

She threw her arms around him, and he caught her around the waist, picking her up, burying his head in her shoulders. "I'm going to take care of you, Red. I promise to make you happy."

"I—I love you, Guthrie."

He set her down, touched her forehead to his. "One day you'll mean that."

She started to protest, but he covered his mouth with hers, his hand on her unhurt cheek, kissing her. Sweetly, with his whole heart.

And, she kissed him back just the same, without a measure of charade.

Guthrie. His name was on her lips when she pulled away, caught in his gaze. He took her hand. "Let's go home."

He picked up his suitcase and retrieved her coffee. She took a sip, relishing it as they walked into the ticketing area, toward their platform. Light washed through the half-moon windows high above, like streams from heaven. Guthrie took her hand, holding it tight.

Home. Yes.

"Red. No wonder you fought me. You've been saving it all for baseball."

The voice knotted in her stomach. She turned, and Cesar stood in the center of the terminal with several men grouped behind him. A bandage covered his nose. He pinned her with his dark eyes, a smirk on his face as he advanced toward her. "Did you think you could run from me? That I wouldn't find you?"

Beside her, Guthrie took a long breath. "Leave her alone, Cesar. She's leaving with me."

Cesar raised his eyebrow. "Really?" He motioned to one of the men, who edged up behind Guthrie. "I don't think so. See, she's my new leading lady, and I'd hate to have to close the show." He reached up to the string of pearls, grabbing hold as if Rosie might be on a leash. "She belongs to me. Isn't that right, doll?"

She considered his smile, remembered his greasy lips on hers, and shot a glance at Guthrie. He appeared calm, just the hint of a storm behind his eyes, but she'd seen that look before when he was grappling at Vito's.

"No, that's not right." She jerked her arm hard and in that same second threw her hot coffee at Cesar's face, splashing him with the scalding liquid. He cursed, even as he yanked, hard.

The strand of pearls shattered, cascading to the floor.

Guthrie jerked into action, his reflexes quick as he put his fist into the face of Cesar's driver. She saw blood as Guthrie caught her elbow. "Run!"

She took off, Guthrie a step behind her, toward the gated area. The conductor stood at their gate, and Guthrie shoved the tickets into his hand. She dared a look behind her and saw the driver scrambling to his feet, Cesar wiping his face with his coat, searching for her.

They were through the gate before he found them. "Red! I swear if you ever come back to New York, I'll kill you dead!"

"Don't listen to him," Guthrie said as he lifted her onto the train stairs.

But she stood at the window of their car, watching as Cesar glared at her from the gate, and tried to pry the words from her soul.

Guthrie drew the shade. Then he unwound the remains of the shattered pearls from her neck. They made a well of shiny broken eggs in his hand. He tucked them into his jacket pocket then pulled her against him, his amazing arms tight around her shoulders. "You're safe now, Red. I promise, no matter what happens, I'll keep you safe."

Chapter 12

Finally, they were headed west.

"Lusk, Wyoming?" Lilly climbed out of the cockpit and landed on the dry, dusty ground. A tumbleweed chased the wind down the runway. Still, despite the dry, chilly air, she breathed in the smell of the West—sage and prairie grasses and bitterroot flowers. To the north, she could make out the hazy purple cutout of the mountains against the sky, white-capped and breathing winter upon them.

"Listen, I got wind that Daily's Air Devils is coming in next week, and we need to make sure that everyone in the town of Lusk spends their cash on us. We need the money to head south for the winter." Marvel shucked off his leather jacket, shoved it into his airplane. "It'll take a couple of days for Rango to find us. In that time, I need you two lovebirds to figure out a new act. Something that will really rake in the dough." He pointed at her, then at Truman, and raised a dark eyebrow. "No honeymooning on this hop."

Lilly turned away, heat climbing up her neck. Truman had been rather demanding of their time alone—using their combined cash on hotels and the occasional fancy meal, as if trying to make up for their hasty wedding in Detroit Lakes in front of the local justice of the peace.

A month later, it was just starting to sink in. Mrs. Truman Hawk. Lilly Hawk. The name felt unwieldy on her, despite the fact that slowly she'd begun to feel connected to something bigger than herself. Mr. and Mrs. Truman Hawk.

She said it again under her breath as she pulled her belongings from the cockpit. "We need to get into town and see if we can find a place to stay. Nothing fancy, not with Marvel breathing down our necks. Someplace cozy." He smiled at her, and it could still stop her world.

"Then we should come back and practice something new. Something fabulous."

He turned, still holding her bag, his smile gone. "No, Lilly."

"You heard Marvel. We need to be spectacular—"

"No." He dropped her bag, his. Came over to her and put those huge hands on her shoulders. "I don't want you to get hurt."

She caught his face between her hands. "You won't let me get hurt. C'mon, we can think of something. How about a ladder trick? You could attach a ladder to the bracing between the wheels, with a rope holding it up to the wing. I'll climb out, untie the rope, and swing down."

"Lilly—"

"Or a car-to-rope transfer? Rango could drive the truck, and I'll stand on the roof, you swoop down and I'll grab a hold of the rope—"

"I don't want—"

"Oh, how about an outside loop? You were going to do it with Moseby, remember?"

"No!" His tone rocketed through her. "Listen, the outside loop is hard enough to pull off without a wing walker. That's why they call it the *suicide loop*. No. Over my dead body."

She occasionally saw him like this. Like when Suicide Dan's shoot hadn't opened and he'd had to deploy his second one, barely getting it out before he hit the ground. And when Rango's motorcycle stalled and threw him into the ring of fire in front of five hundred people. He'd been the one to drag the kid out before he burned. Or the time she'd put her foot through the top fabric of the upper wing. He'd grounded them for three days while he replaced the entire section.

"Nothing is going to happen to me, Tru," she said softly.

"You're making promises you can't keep." He turned and picked up the bag and walked away from her.

"I'm a wing walker, Truman!" She ran after him. "It's what I do!"

He rounded on her, his eyes red. "You're just a girl who's getting in over her head. Again."

She recoiled, stung, and didn't follow him as he stalked away toward town.

He didn't take her up later that day as he practiced his loops and rolls. She watched, her stomach tight, as he executed an outside loop, his head twenty feet from the ground. Apparently he planned on saving their air circus on his own.

They'd found a room in a boardinghouse, the iron bed narrow and squeaky. She lay there, watching the night pass, trying to figure out handholds.

She could do the outside loop. All she had to do was hold on with her legs, like she had that day in Duluth. Truman just needed to give her a chance.

A low drone woke her, something rippling into her bones, down to her core. She opened her eyes and found Truman already up, staring out the second-story window. He let out a word she rarely heard him use.

"It's Daily's. They're here, and buzzing the town." He retrieved his pants, then his T-shirt, pulling it over his head. "I'm going to find Marvel and figure out what to do."

She sat up, threw back her covers. "Let me go with you."

He plowed a hand through his hair. "No. Stay. I'll come back for you." He shut the door behind him.

She got up anyway, probably too fast, because the room swam, turned over. Catching herself on the bed frame, she took a couple of deep breaths. They'd eaten something gamey last night, and probably it hadn't settled right.

Getting dressed, she went downstairs. Marvel and Truman sat at the dining room table, their voices low. Truman was shaking his head. A creak on the stairs made them look up.

"There she is, our Flying Angel." Marvel got up, spread out his arms. "What would you say about flying in your bathing suit today?"

She looked at Truman, who appeared like he might openly tear Marvel limb from limb. "I'd say no. But how about Truman and I do an outside loop?"

Truman stared at her, such fury on his face she had to look away.

Marvel looked like he just might kiss her. "I'll add it to the bulletins! Top that, Daily's!" He picked up his hat. "Now, get dressed. We have to fly through town and drum up some business. It'll be the battle of the air shows today, and I intend to win."

He walked out, and Lilly couldn't look at Truman. Instead she held up her hand. "I know you're against this, but the bigger question is, can you do it? Can you pull us up, out of the loop, with me on the wing?"

"Can you hang on?"

She looked up at him. She hadn't seen that curious, enigmatic look for months, but there it appeared again, as if he didn't know, or couldn't understand her. As if she amazed him.

"Yes."

"Then I'll keep us in the air."

It was a gorgeous day for flying, the wind cooperating, and when they arrived at the field, three more planes had joined them, painted black along the bodies, with an emblem of fire on their tails. Marvel was arguing with what appeared to be his counterpart, a man in a suit, hat, and a look of annoyance.

Rango's truck was parked behind their planes, Dan and Beck setting up the tent. Lilly followed Truman over to their rig.

"They just got here, but they plan on flying today. Said that the show belongs to them. Marvel is giving them the what for."

"But we were here first."

"But they sent their promoter." Rango squatted, began to pound in a tent pole. "A few weeks ago. He said, by rights *they* were here first."

"So, what are we going to do?" She gathered the tent pegs from the canvas bag and held the next one out to Rango.

"We're going to give them a show," Dan said, and pointed to the boil of dust rising from the town. Cars, motoring out to the field. "Better get ready to hop."

She handed the pegs to Rango and went to find Truman. He was fueling his plane, his hands greasy from where he'd checked the engine. "Here they come. I'll round them up for flights and we'll have a line across the state of Wyoming. You get in the air and show them what you can do."

There was that smile she knew. And loved.

She propped the plane for him, and he bumped it out onto the grass, picking up speed, then lifting from the ground like a bird. She watched him, her hand cupped over her eyes. He truly belonged in the skies.

He did a few loops and rolls then angled toward the incoming spectators, buzzing by them, wagging his wings. His job was to impress them.

She had to convince them that it was safe.

Running out with a white flag, she waved it above her head. "Fly with the World War One Ace Truman Hawk for the ride of your life! Safe. Exhilarating! Only five dollars."

Not a hard pitch when she meant every word.

Cars lined up, and while the Daily flyer also took to the sky, their ballyhoo drumming up business, most of the cowboys who lined up drifted to her side of the field. Especially when Marvel put up a sign that said MEET THE FLYING ANGEL. She signed autographs as she waited for Truman's plane to set down.

"We'll split today's take, but only one show gets to stay on. The city council will decide," Marvel said as he met them for lunch, handing out the Daily's lineup of antics. Lilly read the menu. "Consecutive loops, tail spins, whip tails, a stall, barrel rolls, and inverted flying. A five-thousand-foot parachute jump. And thrilling, dangerous stunts by their wing walker, a man named Geronimo." She shoved the menu back into Marvel's hand. "We can outfly them and outstunt them. The city council will be begging us to stay after they see what Truman and I have put together."

Truman's mouth tightened into a dark line.

She'd never seen so many airplanes at once taking to the sky. Perhaps it had been like this over Germany, planes chasing one another, twisting, looping. She cupped her hands over her eyes, watching Truman's plane barrel down on one of Daily's; if he'd been a gunner, the plane would have become shrapnel. It seemed the entire town, and then some, had come out to sit on the hillside. Marvel charged them a penny per pound if they walked in. Cowboys arrived on their horses, and they reminded her of Abel and how long it had been since she'd ridden Charity.

The air reeked of gasoline and exhaust, and she could taste adrenaline lining her stomach, rising to curl around her heart. She could do this. She'd already mastered the inside loop and Truman's barrel rolls. She just had to hold on and not look down. What had Moseby said? Be who she was searching for?

Today she would be brave. More than that—a daredevil. Truman's Flying Angel.

Dan leaped from the sky, so high that he was a speck of white. His trick of cutting the flour bag on his back worked to follow his trail down until his parachute pillowed out at the last moment. She could almost hear the crowd begin to breathe.

Then, suddenly she heard her name, and it was time. She paraded out onto the field, watching as the other wing walker, a lanky boy no older than herself, did the same. They waved to the crowd then she climbed into the cockpit. Turning around, she smiled at Truman. "Lola and Hawk!" she said above the wash of the props.

Truman's face betrayed nothing as he lifted them off the ground. As soon as they were level, he maneuvered them in front of the crowd while she climbed out. She always started by waving from one wing, then the next on the following pass. Then she climbed to the upper wing and sat on the leading edge, her legs twined around the rope, her hands holding tight to her lifeline. She couldn't hear anything but the rush of wind, but saw the other wing walker standing behind the upper wing, probably belting himself in.

Watch this. She gave Truman the all-clear, and suddenly she was rolling, over and over and over, a triple-barrel roll. He rolled upright, and she gulped back her stomach, waving her hands in the air. Truman buzzed the crowd once for their approval. Then back up to the sky for an inside loop. She loved this trick, the way he dove straight for the heavens, only to curve them upside down at the top, and then fall back to earth, leveling out at the last moment. She indeed felt as if she might have grown wings.

He buzzed the crowd again, and she waved. Then he flipped the plane and flew low, across the field. She held on, her body lifting off the wing, only the ropes holding her to the plane, her head fifty feet from the ground.

See, they could do this. The suicide loop. It had a showman name too. Truman righted the plane and flew another pass. She watched as the other wing walker finished his course, settled back into the cockpit.

Now. They should do the loop now and show Lusk just what the Flying Stars could do.

Truman buzzed the crowd again, and she waved then shot a look back at him. He didn't meet her eyes.

He wasn't going to do it. But she wasn't coming in until he did. He'd just have to land with her here, on top of the wings.

He buzzed again and she waved both hands above her head.

And then, she felt it—his ascent into the skies to start the loop. She wrapped her legs around the rope, tightened her hold, her stomach dropping out of her body. Then, suddenly, he crested the top of the loop and dove for the earth. This felt different than the inside loop that curled forward. This loop began to duck her underneath, invert her, and if he didn't have the speed, he'd never be able to pull up and out.

She gritted her teeth, too aware that the ground came up to meet her, only twenty feet, maybe less. She refused to scream—it would only jar Truman.

He needed his full concentration.

Again, gravity pulled her from her perch, but she held on, her arms, hands burning. Then, just when she thought she would break free, go skidding across the earth, the plane began to arch up. She saw sky as they started to climb. The propeller churned in front of her, and she willed the plane skyward. It seemed to slow down, to crawl out of the turn.

C'mon, fly!

And then, just like that, they stalled. Fifty feet off the ground, the air pressure above the wind equalized, stopped sucking them into the sky, and they dropped like a rock.

She might have screamed, she didn't know, but she let go of her rope, clawing at the air, as if swimming as the plane fell, exhausted, and smashed into the earth.

* * * * *

She couldn't breathe. Every time Lilly inhaled, pain speared through her, turned her inside out, made her moan. It was the moaning that brought her out of the darkness into the gray wash of the room. She smelled it, the antiseptic, the odor of the dying, and another moan elicited when she realized she was in the hospital.

Light streaked through a window beside her bed, and at it stood a man, wide shoulders, dark curly hair. "Truman?" she said, trying to focus her vision. He turned at her whisper. She took a breath and wanted to cry with the agony of it.

Oliver.

He appeared older than she remembered, lines drawn around his mouth, his eyes. He still, however, held power in his aura, and she felt it as he strode over to her. "Lillian, thank God. You've been in and out for the better part of a week. I got here as fast as I could."

She tried to sort it out, to unscramble her memories. Flying, and then… "Oh no. We crashed."

He pulled the chair up next to her bed. "Yes, it was a terrible accident. You broke three ribs and your collarbone, your right arm, your left leg. They thought…." He shook his head, looked away. "I'm so sorry, Lilly, but you had a miscarriage."

She stared at him, wrapping her mind around his words. "I was pregnant?"

"According to the doctor." He shook his head. "I don't need to ask what possessed you to start wing walking. You have too much of your mother in you for me to wonder, but…" He got up. "I'll be right back."

He strode from the room, and she watched him go, listening to his steps in the hallway. Then, suddenly, something like a cry erupted from the corridors. Loud and ferocious, it wheedled through her, held her fast.

It sounded like a man being broken asunder.

And then...*Truman.* Where was Truman? No. He was indestructible. He owned the skies.

"No." She said it aloud because it helped keep the truth away. "Not Truman." Her throat filled with acid, her chest tight. "You can't have Truman."

"Miss Lilly?"

Mr. Stewart. Oliver's father. She should have guessed. She covered her mouth, a thousand fragments breaking through her. "I..." She closed her eyes. How was she supposed to live without Truman? Without him tucking her into the cockpit, his sturdy hands showing her how to fly, his smile that turned her life whole?

She'd done this. This was her fault, trying to save their little show. Trying to be the Flying Angel.

Sobs bubbled out, and she put her hand over her eyes.

"Miss, why are you crying?"

"I..." She couldn't say it. *I killed my husband.*

"If you're wondering about your young man, he's alive." Mr. Stewart poured her a drink of water. "Although, I think his troupe is about to pull out of town."

She stared at him, his words noodled in her head. "What?"

"Truman Hawk." He sat down, held the glass out to her. "You're wondering about the pilot of your plane."

"He's my *husband.*" She'd never called him that before. Now the word emboldened her. "Where is he?" She let him help her with a drink.

"I suppose he's at the airfield, although I did see him earlier today, right there." He pointed to the chair opposite her bed.

"He survived." Her vision blurred. "How?"

"He was thrown clear. You were attached to the wings, but they broke off and tossed you, also. Good thing, because apparently the plane exploded. No wonder your father had words for him when he arrived." He wiped her chin, and she stared at him.

"They had *words*? What *kind* of words? This wasn't Truman's fault. He didn't even want to do the trick. I did."

"That's not what he said." Oliver stood again at the door, his eyes reddened. "He told me that this was all his idea, that you were against it."

"That's not true."

"Of course it's not." Oliver sat down near the bed. "But it might as well be for the guilt the man is suffering. I saw a man torn up about your injuries, a man ready to crawl out of his skin. I didn't realize that he truly had come to care for you. That wasn't our agreement."

"What are you talking about?"

Oliver glanced at his father. Mr. Stewart put down the glass and turned back to her.

"I met him, that morning when you left Mobridge. He was buying gas, and after seeing you at the air show the day before, it didn't take much to figure out where you'd run off to. I knew you wouldn't return willingly to New York, and I knew that if you left with the air show, it might make it very difficult to find you. So I offered him a deal."

"A deal." Her voice turned flat. She glanced at Oliver, who met her eyes, unflinching. "What kind of deal?"

Mr. Stewart made to speak, but Oliver held up his hand.

"Nothing but information. He was to call in regularly and tell us where you were. I was worried about you, Lilly, and just couldn't bear it if you disappeared again. Of course, I had no idea he'd allowed you to start wing walking. If I had, I would have hopped the first train west. Of course, the news of your marriage should have surprised me, but I was a fool to think that wouldn't happen."

If her chest didn't hurt before, it burned now. "Why?"

Oliver pressed his lips together in a tight line. "Please, Lilly. Truman is an opportunist. He looked at you and saw a future."

"With a woman he loves."

"Perhaps. Or just a girl away from home with a rich father."

Her voice strung low. "You're not my father."

"So you are trying to prove to me." He got up. "Lilly, I've arranged passage on the next train out. You'll have a hospital car, and in New York the best doctors waiting."

"I'm not leaving my husband."

"Funny, because he's at the boardinghouse, leaving *you*."

She refused to let those words coil around her, burn. Instead, she turned them out onto Oliver. "Did you pay him to leave me?"

Oliver closed his eyes. Ran his hand along his forehead. Shook his head. "I often wonder just why you think so little of me." A muscle pulled in his jaw as he looked up. "And why, when I've only wanted the best for you, it's so hard for you to believe that I love you."

He brushed past the bed, past Mr. Stewart, and out of the room.

She leaned back into the pillow.

"He loves you, more than you know."

"He's driving Truman away from me."

"I believe Truman is not the man you think he is." Mr. Stewart sat on the bed. "But, because your father does not want to take you prisoner, despite what you believe, I feel certain he would allow me to take you to Truman. If you insist on staying with him at that time, I believe I can convince Oliver to let you live your own life, however you choose."

She stared at Mr. Stewart and saw the tremble around his mouth. Sometimes she forgot that, if Oliver was her adopted father, Mr. Stewart was her grandfather.

"Please, take me to Truman."

He hailed a nurse, and despite the nurse's protests, she helped Lilly dress. Oliver came in after she'd dressed and, without a word, scooped her into his arms.

She met his eyes. "Thank you."

"I truly hope I have misjudged him, Lilly."

Then he carried her out of the hospital and down the street to the boardinghouse. He came up the porch stairs and paused at the door, wedging his foot in to open it.

Voices tumbled out, and she stiffened, recognizing them. Oliver moved her into the foyer, and she could see Truman and Marvel inside the parlor, Truman's back to her. He had that tone, the one that raised the hair on the back of her neck. The one accompanied by "over my dead body." "You're the one who put the idea into her head—"

"Yes, but you knew that if you refused, it would only make her do it. Just like the wing walking—the more you refused, the more she wanted it," Marvel snapped.

"I didn't want her to wing walk in the first place!" Truman's voice rose, clung to the ceiling.

"Really, Truman? You didn't see that as a way for her to fall for you, for you to get your way? You always knew how to manipulate the women in your life."

Lilly stiffened in Oliver's arms.

"I have to admit, I never thought you'd go so far as to marry her."

She waited to hear Truman say it—"I loved her, I wanted to marry her"—even held her breath for it, but nothing came out.

"Yeah, well, I had my reasons." Truman snaked a hand behind his neck, rubbed a tense muscle.

"I hope they were good ones, because I'm cutting you loose. I'm flying with Beck and Rango south, to Texas, to try and salvage what's left of my circus."

"What—you can't leave without me. I'm your star flyer!"

"A star flyer that cost me a plane!"

Truman shook his head. "No, listen—Lilly's rich. Or at least her father is. He'll get me a plane."

She held back a cry as Marvel considered him. "I get it. Finally this all makes sense. She's your meal ticket out of my circus."

"Listen, Marvel—"

Marvel held up his hands. "No, I get it. I hear the rumors. I know you always wanted to start your own show. Maybe you even planned this."

"Planned on nearly killing Lilly?" Truman had that tone again. "Plan on losing the baby she was carrying?"

So he knew. Oliver looked down at her, his eyes glossy.

Marvel should shrink before Truman, with that tone, but instead his voice grew low. "I was just like you, once upon a time. I would do anything to fly. Maybe even marry a girl I don't love."

"It's not like that."

"Really? Well, I hope you two live happily ever after." Marvel pushed past him, but Truman caught his arm, held him fast.

"Don't leave me here, Marvel. Take me with you."

She heard Moseby's words, richer now with the truth, roil inside her. *Truman will do exactly as Truman wants. Truman is all about flying. It's all he has, and he's not going to give it up for anything...or anyone.*

"And Lilly, what of her?" Marvel's gaze filtered out into the foyer, latched onto her. He gave her a look.

Truman shook his head, not seeing her. "It's time—it's time for Lilly to go back to New York, where she belongs."

She closed her eyes against his words, hearing the truth. Indeed, yes it was.

Baroness

NEW YORK CITY, 1927

Chapter 13

It had taken four years, but Truman had finally landed his own show.

Lilly stared at the advertisement in the *Chronicle*, something his advance man had placed last week. The Flying Daredevils. Seemed apropos, because the advertisement highlighted Truman and his stunts—midair stalls, mock aerial battles, barrel rolls, inverted flying, and, of course, the suicide loop.

And, he'd replaced her with some bimbo named Agnes the Angel.

She closed the paper and slid it onto the desk, staring out the window of her tiny associate publisher's office as the sun simmered between the buildings off the Avenue of the Americas and Broadway, the rays dissected by Macy's, Gimbels, and Stern's, the six- and nine-story monoliths that grew up around the *Chronicle*. The newspaper building now sat in shadow, the statue of Minerva, the Bell Ringers, and Owls draped in darkness even on the sunniest days. Downstairs, the smell of turpentine, graphite, and beeswax rose from the electrotyping of the plates, combining with the redolence of the ink from the rows and rows of linotype machines. Soon the presses would run, shaking the entire building in preparation for tomorrow's edition, rattling her from the inside out. Lilly picked up a cloth napkin and wiped the greasy newsprint from her hands, leaving the smudges in the folds. The torn parchment of an orange skin lay piled on a salad plate, her tea cold in the half-drunken cup, her lipstick pressed along the rim.

The debris of another attempt at her daily column.

Oliver's nod to Esme's request that Lilly join the ranks of the newspaper world.

Lilly wanted to love the life her mother left her, she really did. Wanted to understand how the odor of newsprint, the clatter of linotype machines, the incessant shouting, the roar of the presses, had ignited her mother's passions. How the call of the daily news had driven Esme to launch her own newspapers out West before returning to New York City to helm the *Chronicle*, turning her back on their life in Montana as if it might have been a figment of their imaginations.

Sometimes Lilly thought it might be. She'd long ago lost the fragrance of the West—the sweat of animals, the redolence of buffalo chips, the tangy sweetness of prairie grasses in the wind. She could no longer imagine the Montana sunsets, hear the cry of a wolf wheedle through her mind as she lay in bed.

New York City had finally flushed from her the memories that had stirred her to flee four years ago into a life that now seemed dangerous, even foolish.

Wing walking. Trusting Truman Hawk.

Believing her own press. The Flying Angel. As if she might truly belong in the skies and save their little circus.

Clearly, Truman hadn't needed her. Hadn't even wanted her. Four years, and he hadn't come after her. Had simply flown out of her life, just like she knew he would.

Agnes the Angel. What a horrid show name.

She picked up the paper and dropped it into the wire trash bin under her desk.

"The news not fit to print?" Oliver stood in her open doorway, his arms folded across his chest, his shirtsleeves rolled up at the arms, showing a hint of tan. She knew others considered him a handsome man, his dark hair bearing just a hint of sand around the temples, his body lean and strong from his yachting. She knew he had women who admired him—she couldn't attend the theater with him without the eye of every society maid upon her, without the casual inquiries of even her friends about the state of his bachelorhood.

Oliver would probably never marry again. He still visited her mother's grave every week, still kept her picture on his night table. Still listed her name on the masthead of the *Chronicle*. And, it seemed, in Lilly, he intended to keep every promise he'd ever made to Esme.

She glanced at the paper in the wastebasket.

Now, he stepped up to her desk. "I saw it too. I'm sorry. If I had the power to keep him out of New York, I would."

She knew he meant the words to comfort her, to protect her. Oliver had arranged the quick divorce from Truman, bringing her papers while she still convalesced at home after the crash. She hadn't wanted to imagine Truman's relief, and refused to ask after him.

She just wanted to forget him, to erase the memory of his voice, the way he lifted her to the stars.

The way his final words skewered her clean through.

However, she harbored a secret, burning hope that Truman hadn't raced after her to New York because Oliver had threatened him, or paid him off. She told herself that Truman regretted his rash words, and that after she'd left, he'd searched frantically for her, but…well, now he had Agnes the Angel, and that should shout volumes.

"Let's take *The Esme* out, shall we?" Oliver said. "Escape to the sea for the weekend?"

The sea. That much they could share. Besides, riding the yacht almost felt like flying.

Two hours later, Lilly sat on the prow of Oliver's twenty-eight-foot yacht and leaned back on her hands, lifting her face to the sun as the boat skimmed across the waves, heading out of New York City harbor toward the freedom of the Atlantic.

Oliver stood at the wheel behind her, his crew having already tied off the sails. He had a captain, but Oliver loved to sail the yacht out of port himself, the wind lifting the collar of his shirt, parting his hair from behind, as if he might be racing the sun into the horizon.

But that was Oliver. Always charging ahead to control his world. If she'd learned anything about her stepfather these past four years, it was that he left nothing to chance. Like tracking her across the country and hiring the best doctors to help her find her strength again. When she'd agreed to learn the ropes at the paper, he'd cleared out an office for her and given her an assistant in the faint hope she might find some useful niche at the *Chronicle*.

She spent the first six months reading every article her mother had written, starting with the scandal of her uncle Foster's murder, through the short trial, and then every issue after that, until her mother took on the daily publisher's column, an analysis of politics and society that taught Lilly more about her world than any finishing school class.

Lilly finally started penning her own column. Clunky and far from eloquent, the words simply took up space, but Oliver published her thoughts anyway, as if they mattered.

She had to tell him the truth. She couldn't bear to see her name in print one more day. She wasn't—would never be—her mother.

Esme Price Hoyt Stewart had been brave and beautiful, had been loved by two amazing men. She'd run after her dreams and become the woman she was looking for. Her mother hadn't a clue what it felt like to be lost, to not know—or perhaps even like—the person she'd become.

They cleared the narrows and entered the lower New York Bay; Sandy Hook, New Jersey to the west, Rockaway Queens to the east. The bay emptied into the Atlantic farther south.

She heard Oliver hand the wheel to Captain McIntire, then he picked his way up to the prow and slid onto the smooth wooden surface. Water soaked the hem of his white linen pants, the leather of his boat shoes darkened from the sea. He leaned back, raising his hands over his head. Closed his eyes.

"Listen to it, Lilly. The sound of the ocean on the hull, knocking, like it's trying to get in. The cry of the seagulls, envious." He drew in a breath. "Your mother loved the sea. She'd beg me to take her out, to escape the city, if only for a few precious hours. You remind me of her most when we're yachting."

She tried to smile at his words. Sometimes, out here, she could close her eyes, and she'd be back on the wings, the wind on her face stirring up the taste and smell of the sky, of gulping in so much freedom it could nourish her for days, perhaps even years. "I thought Mother spent every free moment at the *Chronicle*."

"She loved the *Chronicle,* for sure. But it was only one of her passions. She had so many faces—I wish you could have known her better. Longer. And I wish she'd seen the woman you've grown into." Lilly swallowed back any comment. Oliver had been so good to her, she couldn't bear to tell him how working at the *Chronicle* gnawed away a little more of herself each day. But what else did she have, really?

Oliver roused her from her spiral into herself, reliving the betrayal. "Your aunt Jinx has asked me if you might be interested in summering with her in Newport."

Lilly made a face, and Oliver laughed. "I know. Ever since Rosie ran off with that ballplayer, it seems Jinx has made it her mission to marry you off."

"She'll have a schedule of summer teas and parties that I must attend, along with a list of the current eligible bachelors—do you think it's possible for me to decline?"

Oliver raised his face again to the sun. "I do. But only if you have a good reason."

She pushed herself up to the rail as the yacht skipped over the waves. The water, translucent in the afternoon sun, appeared so inky blue it could be the sky, pulling her to the heavens. She sat on the edge, let the foamy spray splash on her bare legs, icy droplets that made her shiver. She'd taken to wearing pants in the office—thank you, Moseby—and even embraced the skin-baring bathing suits fashionable now. Oliver had turned away, his face pinched and red the first time she skimmed off her dress at sea, but had said nothing.

"Perhaps I could fall ill?"

Oliver's laughter rose behind her and she let it inside, let it stir a smile. "I fear she would only hire you a nurse and post her outside your door."

Aunt Jinx did seem to have a desperate need to fill Esme's shoes. Then again, with Rosie living in Chicago and estranged from her family, Jinx had endured too much loss for blame.

"What if I could offer a solution, something a bit less drastic?" Oliver said.

Lilly leaned her head back and looked at him.

Oliver came to sit with her, his hands curled into the ropes. The captain had slowed the yacht, looking for a place to throw anchor. "I need you to go to Paris."

She let his words sink in, searched his face for guile. "Paris? Why?"

The chain for the anchor channeled into the ocean.

"Everyone is buzzing about this Lindbergh fella attempting a flight across the ocean, and just in case he makes it…I'd like someone there who can get an audience with him. Someone like—"

"Like a reporter with the *Chronicle* who knows how to fly?"

Oliver lifted a shoulder. "I don't like to remember how you risked your life, Lilly, but I know you miss it."

She couldn't let him see the way his words worked their way inside, like he really understood her. Like he knew how she stole away to the tower of the Woolworth Building, fifty-seven stories over Manhattan, and imagined herself rousting out of the cockpit to venture onto the wing, to raise her hands to the wind.

"I believe you could deliver the kind of insight into Lindbergh's flight that only a pilot could muster."

A pilot. She knew what it cost Oliver to say that.

"You could check in on our bureau, make sure everything is running smoothly."

And there it was, his attempt to include her in a business that she hadn't a prayer of understanding.

Still, she'd first glimpsed the person of courage she'd wanted to be in Paris. Sometimes when she stood at her window, staring out at the lights of the city, she could trace all of Paris, the molten streets threading their way through the city, the Eiffel Tower like a lantern high above. She could even taste her heartbeat as she gulped in freedom for the first time.

Yes, Paris.

And, Rennie. What if he was still there? She hadn't thought of him in years—not since Truman had filled all the empty spaces in her life. But what if she found him, the flyboy who'd first given her a taste of the skies? What if she looked into his eyes and saw that he missed her?

What if Rennie could make her forget?

Oliver turned away, staring out into the ocean. "Lilly, I know what it's like to miss someone so much it feels like you're caving in on yourself."

He played with his wedding ring, still on his left hand. "When your mother left for Montana, when I realized she wasn't returning, it cut me so deeply, I felt as if I'd never heal. I couldn't stay in New York. I had to leave. I had to figure out the person I was going to be, without her."

He looked at her then, his face twisted, as if in pain. "I…am still trying to figure that out, Lilly."

She held out her hand, tried to catch a wave. "Do you ever wonder why God took her away so soon?"

She glanced at him and the hard set of his jaw as he drew in a breath. "I am just glad I had her for the few years I did."

"But if He loves you, wouldn't He have given you more time?"

"God never promised me a long life with your mother, Lilly. Just eternity. I'm believing His love, that He's going to give us that. If there's one thing I learned from Esme, it's that we are safe in His hands. His love. That we belong to Him, and He doesn't fail us."

The yacht rocked as the waves lapped against it. A gull cried from the skies above them, swooping into the troughs between the swells. The sun pressed upon her face, her nose, trickled sweat down her back.

"God failed me, Oliver. Over and over and over. He's taken everything from me and left me nothing."

He glanced at her, his eyes watering, probably from the wind. "I'm so sorry you feel that way."

Lilly licked her lips, tasting salt.

He surprised her then by touching her arm, something he did so infrequently, it left heat behind. "You don't have to go to Paris— I just thought it would be easier. You need to learn how to live without Truman."

His words landed like a slap. So rarely spoken, Truman's name shouldn't have so much power over her after four years. Not after she'd wept herself dry, not after she'd changed her name back to Hoyt, not after she'd traced the scars of her wounds in the mirror and realized how close she'd come to dying.

But in Oliver's statement, she heard his name echo back to her the wind, and behind it, his voice. *"Marry me, Lilly. Right now. We'll put our act together and set out on our own.*" The wind bit her eyes and they burned. She blinked moisture into them, wishing she had her goggles.

She watched another yacht slicing through the waters, its bow clean and white, the name in red script on the hull, the sails like surrender flags against the creamy blue sky.

"When is Lindbergh's flight?"

"In two weeks."

She said nothing. She got up and unknotted her swim robe. "When do I leave for Paris?"

"As soon as you're ready."

She dropped the robe and stared at the ocean, knowing the bracing waters would bite, burn through her, steal her breath. "Arrange my passage. I'll write you the best article you've ever read."

Then she took two steps and dove in.

* * * * *

Rosie didn't deserve to be this happy, and she knew it. Sure, she and Guthrie still lived in the three-room brick walk-up in Lincoln Park, with the reek of Vinnie's Italian Deli drifting up through her windows in the summer to sour their apartment, the dust from the delivery trucks churning up onto her furniture, the shouts of boys in the vacant lot next door playing stickball keeping her awake as she waited for Guthrie to return from one of his road trips. But living in the dark heart of Chicago, with the dangers of the mob wars, couldn't destroy the seed of joy that had taken root inside her the day she escaped New York City in the arms of Guthrie Storme.

She stood at her second-story window, watching the dusty street, now draped in shadow, lamplights like spotlights upon the men returning home for the night, dressed in suits, vests, and fedoras. Below their apartment, Vinnie ran the grate over the deli window, and across the street, the Fifth Street Bakery turned off its lights. Next door, Mrs. Kaminsky must be frying up pirogues, because the smell of sunflower oil slid under the door, saturated the walls. Outside, she heard the crack of a bat, voices raised in competition. Sometimes she watched the boys out of her bedroom window and imagined a younger version of her husband, the one Guthrie's mom described for her when they visited after his first season with the White Sox. She could see his dishwater-blond hair unruly over his eyes, wearing a soiled cotton shirt and a pair of knickers, darting around bases made of old tires, scraps of wood, perhaps a flour sack filled with dirt in a field near his house in Kansas.

Rosie ran her hands over her swollen belly. She'd expected Guthrie's train earlier, and now the roast and potatoes cooled in the oven, the taper candles waiting to be lit at the tiny square table in the center of the kitchen. However, she knew sometimes the train pulled in late, or Comiskey, the owner, had a sit-down with the players.

Occasionally, the fellas even went out, celebrating a win at one of Chicago's dark, seedy gin mills, the ones where flappers waited to remind them they were champs. Even the ones who had wives waiting at home.

But not Guthrie. He called her from every city, sent her telegrams, and always brought her flowers, win or lose.

No, she didn't deserve this happiness, but she intended to hang onto it with both fists and not cheapen a moment of it by doubting.

Especially since this time the child inside her had lived past the scare of miscarriage, all the way to eight months of pregnancy. More than lived—thrived, by the way he shoved a foot into her ribs, a knee into her bladder. She'd taken to sleeping sitting up, although she never truly slept from April to October. Not with Guthrie talking in his sleep, or the vast emptiness on the other side of her bed during away games.

The baby moved inside her and she braced herself on the table, blowing out a breath at a small contraction. She'd heard that during her mother's pregnancies, she'd taken to bed for the first duration of the nine months. No wonder she'd been so afraid when she was pregnant with Finn.

Sometimes she missed her little brother so much it made her ache to her bones.

After the first miscarriage, Rosie thought she'd have to take to bed too, but baby number two was still growing, kicking inside her, and she wasn't going to ask any cosmic questions.

She lived in a precarious state of blessing and didn't want to stir the Almighty's ire.

She waited for the contraction to pass before pulling out the roast from the oven. She'd slice it before it got too dry, just the way Flo Humphries, the catcher's wife, taught her. She'd miss the Humphries—apparently after this season, Skip planned on retiring and heading back to Hoboken to coach.

Maybe someday she'd be the team matron, like Flo. Teaching the new wives how to cope with the press, how to massage hot, soothing oil into a man's throwing arm, how to offer comfort when he played a game of errors, or inspire him to homeruns.

She fixed Guthrie a plate and slipped it into the icebox. Then she cut herself a slice of peach cake before covering the rest with a paper bag. She avoided the mirror—she'd become as large as one of Lilly's beloved buffalos—as she sat down in the living room, picked up the paper, read the article of yesterday's win over the Yankees again.

It came after a two-day shutout. Eight-to-nothing, nine-to-nothing, a wretched showing for the Sox.

She could see Guthrie as he took the mound yesterday, his hat over his close-cropped blond hair, his jaw tight, his green eyes missing nothing. Early in their marriage, she'd found him pacing the living room on the eve of a game, the fourth in an at-home series, holding the wastepaper basket.

No wonder he didn't drink with the guys between games.

He'd be pressed and clean, his uniform shiny and white, THE SOX written on his chest. The band would be playing, warming up for the national anthem, and the hawkers would walk by with popcorn and cotton candy, hot dogs and beer. If they were at home, she'd wear her best dress, something that Guthrie could spot when he searched the stands for her, right before the first pitch. She usually stood, but didn't wave, allowing his smile to seep through her and remind her that, indeed, she was his lucky charm.

She'd started to believe it after the first season, when he'd batted a .347 and pitched two no-hitters. Comiskey offered him a bonus if he managed thirty regular season wins—Guthrie came close with twenty-seven. This year, he'd helped shut down the Tigers with two wins out of a four-game series, and managed to pull out a couple of games from the Indians and the Browns. But the Yanks...the Yanks always managed to best them.

Until yesterday. She imagined him on the mound, firing knuckleballs and sliders, fastballs and curves, his body strong and sharp, his reflexes tight as he threw men out at first or stared them down over the plate. *Baseball is all about strategy. You gotta outthink the guy at the plate. You can't let him get in your head.* That first year, he'd taught her everything he knew about the game, and she learned how to be a ballplayer's wife. How to sort out myth from superstition, how to ignore the bad press, the bimbos, and the scandal. She knew which players cheated on the road, and which stayed true. And, she knew that she had married a man of honor.

It took her a while to recognize.

Even longer to trust.

But Guthrie never came home with anything but the smell of popcorn, hot dogs, dust, and sweat on his clothes and an honest game on his tanned face.

And they had a perfect life ahead of them. She set her empty cake plate on the table and patted her stomach as she rocked the baby inside to sleep. A perfect life.

If Guthrie won his allotted thirty games, he'd land that ten-thousand-dollar bonus and maybe they could buy a little house outside the city. Sheila and Joe had a house like that, something with a patch of grass out back where Joe could teach his son how to catch.

She could already see Guthrie lining up behind little—Claude, or maybe Phillip—circling his arms around him, helping him hold the bat. "You're going to have his eyes, aren't you, little one?" She heard more shouting from the yard. Getting up, she went to the bedroom and sat in the darkness on the side of the bed, watching the boys scramble around their makeshift bases in the twilight.

Guthrie liked the name Charlie.

Sliding back on the bed, she drew up her knees, curled her hand over her tummy.

"She belongs to me. Isn't that right, doll?"

Sometimes when Cesar slid into her thoughts, her dreams, she could shake herself awake, remind herself that he couldn't find her.

Tonight he had an unexpected hold on her, his hot breath in her face, smelling of whiskey, his hands on her throat, squeezing.

No. No—

I swear if you ever come back to New York, I'll kill you dead!

"No!"

"Rosie—wake up! Shh, you're having a nightmare."

Guthrie's voice rocked her out of the moment where she stood at the window of the train, Cesar's eyes burning into her, his voice twisting her breath dry inside her.

Guthrie. Handsome in a pin-striped suit and tie, still smelling like cologne despite the long train ride. He flicked on the light and pushed her damp hair back from her sweaty face. "Sorry I'm late. I—I had to meet with Coach."

"I missed you." She pushed herself up, into his arms, held him around the neck, probably too tight, but Cesar's voice could still strip her bare.

"I missed you too, baby." He pressed a kiss to the side of her neck. She leaned away and ran her hand down his face, five-o'clock stubble scratching her palm. Then she kissed him.

Guthrie had insisted on separate cars until they reached Chicago. Then, he'd found them the first justice of the peace he could find and checked them into the Palmer House hotel.

She hadn't realized just what it might be like to be married— she expected the vulnerability, but not the satisfaction it gave her to know how he needed her. How she held the world for him in her response to his affection. He drank in everything she gave him.

Now, he leaned her back into the pillows, caressed her face with his hand, rubbing his thumb down her cheekbone as he lingered, kissing her like he had in their newlywed days. She relished his touch more every day, the sunshine embedded in his skin, the curl of his hair in her fingers, the way he tasted sweet, like bubblegum, his chew of choice.

He leaned away, found her eyes. "I don't want to hurt the baby."

She cupped his face in her hands. "I don't think he'll mind."

"He? What if it's a she?" He stood up and shucked off his jacket, tucking it over a chair. Then he pulled free his suspenders and toed off his loafers.

She leaned up on her elbows. "Then we can't name her Charlie."

He crawled onto the coverlet beside her, and she turned into his arms. He ran his hand over her belly, warming her clear through. "Why not? Charlie is a swell name for a little girl. Maybe she'll have a pitching arm too."

She looked up at him, shaking her head, and he kissed her on the nose. Then he nudged her chin up and found her mouth.

So much for his supper in the icebox, the cake. Apparently he wasn't hungry.

The sun had disappeared, night pressing through the windows, when she nestled back in his arms.

"I can't believe we're having a baby," she said as he ran his hand over her skin.

"I still can't believe you married me, Red," Guthrie said. "I took one look at you and saw a woman so far out of my league I wasn't sure if I could get up the nerve to talk to her. I was this country boy from Kansas talking to this classy lady, someone who by all rights shouldn't have given me a second look."

"You didn't seem to have any problem charming me right out of Cesar's palace and into your arms."

"It wasn't quite that fast," he said. He leaned up, found a lock of her hair, twirled it between his fingers. His expression turned solemn. "Truth is, Red, every day that I wake up beside you I can't believe how lucky I am. I'm afraid that one of these days you're going to figure out how far below yourself you married and send me packing."

"I am never going to send you packing, Guthrie Storme." She kissed him, and it seemed that he breathed her in.

Then, he pushed himself away from her. "I need a shower." He got up and stood in the threshold of the bathroom door, his gaze roaming over her. "And then we have to talk, Rosie."

Something in his eyes—she pulled the sheet over her. "What is it?"

He seemed to debate for a moment then came back and sat on the side of the bed, his back to her. Then he scrubbed his face with his hands.

"You're scaring me, Guthrie."

He turned to her then, the lamplight turning his hair to gold, his eyes soft. "I'm being traded, Red. That's why I was late. The coach wanted to see me."

"Traded? But the season just started."

"They need cash, and apparently, I'm the hottest ticket they have."

She ran her hand down his arm, sinewed with muscle. "I'm not surprised. You're only getting stronger. And I suppose this comes with a bonus?"

"A nice one. I might even be able to buy you a real ring, one with a big diamond."

She didn't need a big, fancy diamond. The slim gold band with the dot of glitter fit her perfectly. "Where are we going? St. Louis? Cleveland? Detroit?"

He caught her hand, and then his face twisted. She knew it before he said it, tasted it in the back of her throat, felt it in the clench of her chest.

No.

"We're going to New York City. I've been traded to the Giants."

Chapter 14

If she wanted to forget Truman, Lilly had come to the right place. The moment she stepped off the plane, the memories shone in her mind, like jewels she'd tucked away, afraid to retrieve lest they lose their luster.

She instructed her footman to put her bags in the room where she'd sat at the windowsill, watching Sarah Bernhardt's funeral so many years ago on the Champs-Élysées, reading her Zane Grey book and longing for the wide spaces of Montana. She lunched at the Café a la Paix then strode down the avenue to the gardens of the Palais Royal, remembering how the statues had enchanted her.

The entire city had enchanted her, perhaps, the peonies and climbing roses fragranced the boulevards, the smell of café au lait from the bistros, and everywhere she walked, men in suits and derbies, reminding her of Rennie.

She found herself looking for him, searching for his dark-chocolate eyes, the tweed jacket, the derby that he wore at a rakish angle. She stood across the street from the Café a la Paix, watching traffic, hearing him in her past.

"Rennie Dupree, flyer and lifesaver at large."

"Lilly...Hoyt. Daredevil."

If he only knew. She bought a copy of the *Chronicle* in English and walked the length of the boulevard, over the bridge and into the gardens of Luxembourg, along the pathways brushed by eager willows, inhaling the cherry blossoms. She sat at the lake, watching children float sailboats into the glistening waters, the sun turning the water molten until the rays slipped behind the regal skyline of Paris.

She took a cab then to Montparnasse and stood outside Le Select nightclub, her gaze upon the zinc bar, imagining Hem and Presley queuing up for drinks. The jazz threaded out into the night air, tugging at her, hot and chocolatey like she remembered.

You make me better, Lilly. Make me the person I should be.

Rennie sidled up beside her in her thoughts, and she put her hand to her mouth, his lips suddenly against hers, sending heat through her.

She'd been so young, so fleeced by his charm.

Flyers. She should have realized then the magic they had over her. Truman had only been a younger, brasher version of Rennie, poised to steal her heart.

And probably, this Charles Lindbergh was exactly the same sort. Arrogant and flashy, driven by fame and the pull of the heavens.

Not to mention foolish.

She'd done the calculations herself: thirty hours over the Atlantic, perhaps with five hundred gallons of gas. He must have had to empty out everything but his skivvies to get the plane off the ground. She'd flown over lakes, sometimes fifteen or twenty feet above water, knew the dangers of the air currents that could snag a wing, pull the wheels into the sea.

And last night, as he'd departed, they'd predicted fog off the coast of Ireland.

She hailed a cab and climbed into the backseat. "Five Eighteen Avenue des Champs-Élysées, s'il vous plaît."

"Very good, ma'am."

His English surprised her. "Where are you from, sir?"

"Ireland. Was shot down in France and stayed." He glanced back at her, smiling. "Fell in love with my nurse."

"Of course you did," she said. He motored her over the Rue du Bac bridge and then down the Champs-Élysées. Across the river, the Eiffel Tower arched over the city, shiny and bright.

A lighthouse.

"Any news on Lindbergh?" she asked, leaning forward. All of France buzzed about the attempt; some said he had even left early in hopes of beating the weather.

"Aye, they spotted him off the Emerald Coast a few hours ago."

She let the words sink in.

"Can you take me to Le Bourget, instead?"

"Oh, ma'am, there's a hundred thousand people there—you won't see a thing—"

"Please, sir. I made a promise to my father to watch Lindbergh land." The words just slipped out. Her father.

He gave her a smile. "Ah, that I might be so fortunate someday to have my daughter think so much of me."

Like eyes, the windows along the boulevard watched her, bright and unblinking, their reflection glistening upon the cobbled street.

"I can't believe this Lindbergh has the spine to fly all the way over the Atlantic. Not with two Frenchmen that went down only last month. Daft."

She made a noise that sounded like agreement.

"Or maybe dedicated," he said as they eased out of the city. "There's power in commitment. It turns you into the man you hope to be. The man you can live with. Maybe even a hero."

She glanced at him, noticing now that only one hand gripped the steering wheel, the other absent, his sleeve folded up into itself.

Le Bourget had turned the night sky to daylight with the beacons streaming to the heavens. Cars clogged the roadway, so the driver let her off to walk. "Do you need me to wait?" he asked.

She shook her head and paid him. Her position at the *Chronicle* had purchased a spot for her in one of the hangars and an interview with the aviator when—or perhaps if—he showed. She wheedled her way around the cars—Peugeots and Benzes, along with Citroens and not a few horse-drawn carts and buggies, driven from nearby farms. Adventure showed no social prejudice.

As she drew nearer, the light betrayed the crowd, an immensity of people pressed up against the iron gates that surrounded the field. A row of hangars beyond showed more people—probably the flyers who worked out of the field, along with mechanics, and not a few men in tuxedos—probably local dignitaries.

An explosion downfield startled the crowd and a rocket flared into the sky. Search beacons for Lindbergh. People holding onto the faint hope that he might actually keep his word.

She pushed her way along the back, saw people hanging from the iron staircases that roped up the side of the hangars. She tried to edge her way to the front.

French epitaphs landed behind her, and she gave thanks for her too-rusty French. Still, the crowd seemed to work in unison and closed around her.

So much for her interview. Oh, why had she allowed the nostalgia of the city to woo her away from the field? The one thing Oliver asked of her and she couldn't manage it. Who knew that Lindbergh might prove to be the hero he set out to be?

And then she heard it, the distinct rumble of a motor. The crowd roared in reply until the noise grew above it, thunderous.

Then the silver bird dropped from the night and into the stream of light, gliding. No one moved, no one breathed, and in that moment, Lilly felt it.

The magic. The ethereal sense of being able to rise above the clouds, to see the world as a thumbprint. The power of climbing out of an airplane to stand on the wing, press her hands to the wind, gulp it in.

As if she only need close her eyes and lift her arms and she'd be flying.

She heard him then, as if he'd never left, as if he'd chased her all the way to Paris. *"I guess the only question left is...what are we going to call your act?"*

"Lola," she said softly as Lindbergh's plane drifted down onto the swath of light in the middle of the runway. "The Flying Angel."

Lindbergh's plane bumped along the ground, the prop still whirring, but the crowd caught its breath and surged forward, a mass of people climbing the six-foot fence.

"Stop! Wait!"

But the iron fence collapsed as they churned forward, running toward Lindbergh's triumph. She heard choruses of *Vive!* but only tuned her ears to Lindbergh's prop chopping the air.

"Wait!" How many times had Truman told her to stay clear—she'd heard too many stories of wing walkers and ground crew walking into a churning propeller. "Stop!" She tripped over a mangled, deserted bicycle and went down on her hands and knees.

She looked up just as the plane turned and charged toward the crowd. Lilly screamed as the mob turned, scattering. Lindbergh's plane rambled toward them.

Cut the engine! Cut—but even afterward, the prop would continue to skewer the air—

She found her legs just as the machine ground to a halt, rocking back as if exhausted. The propeller died with a splutter.

Thirty-three hours in the air.

The crowd went berserk as Lindbergh opened the hatch of his plane. They pulled him from the plane, carrying him across the tarmac. She caught a glimpse of him—towheaded, tall, and lean. Probably handsome. Most flyers were, if you added in the twinkle of danger in their eyes.

In that moment, she could almost see Truman, waving, his grin broad and white in this moment of triumph.

Souvenir hunters cut pieces of fabric from the plane—the *Spirit of St. Louis*. The police rescued Lindbergh and delivered him to the dignitaries in the hangar downfield. She followed and tried to move in to hear the loudspeakers, but after an hour, she gave up trying to get closer to hear. She'd hunt him down in the morning, perhaps use Oliver's connections.

Meanwhile, the exhausted *Spirit* sat tended by a handful of gendarmes, the souvenir hunters having been chased away. She wandered toward it and informed one of the guards of her credentials. He allowed her passage to the airplane, and she climbed up on the wing—she should have worn trousers—and hauled herself into the cockpit.

She lowered herself into the wicker chair of the cockpit, still feeling the heat of it, the weight of Lindbergh's body on the fibers. An empty canteen of water lay on the floor near the pedals. Under the seat, a crumpled paper bag rustled against her foot. She took it out and opened it.

Two uneaten sandwiches.

Uneaten, after thirty-three hours. She closed the bag then gripped the yoke, the cool polish of it fitting into her hands. She imagined herself over the ocean, fighting the wind shears, leaning into the currents.

What had her driver said about commitment? It turned regular men into heroes.

And women?

She leaned back into the seat, closed her eyes, listening to the wind through the trees at the far side of the field.

Be who you're looking for. Don't spend your life looking for what you want to be, or you'll never stop searching. She wasn't sure why Moseby's voice, a haunting from the past, found her, but she settled into it. *You are who you commit to be, doing what you commit to doing.*

Oh, how she loved to fly. In fact, maybe one of the local pilots would let her borrow a plane, take it up over Paris.

She climbed out and headed to the flight office. A congregation of French flyers, some of them drinking hot coffee, others talking about Lindbergh's trip, looked up as she came in and found her way to the counter. Behind them, maps of the French, English, and Austrian countrysides, along with a huge expanse of ocean and the eastern American seaboard, papered the walls, with a red thread marking Lindbergh's route.

"Bonjour," she said, resurrecting her French. "I...I'm looking to hire a plane for the day tomorrow."

"It can't be!"

The voice startled her, and she looked for the source. For a moment, she didn't recognize him, not with the scar along his chin. But the dark smudge of a smile hadn't dimmed from her memory, nor his green eyes and the power they once had to turn her inside out, steal her thoughts.

"Rennie?"

"Lilly Hoyt, what are you doing here?"

She had no words for this, not sure where to even start. He parted his way through the crowd and offered his hand and she took it, rough as it was in her grip. She'd forgotten the feel of a pilot's hands, the chips and digs in his skin from his hours overhauling his plane. Truman had those hands.

"Ray, come and see who I found!" He turned toward the door to the weather office. An older woman wearing jodhpurs sauntered in from the next room.

Ray? The woman looked familiar. "I'm sorry, I don't remember—"

"Baroness Raymonde. I'm one of the flyers here at Le Bourget. Are you here for the flight?"

"I'm a reporter—yes, but—"

"And she's come back to me!" Rennie nudged Ray out of the way. "Remember her, Ray? She went to the bullfights with me and Presley in Spain." Around her, others had turned to watch. Probably they could see her face flaming. He wore a sleek leather jacket, longer than Truman's, a white scarf at his neck, derby cocked on his head. As he leaned close, she caught a whiff of something from the past, absinthe, perhaps, and the faintest hint of cigarette smoke lifting into the wind. He remembered her too, his gaze upon her familiar, even intimate.

"I always knew you'd come back to Rennie, ma chérie," he said, and winked. "I've missed you so."

* * * * *

Rosie just knew that any day, she'd come home to their little flat in Queens and find Cesar on her doorstep, ready to make good on his dark promise. Every time she opened the door and stood in the quiet hallway of their three-room apartment, her heartbeat thundering in her chest, she listened for his breathing, searched the air for the aroma of his Cubans.

It was only a matter of time.

Her fight with Guthrie still had the power to stop her cold, shake tears from her. *I want more for you than this pitiful apartment in the middle of Chicago! Pitching for the Yankees means a better life for both of us.*

You just want to be a star. You don't care if it's going to get us both killed!

He'd winced, and she longed to yank back her words.

No, if she hadn't wanted to be a star, maybe she wouldn't have fallen for Cesar, let him dig his claws into her life.

Yet again, perhaps she would never have had to escape with Guthrie, and found this surprising place of joy.

I'll keep you safe, he'd said when he'd shown her their new apartment, the locks he installed on the front door. Such a smile on his face when he walked into the big white kitchen then opened the door to two tiny back bedrooms. *One for Charlie.*

The place came with a postage stamp–sized, weed-riddled courtyard in back where he'd found a secondhand table and chairs, and a front bay window off the family room. In the morning, the sun turned the hardwood floors a rosy gold.

She set her groceries on the kitchen table and slid onto a chair. Her legs hurt, and her entire body had turned into an incubator. What she wouldn't give for a day at the sea, at her mother's estate in Newport, lounging on the patio chairs, a cold lemonade at her merest beckoning.

She unbuttoned her shirtwaist, letting the collar hang open, got up, and wandered over to the fan, turning it on. The blades churned the air, and she leaned into it, letting the whir fill her thoughts, settle a cool breeze over her body.

Two weeks since she'd returned to New York City, and she still hadn't the courage to track down her mother. Because that would mean an apology. And introducing Jinx to her husband.

She couldn't bear to put Guthrie through that, to hear the disdain in her mother's voice. *He isn't our set, Rosie.*

Maybe not. But maybe she didn't want to belong to that set anymore. Maybe…maybe she'd found a better set, a new place to belong.

It didn't keep her from wanting to see Finn, however. Maybe after the baby was born she might introduce the child to his or her uncle. This little one might bring reconciliation to them all.

The baby turned inside her and she pressed her hand against her stomach, sitting down on the sofa. Maybe she'd just put her feet up for a moment, lean her head back. A few moments' rest before Guthrie's game this afternoon.

The noon chime woke her and Rosie blinked her eyes open, a chill running over her from the breath of the fan as she found her bearings.

Guthrie's game started in an hour; he would already be looking for her in the stands. She splashed water on her face then tidied her hair and pulled on a long-waisted dress that stretched over her belly. One glance in the mirror told her she looked like a seal, bleached and dragged in from the sea.

A fine sweat filmed her back as she tucked on a canvas cloche hat, an orange silk pansy in the brim. Then, picking up her fan and her handbag, she locked the door.

She had a vague recollection of how to find the Polo Grounds in Manhattan where the Giants played, but Guthrie's directions tangled in her thoughts, a product of the heat and fatigue.

She got on the Roosevelt Avenue Corona Line at Elmhurst Avenue, rode it through Long Island City, over the East River, through the 60th St. Tunnel until she saw the signs for Fifth Avenue.

Fifth Avenue, across from Central Park, where she'd grown up in the Worth family chateau. Oliver and Esme had owned a home just down the street before her mother had sold the estate and moved into rooms farther down on Fifth Avenue, in the Warren and Wetmore Building.

Lilly might have married, maybe even lived in one of the gallant houses on Fifth. *I'll forgive you someday...* Lilly's words on the boat so long ago could still brush tears into her eyes. *Please, Lilly. Be happy.*

The urge to disembark at Fifth pulsed inside Rosie until the doors closed and the train rumbled forward, the curtains at the windows shivering with the movement.

Guthrie would be looking for her, needing her smile as he took the mound.

She thought she remembered him saying this line turned north, toward Harlem and the Washington Heights district where the Giants played. It took her two stops before she realized the train had veered onto Broadway, passing 48th Street, then Times Square.

As she read the electronic marquees, her chest tightened. She needed to get off, perhaps take a taxi down to the stadium.

She checked her watch. The game had started five minutes ago.

She got off at the next stop—34th Street, and stood on the sidewalk, smelling the exhaust of the Packards, the Fords, listening to the buzz of the city wheedle through her. She'd forgotten the electric hum of the city, the fragrances of the bakeries, the sound of horses and pedestrians and buses. A fever flowed through Manhattan different from that of Chicago. Almost an anticipation, even an arrogance.

How many times had she traveled down Broadway in her mother's Duisenberg, watching the peasants disembark from the train?

A florist had set up a stand on the sidewalk, hawking roses and peonies, lilies and tulips. Next to him, a newsie held up a paper from his stack, announcing the headlines.

She paid him a nickel and read the headline. LINDBERGH DOES IT! TO PARIS IN 33 ½ HOURS; FLIES 1,000 MILES THROUGH SNOW AND SLEET; CHEERING FRENCH CARRY HIM OFF FIELD. PARIS BOULEVARDS RING WITH CELEBRATION AFTER DAY AND NIGHT WATCH. She read the masthead and found Oliver and Esme's names, and on the article the initials at the byline made her smile. L. J. Hoyt.

So Lilly hadn't married. But she'd managed to fill her mother's shoes. Perhaps she would finally forgive Rosie. Perhaps both their lives had turned out exactly as they should be.

Rosie looked up and found herself on the corner of 40th Street. She stopped for a moment on the edge of the theater district. Ahead, the marquees of the Majestic Theater and the Gallo Opera House beckoned, the old pulse inside her pushing her forward. She stood across the street from Times Square, voices in her head.

You, a star? Dashielle's laughter that night in Paris.

I'll make you my headliner. Cesar's voice, dark and too alluring in those early days.

A playbill tumbled by on the wind and she stamped her foot on it, reading the name. *Tommy*, performed at the Gaiety Theater at 46th and Broadway.

She would like to see that.

She checked her watch again. Even if Guthrie hadn't taken the mound, he would be searching for her from the dugout. But she needed to sit, perhaps drink some water before she found her way back to the subway. Already, she ached all the way through to her bones, and Charlie wasn't helping, the way he moved as if anxious to get to the game.

A red canopy over a nearby restaurant suggested shade, and she wandered over and settled down on the bench by the door. A doorman gave her a look but she leaned back, closing her eyes, fanning herself.

The smells drifted out—roast pork slathered in rosemary and garlic, new potatoes in butter, dark red wine—perhaps she just imagined it all, but she could nearly taste the meal. How long had it been since she'd dined out?

"Rosie Worth?"

The voice roused her out of her hunger, her fatigue, and she managed to open her eyes.

"Blanche?"

She looked every bit as beautiful and daring and flamboyant as she had the day Rosie left her in Paris, with siren-blond hair, those green eyes, sharp and bright, missing nothing. She wore a rose-colored linen dress with a low sash, and a gray low-brimmed hat, a satin ribbon around the brim, and three strands of pearls at her neck. Her kohled eyes scraped over Rosie, her lips a perfect surprising pout of shock, traced in lipstick so red they glistened like blood. Had Rosie even remembered lipstick? Her hand nearly went to her mouth to check.

"It is you. Oh my." Blanche slid down onto the bench beside her. "What are you doing outside Sardis? And..." Her gaze trailed down to Rosie's protruding belly. "In such a condition? Why aren't you home, in bed, or perhaps down in Newport, and out of this heat?" Blanche looked closer, her voice dropping. "You're sweating, dear. And you don't look well. Who are you waiting for?" Her gaze dropped to Rosie's finger. "And who on earth did you marry?"

Rosie slipped her hand over her plain gold band, her own gaze darting to the glittering stone on Blanche's finger. "Who did *you* marry?"

"Why, Pembrook, of course." She glanced away from Rosie, toward the restaurant. "In fact, I'm meeting him for lunch. Why don't you join us?"

Oh. "I...can't. My husband has a game." Funny to say that out loud, a sentence that had come so easily to her in the past three years. Now it seemed out of place, even vulgar. Indeed, Blanche raised a perfectly penciled eyebrow.

"What kind of game?"

"He plays baseball. For the Giants."

Blanche said nothing for a long moment, just swallowed, and her smile seemed tugged out from some place of shock. "Baseball?"

"He's a pitcher. Today's his first home game. He was traded from the White Sox in Chicago a few weeks ago."

"So that's where you've been? Chicago?" Blanche shook her head. "Darling, no wonder we haven't seen you. Chicago! A mobster's city from what I hear." She hooked her arm through Rosie's. "You look positively peaked. Let us lunch and you can catch us all up."

"Us?"

"Me and Pem...and we expect Dash, also."

Dash. The name jolted her forward, sizzled inside her. Dash.

You're my good-time girl. But I don't want to get married.

She settled a hand over her stomach. "I don't think—"

"I absolutely insist." Blanche rose, pulling Rosie to her feet. "At least a lemonade, okay? My treat."

She wasn't sure if Blanche had quickly assessed her financial situation or simply wanted to be generous, but the kindness of her friend wooed Rosie into the cool interior of Sardis.

The place reminded her of Delmonico's, with the white tablecloths, the bright lamplights, and the clientele—men in suits and ties discussing business, women from the upper Eastside decked out in pearls and gloves, the latest hats, cool dropped-waist dresses. White-gloved waiters moved in and out of the tables carrying salads and luncheon plates.

Charlie kicked her empty stomach.

Blanche waved to someone across the room and Rosie followed her gaze to Pembrook. He met Blanche's wave with a smile. And then his gaze landed on Rosie.

She hadn't expected to appear so much different that she would elicit such a look of shock on Pembrook's lean face. He too appeared older, his brown hair thinner on top, perhaps more tone and confidence to his body as he stood and walked out to greet them.

"Look who I picked up off the street!" Blanche said.

She didn't have to phrase it quite that way. But Rosie urged out a smile. "Pem." She leaned in for his kiss on her cheek.

"Rosie, you look—"

"Enormous," Blanche said, giggling, and Rosie shot her a glare. "I can't help it. It's just…well, most women would be at home in this state." Blanche sat down as Pembrook held her chair. She tugged off her gloves. "But apparently this isn't our little Rosie from Paris." She leaned toward Pembrook as he held out the chair for Rosie. "She's run off with a baseball player!"

Did she have to phrase it like that? "Shh, Blanche."

"Really?" Pembrook said, sitting down. He still had his gaze on her, as if he'd never seen a pregnant woman in public. Rosie grabbed her napkin and draped it over her belly. "Did you marry a Yankee?"

"He plays for the Giants." Rosie didn't look at her watch. "Right now, in fact. I'm missing his game."

"But I convinced her to dine with us," Blanche said, wrapping her hand around Rosie's wrist. "We all need to catch up! Wait until I tell you about the wedding."

Blanche raised her hand to summon the waiter and launched into the story.

Pembrook played with his fork, stealing glances at Rosie.

Rosie ordered lemonade, sipping it slowly, and then allowed Blanche to add a salad.

Second inning, for sure. If she didn't show up by the fourth, she might as well not go at all.

Her salad appeared, and she tried not to devour it. But when she looked up at Blanche's silence she realized she'd been inhaling her food. "The baby makes me hungry."

Blanche leaned back, her Waldorf salad half-eaten, and pulled out a cigarette. "Really, Rosie, I never thought I'd see you like this." She lit it, blew out smoke. "Somehow when you returned to New York, I thought I'd see your name on the marquee of the Majestic."

Rosie put down her fork, wiped her mouth, the salad filling the crannies in her stomach. "I found something better," she said, the words settling inside, deep and true.

Blanche quirked an eyebrow, glanced at Pem.

But his gaze fell beyond them and he raised his hand, waving.

Rosie steeled herself a moment before she turned.

He'd only grown more handsome. Taller, his dark hair clipped tight to his head, those smoky eyes dark and with a hint of danger, his smile at an angle that suggested he knew the game and how to play it. He wore a black suit, a matching black tie, and a white dress shirt, and she could smell his exotic French cologne from across the room.

Slick. Polished. Dashielle Parks.

Dash's gaze landed on Rosie and he slowed for a moment, clearly rattled.

She smiled at that. It raked up the old Rosie, the one who had once made him chase her across Paris, the one who knew how to walk into a room and elicit the attention of every man. She lifted her chin and extended her hand. "Dashielle Parks. What a pleasure."

He ran a hand down his suit, smoothing his tie, a perfect smile forming on his lips. "Red Worth." Then he took her hand, bent and kissed it.

She expected some tingles perhaps, warmth at his touch, but even as he stood and surveyed her with those burning eyes, she let Guthrie walk into her thoughts.

Guthrie, blond and passionate, with his easy smile, the way he could turn her world safe.

"Rosie Storme," she corrected for him.

He said nothing, nonplussed, then nodded. "Of course." His gaze traveled to her shape. "Congratulations?"

"Indeed," she said, and allowed him to tuck her back into her chair.

He greeted Pem and Blanche then sat down, angling his chair toward her, his legs crossed. A waiter came over and he ordered a brandy, turning down a menu. "I already ate." He pulled out his cigarette case and retrieved a Pall Mall, tapping it on the end of the slim silver box. "Married. With child. What other surprises does Rosie have for us?"

"She married a ballplayer," Blanche supplied.

Dash lit his cigarette. "No wonder I didn't see your name in lights when I returned from Paris."

Had he looked for her? She shook away the thought.

"I was going to be a headliner at Valerie's. And then I met Guthrie."

"Swept you off your feet?" Dash wore mocking at the corners of his mouth.

"Something like that." She refused to allow his ridicule and put on her best society girl, leaning forward to nestle her chin into her hand, her elbow perched on the table. "But enough about me. Dash, please tell me you're not a banker."

Blanche giggled. "Heavens, no! Dash is making moving pictures."

Rosie kept her smile.

Dash's gaze upon her never wavered, his eyes so dark they seemed to pin her. "I came back to New York looking for you, Red. Thought we could make a splash out West, in California."

"You're making movies?" She kept her voice cool.

He flicked off his ash onto Blanche's plate. "I'm financing movies. But I have my say." He smiled again, something she'd seen before. "For the right girl."

She didn't have to work hard to read between his words. For *my* girl. The good-time girl, the one who swooned at the very mention of his name.

She leaned back, wiping her mouth. "Have you found her?"

He glanced at Pembrook, winked. "I'm still auditioning."

Same old Dash. She picked up her lemonade as his brandy appeared. "Here's to Dash and his never-ending quest for the right girl."

She drank, but Dash held onto his glass, his smile falling. "Red. Don't be like that. It wasn't my fault things went sour between us."

She put down her lemonade. "Thanks for lunch, Blanche, but I am sure Guthrie's in the fifth inning by now."

"Don't go, Rosie." The sincerity of Dash's tone stopped her.

She met his gaze. "Dash, believe it or not, I'm not just a good-time gal. I'm Guthrie's lucky charm."

A muscle pulled in his jaw, and his smile vanished as she got up and worked her way outside. The heat hit her like a slap, but she stepped out onto the street, trying to find her bearings. How could she have let so much game time pass?

She would have to take a cab. She motioned to the footman, intending to request a cab, when Dash pushed out of the doors behind her. "Red!"

She didn't turn. "Dashielle, really. I'm not angry—"

He caught her arm. "But I am! You left Paris, never let me explain, never let me think about your offer—"

"Would you have taken it? Please. I rue that day in the park. I just— I just thought we had something."

"We did have something." His eyes were red. "We had more than something. And I was foolish to laugh at you." He shook his head, his voice low. "Forgive me for hurting you, Red?"

Oh, Dash. She'd lived with honesty for four years now and knew how to recognize it. "It's okay, Dash. I'm happy. I married a man who I trust, who makes me feel beautiful."

"You are beautiful, Rosie." He had her eyes now. "I wish you'd waited for me."

"I couldn't wait. My mother wanted to marry me off to a duke."

"So you ran away with a baseball player instead?" His voice shook.

"I fell in love with a baseball player." She heard the words, smiled at the truth in them. Yes. She'd fallen terribly, deliciously in love with Guthrie Storme. And, she was missing his first home game. "I have to go, Dash."

"Let me drive you."

She considered him a moment, then nodded. He directed his footman to retrieve his car and she shouldn't have been surprised when he took the driver's seat of his sleek roadster, the red velvet seats embracing her as she settled inside. Oh, the plush comfort could make a girl lose herself in slumber. Five minutes in the heat and she turned into a rag, not to mention the baby banging around inside her. She made a face as he pressed into her ribs.

"Are you in pain?" Dash eased out into traffic.

"Sometimes."

"I should take you home." He braked at a light and wore what looked like worry on his face.

"I'm fine, Dash. Guthrie will be expecting me at his game."

"He wouldn't want you to collapse, and you do look exhausted."

She pressed her hand to her forehead. "I hiked from 34th Street to Times Square."

He gave her a look that made her turn away in shame. "I'm taking you home. The game is about done anyway, I would wager." He pulled out his pocket watch. "It's nearly four."

Had she truly sat in the restaurant for two hours? She leaned her head back against the seat. "I feel ill—"

"Is it the baby?"

The panic in his voice made her smile. "Calm down, Dash. I just meant that I'm sick to miss Guthrie's game."

Dash said nothing.

They drove down Broadway to Fifth Avenue, and an errant curiosity made her suggest they drive along the park. Dash pointed out all the current inhabitants, including Esme and Oliver's house. "He's never remarried. Lilly lives there with him, now. Writes a dreadful column for the paper each week."

"Dash!"

He grinned at her. "I'm being kind, I promise."

She let herself smile. "Apparently Oliver finally found her, brought her home. He always wanted her to work for the paper. I always thought Lilly had more adventure in her though."

He turned off Fifth Avenue at the end of the park. "And I thought you had less of it in you."

She would take that as a compliment. "I live in Queens."

He took his time, weaving through East Harlem, then back through the upper East Side, pointing out the now closed Delmonico's then driving over the 59th Street Bridge into Queens. She let the wind cool her, holding onto her hat with one hand. Dash drove her around the new Yankee Stadium on the other side of the river as she told him about life with the White Sox, Guthrie, finally weaving in the sordid incident with Cesar.

"So, he said that if you ever return, he'd find you?"

She managed a nod. "It's been two weeks of looking over my shoulder, waiting for him to appear on my doorstep."

"Aw, Red, I'm sorry."

He slowed as they turned onto Elmhurst. The twilight draped long shadows across the streets, into the alcoves of the brownstones. She pointed out her building, and he pulled up to the curb. He jumped out, walked around to her side, and opened her door, helping her from the truck.

She retrieved her key.

"Wait here," he said, taking it from her. He bounded up the steps then unlocked the door, easing it open and disappearing inside.

When he returned he flicked on the outside light. It bathed the street in a wan, diffused glow. "All clear. No nasty mobster waiting to slit your throat."

She shook her head. "You're mocking me," she said.

He came down the stoop, his smile gone. "I'm not mocking you, Red." He pressed the key back into her hand then lifted her chin. "If you ever need anything—and I mean *anything*—come to me." He met her eyes, and she saw in them an unfamiliar softness. "I told you once that

I was halfway to falling in love with you. When you asked me to marry you, then left Paris brokenhearted, I realized that I was already there."

She swallowed, looked down, her eyes heating.

He pressed his lips to her forehead. "Take care of yourself, Red."

Then he left her there on the curb, his roadster pulling away with a purr as the night fell around her. She was walking up the outside stairs, her hand around her key, when she saw him. Movement out of the corner of her eye, a man standing just outside the street light.

A chill bled through her.

But her eyes adjusted to the darkness. And—it was only Guthrie, his hair slick, wearing the suit he'd left in for the game. She raised her hand, a greeting on her lips, when she saw him turn.

He walked away from her down the street and into the clasp of darkness.

* * * * *

Rennie had changed. Subtle edges to his personality, perhaps, but his jokes cut deeper, his laughter rang sharp and raucous, his eyes in hers glanced off, settling only occasionally to stab at her, as if trying to read her. He'd become jaded and sharp, and he dragged her back to Montparnasse, showing her off like some treasure he'd stolen.

"I always knew Lola couldn't live without me." He draped an arm over her shoulder, pressed a kiss to her cheek, hot and lingering, so long that she pulled away. "Where have you been for four years? Breaking my heart?"

His hair had thinned, his face drawn, his skin pale, probably from too many tight nights.

"Actually...? I learned how to fly."

"Fly?" He rolled his eyes, smiling wildly. "As in airplanes?"

"I was a wing walker with an air show, and I learned how to pilot a plane."

He laughed then, flapping his arms. "Lola of the skies."

She tried to keep the hurt out of her voice. "You were the one who started it. You said I belonged in the heavens."

He slid out of the booth. "I said a lot of things, Lilly. Not all of them are true." He staggered, wobbly on his way to the bar where he leaned against it, gesturing to the keep.

"He really did miss you," Presley said. Lilly still couldn't believe she'd seen Presley, like a fixture at the zinc bar, when she'd walked into the club. As if she'd faded back into time, complete with smoky music, flashy women with sequined and feather headbands, absinthe flowing like water—not a hint of prohibition this side of the ocean. Presley, too, seemed sharper, her hair redder, her body thinner, her smirks less generous. She wore a deeply V-d black dress with rosettes at the shoulders and a tight black cap on her head, her eyes so black they seemed to peer out with horror at Lilly across the table. "I don't think he was prepared for you to break his heart."

Lilly traced her finger around the rim of her highball. She'd taken a sniff and her stomach lurched at the memory of the licorice touching her lips, swilling her stomach. "I think he was in love with a younger, more naïve version of me that he could impress."

Presley drew on her cigarette. "Did he?"

"Impress me?" Lilly lifted a shoulder. "I'd never seen a bullfight before."

"You mean the bullfight between Ren and your father?" Presley giggled. "I thought your old man was going to sort him out right there. You should have seen the look he gave Rennie—he could have turned him to ash right there in the middle of the verandah. He told him that if Rennie had stolen your honor then he would be back and Rennie wouldn't leave standing." She leaned close, her eyes in Lilly's. "He didn't, did he?"

Lilly shook her head, still caught in Presley's words. "Oliver said that?"

"Sat in the bar all night, nursing a lemonade, watching Rennie to make sure he didn't sneak up to your room. I think Rennie was scared of him. I know I was."

Scared of Oliver? "Oliver wouldn't hurt anyone."

Presley tapped off her ash and lifted a shoulder. "Never know what a father will do for the daughter he loves."

Lilly had nothing for those words, letting them seep inside her. Oliver...loved her? Somewhere in the back of her heart she'd always thought he'd simply tolerated her, looked upon her as his responsibility, a byproduct of his marriage to her mother.

Even if he had adopted her, he'd done it out of obligation, not love, right?

But hearing it from someone else, not her cousin, or her grandfather, or even Oliver...

"But now you're back, and Rennie looks happy." Presley grabbed Lilly's hand. "Please tell me you're staying."

Lilly stared into her glassy eyes. "I—I don't know." Paris had a way of making her forget, but despite the sultry jazz, the lure of adventure, she couldn't break away from the sense that the woman she'd been four years ago had vanished.

"Of course she's staying!" Rennie came over, sliding into her booth, his arm around her shoulders.

A couple of people she didn't know scooted beside Presley. She noticed one of the men hung his arm around Presley's shoulders. Presley looked up at him and smiled, too much hope in her eyes.

Perhaps someone didn't have to be young to be naïve.

"I only came to do the story on Lindbergh," Lilly said. His interview yesterday lingered inside her as she wrote the article. When she'd turned it in, only to have the Paris bureau telegraph it to New York, she almost didn't recognize the writing.

What had Oliver said about throwing passion into her writing? Lindbergh had given her that in his quiet, courageous demeanor, the way he explained his flight.

"About halfway through the flight, in the dead of night, I found myself trying to climb through a patch of clouds. Sleet began to form on the wing and forced me down. I had to turn around to find a way through."

His words conjured up that day when she'd climbed out onto the wing with Truman on the way to Duluth.

"I debated right then whether I should turn around and make another attempt. But I'd mapped it all out and I believed I could make it. I decided not to think any more about going back, that I must press on. A few hours later, I found Ireland."

She knew about pressing on, believing she could find a way through.

"There's power in commitment; it turns you into the man you hope to be. The man you can live with."

Lola the wing walker. There, on the edge of the plane, holding on to the wing wires with everything she had, she'd become the women she'd wanted to be.

The woman her mother had been.

Perhaps she could become who she was looking for. Perhaps that woman just waited for her to reach out, hold onto it, and not turn back.

"No, Rennie, I'm not staying. I need to go home, where I belong."

"I think you belong here." He winked at her, but she didn't smile. He searched her eyes a moment then grinned, something sloppy and arrogant. "Would you like to see Paris at night?"

She put her hand on his chest, pushing him away. "No, Rennie, I believe I already have. Once is enough."

Chapter 15

She'd lost him.

Rosie stood outside the Cotton Club, watching through the window as the rain pattered on the sidewalk, into her hair, through her cotton sweater.

She ached, right down to her bones, from sitting in the chairs at the Polo Gardens cheering Guthrie to his first no-hitter. Except, sitting there, the tang of popcorn in the air, the smell of the dirt and sweat rising from the field, she didn't feel like his lucky charm.

She felt like something he dreaded. For two weeks—and she could pinpoint it to the day that she saw Dash, to the day when she got out of his shiny roadster, let him kiss her, that Guthrie had decided not to love her.

She'd tried to explain, but Guthrie insisted that it didn't matter, that he knew that Dash had meant nothing to her, that in fact, nothing had changed between them.

But she knew. At night, he lay with his back to her, his body cold, his shoulders stiffening when she ran her hand down his arm. Twice last week after practice he'd stumbled home late, forbidden whiskey on his breath. And, when he left for a short road trip to Boston, he landed the merest peck on her cheek. She found no satisfaction that they'd lost half their games to the Braves. Most of all, he hadn't even looked at her at today's home game.

She didn't know if he saw her, or even if he knew she sat in the stands, cheering him on as she stood at the beginning of the game, smiling, waving.

He pitched brilliantly, winning by one run over the Braves at home. As if, indeed, he'd seen her.

She waited for him outside the stadium, on a bench, just like she had after his Yankees game so many years ago. Waited while the other players emerged from the locker room, freshly showered, opening their arms for their wives, their families.

The players came out in groups—Jack and Mickey, catchers, and infielders Doc and Rogers, Tex and Edd, both outfielders. She lifted her hand to Buck, Smiley, Dutch, and Ned, who looked at her with a frown when they got into a hired car and motored away, probably heading for a club.

She'd waited until night dropped around her, the skies opened up and cried. Until the janitors turned off the stadium lights. Until the Giants' manager John "Muggsy" McGraw emerged from the darkness. She dredged up her courage and caught up to him.

"Rosie, what are you doing out here in the rain?" Muggsy took off his hat, held it over her head.

"Hey, Muggsy." She ran her hands up her soggy arms. "I…have you seen Guthrie?"

Muggsy stared at her with a frown. "Two hours ago. He left right after the game. Seemed to be in a hurry—he didn't even shower."

Funny, he hadn't even sent her out a note with one of the players to tell her to go home.

"Do you know where he might have gone?"

Muggsy walked her to the curb, hailed a cab. "I heard rumors of the fellas heading out to the Cotton Club up in Harlem. But you get on home now. The rain is no place for someone in your condition."

A cab pulled up and he opened the door, settled her into the backseat. She thanked him as he closed it then directed the cabbie to the club.

If he wouldn't come to her, then she'd find him. Drag him home. Remind him that he had a family, a wife who loved him.

She had something to give him now. A child.

But, as she stood outside the club, the bright lights of the marquee listing Duke Ellington's band and the Jubilee Jumpers, she couldn't bear the scene she saw in her mind. Walking into the club, soggy, enormous, angry; while around her, thin, flashy women would be sidling up to him, cooing into his ear. In her worst nightmares, he ignored her, perhaps drew one of the flappers onto the dance floor.

She'd been one of those flappers, once upon a time.

She stared at the patrons standing under the awning, their coats wrapped around them as drivers bearing umbrellas fetched them to their vehicles. Music twined out, and she had no doubt that inside she'd find a back room flowing with bootlegged whiskey.

"Can I help you, ma'am?" A young footman—he resembled Cesar in too many ways, groomed dark hair, Italian-accented English—approached her. "Perhaps hail you a cab?"

She pressed her fingers to her eyes, glad that she hadn't applied much kohl, aware that every day she became larger she lost a little bit more of her glamour. "Yes, please."

She climbed into the cab and directed him toward Queens, staring out the window as the rain slid down the dark pane, the bright lights of Harlem turning the world fuzzy. What if he never came back? What if she *had* lost him? She knew the stories about other ballplayers, the ones who had a lady in every city. Worse were the ones who quit after their baseball career dried up, unable to face a life without the game they loved.

What would she do without Guthrie? Return home?

She ran her hand over her belly. She didn't care what it took, she'd find a way to win back Guthrie's heart.

The cab pulled up to her brownstone and she paid him, climbed out. The house seemed dark, even unfriendly, the windows unseeing, the porch light off. Her footsteps echoed across the pavement as she climbed the stairs, pulling out her key.

Except…except the door stood ajar, the faintest crack betraying it. She put her hand on the handle, her chest full. "Guthrie!"

She pushed open the door, closing it behind her. Maybe he'd come home to surprise her—he did that once after he'd won, bought roses and scattered them around the house. "Guthrie?"

She flicked on the light.

She slammed her hand against her mouth to press back her scream.

Guthrie lay thrashing on the floor of the foyer on his stomach, one man twisting his hand behind his back, pinning him, another with his knee in his back, his hand clamped to his mouth. Blood dripped from a cut over his eye, his nose bled over his captor's hand.

He shook the man away. "Rosie, get out of here!"

The man wrenched his arm harder, and he yelled in agony.

"Stop—you're going to break his arm!"

"It's not his pitching arm," said a voice from behind her. She froze.

She steeled herself as Cesar walked out of the shadows. He held a bat—one of Guthrie's—in his grip.

"Hello, Rosie."

"Leave her alone! This doesn't involve her!"

She glanced at Guthrie. What didn't—

"It absolutely involves her, Guthrie. How stupid are you? This is all about me losing my star." Cesar stepped up to her, tucked his cold hand under her chin. "I've missed you, Red."

Then he kissed her. She jerked herself away from him and threw her hand up in defense when she saw him curl a fist.

"Don't you touch her!"

She heard a pleading on the tail of Guthrie's voice that made her want to weep. She dropped to her knees, crawled over to him. "What's he talking about? How did he find us?"

"C'mon, pet, I read the paper. Guthrie made all the headlines when the Giants bought him." He tapped the bat in the palm of his hand. "Perfect timing too, because my ace at the Yanks had started to dry up."

She shook her head.

"Do the math, sweetheart. You cost me a hundred grand in bookings. I need recompense. Guthrie here agreed to throw a few games, work off your debt."

She stared at him. He looked away from her.

Oh, Guthrie. So that was why he couldn't bear to talk to her. She'd turned him into a cheat.

"Except for today, see. Today, he decides to win. So I had to remind him just what he had to lose."

Guthrie howled as Cesar's man twisted his arm.

"Leave him alone! I'll get you the money—I have the money. Please. Don't hurt him."

Cesar crossed the room in one step and grabbed her by the hair, yanking her to her feet, putting his face in hers. "I know you do." His breath bore the stench of whisky. She turned away from the spittle on the sides of his mouth, and he dropped her back on the floor. "You've got two days." He tapped his enforcer on the shoulder, and he released Guthrie.

Guthrie turned over, and she saw the fury in his eyes. She grabbed his hand, pulled him to her. "You'll have it, Cesar. I promise."

"Good." Then he crouched next to her and pressed his hand on her belly. "Because we wouldn't want anything to happen to Junior here."

Guthrie lunged at him, but the muscle behind Cesar landed a kick on his jaw, slamming him back into the wall.

Cesar smiled. Held up his fingers. "Two days." He touched her on the cheek. "You're still so beautiful, Red. Such a shame."

Then he got up.

As soon as the door closed behind him, she pounced from the floor and locked it.

She began to shake as she turned. Guthrie sat against the wall, his face battered, his shirt ripped, breathing hard. He looked up at her with eyes that apologized.

"I don't understand. How did this happen?" She fell to her knees, catching herself on the floor, scrabbling over to him.

Guthrie looked away. "You were right, Rosie." Then he cupped his face with his hand, covering his eyes. "I should have listened to you."

"How long have you been throwing games?"

It seemed he couldn't look at her. "About a month."

She did the math. Right about the time he'd seen her with Dash.

"And not every game—just the ones Cesar told me to. He found me after a practice one day, told me that if I didn't work with him..."

"He'd kill me." She sat back, hearing her nightmares play in her head.

Guthrie took her hand. "We can leave. Disappear. I don't have to play baseball. I can farm, or work on the docks. Maybe become a fighter—"

"Stop. Guthrie. Please."

"No, listen to me, Rosie. I got a little stashed away. See, I figure that Cesar wasn't the only one who could make good off me. I figured it out that every time I threw a game, he bet against the Giants and made a bundle. So...I did the same. I...used the pearls left from your necklace as seed money and created a little nest egg."

He tried a smile. "I figured he had it coming."

Oh, Guthrie. She pushed herself off the floor, held onto the wall as she made her way to the kitchen and dug out a rag. Wetting it, she returned to where he sat on the floor then pressed the rag to his nose, his eye. The welts on his knuckles. "How much do you have?"

"About five grand."

Five thousand dollars? "That's a lot of money."

He brushed her hands from their tending. "I know. It'll get us to Chicago, maybe even out to California. We'd be safe there."

How she wanted to believe him. He had electric eyes, the kind that could spark her own hope, the eyes that made her believe she could run away with him, marry him, live happily ever after. But, "I know Cesar. He'll find us. And kill us all." She pressed her hand over her womb. "Charlie needs his father. And his father needs baseball."

"I don't need baseball. I have you." He drew her down to him. "I'm sorry I didn't tell you."

"I thought you were angry about seeing me with Dash."

She heard his chuckle deep in his chest.

"I have no fear of Dashielle Parks." He pressed a kiss to her head. "I just wish I had the money to keep you safe."

But, see, she did.

* * * * *

So this is what it felt like to want to go home. Lilly stood at the rail of the S.S. *Majestic* as the fog cleared the New York Harbor. Lady Liberty gleamed under the cast of morning light, rose gold and orange, as if a torch guiding them home. She raised her face to the salty wind, breathing in the taste of the sea, the cry of the gulls over the ship. How could it have been only four years ago that she had stood here detesting Oliver, blaming him for stealing her future, ripping her out of Rennie's arms?

She should throw herself at his feet and thank him. Too easily she'd seen the life from which he saved her. Hollowed out from too many careless nights like Presley, or pregnant and abandoned like Hadley, Hem's wife. No doubt, Rennie would have broken her heart too many times over before Lilly realized the truth.

She belonged in New York, with her family. With Oliver.

Never know what a father will do for the daughter he loves. Presley's words had embedded inside her, and since that moment, as she'd steamed across the Atlantic on the *Majestic*, she'd suddenly seen everything— Oliver presenting her with pearls on her eighteenth birthday, arriving in Spain, fury on his face, his head in his hands, weeping as Esme died.

"It's just you and me now."

Oliver and his cry of pain outside her hospital room in Wyoming.

"Why is it so hard for you to believe that I love you?"

Because she didn't belong to him. She wasn't his flesh and blood, his responsibility. His real daughter.

But perhaps it didn't matter. He'd adopted her—nearly against her will—and then committed to loving her. Despite her anger. Despite her rebellion. Despite the fact that she'd spent so much time running from his love.

The ship parted the fog, rolling it back as they entered the harbor. She waited until they docked then returned to her stateroom, where she instructed the porters to deliver her cases to Oliver's chateau— no, her *home*—on Fifth Avenue. Then she caught a cab and headed to the *Chronicle*.

She wanted to see him. To knock at the door and enter his office and have him look up when for the first time—probably ever—she would greet him with kindness.

Like a daughter would.

She never thought she'd miss the sounds of the *Chronicle*— the newsies who greeted her as she entered the round entryway, the linotype machines, the rumble of the presses, the acrid pinch of the chemical baths from the photo department. She climbed the stairs and didn't even bother to stop at her office, just headed right to Oliver's suite.

His receptionist greeted her, turning from her typewriter to face her. A little older than she, Madeline, with her dark, pinned-back hair, her steely eyes, had a way of dressing down someone with a look, making sure they had a sound reason for disturbing her publisher.

Lilly debated, then headed right for his door. She was his daughter, after all. "Is he in a meeting?" She reached for the handle, her hand raised to knock.

"He's not here."

She stilled, turned. "What?" Oliver never took off time from work—he practically lived at the paper. "Where is he?"

"I don't know, ma'am. He told me he'd be out of the office all day."

Lilly pressed her hand on his door, then, "I'm going to check his appointment book."

Madeline found her feet as Lilly opened his office and stepped inside, but she didn't chase her. Lilly closed the door behind her.

Once upon a time her mother had shared this office with Oliver. Lilly well remembered doing her studies on the tufted leather sofa against the wall, or listening to her mother and Oliver argue about headlines and print runs. She made a point of not entering after her mother's death, the memories too rich to taste. Now, she could almost see Esme, regal and tall, standing at the round window overlooking Chronicle Square, watching the pigeons roost on the arms of the statue cast of August Worth, Lilly's grandfather. She would be wearing a simple shirtwaist, perhaps with a vest or sweater, a dark skirt, her blond hair piled upon her head, or caught at the nape. Sometimes at home, her mother let her hair down, and it flowed like a river of gold. If only Lilly had been born with her heiress beauty. But she'd taken on her father's features—coal-black hair, matching eyes. She looked more like her grandmother, a descendant of the Crow.

Lilly went around Oliver's massive desk and stood at the window, staring down. In this spot, she could almost imagine her mother's voice.

"Whatever happens, honey, don't forget who you are. Don't forget the blessings God has bestowed upon you. Don't forget your name and where you belong."

But, she had. She'd forgotten everything that made her who she was. She'd forgotten the courage born from her mother, the compassion of her grandmother, the honor of her birth father.

Most of all, she'd forgotten the blessings He'd left her with.

Oliver.

Paris had made her remember. She could thank Rennie for that much, perhaps.

She turned away, out of the pocket of memory, and her gaze scraped across Oliver's desk, landing on a trio of framed pictures in the corner. Esme and Oliver on their wedding day, a twinkle in her mother's eye, despite the solemn expression. The next, an arranged photograph taken of all three on holiday in Newport. Lilly looked as if she had eaten something sour for breakfast.

And the third picture? Just of her, a shot taken by Oliver—he was always taking out his camera in the unstaged moments of life. She'd never seen this photograph before—of her, seated on the window seat in the parlor, her knees tucked under her skirt, her hair in long braids, reading a book in the afternoon light.

She looked lost in her own world, oblivious to the fact that Oliver's lens focused on her.

Perhaps she'd always been oblivious.

How had she never recognized Oliver's steadfast love?

Or perhaps she had simply disdained it.

But it hadn't disdained her. His love had followed her across the ocean and back, even out West. What had that preacher said in Minnesota? *And the Word says that neither death nor life, nor angels nor rulers, not things present, nor things to come, nor powers, nor height or depth, nor anything else in all creation will be able to separate us from the love of God in Christ Jesus our Lord.*

Rennie was wrong. God's love was here, in this world, if she just looked for it. He did show up when she needed Him. In Oliver, over and over. And perhaps God kept showing up, despite the fact she'd run from Him too.

She ran her thumb over the picture of her mother, of Oliver, still hearing the preacher. *When God adopts you into His family, you belong to Him. He's stamped His name on you. A name that comes with His protection. And His birthright—which is eternity and the power to live with joy on this earth. It's all yours, just as if you'd always belonged. But the Good Word says that to have this, you must repent.*

Repent.

She sank into Oliver's chair. Stared out toward the city. "O God, I'm sorry I turned away from You. That I ran from You. From where I belong."

In His arms.

And, at the *Chronicle.*

She returned the frame to the desk and headed to the door, opening it to poke her head out. "Madeline, I need Bernie and Mitch in here with a status of today's edition."

The woman stared at her, and Lilly shut the door before the secretary called security.

She hadn't a clue what she might be doing, but she, like her parents, would figure it out, trusting in God's blessing.

Six hours later, she'd put the paper to bed, toured each of the departments, and written a column that she might actually read. Especially after Bernie complimented her on the Lindbergh piece. Commitment. It felt like fire in her veins.

She took the train home then walked through Central Park, through the column of arching elms along the pathway, breathing in the lazy fragrances of the pear and cherry trees, the pink magnolia blossoms. Sometimes she could still smell the prairie on the wind, but Central Park conjured its own magic, with the mounted police patrolling the park, the scurry of squirrels upon the willow oaks.

How many times had she strolled through the park with her mother, capturing the memories of her childhood?

Yes, she belonged here.

She exited the park and crossed the street to the Price family chateau. Once upon a time, footmen—Oliver, in fact—stood at the door to attend guests through the iron gates. When Oliver married Esme and moved into the chateau, he'd retired many of them, given others a job at the paper, manning the presses or working delivery. Now, only a handful of staff remained—the cook and two scullery maids, her mother's lady's maid-turned-housekeeper, Bette, and her two assistants, and Mr. Stewart, Oliver's father and butler, who had resisted his son's insistence to retire.

Apparently, in the golden age of the Price family, Phoebe Price employed a small army to keep the grounds running, her parties on the social register of must-attend events. Even Aunt Jinx had a larger house staff, despite her smaller assembly of rooms in the Warren and Wentworth Building at 927 Fifth Avenue.

Lilly opened the door, the lilac trees in the courtyard of the house scenting the July air. Still, the silences, marred by only the ticking grandfather clock in the foyer, drilled through her, especially when she dropped her handbag and pushed open the doors to Oliver's office.

Once upon a time, her grandfather, August, occupied this space.

After he passed, Esme had remodeled with white wallpaper to contrast the dark mahogany wainscoting, opened the velvet drapes at the windows to allow in the light, and replaced the family picture over the fireplace with an oil duplicate of the sitting trio of their family on Oliver's desk. Photographs of the city, from vagrant children to crime to architecture, hung on the wall opposite his desk. Apparently in his youth Oliver had worked as a photo stringer for the *Chronicle*. She barely believed it.

Behind his desk he'd hung her mother's debutante picture. Lilly could never reconcile the buttoned-up young lady with the woman she knew, the one as comfortable on a horse as she'd been drinking tea.

Lilly had made a point to never enter Oliver's lair, and now, just standing in the opening of the double doors felt too intimate.

Even, invasive.

"Ma'am, can I help you?"

Bette had served her mother in her youth and knew the secrets of the Price family better than any of them. White streaked her long black hair, netted at the back of her neck. She wore the requisite housekeeper's black dress minus the white apron of her assistants. She had always frightened Lilly, just a little.

"I was hoping to find Oliver."

It just might be the first time she'd ever said that, but Bette didn't comment. Simply, "I'm sorry, ma'am. He left last night after work without a word. I don't believe he was expecting you back so soon."

She wasn't expecting herself back so soon. Or, ever. Still, "I sent him a telegram from the Paris office. I thought he might have received it." Of course, it had been a little vague. *Finished in Paris. Coming Home.*

"I'm sorry, ma'am. I'll tell Cook you have arrived and will be needing dinner."

Lilly tried not to taste the bitter swell in her throat as she climbed the stairs to her room. He would return…and she would be here running the paper and waiting for him when he did.

She had reached the landing when she heard the door open and footsteps in the foyer. She turned, her hand on the rail, and warmth spread through her, something new and brilliant as Oliver walked into the room holding his fedora and a small satchel.

"Oliver!"

He looked up, and she didn't know why it had taken her so long to see it—the warmth in his eyes, the delight. "Lilly!" He set down his bag and opened his arms.

She'd never had a father. Not until this moment when she wrapped her arms around his waist, let the warmth of his embrace speak to her. Safety. Protection.

Love.

Why had she been so afraid of it?

She stepped back, smiled into his eyes.

"I read your article. Magnificent, Lilly. How was Paris?" Despite his warmth, as he stepped back, she saw something flash through his eyes. Concern? Even, panic?

"Paris was Paris," she said as she heard another footstep, as she looked past Oliver to the man coming up behind him, into their home. "But I belong here…."

Her words ended with a gasp.

"Hello, Lilly." Truman pulled off his hat and looked at her with an intensity that could always unravel her just a bit.

Truman.

And he looked good. Time had been generous. His shoulders seemed broader under his faded leather jacket, and he wore a crisp white shirt and black tie, dark trousers, a spiffy rendition of the renegade flyer he'd been. He was even clean-shaven—no more raze of dark whiskers. Still, that unruly lock of black hair hung over his gray-blue eyes, and he gave her the slightest rakish smile, the one that never ceased to sweep words from her mouth.

She stood, mute, in the foyer, her gaze returning to Oliver.

"I should have done this years ago." Oliver ran his hand along the brim of his hat, considering her, then Truman for a moment. Finally, "I'll be in my study should you need me."

She wasn't sure just whom he might be talking to. Still, she had the crazy urge to lunge after him as he disappeared into his office.

She didn't want to guess at how she looked after two weeks' passage and a day at the *Chronicle*. For all she knew, she wore newsprint down her face, her hair in tangles.

"I know this is a surprise."

She looked at him, then, trying to choose which words to start with. She managed an unladylike, "Uh…"

He smiled, too much charm in it, and she wanted to slap him. Perhaps she *could* find the correct words. "What are you doing here, Truman?" She shot a look at the closed door to Oliver's office.

No, not closed. Slightly ajar. She remembered Presley's description of him sitting in the tavern in Spain. Perhaps he had his ear pressed to the door, waiting in the wings. The thought propelled courage into her veins. "Finally, after four years, you track me down?"

"Your father came to my air show."

She didn't bother to correct him, because yes, Oliver was her father. Except…so he hadn't tracked her down. Still, "I don't understand."

Truman set his hat on the foyer table and reached inside his jacket. "He came to inquire after these." He pulled out a folded wad of papers. "It's our divorce papers. I haven't signed them."

His words stilled her, all the way through. "You mean we're still—"

"Married. Yes." He curled them into a tube in his strong hands, drew in a breath, looked away from her, and it reminded her of that shaken expression after she'd climbed out onto the wing in the fog, when he'd depended on her to get them safely to ground. "I couldn't, Lil. Not when I still loved you."

She stared at him, his words like a flame through her.

Any time Oliver wanted to burst through the door and throw Truman's hide from their house would be fine with her. Her entire body thrummed.

"Love me? Truman, you threw me away like an old piece of fabric, patched up your wounds with a new plane, a new air show. Let's not forget Agnes the Sky Angel."

He held up his hand. "Lilly—"

"Do you even know what love is, Truman? Because guess what? Love sticks around. Commits. Love doesn't run."

At least, that's what Oliver—what God—had taught her.

Every word appeared as a blow on his face and he winced, looked at the ground. "I know."

"You know? What do you know? That you betrayed me? That what you did was—"

"Unforgiveable?" He said it so softly it shouldn't have silenced her, but she stood there as memory rushed back at her. *There's no forgiveness for me.*

She turned away, her back to him, hating the answer. "No. Not unforgiveable. Nothing is unforgiveable." She wanted to say the words— *I forgive you*—but they lodged in her throat.

He took a step toward her. It seemed the door to Oliver's office had cracked open just a bit wider. "Lilly, the day we did that suicide loop, when you nearly died, I nearly died too. The thought of losing you the way I'd lost my brother—because of my stupidity, my arrogance—

I couldn't bear it. I don't know what Oliver told you, but I begged him to take you back to New York City, away from me. I was afraid of what could happen to you, with me. I asked your father to make you forget about me."

No wonder Oliver had delivered the divorce papers. No wonder he never spoke Truman's name. She closed her eyes. "Then why are we still married? What are you doing here?"

Truman came up so close behind her she could smell the sky on him, the touch of the sun on his skin. If she turned, she might step right into his arms. She edged away from him.

"I'm here because nothing is right without you," he said softly. "We belong together. Since you left, everything feels off balance."

She rounded on him. "You have your own show—it's everything you ever dreamed of! I'm not stupid, I know that's why you married me. So that someday Oliver would buy you your own plane."

He stared at her, his mouth open.

"That's not true, Lilly." Oliver stood at the door now, his hands in his pockets. "I accused him of the same thing, and he told me he didn't want my money. I told him that he could have it anyway, as long as he loved you, kept you safe. That's why he told Marvel he could buy a plane."

"But you let me believe—"

"That was my doing," Truman said. "I knew that you would only leave me if I betrayed you. I knew you would find out what I said to Marvel, and I...didn't care."

He didn't care that he'd hurt her. "Well, it worked."

His lips tightened into a tight line of regret. "Yeah."

"So you came back because—"

"Did you not hear the part where I told you I am still in love with you? That nothing is right without you? That when Oliver showed up to retrieve the papers from me—the ones I've been holding onto for four years— I couldn't bear not seeing you? I begged him to let me see you, and he agreed."

"What if *I* didn't want to see you?"

Truman flinched. Glanced at Oliver. Then he nodded. "Okay. I deserve that. But I'm not signing those papers until I know you really don't want me."

She hated the look on his face and the way he so easily stirred her heart. *I want you, Truman.*

But then what? Live on the road with him, flying from one air show to the next? A vagabond life until one of them died?

She couldn't live that life. She glanced at Oliver, and he met her eyes. Not anymore.

Truman was her past. New York, the *Chronicle* was where she belonged now.

She turned away from him. "Sign the papers, Truman." Then she walked up the stairs to her room and shut the door.

Chapter 16

Her courage, whatever remained of it, failed her.

Rosie stood across the street from the Price family chateau, in the shadows of the late hour, watching as a man stalked out the front door, then turned and stared up at the house as if he meant to scale the walls.

He stood there so long she could nearly feel the frustration pulsing inside him. Then, just when she thought he might be leaving, he sat on the front steps, his head in his hands, until she thought he'd stay so long she might have to find a bench and rest her swollen feet.

He finally got up, took another look at the house, and strode into the night.

She watched him go, and his stance reminded her of Guthrie when she'd turned him down so many years ago on the boardwalk.

Or, when he realized that she intended to pay Cesar every cent he demanded. She wasn't going to run and spend her life looking over her shoulder. After having a taste of happily ever after, she intended to protect it with everything she had.

And, as the daughter of Foster and Jinx Worth, she had a considerable amount. She just needed to access it.

Which started with Lilly. Lilly had clearly returned and made amends with Oliver—Rosie had seen her one day, looking smart in a pair of camel trousers and a crisp white shirt. She might not be on the *Chronicle* masthead, but she looked like a publisher.

A publisher with access to the *Chronicle*'s considerable funds should Bennett and Jinx turn her away. It made the prospect of facing her parents less desperate.

Rosie wanted to throw herself in her cousin's arms. Instead, before she could stir up her courage, Oliver had returned home, the dejected young man in tow, and she'd had to wait until he left.

Now, she fought Guthrie's voice in her head and crossed the street, striding up to the door, nearly out of breath as she pulled the bell cord.

It chimed deep in the house, and Mr. Stewart, Oliver's butler, opened the door. He started at her appearance, despite his training. "Miss Rose. What a pleasure to see you." His gaze dropped to her condition.

"Can I come in? I'm here to see Lilly." She didn't sound at all like her stomach churned, her body flimsy.

"Of course." He opened the door wider, and she shuffled inside, aiming for the bench in the foyer.

"Rosie?"

Oliver had opened his study door. The last time she'd seen him, he'd taken a room in her mother's house, dragging himself in long after midnight, fatigue etched on his face. Now he appeared tan and robust, looking handsome and even young in a suit. Shame that he'd lost his wife so early. Now that she knew what love felt like, that kind of blow seemed unbearable.

"I can't believe it's you." Oliver walked over to her, pulling out his handkerchief. She took it, folded it neatly, and pressed it to her brow. He addressed his butler. "Father, can you fetch her a drink?"

"I'm here to see Lilly," Rosie said.

"Of course you are." Oliver stood aside as the butler handed her a glass of water from the side table. She drank it, surprised at how parched she'd become. She returned the glass to Mr. Stewart.

"Lilly's upstairs," Oliver said. "Father, can you inform—"

"I'll go talk to her." Rosie pushed herself up, belly first, aware that her actions had silenced both Oliver and his butler. Apparently neither had seen a pregnant woman in such close proximity. Or perhaps in public.

She placed a hand on the small of her back then waddled over to the stairway. Maybe she'd just lie down for a moment…

Lilly had taken her mother's former room, the one overlooking Fifth Avenue. Rosie knocked on the door, and, hearing nothing, eased it open.

Time cascaded away, and in that moment Rosie flashed back to Paris, to Lilly sitting on her windowsill, her legs pulled up to herself, staring outside, perhaps seeing nothing.

"Lils?"

Then time broke away and Lilly turned, bringing the time with her. She'd aged, cut her hair short into a perfect, fashionable bob. She wore trousers, and the naïveté had dropped from her expression, leaving behind only what looked like tears.

Indeed, she'd been crying. Rosie heard it in her voice, saw it in how she wiped her cheeks as she got up. "Rosie?"

She nodded. "Hello, Lilly."

"Rosie!" Lilly crossed the room in a moment and threw her arms around Rosie's neck. "I thought you moved to Chicago!"

Rosie closed her eyes, pulled her cousin close, inhaling the sweet reunion. "Oh, I've missed you."

Lilly pulled away, caught Rosie's hands. "And look at you."

"I'm one of your buffalo."

"You're glorious!" Her hands hovered above Rosie's stomach until Rosie took them and pressed against the baby moving inside.

Lilly's eyes widened. "Oh my. Does it hurt? When is your time?"

"Not for another couple of weeks. And it only hurts when I hike across town, get on a subway, or tromp through Central Park."

Lilly stared at her, as if trying to dissect her words, then pulled her over to the sofa in front of the fire. Rosie had always liked this room, the tiny rosebud wallpaper, the elegant Queen Anne bed on a riser in the middle of the room, the dressing table with the three gilded mirrors, the connected bathroom, updated with tiny Italian ceramic tiles. The boudoir bespoke an era of luxury, the boudoir of an heiress. Probably, Rosie could climb inside that gigantic bed and sleep for a year.

But she didn't live in this world anymore. And perhaps, if she had to choose—

"Lilly, I need your help."

Lilly sat next to her. "Anything."

Rosie blew out a breath. "Really? How about a hundred thousand dollars?"

Lilly eyes widened. Rosie met her eyes, nodded. "I'm in big trouble and I don't know what else to do."

"Tell me what happened."

She started with Cesar, then Guthrie, her escape at the train station, Cesar's threat, then adding in the years in Chicago, and finally Guthrie's trade to the Giants. "He's been throwing the games for Cesar, so Cesar can rake in bets. But it's killing him, Lilly. Guthrie is a man of honor, and he couldn't do it anymore. So he pitched his heart out in the last game, and now Cesar wants cash—a lot of it—or he's going to kill Guthrie." She ran a hand over her stomach. "Maybe even the baby. I have until tomorrow to raise the money."

"Oh, Rosie."

"It's worse. Guthrie thinks we should run. But he doesn't understand Cesar. He'll find us. And then..." She raised her chin, refusing to let her voice, her fears, rule her. "I will do anything to protect Guthrie. I love him."

Lilly said nothing, as if weighing her words. Then, she got up and walked to the window, staring out into the night, her reflection staring back at Rosie. "I can get the money from Oliver. But it'll take time."

"You sure he'll give it to you?"

"Just as sure as I am that Bennett will give you the money you need."

Bennett. Rosie had let that scenario into her mind too many times last night. The one where she appeared on her mother's doorstep, pregnant and desperate—her mother's greatest fear—and asked her stepfather— no, groveled in front of her stepfather—to give her the money to save the man she loved.

But, for Guthrie, she would do it.

And then…and then Bennett would stare at her with that cold disdain, the one that told her she wasn't his child. He would close the door on her, leave her sobbing on the doorstep, and never spare a moment of regret.

She deserved it, probably.

"Of course Bennett will give it to you. He loves you."

"He doesn't love me, Lilly. I'm not his child. I'm a reminder of the years he spent away from my mother."

Lilly came to her. "You're the daughter of his wife. How do you know if you don't ask? Of course I'll get the money—if I have time. But Bennett has the resources you need."

Rosie closed her eyes. "I don't know what to say to them."

"How about 'I'm sorry'? How about 'I love you'?" Lilly sat down beside her again. "The words I mean to say to Oliver." Lilly took her hand. Squeezed. "I will go with you if you want me to."

"I know," Rosie said. She touched Lilly's cheek. "But I think you have your own problems to chase after."

Lilly frowned.

"I saw a handsome man storm out of your house who looked like he wanted to tear down the door and carry you away."

"More like shove me into the cockpit of his Travel Air and barnstorm across the country."

"What?"

Lilly held up her hand. "Nothing. He's…well, he's my husband." She rolled her eyes.

"Your *husband*?"

"I thought we were divorced."

"You're divorced?"

"He never signed the papers, and he had the nerve to come back here and tell me he still loves me."

"Lilly, what is wrong with you?" Rosie stared at her. "Don't let him walk away."

"Why not? He let *me* walk away."

"Not if he came here to declare his love for you." Rosie shook her head. "What is it going to take for you to recognize love?"

Lilly drew in a long breath, her eyes clouding. "You don't understand, Rosie."

"What I understand is this: It's worth fighting for. It's worth dying for." She got up, pressed Lilly's cheek. "Why is it that we have such a hard time believing in our happy ending?"

Lilly cupped her hand over hers. "Because we didn't pay for it. We don't own it."

"Not anymore. I'm going to make sure this happy ending belongs to me." She leaned down and kissed Lilly on the forehead. "I love you, cousin."

"What are you going to do?"

"What I should have done a long time ago. I'm going to talk to my parents."

When Bennett first married her mother, Rosie believed everything the press said about him, everything Jack had accused him of as he'd packed his things and left.

She'd blamed Bennett for destroying her mother's marriage, even for killing her father, despite the truth. Although she'd lived with her father's abuse for years, Bennett seemed an interloper, a convenient escape for her mother's tears.

Then she'd met Guthrie.

An escape for her tears who'd turned into the man she couldn't live without. Perhaps she and her mother weren't so different after all.

Rosie churned that all through her head as she took the elevator to her parents' fifth-floor apartment. It overlooked Central Park from the west and, with sixteen rooms, managed to satisfy Jinx's need for spaciousness. After all, she still owned their cottage in Newport, even if she had sold the chateau on Fifth Avenue.

No doorman, but she stood in the corridor like a convict waiting for someone to yell her name down the hall and send her running.

Footsteps inside responded to the ringing of the bell, and she imagined at this late hour her mother had debated answering the door herself, her tendency to send the housekeeper away at an early hour.

She prayed for it, in fact.

The door swung open, and Bennett stood in the frame.

He so strongly resembled her father that for a moment, Foster stood there, tall, forbearing, staring her down with his dark eyes. Then, Bennett smiled, a warmth in his blue eyes that she realized she'd seen before, and the memory of her father vanished.

"Rosie!" Bennett glanced back over his shoulder. "Jinx! It's Rosie!" He seemed to want to reach out, to put his arms around her, but hesitated. Still, the action eased the breath inside her.

"Rosie?" Jinx appeared behind him, her black hair swept tight to the back of her head, dressed in a lavender silk robe, a strand of pearls at her neck. Her hands shook as she reached out to her, pulling her into the apartment. "Finally," she said, closing her into her arms.

"Mother," she said, breathing in the powder on her skin, settling into the softness of her embrace. "I need help."

Bennett closed the door behind her. "What took you so long?"

* * * * *

"Don't make the same mistake your mother did."

Oliver's voice haunted Lilly as she rode in the cab to the airfield just beyond the Queens bridge.

He'd visited her office at the *Chronicle,* shutting the door behind him, and she knew, right then, they were having another father-daughter talk.

This time, she tried to listen.

"I know I blindsided you with Truman. But I thought you needed an opportunity to hear the truth."

"Why didn't you tell me he sent me away on purpose?"

"And hurt you more?" He sat on the side of her desk. "I couldn't bear it. You wanted a divorce, and I was willing to see this through if that was what you wanted. But I—I was wrong, Lilly. I let you repeat the past." He picked up the paper from her desk. "I loved yesterday's column. Even better than the Lindbergh piece." He tucked it under his arm. "You are more like Esme every day. But please don't make the same mistake your mother did."

She assumed that meant leaving the man she loved in New York City, namely Oliver. But she wasn't her mother, and she wasn't leaving. It was Truman who would do the leaving, and she had to let him go.

"His show is playing for one more day in Queens," Oliver said, and winked.

Her stomach roiled as she headed over the bridge toward the airfield. Truman had crafted an air show deserving of New York. Gone were the days of the buzz through town to gather in townspeople, racing them back to the field to offer rides for five dollars a pop. His advance man placed ads in the *Chronicle*, the *Sun-Times*, and on bulletins pasted to street corners around the city. Now, as she approached, she made out a biplane in bright orange looping high above, disappearing behind the buildings as it dipped down to the airfield.

She wasn't surprised to find the field full of spectators, most of them sitting on blankets or on the hoods of their cars, maybe a thousand of them. Concession workers moved through the cars selling peanuts and popcorn, programs and playing cards. The cab dropped her off at the outskirts and she walked in, paying her dollar walk-in fee and finding a spot on the far edge of the field just in time to watch Agnes the Sky Angel climb out onto the wing and prop on the leading edge while the pilot did an inside loop, then a series of barrel rolls.

She could almost taste the wind in her teeth, the rush of adrenaline, feel her stomach climb up into her throat.

She didn't even realize she was holding her breath during the ladder act, when the wing walker climbed down to a car and sped off, her arms waving.

Well. Lilly hadn't mastered that move. Yet.

No, there was no *yet*. That life was over. She didn't long for the danger, the sense of power. Didn't long to look back and see Truman grinning at her, pride in his eyes.

Didn't long for—

"Lola the Flying Angel, I can't believe it!"

Lilly looked up at the man that blotted out the sunshine and grinned. "Rango." He wore a white shirt, a pair of canvas pants, suspenders holding them up. He still brilliantined his hair back with enough grease to power a small engine. "Still hawking popcorn?"

"Naw. Only when we're busy."

She bounded up to him, and he gave her a hug. She smelled the gasoline on him, reached up and scrubbed a smudge off his face.

"What are you doing here?"

"Marvel sold the show to Truman. Said he was the only one who he trusted to keep it flying."

"When?"

"About a year ago. Truman's still making payments, but he finally got his own plane." He pointed to a black biplane, now playing daredevil fighter in a mock battle against the other orange biplanes. "He's still the best I ever seen."

She shaded her eyes, imagined him at the controls, in the back cockpit, his eyes fierce, pushing his aircraft to the limit. "He never does anything halfway, does he?"

Rango looked at her, his smile gone. "Nope."

"Can I ask you something?" She looked back at the black hawk in the sky. He'd rigged something to his engine that released flour, just like their jumper once had, and the trail of white sketched his movements in the heavens. "Has Truman moved on since me? I know he was once a ladies' man."

"What?" The noise he made turned her attention to him. "No. Not even one. I promise, only one he's ever fallen for is you, Lilly."

She drew in that information, swallowed it down, blinked her eyes against the glare of the sun.

"Ever," Rango added as he picked up his concession box. "Stick around for after the show?"

She nodded. Absolutely.

They played in the sky for over two hours to the crowd's delight, and afterward, a line rushed the pilots, Agnes, and the parachutists. Lilly watched from afar as Truman signed autographs, his face tan outside the lines of his raccoon eyes, smiling as women all but swooned next to him.

She moved away from him, wandering to the fleet of airplanes. Five of them, four dressed in orange, the last in black. Truman's Hawk. She climbed up onto the wing, peered inside to the cracked red leather seats. Then she turned and scrambled onto the wing. On a tail dragger, she could upset the entire plane with her weight, so she simply stood at the far edge, holding the rope. Closed her eyes. *You're a natural, New York. You belong up there.*

"Lilly?"

His voice startled her out of herself. She looked down, over her shoulder.

"Did you hear me? You belong up there." Truman held his gloves in his hands. He piled them into his leather helmet and dumped it into the cockpit.

"I..." She shook her head. "I don't know. Maybe not."

He stepped up, offered his hand to her. She considered it a moment then took it. He caught her as she jumped down.

She disentangled herself and stepped away, too aware of how easily memory swept her back. He still smelled fresh and strong, like the sky, like freedom. But she wasn't that girl anymore. Wasn't his girl. "I was young, and really naïve."

"I thought you were brave."

She couldn't let him see how his words tunneled deep inside her, how he could still make her heart pulse to life. "You have an amazing show, Truman."

He sighed, something so long it could make her cry. "Thank you."

"It's everything you hoped for. A fleet of planes, a daring wing walker, your name as owner."

"No, that's not everything, Lilly," he said softly.

She closed her eyes, shook her head. "Truman—"

But he grabbed her arm, spun her around. And, as she opened her eyes, she hadn't even a moment to brace herself before he kissed her.

He simply slid his hand behind her neck and pressed his lips to hers, an urgency, even desperation in his touch that shattered all the arguments she'd come armed to wield. He tasted of their past, the sweet moments of discovery, of the too-vulnerable intimacy, the delicious safety of being in his arms.

She had no power to resist him, not when he softened his kiss, moved his arm around her waist, drew her into the pocket of his embrace. Not when he came up for air whispering her name, pressing his forehead to hers, then dove back in.

Truman. She tasted tears and realized they were his. Oh, Truman. She slid her arms up around his shoulders and simply hung on, losing her grief, forgiving him, needing him to be everything he promised with his touch.

"Please, Lilly," he said as he pulled away again, finding her eyes. She could fly forever inside them. "Please say you still love me."

Oh, she wanted to. It was right there, the last pulse between what she wanted and the fears that choked her. She caught her breath, tried again. But the smells and sounds of the airfield rose around her, reminded her of the truth.

Flyboys flew away.

She said nothing.

He slowly released her, back to the ground—she hadn't even

realized that he'd picked her up—and stepped away from her, holding up his hand as in surrender.

He shook his head then, trying a wry smile. "Can't blame a guy for trying."

"Truman—I... don't you see? You'll always be a barnstormer, always the scamp that flies away with my heart. I can't live this life with you. I can't love a man who needs flying more than he needs me."

And, she couldn't run away from Oliver, again.

He swallowed and looked away. Ran a thumb under his eye. "How about I give you a lift home?"

"I can take a cab—"

"I insist." He didn't look at her again as he rounded up the keys from Rango, who glanced at them both with something of confusion.

She gave him a kiss on his ruddy cheek. "Good to see you again. I'm still holding out for that dance."

He tipped his hat to her, his smile half-hitched.

She climbed onto the truck bench and Truman motored them out of the airfield toward Manhattan.

"Where to next?"

His hands on the wheel whitened. "West. Philadelphia, then across to Pittsburg. We have permission to play all the big cities."

"That'll put you in the black."

He nodded, still not looking at her. "I've nearly paid off Marvel."

"Rango told me."

He said nothing as they crossed the bridge, the sunset bleeding through the streets, over rooftops.

"Truman, I'm sorry."

He held up his hand. Then, he leaned over and tugged out from below his seat the curl of papers. Tossed them on the seat. "Don't worry, I'll sign them."

She picked them up, smoothing them out on her lap, swallowing against the great well of emptiness consuming her. She could hear the roaring inside, and with everything inside her wanted to tumble out of his truck at the next intersection and run.

They finally turned onto Fifth Avenue, the streetlights splashing into the streets. As they neared the house, she drew in a breath. "You can sign these inside."

His lips knotted into a tight bud. He pulled up to the curb outside her house then got out and came around the truck and opened the door.

The gate hung ajar and he pushed it open, following her up the stairs, his shoes scuffing on the marble.

She put her hand on the handle to open it and jerked. Her hand came away sticky, and she stared at it a moment, at the smear of red embedded in her palm. "What—?"

"Stay here," Truman said and pushed past her into the foyer.

She stood there, dumb for a moment, unable to move. Blood. Her hands began to tremble. "Oliver!" She stumbled inside, saw more of it, a smear across the floor, footprints tracking it into the hallway.

"Oliver—where are—"

She stopped at the sight of Rosie, blood saturating her dress, leaning over a man sprawled on the floor, his body writhing as Bette and Oliver tried to press towels to his wounds—so many of them, seeping blood onto the marble floor. Rosie held his face in her bloody hands, staring into his eyes, speaking quietly.

Truman stood above them, not moving. But he turned when Lilly gasped, catching her a second before she slid to the floor. "What happened?"

"It's Rosie's husband," Oliver said. "He's been shot."

"Shot? How—"

Oliver turned to Rosie. "Just breathe. It's going to be okay."

But one look at Rosie told Lilly that no, it would never be all right.

"Truman, call an ambulance," Oliver said.

"I already called them." Mr. Stewart appeared with more towels.

"I have my truck out front—we can take him!" Truman still had his arms around her.

"Please, Guthrie. Please. Shh, listen to me. You're going to be okay." Rosie put her face down to the man's. "Shh. I'm sorry. I'm so sorry."

Lilly untangled herself from Truman's grip and edged over to Rosie. Her hands were bloody to her wrists. "Rosie, let Bette in here. She and Stewart know what they're doing." She reached for Rosie's hands, but her cousin slapped them away.

"Guthrie!"

Guthrie was pale, his lips a horrid color of gray. His breathing emerged shallow, if at all, his eyes drifting closed, back open again when Rosie shook him. "Guthrie! Don't leave me!"

He seemed to gasp then raised his hand and clasped Rosie's arm. There was so much blood, it slicked the marble floor, saturated Lilly's skirt.

"I'm sorry, Red." His voice was so faint, Lilly wanted to weep. "I thought I could fix this."

"I told you I had the money." Rosie was beside herself, her words nearly intelligible. "You didn't have to do this."

"I didn't want your money, Rosie. I...wanted...us. You. We had to be free of him. He'd never let us go." He reached up around her neck, pulled her forehead down to him. "You have to be free, Red. For Charlie."

Rosie had begun to weep, to unravel, her words unintelligible.

"I love you, Red." His arm slipped down, landed on her hand. "But... you—you gotta leave. He'll find you. He'll find the baby. Save Charlie."

His eyes closed, his body shuddering.

"Don't leave me, Guthrie. Don't you dare leave—Guthrie!"

Lilly wanted to press her hands to her ears, to close her eyes, to curl into a ball at the stench of death, but Rosie's wail shredded through her, lifting her out of her horror.

"No—no, God! No!"

Rosie had Guthrie by the shoulders, was shaking him. His hand flopped onto the floor.

"Rosie—stop. Rosie!" Oliver reached for her, put his arms around her, pulled her back from Guthrie just as Truman appeared with two men carrying a gurney. Rosie fought Oliver, twisting in his arms, landing an elbow in his chest. Oliver just held on, scooting her back from the corpse as she writhed in his arms, hysterical.

Oliver met Lilly's eyes, shaking his head.

Lilly scrabbled over to Rosie and caught her face between her hands. "Rosie, shh…they're working on him. Shh. You're going to hurt the baby."

The words seemed to capture her, because she stopped struggling, fixed her eyes on Lilly's. "My fault. This is—this is my fault."

Oliver still had a grip on Rosie, his white shirt dripping, his arms around her. Lilly looked up and found Truman standing above them. "Help me get her into the study."

He nodded, then bent down and swooped Rosie into his arms, as if she weighed nothing. She curled into a ball against his chest, starting again to unravel.

Lilly cast a look back at the ambulance drivers and wanted to weep at the loss of urgency. Guthrie's body lay still, already dissolving of color.

Truman set her on the leather sofa and Rosie began to shake. "Guthrie—he needs me."

Lilly caught her hands, held them together. "Rosie. You have his baby to think about right now. You have to calm down." Her words, but they didn't seem to issue from herself, because inside she was still screaming.

Still seeing Guthrie writhing through the last throes of his life.

Still listening to Rosie's world shatter.

Truman appeared with water. He must have also closed the door, because the voices outside muffled.

Rosie's hand shook as she drank, and Lilly steadied it. She took the glass and gave it back to Truman. "What happened?"

"I...I...I had the money. And Cesar told me to meet him at the park. I thought Guthrie had practice, but...Guthrie was already there. How did he know I was to meet Cesar there? And he'd brought some of his fellow players with him. Mugs and Smiley and—and then Cesar and his men had guns and they just started shooting them. Shooting Mugs. And Smiley—they shot him in the head. And..." She pressed her hand to her mouth, shaking her head. "But Guthrie didn't run. He ran at Cesar with a bat—a *bat*—and hit him. He hit him again then..." She swallowed, looked up at Truman, back to Lilly. "They shot him. Cesar's men shot him. And he kept hitting Cesar, getting up until they shot him again—" Her voice raised, on the far end of sanity. "They kept shooting him until he just lay there, bleeding. So—so much...blood."

"How'd you get him here, Rosie?"

"I got Oliver. I had to leave Guthrie, but I had no choice. He and his father brought him here."

No wonder Oliver was sopping with Guthrie's blood.

Rosie looked up then, toward the closed study doors. "I have to go with him. I have to—" She started to rise, but her legs collapsed under her, and she groaned, her hand over her stomach.

"You stay right there, Rosie." Lilly got up, turned to Truman. "She needs a doctor."

"There's blood on the street and on the front steps," Truman said quietly. He took her arm, pulled her away. "Who is this Cesar?"

"He's a mobster, owns a club Rosie used to work for. She ran away from him to marry Guthrie. He told her that if she didn't cough up a hundred grand he'd kill Guthrie and her baby."

Truman's mouth tightened in a grim line. "Apparently he's a man of his word."

Lilly glanced back at Rosie, the way she tucked her arms around herself, her face twisted.

Truman leaned closer, spoke directly in her ear. "We don't have a lot of time. I know men like this Cesar. He's not going to let her stay alive after this. You need to get her out of here."

His words went through Lilly like a knife. "You think he'll come here?"

"Shh." He glanced at Rosie, back to her. "Maybe. Probably. Which means you need to leave, now. And I'm not just talking this house. You need to get out of New York."

"Out of New York. But—"

"Go to Montana." Apparently Oliver had come in, had been listening, and now moved into their conversation. "Go to the ranch. He won't find you there."

"The ranch? My mother's ranch? But I thought—"

"I didn't sell it, Lilly."

Oliver could have slapped her with less of a blow. She stared at him. "But you said it was gone."

"I—I leased the land, but I didn't sell it. And the house is still yours."

He drew in a breath, glanced at Truman. "I just felt like if you knew it was there, I'd lose you all over again. I was going to tell you when the lease came up. I just wanted you to give this life a try. Give your mother's hopes a chance."

"The hope that we might share the paper?"

"The hope that we might be a family." He looked back at her, tried a smile. His eyes glistened.

She forgave him. How couldn't she? Her affection ran deep, the kind of affection adopted, not birthed, the kind of affection that told her that this was the father she'd longed for. The father she'd found. And after everything, he'd preserved the very thing he thought he'd lose her to. "We are a family." She wrapped her arms around his waist, holding on. "I love you, Father."

He stood a moment, as if rattled, then wrapped his arms around her. "I love you too, Lillian Joy. You are everything to me."

Everything. The word went through her, and she believed him.

Then he held her away. "But Truman's right. You have to go. Take the Rolls to the station, get on the first train west—"

"No." Rosie's protest made them all turn. "No. He—he found us at the train before. When I escaped with Guthrie. He'll find us again. He'll kill us. He'll—"

"You could fly." Truman was nodding, first to Oliver, then to Lilly, as if convincing himself. His voice warmed to the idea. "You're a pilot, Lilly. You were born to fly. You could go to the air show and take my plane. Fly it out to Montana. Your father's right—Cesar will never find you. And we'll stay here and make sure he doesn't follow you."

Fly. The idea rooted inside her, stirred her. Yes, they could— "What do you mean *you'll stay here*? You can't stay here! What if Cesar shows up?"

Oliver glanced at Truman, back to her. "We'll be fine, Lilly. Trust us."

"But—"

"I swear, Lilly, you are the most stubborn woman I've ever met. Get in my plane and get out of here."

Truman wasn't kidding, his blue eyes fierce in hers.

She had no words. So she rose up on her toes and kissed him, something quick and sharp and true. "I'll take care of her."

"Rosie?" Truman asked.

"Your plane."

He shook his head. "I don't care about my plane, Lola. Just the pilot."

Oliver had flung a blanket around Rosie's shoulders, was helping her off the sofa. "Close your eyes, Rosie. We're going to get you out of here."

Chapter 17

She just wanted to stop hurting.

Or feeling like the world had dropped out beneath her.

It would help, too, if she could keep down her lunch. But four days of nausea, sickness, and traveling had turned Rosie inside out. She ached from her feet to her hairline, and no amount of blankets or sitting in front of Lilly's massive green marble fireplace, watching the flames devour the pine logs, snapping and growling, could warm her.

The morning sun slid fingers through the room, touching the dark side tables, turning the crushed red velvet on the divan and side chairs shiny, like blood.

She leaned back into the rocking chair, wishing she could shake the hum of the prop from her brain or erase the feel of the wind seeping into her ears. No matter how well Lilly tucked the blankets around her in the cockpit, the breeze found the holes and drilled the cold into her body. She'd never be warm again. But perhaps it had nothing to do with the four-day flight to Lilly's ranch.

Probably the cold came from leaving behind everything good and honest and right in her life. From watching her husband's eyes glaze over, feeling life spill from him onto Oliver's white marble floor.

She stared at her hands. She still had his blood embedded in her pores.

"I didn't want your money Rosie. I...wanted...us. You."

Why, Guthrie? Why? If she closed her eyes even for a moment, she saw him there, in Central Park, near the carousel, the shadows of the horses distorted against the eerie lamplight. She could only imagine that he'd followed her. Or maybe he'd heard her telephone Cesar from the next room as he lay in their bed, recovering from Cesar's beating. But she saw none of it in his beautiful eyes when she'd kissed him good-bye and lied to him.

He'd lied to her too. Told her that everything would be okay. That he would protect her, that they would be safe, live happily ever after. He'd kissed her sweetly, and for a moment, she'd leaned into him, believing him.

It gave her the courage to untangle herself from his arms and try to buy their freedom."Ma'am, perhaps some tea?"

The voice rescued her and she found Dawn, Lilly's housekeeper, bearing a tray with tea, some crackers. Apparently Oliver had telegrammed ahead, because the house awaited them with a complement of staff, every cobweb swept clean, and smelling of cinnamon.

In a different life, with Guthrie beside her, Rosie might like the ranch home. Two stories, with a grand entrance, the dark, tooled banister curving up to the second-floor landing. Gleaming golden wood floors, the oval grand room, the warm parlor with the red velvet settee—it all suggested she might be back in New York City, sitting in her mother's great room, with the exception of the oil portrait of an Indian woman over the mantel. She stared down at Rosie with what seemed kind, black eyes and Rosie couldn't look at her.

Likewise, she could hardly bear the kindness of Dawn, who resembled the woman in the portrait so much they might be sisters. She'd tried to ladle soup into her mouth, rubbed her frozen feet, and sat with her into the night, pressing a cool cloth to her face.

"I—I don't know if I can keep it down."

Dawn set the tray on the side table. "You need to eat something, Miss Rose, for the child."

How many times had Lilly said that on their trip west? Rosie ran her hand over her belly, aware that the baby had quieted, probably from the lurching landings, the vibration of the plane. She could still taste her fear as the ground dropped away, as she glanced back at the surreal image of Lilly in the pilot's seat.

Lilly had also turned into her nurse. When they landed in Philadelphia where they spent the night, then in Ohio somewhere, then over to Indiana and Illinois—every night she tried to coax food in to Rosie. "You'll feel better with some food." She finally managed to get some soup down at the hotel in some prairie hideaway. It only returned an hour later. Lilly put her to bed in the boardinghouse and fetched a doctor.

He found the baby's heartbeat and suggested they spend a few days, but Rosie pushed them on to Nebraska, across southern Colorado to Wyoming, then north to Butte.

It seemed familiar terrain to Lilly, who only grew fiercer, the sun turning her skin leathery except for the white rings around her eyes. And every time they landed, she apologized.

"You'll feel better when we get to Montana."

She'd never feel *better*. How did one feel better when life—when God—had betrayed her?

She'd simply been too happy. She'd simply forgotten that she had nothing with which to barter for the graces of the Almighty.

She'd turned into her mother, broken. Weeping in her bed at night, without comfort.

Now, she answered Dawn.

"I don't want to eat."

"Not even for your child?"

Rosie looked away. How was she supposed to raise a child without Guthrie? She shook her head.

Dawn made a noise then got up. "I'm drawing you a bath. See if we can't work some of those tangles from your hair."

Rosie closed her eyes, leaning her head back. She didn't care what she looked like. She'd never be clean, be whole again.

Not after watching Guthrie's face as he swung his bat at Cesar. She didn't know him then. And perhaps her scream had jolted him, jerked him away from his fury.

Perhaps it had cost him his life, because in that hesitation of the second swing, one of Cesar's men had found his gun.

She jerked, watching him stumble back, the shot sharp and acrid through her. She pressed her hands to her mouth, seeing Guthrie fall. She shuddered as he got up, swinging, then as the man shot him again.

About then she'd stumbled, screaming, out of the shadows where she'd hid, and had run to her husband, broken on the path.

Cesar's men picked up Cesar and ran.

Only the shivering trees remained to witness her grief as she gathered Guthrie into her arms. Still breathing. Still alive.

Lilly. Lilly would help her.

"Ma'am, your bath is drawn." Dawn again. Rosie opened her eyes from the trauma. Dawn wore a white cloth tied around her black hair, pinned at the nape of her neck. Unlike Amelia, her mother's housekeeper, Dawn wore a gray cotton dress, no apron, informal. As if she might be Lilly's spinster aunt.

"Where's Lilly?"

Lilly had vanished shortly after they'd landed on the strip of road outside the house. She'd motored the airplane up the driveway toward the barn, the sun still simmering high over the horizon, rousing Rosie from her slump in the front cockpit.

As Lilly tried to help her out, a lean, dark-headed man rode in, reined his chestnut mount, and climbed down. Older than Lilly, with a deep tan, lines on his face, he pushed up his hat with one gloved finger and stared at them as if he'd never seen a plane before.

Perhaps he hadn't.

Then, Lilly climbed down, and something about the greeting between Lilly and this man, as Lilly dove into his embrace, heated her eyes, made her look away.

Lilly called him Abel, and it roused a memory tucked inside Rosie. Abel—their hired man? The one Lilly had written to in her childhood?

Rosie had no words for the way this same man climbed onto a hay bale, leaned into the cockpit, and lifted Rosie into his arms. He smelled of sweat and the prairie grasses, the heat of the sun, wild and uncouth, but she didn't care as he carried her inside and into a room decorated in teacup rose wallpaper. Dawn had appeared and tucked her into a featherbed. As the housekeeper had pulled the green velvet drapes of the bedroom, blotting out the Montana landscape, Rosie had sunk into the pillows and imagined everything away.

Imagined herself safe.

Imagined herself in Guthrie's arms.

Until she woke the next morning and found the house quiet, the sun shining, a new, fresh day of agony. She'd been restless since then, unable to find a comfortable spot. Even the rocking chair now pressed into her bones.

"Miss Lillian rose early, and is out on her land with Mr. Abel."

Rosie allowed Dawn to slip an arm behind her as they mounted the stairs for her bath. "He's the hired man?"

"He's leasing this land, and was a dear friend of her mother's. He tends the house, also, although he has his own homestead just south of here."

"What happened to his hand?"

Dawn tucked her close, her arm around her waist as they worked their way up the stairs.

"He was in a terrible mine fire, the one that killed Daughtry, Lilly's father. Esme took him in after he recovered. He's part of the family."

Pictures hung on the wall, oils of Esme and Lilly in her christening gown, the long lace flowing down over Esme's lap, Lilly's chocolate hair, dark eyes so full of fire, even then.

"Such a painful and yet joyous season. Mrs. Hoyt had lost Daughtry in that terrible fire and she didn't even know she was carrying Lilly. The day she discovered she had Daughtry's child within her, she sat in that very rocking chair, just like you, and stared at the fire. As if trying to perceive God's mind."

Dawn slowed halfway up, as if sensing Rosie's fatigue. "I helped Mrs. Hoyt when her time came, and I'll help you too, Rosie."

They had reached the top. The exertion of the climb knotted Rosie's body and she stopped, groaning.

Dawn held her as she clung to the wall, breathing through the ache. It seemed to subside enough for her to take a full breath.

"How soon before your time, Rosie?"

"Maybe a week or more."

Dawn said nothing as she hiked Rosie back into her arms and delivered her to the bedroom. Rosie could smell the scented oils Dawn added to the bath, floral and light. As if trying to soothe the darkness from Rosie's spirit.

She settled Rosie onto the bed and left her to fetch her robe.

Rosie ran a hand over her stomach as the baby shifted inside her. Another fist of pain followed the kick inside. She caught her breath.

Dawn returned, watching her with a frown. "Are you sure—"

"What did Aunt Esme decide?" Rosie said, her hand tightening around the brass frame. "Did she perceive the mind of God in taking her husband so early? In giving her a fatherless child?"

Dawn began to untie Rosie's hair, letting it fall, her hands gentle. "Perhaps it wasn't the mind of God that she discovered, but His love."

His love. Like Lilly. And Oliver.

But Rosie had no Oliver waiting for her, and this child needed a father, a family. He needed a mother who wouldn't look at him and see grief.

There was no love for Rosie to discover.

Another pain coiled around her, bending her over, and in that moment she felt a kick, even a pop, deep inside.

Wetness saturated the damask coverlet of the bed.

Rosie jerked, moaned as the coil around her belly tightened, stealing her breath.

Dawn knelt before her, took her hand, and squeezed. "I believe your time has come."

No. Rosie stared into Dawn's eyes, a darkness seeping through her, turning her numb. "No. I'm not having this baby. You don't understand. I can't have this child without Guthrie. I *won't.*"

Dawn smiled and patted her cheek. "Miss Rosie, you're going to be a mother whether you want to or not."

* * * * *

Deep inside the caverns of sleep, and caught in the tangle of prairie smells and the warm rush of wind over her skin, the mourning cry resonated as timber wolves on the far ridges. The sound of it tunneled inside her, resonated, drew her out of slumber in a rush, her heart in her throat.

Lilly stilled in the padding of the night, listening. She was fifteen again, and wolves stalked the herd, thirsty and brutal, ready to devour. She should pull on her boots, grab her rifle, wake Abel, and ride out to protect the calves.

She heard the sound again, robust and high, panicked and angry, and time bled away.

"Charlie!" Lilly threw off her quilt and didn't mind the cool lick of the wood floor across her feet as she grabbed her robe, pulling it on. The cries resounded down the hallway, so loud they could sheer clear through to her bones. She tied the belt, cinching it around her before she stopped at Rosie's door, not sure whether to knock.

A breath, and another loud bellow made her turn the handle.

She pushed into the room, the cries from the cradle at the end of the bed nearly deafening. Rosie lay curled in the center of the bed, her knees to herself, the covers over her head. Lilly stood above the cradle, hesitating only a moment before she scooped up the infant.

"Shh, Charlie. Shh." She tucked the little one against her chest, her hand finding the wetness of the cloth nap. No wonder the child sounded miserable. She grabbed up the quilt, tucking it around the baby as she found the dressing table. The infant continued to scream, its little mouth wide, its entire body trembling. Lilly unpinned the cloth, found it only wet, cleaned the child, added powder, then pinned on a fresh nap, swaddling the baby back into the quilt.

For a little girl, Charlie had the lungs of a buffalo. She continued to squirm, arching her back, her eyes closed, her hands in tiny fists.

Oh, how Lilly loved her. From her fuzzy prairie-brown hair to her blue-as-the-sky eyes, the red little fists, her round tummy, every petite appendage including her delicate nose, little Charlie seemed nothing short of a miracle.

Just think, she might have had a child like this, soft and downy, with Truman's dark eyes.

No, that dream had died. She couldn't dwell on the things she'd lost. None of them could.

Lilly held the infant in her arms and sat down on the bed. Rosie didn't move.

"Rosie. Charlie's hungry. Are you sure you don't want to try—"

"Go away."

So she wasn't sleeping.

Lilly bit back her ire, kept her voice kind, patient. What had the doctor said? Depression? But this didn't feel like depression. It felt more lethal, like grief. Like losing Guthrie had destroyed Rosie, and with it anything she had to give to her child.

"Rosie, she's so beautiful. Look at her. Just one look. I promise, she's worth it. She has these amazing fingers, they curl right around your finger. And this nose—it's your nose. And she smells delicious." She pressed her lips to Charlie's forehead, inhaling. "Shh."

"I don't want her." Rosie rolled over, her back to her. "I can't."

Lilly drew in a breath and couldn't keep the frustration from her voice. "I don't understand you, Rosie. You have everything to live for. This child is here because Guthrie loved you. You're not alone. You have me and my father. We're going to help you. And you're not destitute. Your mother and Uncle Bennett wired that you could come back to New York, live with them. You still have the money they gave you. And look at your precious, beautiful daughter—"

"Get out!" Rosie sat up, glaring at her with reddened eyes. "I don't want her. I don't want any memory of Guthrie, or the life we were going to have. I don't want any help. I just..." She closed her eyes, held up her hand as if to push them away. "I just want to forget." She lay back down, pulled the covers up over her head. "Please, leave me alone. And stop calling her Charlie. That's the name Guthrie wanted for our child. This child is an orphan."

Charlie writhed in Lilly's embrace, one skinny arm snaking out, fingers splayed as if grabbing for something unseen. "We'll be downstairs when you change your mind," Lilly said softly. She got up and found Dawn in the hall, also in her bedclothes and robe, her long black hair down to her waist.

"I'll warm some milk," she said.

Lilly descended to the parlor, stood by the window, staring out as the dawn pushed back the darkness. A sliver of gold simmered against the horizon, the sky a slate gray. She put the baby against her shoulder, rocking her, singing softly.

A miracle child, and Rosie didn't want her. After two days of labor, after Lilly drove to Silver City in Abel's Packard to fetch the doctor, after turning the baby out of the breech position, after nearly dying from exhaustion, the loss of blood, Rosie didn't want her child.

Lilly heard footsteps, light on the floor behind her. Dawn bore a bottle of milk. "Shall I feed her?"

"I can. You go back to bed. We'll be fine." Lilly sat in the rocking chair and nestled Charlie on her lap. The baby's mouth opened for the bottle and she sucked hungrily, her eyes closing, her sighs shuddering out of her.

Dawn stood above them, arms akimbo, shaking her head. "I've never seen the sickness this bad. Already nearly two weeks and she still can't bear to look at the child."

"She'll get better," Lilly said.

Dawn sank down onto the velvet divan. "I don't know, Lilly. She's all healed up, yet she refuses to leave her bed." She ran her hand over Charlie's head. "It's nice to have a baby in the house. To have you back."

Lilly met Dawn's eyes, found them shiny. "I missed you too."

"I long dreamed of looking up one day and seeing you ride down the driveway on Charity, as if you were just out overlooking the herd with Abel."

"I'm sorry it took so long for me to return. I tried, years ago, but then my father needed me after Mother died."

"I'm so sorry about your mother, Lilly. She was like a daughter to me. She wrote to me often after you left the ranch, told me about your life in New York. I never could see you in those fancy dresses. In my mind, you will always be riding Charity across the hills, your long braids stringing out behind you. Scared me to death when you showed up in an aeroplane."

"It's not mine. It belongs to…" She wasn't sure what to call Truman. Husband? Friend? Pilot?

"The man you love?"

Lilly stared down at the baby, jostling her a bit to keep her awake, still suckling. "Why do you say that?"

"Because every day you stand on the porch, watching the road, and I'm wondering who you are waiting for."

"My father." She removed the bottle, still half-full, and handed it to Dawn. Then she turned Charlie over on her knees, resting her face in her hand, rubbing her back for a burp. "I left him in New York in a rather precarious situation. He told me he'd come when he could."

But Dawn was shaking her head. "Oh, Lilly, you're so much like your mother. I knew her before she and Daughtry were married. I know the look of a woman in love. A woman with her hopes upon her countenance."

Charlie emitted a tiny pop of sound, startling herself awake. Lilly rolled her over, nestling her back into the cradle of her arms before she could start to wail, and took the bottle from Dawn.

"What you see, Dawn, is what can never be. I do love this man. His name is Truman, and I married him years ago. He's the one who taught me to fly. But that's the problem—he's a barnstormer, a risk taker, a man who belongs in the skies."

"And you are needed here."

She couldn't agree, not really. "The buffalo herd has nearly doubled in size. Maybe I belong in New York."

"Abel tends the animals with your heart. It's why he leased the ranch from your father. Perhaps the buffalo don't need you, but yes, this little one does. You've always been a nurturer, Lilly. Perhaps this is the mind of God, bringing you back here, now, with Rosie, for this child."

"This child has a mother, Dawn, and it's not me."

Dawn ran her hand over Charlie's forehead again then nodded. The baby had fallen asleep with the bottle in her mouth. Lilly removed it.

"Would you like me to return her to Rosie?"

"Let Rosie sleep. I'll put her down in the bassinet." Lilly got up and put the baby in the wicker Indian basket Lilly had found in the attic and cleaned, the one she set on the window seat for moments like these. "I'll just nap on the divan in case she wakes."

Dawn took the bottle but paused at the door. "This house still echoes with the laughter, love, and dreams of the people who loved you. I saw the paper, I know this Cesar fellow is dead. But Montana is not a terrible place to raise this child. You might tell Rosie this."

Not a terrible place, indeed. Riding through the prairie that first day back with Abel stirred up the taste of galloping Charity through the tall grasses, the odor of sun-baked cow pies saturating the air. She loved this land, the sky, so deeply blue, so wide it might be the sea, the gray-black ripple of foothills feeding into the white-laced mountains to the north. Sparkling rivers, the lush paint of the pink bitterroot flowers, the yellow buttercups, lavender clover.

And, the buffalo. The shaggy-coated beasts roamed over the land, no longer corralled in the canyon bordered by the meager river. "The drought pushed them out, in search of water," Abel said, sitting tall in his saddle, his once-dark hair now sanded with white. He was every bit as wide-shouldered and wise as she'd remembered. "Now, we have to ride for miles to find them, and camp out during calving season to watch for wolves, cougars. They still roam our land, however, and for now, they're safe."

Truman's plane might help in the search in the spring. The thought tripped into her head, and she shook it away.

Truman would return, yes, for his plane. Then he'd hand her the signed divorce papers and fly out of her life, and she wouldn't blame him. She'd nearly gotten him killed. Again. And now she had Rosie and her child to care for.

She would care for Charlie until Rosie broke free of her grief. As long as it took. And then she'd return to New York where she belonged and help Oliver run the paper.

Leaning over the basket, she kissed Charlie's tiny nose then curled up on the divan, pulling her robe over her. From here she could hear every rustle, even a feeble cry.

She sank into sleep despite the plume of morning sinking into the room, yet lightly because the house creaked and it roused her. Lilly listened, her eyes blinking in the rose-gold light, but perhaps it was only her imagination. Getting up, she tiptoed to the baby, found her still asleep, beautiful translucent eyelids closed, tiny rosebud lips open, her quilt still tucked around her.

So precious.

Lilly lay back down, closed her eyes. Yes, for as long as Rosie needed her, and then some.

Another creak of the floor and this time a footstep accompanied it. Lilly opened her eyes, realized that morning had parted the curtains, the room lit and warming. She pressed a hand to her cheek, found the creases of the divan pillow in it.

"Rosie?" She sat up, hoping to see her cousin in the hallway, searching for her daughter.

Instead, in the middle of the hallway, under the gleam of the sun, wearing a sharp black suit and tie, his hat in his hands, stood Truman.

Truman.

Alive and well and unscratched, looking so painfully handsome that for a terrible moment she thought it might be a dream.

And as long as she was dreaming, she imagined herself launching into his arms and holding on. Dreamed of hearing him say that he'd returned for her, that he loved her, that she was everything to him.

For a moment, as she dreamed, silence thudded between them. Then a devastating smile twitched up his face. "Hello, Lola."

Lola. She drew in a quick breath.

Real. Not a dream. So she shook herself free and held onto the brutal truth. Truman wouldn't stay here, wouldn't commit to live this life, or whatever life lay before her. "I suppose you're here for your plane." Oh, that hadn't emerged quite like she'd intended, but he didn't flinch.

"Maybe."

See. She shouldn't expect anything different.

"Is it in one piece?"

She glared at him, tucking her robe around her, got up, and padded over to the basket.

Charlie was still sleeping. Lilly laid a finger to her mouth then tiptoed out into the hallway. "Of course it is. When did you get here?"

"Last night, late. I stayed in town then hired a car this morning."

He'd said *I*. Not we. Not her father. She braced herself. "Where's my father? The paper said that Cesar was killed, but—" Oh, please—

"Oliver's fine. He'll be out in a day or two, I promise." Truman pulled his trilby off his head, ran his hand around the brim. Looked out the window.

"What aren't you telling me?" She stepped up to him. Saw the remnants of a bruise on his jaw. "Truman?"

"He got a little banged up."

"What—"

"He'll be fine. Cesar's men brought the heavy artillery, and although your father had called in some favors with pals in the police department…well, they fired the house, Lilly." Truman shook his head. "It's gone. Your chateau on Fifth Avenue burned."

The Price home, turned to ash. She had to reach out, to hold the doorframe. Her mother's portrait, her books and journals, Oliver's photographs, the family heirlooms.

"Was Oliver—"

"He's going to be okay. He was burned trying to retrieve a few items, but the fire department pulled him out."

She sank down onto the stairs. "How did Cesar die?"

"From the beating Guthrie gave him. And the Napoli gang—all arrested." Truman seemed to want to take a step toward her, almost gave a start. Then, "You're safe, Lilly. You and Rosie are safe."

The nearness of him buzzed through her. He smelled good, some sort of soap, and had brilliantined back his gleaming black hair, capturing that rebellious lock, as if trying to make a good impression. He set his trilby on a side table.

"This is a beautiful place, Lilly. No wonder you wanted to return home." He stood there talking to her like a salesman, or an old family friend, shifting from side to side as if nervous.

She'd never seen him without his cocky smile and the "over my dead body" stance, except, of course, two-plus weeks ago when he'd suggested he loved her. That he couldn't live without her. That he'd do anything to prove it.

Without his trilby, he had nothing to do with his hands and slipped them into his pockets.

She wanted to weave her fingers through his, wrap them around her. Lie to herself that he hadn't arrived for his airplane, but for her.

But she wasn't that stupid.

Lilly didn't want to imagine what she might look like, the lines in her face, her reddened eyes, the disarray of her hair.

A noise emerged from the basket, the smallest of whimpers.

"Is that Rosie's child?"

"A little girl. She hasn't officially named her yet, so we keep calling her Charlie." She picked up the infant, cradled her in her arms, hoping she might fall back to sleep. "I remember Rosie telling me that Guthrie wanted a son named Charlie. I didn't know what else to call her."

"Where's Rosie?"

"She's upstairs sleeping." She patted the baby's diaper as Charlie began to squirm, as the first little squeaks came from her. "I need to change her diaper."

"I'll help."

She stared at him, her mouth forming a question, when little Charlie woke with a start and began to wail. Wetness soaked through the blanket and into her nightclothes.

"Excuse me." She brushed past him, heading up the stairs, and noticed that he followed her. When they reached Rosie's room, she turned. "Rosie's sleeping. Stay here, I'll be right back."

He nodded, and she eased open the door.

Then she simply stood there in the threshold as Charlie screamed. Rosie's bed wasn't just empty, someone had made it.

As if she'd never been here.

She stepped inside.

"Is she here?" Truman said, right behind her. "Because I don't see her."

"Maybe she's downstairs," Lilly mumbled and went to the dressing table.

Truman fetched a dry diaper. Lilly cleaned Charlie, powdered her, then replaced the saturated diaper.

"She's so little."

"Nine pounds when she was born."

She had no words when Truman reached over, sliding his large hands under her, and picked her up. He held her close, tucking her into the crook of his arm.

The sight made Lilly want to weep.

He would have made a delicious father, with little boys to teach to fly and a little girl to dance on his shoes.

No. She couldn't think this way, and the sooner he left— "I gassed up your plane. You can get Abel to help you push it out of the barn to the road."

Emotion pulsed at the edge of Truman's eyes. "What if—"

"Lilly!" Dawn's voice cut through his question. She wore a clean brown dress, her hair now neatly pinned back in a bun. She didn't even cast a look at Truman as she strode into the room, looking shaken, holding a piece of stationery.

"She's gone."

Lilly frowned.

"Rosie's run away." Dawn shoved the paper at Lilly.

She took it, cold fingers pressing into her with each word.

Dear Lilly,

Once upon a time, you promised to forgive me for betraying you. I believe you may have to work harder at it now, for I know my next sin to be much greater, perhaps even unforgiveable.

I cannot care for the child I birthed.

I have lain in bed for ten days watching you bathe, diaper, and feed the child, and have discovered one thing: you are her mother. You are the one who wakes at night, you are the one whose heart is moved by her cries, who inspected her tiny fingers and toes upon birth. You may not have carried her, but you were meant to be this child's mother by the very fact that you have taken her into your heart.

I know you would give your life for this child.

I cannot even look at her. Not when she has Guthrie's lips, his eyes. Not when I must bear the day when she inquires about her father, and I must keep him alive in her heart. Your mother had a strength I do not possess. In fact, I do not want it.

If I am to survive this grief, I must erase it. Do not try and find me, for I do not wish to belong to the world I had, the woman I was.

I give you this child as your own, Lilly. I pray someday you will forgive me yet again for this betrayal, this weakness. If I know one thing, however, it is that only you can understand what grief this daughter of yours will bear. And that, I know, will be her salvation.

Gratefully,
Rose

"How could she do this?" The words shook out of Lilly, just a whisper, growing louder the second time around. "How could she do this?"

Dawn's eyes widened as Lilly shoved the letter back into her hands. She rounded on Truman. "We have to find her. Stop her. Dawn, take the baby—"

She went to retrieve Charlie from Truman's arms, but he stepped back. "Lilly, stop." His low voice cut through the whirr in her head. "She doesn't want to be found."

"She doesn't know what she's saying! She belongs here, with this child. Her child!"

"No, Lilly. *Your* child. You can't force her to be something she doesn't want to be. Just like Oliver couldn't force you to be a newspaper woman. She has to want it. Commit to it." He nudged Charlie, now sucking her fist, into Lilly's arms. "Lilly, your heart is broken for those in need—Rennie, and your buffalo, and even me. I was broken until I found you. I didn't believe that I could be loved, but you changed that. You made me believe, even for a little while, that someone could love me, despite my mistakes, my sins."

Just like Oliver had for her. "Truman, I never stopped loving you."

He touched her cheek, his eyes soft. "You can be this child's mother if you want to."

There's power in commitment, it turns you into the man you hope to be. The man you can live with.

The mother she hoped to be?

"I—I don't know..."

"What if you didn't have to do it alone?" He ran his thumb over Charlie's delicate fingers. They opened and wrapped around his, holding on.

She looked up at him. His eyes glistened. "I didn't come back for my plane, Lilly. I came back for my wife, if she'll have me. Please forgive me."

"I forgave you long ago, Truman. But..." Oh, it felt good to finally say that. And she longed to step into the dream, but— "What about your air show and flying and—"

"I sold the air show back to Marvel. He wanted it anyway. I'm out, Lilly. And I came here with the hope that you'd let me prove every day that I love you. That I'm not going to leave you."

"You're not going to get into your plane and fly out of my life?"

"It's your plane now—I bought it for you. I'm grounded."

He caressed the baby's head. "It's taken me ten years for it all to sink in. God walked back into my life the day you asked me for a ride. I just didn't see Him until you left." He cupped his hand under her chin. "Flying Angel."

She blinked against the burning in her eyes. Charlie began to squirm in her arms.

"I'll heat up some milk," Dawn said from behind her. Lilly had forgotten she'd been standing there.

"And I'll feed her," Truman said. "Please?"

He wanted to feed her? "Who are you?"

"Her...father?"

She swallowed, nodded. "Yes."

"Yes I can feed her?"

"Yes, you can stay. You can be her father." She couldn't look at him, but he stepped close, putting his arms around both of them. "But only on one condition."

"I have a feeling I'm not going to like this."

"You're not grounded. I have uses for that airplane, sir. I'll need to track the buffalo, maybe fly into Butte and check on the family paper. The *Chronicle* needs a good editor out here."

"Please don't suggest wing walking." He curled his hand behind her neck. "I love you, Lilly Hoyt. From the minute you walked into my life and hitched a ride. I've never stopped loving you." He smiled then kissed her, his lips warm and soft and perfect, so familiar, so right, and she tasted everything they'd had, everything they would have.

In his arms, yes, she could fly.

When he released her she smiled into his eyes. In his reflection she saw a woman, her dark hair tousled, a baby on her shoulder, a smile in her eyes. A woman she finally recognized.

A woman in the embrace of her God.

Epilogue

Here, in Hollywood, Rosie could glitter again. She stood in front of a shop window, staring at the dress, the shiny fringes along the bodice and hem, the feathered headband, the long gloves, and saw herself sliding into it. Saw herself sashaying onto stage, maybe singing something smoky into a microphone. But more, she saw her name on one of those playbills, perhaps even on a movie poster.

She would change it, of course. Not Rosie. Not Red. Roxy maybe. Roxy Price.

She'd reinvent herself in Hollywood and Cesar's men would never find her. Or her daughter.

Lilly's daughter.

Rosie had to train herself to think this way now. Lilly's daughter. She never had a daughter, was never married to Guthrie Storme.

She'd already taken off her ring, hanging it on a gold chain around her neck. She'd hide it after she got settled. After she found a place to secrete it where she'd never accidentally run across it to tear her asunder.

Yes, she'd erase her past. Erase her memory of New York society, a mother who had loved her despite her sins, a stepfather who filled in for the father she'd lost, a little brother who had allowed her to love again.

She'd forget her older brother, sever his memory that lingered like a noose around her neck.

Yes, here in Hollywood, she'd walk into the world reinvented.

Hollywood thrummed with an energy unfamiliar in New York City. Everything seemed alive and new, from the pavement on the Boulevard to the shaggy palm trees, to the fancy women wearing their furs on the sidewalk at the height of the morning. Men in straw boaters and suits hustled by, Ford Model Ts, motorcycles, and trolleybuses motored down the road. Everyone seemed in a hurry, as if life might leave them behind. The place even smelled fresh, a fragrance of sunshine, the ocean on the breeze.

She'd spotted the Knickerbocker Hotel from blocks away, the grand letters rising above the massive building like a map. Now, seeing it across the street, the fringed canopy waving in the wind, the bellhop by the door, she pressed her hands to her stomach, thankful that she'd lost more of her pregnancy weight on the three-day trip down to Los Angeles. Another week of tea and crackers and she might fit into that dress in the store window.

Still, her stomach roiled. She closed her eyes, reached past the last four years to the woman she'd been years ago, in Paris. The woman who knew how to put on a smile, play games. The woman who could reel in everything she wanted.

That woman entered the cool interior of the Knickerbocker, walked past the gilded walls, the gold brocade divans, the gleaming chandeliers, to the elevator. "Eighth floor," she said, not even looking at the operator. He got in behind her, looking sharp in his red jacket and his white gloves, and pushed the button.

This would be her world. Attended by others. Royalty. Like Sarah Bernhardt.

She stepped off the elevator and onto the smooth red carpet that lined the hall. She didn't stop until she reached the far door, the suite of rooms behind 806.

Then, she knocked.

Pasted on the right smile.

Raised her chin.

Betrayed nothing but cool expectation as the door opened.

"Rosie. What a surprise! What are you doing here?" Dashielle wore a blue cardigan, a white collared shirt, an ascot at his neck, a pair of linen trousers. His onyx black-hair gelled back, he sported a tan. He already looked born and bred in California.

She patted his face with her hand then pushed past him into the suite, her heart nearly in her throat. But desperation didn't become a starlet. She dropped her handbag on the long white curved sofa, took in the view of Hollywood from his paladin windows, and then turned, tugging off her gloves, one finger at a time. "Blanche told me where to find you."

He wore an enigmatic smile, as if he didn't know quite what to do with her. "Did she?" He closed the door, his smoky eyes bearing an old twinkle.

"Umm-hmm."

"And why did she do that?"

She dropped the gloves on her handbag. Came close to him, and only felt a slight burn in her throat when she pressed her hand to his chest, right by his heart. "Because, Dashielle, things have changed. It's time for you to make me a star."

Baroness Questions

1. At the beginning of the novel, both Lilly and Rosie are restless. What do they each want? At the end of the novel, did they get what they wanted? Have you ever felt a restlessness and didn't exactly know why?

2. Lilly is easily wooed into a dangerous life that gets her into trouble. Why did this happen? Have you ever been wooed into something you knew wasn't healthy? What happened?

3. Rosie is enthralled by Sarah Bernhardt and her legacy. Why is this appealing to Rosie? Why does she want what Sarah had?

4. Lilly arrives home to a tragedy and makes a snap decision that changes her life. What is that tragedy, and why does she leave and head west? What would you have done in Lilly's position?

5. Rosie lands a job she believes will make her a star, but it comes with sacrifices and compromises. Will our dreams always cause us to make sacrifices? Compromises? Are they worth the outcome?

6. Lilly discovers a flying circus and escapes with them rather than go home to New York. How does this affect how she sees herself? Have you ever been in a situation that causes you to become a person you didn't realize you were? Braver? Stronger? Smarter?

7. Oliver travels to Wyoming to rescue Lilly and helps her see the truth about Truman. Is it the truth? What does Lilly believe about her

marriage that sends her back to New York? Have you ever made a decision about a relationship based on a lie?

8. Rosie escapes New York and marries Guthrie. Three years later, we find her happy and living in Chicago even though she's not a star. Why? What do you think Rosie really wanted? Have you ever received something opposite of what you dreamed, only to realize it is what you really wanted?

9. Lilly is in New York, working at the paper, but she still isn't happy. Why not? What does Oliver recommend her to do? Why? In what ways does Oliver show that he loves Lilly? How do his actions resemble the actions of God toward us?

10. What does Lilly realize when she goes to Paris that changes her thinking about her future? Why do you think Oliver goes to find Truman? Have you ever tried to "fix" a decision you made long ago? What happened?

11. Rosie returns to New York only to have her past find her. When she returns home for help, what kind of reception does she expect? What does she receive? Have you ever received a different homecoming than you expected?

12. Lilly helps Rosie escape New York and ends up taking care of Rosie's child. Why is this Lilly's destiny? Standing where you are today, is it what you expected for your life, or not? Why or why not? What do you think the statement, "Don't forget your name, and where you belong," means for your life?

Bonus: What do you think will happen with Rosie? What do you want to happen with Rosie?

Author's Note

Times haven't changed so much from the Roaring Twenties—a decade where young people peered into the lives of their parents and said, *We want something different.* They just didn't know what that difference was...so they went searching. The Twenties embodied a time of great turbulence and change—from the flappers who went on to be showgirls and even Hollywood stars, to the authors who gave us books like *The Great Gatsby*, and *The Sun Also Rises*, to the pioneers in aviation and technology—they explored life and tried to find a home for their restlessness, tried to figure out where they belonged.

Into this world, I inserted Lilly and Rosie, two very different women seeking the same things—a conviction that they were loved and a place to belong. Lilly believes her place is on the plains of Montana; Rosie believes hers is under glittery lights, surrounded by the adoration of the masses. Both of them come to know the truth: knowing your place comes from knowing who you are and where you belong. The answer is found here:

For I am persuaded, that neither death, nor life, nor angels, nor principalities, nor powers, nor things present, nor things to come, nor height, nor depth, nor any other creature, shall be able to separate us from the love of God, which is in Christ Jesus our Lord. (Romans 8:38-39, KJV).

No matter how far we run, how many "lives" we try on, we will never find ourselves outside of God's love for us. More than that, understanding His relentless love for us—not unlike Oliver's love for Lilly—changes us. Turning around and embracing God's love for us helps us to become the people we long to be. I love what Esme says to Lilly—her birthright, so to speak: *Don't forget your name and where you belong.*

Our name is Beloved, and we belong to the One who loves us. How does that change us? We don't have to thirst for meaning, or identity, or even love—or let that thirst control us. We have all those things, and as long as we hold onto God and let Him work out His good purposes in our lives, we'll become the people we hope to be, one day at a time.

I pray that you know God's relentless love in your life.

Thank you for reading *Baroness*. Will Rosie find her way back to love, to her family, to being a daughter of fortune? Stay tuned for the next chapter of the journey in *Duchess*, Rosie's story.

All the best,
Susie May

About the Author

SUSAN MAY WARREN is the best-selling author of more than thirty novels whose compelling plots and unforgettable characters have earned her acclaim from readers and reviewers alike. She is a winner of the ACFW Carol Award, the RITA Award, and the Inspirational Readers Choice Award and a nominee for the Christy Award. She loves to write and to help other writers find their voices through her work with My Book Therapy (www.mybooktherapy.com), a writing craft and coaching community she founded.

Susan and her husband of more than twenty years have four children. Former missionaries to Russia, they now live in a small Minnesota town on the shore of beautiful Lake Superior, where they are active in their local church. Find her online at www.susanmaywarren.com.